# YOU WERE NEVER REALLY HERE

## GERDEN IBRAHIM

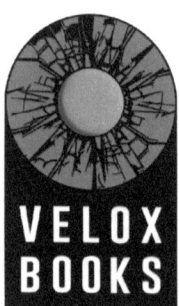

Published by arrangement with the author.

Copyright © 2026 by Gerden Ibrahim.

All rights reserved.

No part of this publication may be reproduced, distributed, or transmitted in any form or by any means, including photocopying, recording, or other electronic or mechanical methods, without the prior written permission of the publisher, except as permitted by U.S. copyright law.

The story, all names, characters, and incidents portrayed in this production are fictitious. No identification with actual persons (living or deceased), places, buildings, and products is intended or should be inferred.

# YOU'RE READING ANOTHER TERRIFYING COLLECTION FROM

**FOLLOW VELOX TO KEEP THE NIGHTMARES COMING:**

# CONTENTS

| | |
|---|---|
| You've Never Been Here Before | 1 |
| For My 26th Birthday, I Got a Cake With Candles I Can't Blow Out | 8 |
| If You Live in My Town You Will Never See Your Grandchildren Grow Up | 14 |
| Something is Wrong With the Snow | 20 |
| Our Local Grocery Store Started Selling Products That Don't Exist | 26 |
| My Dad Has a Second Face | 48 |
| The People in My Hometown Produce Cursed Goods | 54 |
| The First Hotel in Our Town Just Opened, But All the Guests Are Quarantined | 60 |
| Amy's Missing. Have You Seen Her? | 66 |
| There Are Two Versions of My Childhood Tapes | 73 |
| I Woke Up Inside a Replica of My Childhood Home | 109 |
| I'm Playing a Game Called Smile But Nobody Taught Me the Rules | 114 |

| | |
|---|---|
| The Social Experiment | 153 |
| Every Night, A New Woman Dances On Our Street | 183 |
| I Moved to a Neighborhood Where the People Are Too Welcoming | 192 |
| This is Not My Home | 199 |
| My Brother Died But He Never Left Me | 208 |
| There Must Be Something in Our Water That Turns All the People Odd | 218 |
| Somebody Keeps Sending Me the Same Text Every Night | 226 |
| Something Is Not Right with the New Family | 234 |
| I Went Back to Kicky-Kids' Fun Land. It's Not So Fun Anymore. | 254 |
| I Used to Love Watermelons. Now They Smell Like Death to Me. | 262 |
| Nobody Warned Us About the Scarecrow Before We Moved Here | 269 |
| When the Lights on the Street Start to Flicker at Night, It's a Warning to Stay Inside | 277 |
| My Mother Is Performing a Puppet Show for Us. When It Ends, We Die. | 284 |
| Welcome to Heaven | 290 |
| They Were Out of Lemons | 298 |

# YOU'VE NEVER BEEN HERE BEFORE

I was on my way home from work, like every day. Nothing out of the ordinary until I reached my apartment building. The first sign was glued to the main entrance.

**You've never been here before.**

"Weird," I mumbled to myself as I opened the door and made my way to the elevator. Inside, another note was glued next to the buttons.

**All floors will feel right, none of them are.**

I wondered if this was some kind of art project by one of the other people who lived in the building or a prank some teens were playing.

I pressed the button for the seventh floor, and the elevator started moving with a soft hum.

The door opened, and right as I stepped outside, I saw another note, stuck to the floor right in front of my shoes.

**It's not too late. Yet.**

I walked past it with a queasy feeling settling in my stomach. The building I live in has 20 floors in total, and I wondered if there was a note on each floor or whether mine was chosen for a particular reason. But I was tired from work, hungry because I only had a light lunch, and I was in no mood to deal with any of it.

I tried to ignore it until I stepped inside my apartment, where another note was waiting for me. A small piece of paper in the same handwriting as all the others I had passed on my way.

**This is not your home.**

It was glued to my wall right across from the door.

I stood in the middle of the room, my body suddenly frozen and my mind going blank.

Then, finally, fear came over me.

Somebody had been inside my apartment. Or maybe they were still inside.

I live in a one-bedroom apartment, so luckily there weren't many hiding spots. Collecting all my courage, I went to the bathroom, checked my closet, and looked under my bed—all the places a person could hide. It appeared I was alone, so I locked my door and bolted it from the inside.

When I finally felt safe enough, my thoughts started racing, and a strange feeling settled inside of me. The feeling that these notes weren't a threat but a warning.

I decided to knock on my neighbor's door to ask whether they had found a similar note in their home, but before unlocking the door, I checked through my peephole to see if there was anyone outside. I couldn't shake the feeling that somebody could be waiting for me.

At first, the part of the hallway that I could see was empty, but slowly, a shadow started appearing in my vision.

The first thing I saw was a foot stepping closer to the front of my door. Slowly, the rest of the body followed. It belonged to a man dressed in a wrinkled, awkwardly fitting gray suit. His dark hair was parted in the middle. I tried to remember if I'd seen him before, but I couldn't say for sure. A lot of people lived in this building, but I hadn't met many.

At first, I thought he was just passing through, and I tried to control my breathing, fearing that he could hear me through the door.

But then he turned toward me as if he could see me through the other side. His gaze was fixed on mine even though that was impossible. And then he slowly waved.

Instinctively, I stumbled back.

There was a loud knock, but I didn't move. I held my breath, even when I started feeling dizzy. I stood there for a few moments until I finally decided to check if he was still there.

I imagined his face glued to the peephole as I moved closer, but when I looked out again, he was gone.

I couldn't make sense of the strange situation, but I knew I needed to call for help. There had been an intruder in my home, after all. But when I went through my pockets and my bag, I realized I didn't have my phone, and I'd never bothered to get a landline. It was too coincidental that I would lose my phone on such a strange day; somebody must have stolen it from me.

I knew I had to get out and talk to someone, but I was too afraid that I would stumble into the strange man in the hallway.

Before I could think of another plan, the sound of rapid knocking came from my door. This time it wasn't as loud. There was a different undertone to it. Fear.

Carefully, I walked up to the peephole again and saw the face of a young woman who lived on my floor. We'd met a few times in the hallway or the elevator.

The knocking became slightly louder, and I heard a whisper.

"Please, let me in."

Reluctantly, I opened my door. She pushed me to the side as she made her way in, quickly shutting the door behind her.

Her eyes were wide, her breathing fast.

"What is going on?" she cried out. Then her gaze went to the note on my wall.

"Did you get one, too?" I asked.

"I've been hiding in my apartment all day. Something scary is happening," she responded. "I didn't know what to do, but then I finally heard your door. You're the first one I saw coming home." She looked away from the note and met my gaze. "Then I saw that man outside. I waited till he was really gone, and then I came over."

Somebody was clearly messing with us, and seeing the fear in her eyes made me realize that this situation was real and that we needed to get away as soon as possible.

"I don't know what the hell is going on, but we should probably try to get outside. We can take some knives—"

"We can't," she interrupted. "There is no way out."

"What do you mean, there's no way out?"

"Once you're inside, you're stuck."

"What?"

She sighed. "Do you know who I am?"

I'd met her a few times before, in the hallway or in the elevator where we'd chatted a little. "I don't remember your name, to be honest, but—"

"Let me make this quick. You *don't* know me. We've never met before. And we don't live here."

I laughed, but before I could say anything, she continued.

"Think about it. *Really* think. Try to remember. Is this your home?"

I looked around the sparsely furnished room. I looked for photos or mail, but there was nothing. Then I looked at her again. She wasn't much younger than me, maybe early twenties. Her brown hair was long and curly, falling over her shoulders. I tried to think of the few times we met, and then I realized that something was off about the memories. Normally, when you remember moments, you see yourself from a third-person perspective, but everything I remembered was in first person. Like moments happening in real time.

I swallowed. "What is happening? Did I lose my mind?" I finally asked, not really answering her questions.

She shrugged.

I tried to remember my family, friends, and childhood, but there was nothing. My mind was blank.

"What's your name?" she asked.

"Dan. I think."

"I'm Cassie."

"Cassie, why did you come here? Why would you trust me if you don't know me?"

She shrugged again. "I couldn't hide forever. Shouldn't I trust you?"

I shook my head. "No, I'm—" I wasn't really sure what to say. "I'm not dangerous."

She smiled.

"I'm going out," I decided. "Like you said, we can't hide forever."

"You look weak. I think you should eat something, gather your strength, and then we will form a plan."

She was right, but I was suddenly feeling too sick to think clearly. I grabbed a big kitchen knife and made my way to the hallway. There was no one else around, so I quickly walked to the elevator. On my way, I noticed that the note I had seen earlier was gone. I pressed the elevator button, but nothing happened. After a moment, I decided to check the stairs, but the door was locked. Suddenly, there was a noise, and the elevator door opened. I made my way toward it, passing Cassie, who still stood in my doorway. I stopped when I noticed that somebody was inside the elevator. The man in the suit.

Our eyes met briefly, and then he noticed the knife in my hand. He shook his head but didn't say anything. Then he looked behind me, straight at Cassie.

"Come back, quick!" she shouted. The man took a step forward, but before he got too close, I ran back to my apartment. Cassie shut the door and locked it.

I was panting.

"I told you there's no way out," she whispered, turning toward my sofa—well, not really mine—and sat down.

"We can't stay here forever. We'll starve. Or he'll find a way in. He could break the door. We should try to make a sign and hold it out the window. Maybe someone will see it."

Cassie frowned. The man started banging on the door from the outside again. Louder and louder.

"Get out of there," I heard the man's muffled voice. "It's not too late—" His voice broke off.

My eyes moved from her to the door. I wanted to scream, to jump out the window, but it was too high, and I wouldn't make it.

Cassie caught my eye. "You could jump. Try it." A wide grin was spreading over her face.

"What?"

"You told me you weren't dangerous, but you didn't even bother to ask if I was."

She crossed her legs on the sofa, all the fear I had noticed on her face earlier gone. She looked like a happy child, and I realized I had made a big mistake. I trusted her in the first place because I thought she was my neighbor and then because I thought she was in danger, just like me.

The banging on the door was back.

"Did you leave all those notes?" I asked.

She shook her head. "Why would I warn you?"

"Who is that man? Are you helping him?"

She chuckled. I inspected her face again. Something about it was off. It was too perfect.

I tightened my grip on the knife.

Then there was a loud thud. The door had broken. I felt an arm grabbing me and pulling me into the hallway. Before I could defend myself, I was being pulled into the elevator. I fell to the floor and saw Cassie in the hallway, smiling at me, but she didn't move closer, didn't try to stop him.

"Don't be gone too long," she said before the door closed.

I remembered that I was still holding the knife and used all my strength to push it into the man's leg.

His eyes opened wide as he crumbled to the ground next to me.

I pulled out the knife, ready to hit again, when he whispered, "Please don't. I'm trying to help you."

My entire body was shaking with rage, but when I saw the pained look on his face and the blood spilling on the floor, I stopped for a moment.

"She lured me in, just like you. Just like the others that are hiding," he croaked. "Once she makes you eat something, you can't leave anymore, but she can't make you stay by force."

I was lost for words.

The door opened as we reached the first floor.

"Run," he told me. "Try not to think of this place again."

I looked at his bleeding leg and felt horrible. He was trying to help me this entire time. When he saw that I was hesitating, he added, "My leg will be fine. We heal faster here."

"What's your name?" I asked.

"Matteo. Gerrard. It's the only thing I remember."

"Matteo, I can't just leave you."

"You have to, while you still can. And be careful. She will find a way to get you back."

---

The first moments after leaving the building were a blur, but as I got further away, my real memories came back. Of my real home and my past.

The memories of Cassie and my imagined home stayed as well. However, when I tried to find the building again later, I couldn't.

I researched online for hours until I finally found him. Matteo Gerrard had disappeared five years ago on his way to a job interview. He was only 20 then. As I looked further into it, I found that he had disappeared once before after he went to a festival. He was gone for a week when he suddenly returned to his parents.

I can only imagine what happened then. They probably thought he'd taken too many drugs or that he was going through a psychotic episode.

So a year later, Cassie found him again. And this time he couldn't save himself.

He told me not to think about it, but I can't stop. I wonder why she let me go so easily. She was able to control my mind and my memories; there was no way she couldn't stop me.

But then I think of the smirk on her face when she told me to just jump. My fear was all a game to her.

She let me leave because she knows she can get me back. And play another round.

# FOR MY 26TH BIRTHDAY, I GOT A CAKE WITH CANDLES I CAN'T BLOW OUT

The bright morning sun was shining through the crack in my dark red curtains. I didn't like being awake just yet, but the feeling of the sun on my skin somehow almost made up for it. I missed spring. I woke up in my childhood home, tucked gently into my bed with sheets that smelled of fresh lavender and felt as cozy as if they had just come out of the dryer. A pleasant way to wake up. Very pleasant indeed. Until my mind started running, thinking and worrying, and that was always where things began to go wrong. Or when I became conscious of the wrongness.

As my mind woke up just a little more, the intrusive thought dug in like a worm.

*I shouldn't be here.*

The first shot of anxiety rushed through my body, so early in the morning. What a pity.

*I don't live here.*

*These are not my sheets, not my softener smelling like fresh lavender.*

*I don't live here anymore.*

I was twenty-five years old. Last year I was back at home for a few months after I finished college. But after torturing myself with application letters and a bunch of refusals, I finally got my own place a little while ago.

Well, technically, I was twenty-six as of today. As my thoughts became just a little clearer, I finally started to remember that I'd come home for the weekend to visit my parents so I wouldn't be entirely alone on this birthday that I'd much rather just skip. I *was* supposed to be here because I came here last night.

I swear, my morning brain could not be trusted one bit.

Finally, I stretched and shook off those terrible intrusive thoughts as well as I could. Things were much better now, and I should be feeling just swell. I even managed a smile when I heard Mum and Dad knock on my door.

They'd dressed up for the occasion, which was a little odd but also very sweet of them. I supposed they wanted to make the best of this day. I couldn't exactly have a big party with the country in a partial lockdown, after all.

Mum was wearing a pastel-rose dress with tiny white flowers and a wide white belt wrapped around her waist. Her lips were shining with bright lipstick, and she didn't have a single smudge on her paper-white teeth. She was even wearing heels that went with the style of the dress, though we were certainly not a shoes-inside type of family.

Dad put on a nice pastel-green shirt and even had a small bow tie tied around his neck. His face looked freshly shaved, and he had a little spark in his eyes as he brought in the cake they must have baked in secret while I was asleep. Or maybe the spark I saw was just a reflection of the candles on the perfectly delicious-looking cake.

It was mint green with pink frosting flowers smudged around the corners and Happy Birthday written in a squiggly font. The top was embellished with twenty-six candles, thirteen of them green and thirteen of them pink, it appeared. However, it was hard to say for sure since the top of the cake was basically one big layer of fire.

"Very funny," I exclaimed after my fifth attempt at blowing them out. "You do know April first was three weeks back?"

The stupid candles wouldn't blow out. Of course, Mum and Dad had to get trick candles. Neither my lungs nor my mood was ready for those so early in the morning.

Mum smiled, and Dad grinned.

"Come on, honey. Blow out the candles!" Mum said in a melodic voice.

"Make a wish, love! And make it a good one. Who knows how many more of those you'll get!"

They both started laughing.

"Yeah, funny, Dad. I'm old. Just remember, if I'm old, so are you!" I tried to joke, but they didn't respond to that.

"Make a wish!" Mum repeated.

"I wish for you to act a bit more normal." I nervously chuckled. They hadn't stopped smiling since they came inside.

Mum got closer to my face. I could feel her breath against my skin. It smelled like iron and cigarettes.

"When did you start smoking?" I asked.

Mum took a step back. She seemed to be embarrassed. I didn't like her picking up an unhealthy habit, but I also didn't want her to feel ashamed in front of me. However, both my parents lost their smiles when I asked about the cigarettes. Dad pulled the cake away again.

"Well, then I suppose your wish will just have to wait if you find it so terribly difficult to make a decision, young lady!"

"Yes, very true, my dear. You tell her," Mum added. "We will go downstairs for your birthday breakfast, and you can have your cake then."

They both nodded at each other and moved away from my bed. They took the cake that was still burning—the candles should have burned through the cake by now, but they were still standing tall. Then they turned around, without a smile, let alone a word, and left the room.

I heard them go down the stairs, and that was the very strange beginning to the morning of my twenty-sixth birthday. But of course, it didn't end there.

---

The next very strange thing was the gown I was wearing, which I certainly didn't remember putting on. It was white with hints of gold by the collar. I was more than sure that I didn't own a clothing item like that. I didn't even think my grandma owned anything like this. And I would have known if I put on something so terribly odd, which meant my parents had to be the ones to dress me. In my sleep. If this was another prank, then I clearly misjudged Mum and Dad. They were losing their minds.

I didn't bother getting changed, so I could storm down there and confront them about their absurd actions. This was not the birthday party I had in mind. I wanted a nice and relaxed day with cake and maybe a few presents.

As I ran down the last flight of stairs in my strange gown, I heard the music. It was coming from the kitchen. A melody I couldn't quite place. All of a sudden, my anger about the strange clothing vanished, and instead, I felt a miserable malaise. Slowly, I stumbled inside the kitchen, where I was taken aback by everything they had done.

There were balloons in every corner, confetti, and a big paper sign that said HAPPY BIRTHDAY. Fringe curtains were hanging from the windows. Even weirder, it all looked as if it was meant for a child's birthday party. My parents were standing around the confetti-filled table, their smiles bigger than when they had come inside with the cake, which sat in the middle of the table. Around it, however, were items that I believe had once been meant for breakfast.

But they were all rotten.

I instinctively took a step back. "Mum, Dad," I whispered.

"Yes! That's us, your mummy and your daddy. Now, be swift. Make a wish and blow out your candles so we can get to your presents!" Dad said without blinking once.

"What's going on? I don't like this. Please stop," I muttered.

Mum almost lost her smile again, but then she used her right fingernail to pull up the corner of her mouth. "Honey, this is your special day. We will never stop."

My eyes wandered to the telephone on the kitchen counter. It was an old green telephone with a cable, the ones people stopped using more than a decade ago. I didn't even realize we still owned one. It didn't matter anyway; its cord was cut. Or was it burned off?

I'd probably left my own phone upstairs. I needed to get it and call for help. My parents were clearly unwell, and I was getting incredibly worried.

"Let me just... get changed. And then we can have cake. Okay? I'll be right back."

"NO!" they both shouted simultaneously.

"You look perfect," Mum said.

"Now make a wish," Dad added.

Despite feeling incredibly uneasy, I took a step closer to blow out the candles. Maybe cutting the cake would distract them enough for me to go get some help.

This time I took a very deep breath and started blowing as hard as I could.

The fire only seemed to grow bigger.

"If you won't, I suppose we have to blow out the candles and steal your wish," Mum said, chuckling.

"Why yes, Deborah. Would you like to do the honors?" my father asked her.

She got closer to the cake. So close that her entire face was now shining orange and red from the fire. So close that her makeup was even starting to melt.

Or maybe it wasn't only her makeup that was melting.

"Mum, your face," I whispered, in shock.

But she didn't care.

"I wish for our sweet child to forever stay with us," she called out, in glee.

"Moron! You cannot say your wish out loud!" Dad shouted.

Now he was getting closer to the cake. Their expressions became even more forced, and Mum's makeup melted onto the cake until even her hair caught fire.

I don't think I'll ever get the smell of burned hair and skin out of my nose.

"Mum!" I shouted, but she didn't care. Not even when her face kept burning.

I suppose that was what woke me up. Of course, I'd known from the beginning that something was not right, but this moment sent me over the edge.

I shouldn't be here.

I don't live here.

And I have no fucking clue who these people are.

---

I slammed the burning cake into my fake father's face and started running before the wrong mother could do anything.

I got out just in time. I have absolutely no idea how they tricked me into that house or into thinking that they were my own parents. They didn't even look like them, but I had been so sure in the morning that everything was fine. As my thoughts became more my own again, I started remembering that I'd gone for drinks at my friend Clara's house, but I couldn't even say what day that was. How they got into my head and memories like that I will never understand. I was lucky my mind became conscious in time, or it might really have been my very last birthday.

I ran and ran until I found help and was taken to the police.

They went to the house as I'd instructed them. It was currently uninhabited. Apparently, it had only recently been restored after the family that lived there died in a fire. I really can't say if those people were even real, whether they had lost a child and tried to lure a new one in. Maybe I was just an easy victim. Although I'm not sure how they knew about my birthday.

When the police found the house, there was nobody there. The fake parents were gone, but they had left one thing.

A mint green cake with pink frosting and twenty-six burning candles.

# IF YOU LIVE IN MY TOWN YOU WILL NEVER SEE YOUR GRANDCHILDREN GROW UP

I live in a very young town. By young, of course, I don't mean that it is new. No, our people have lived here for generations, just not all together. To someone from the outside, it might sound a little odd, and as we are quite an understanding bunch, we get it. It is a strange concept, though one that has proven to be quite successful.

No, the town itself is not young, but the inhabitants who get to live here are—the ones who get to live in a community of progress, fun, and of course, a little bit of love. Not a single person in this place we call Milton is unemployed; there are opportunities for every individual. Poverty does not exist; there is never a lack of food or drink. Despite the town's small size, we have lively nightlife, wonderful restaurants, and great bars. Hardly anyone is lonely. We are all peers in some way. No one is better than another. Yes, some jobs might be more powerful than others, but those who hold them are often quite visionary. We retrieve our energy exclusively from renewable sources. Big windmills stand tall in the fields surrounding us. Behind the windmills, there isn't much more than a forest that we never cross, as behind it we would find the other place. We call it Sector B.

There are two simple laws where we live, and when we abide by them, we are allowed to live a fruitful life in a place that seems to be more advanced than the entire rest of the world but not accessible to anyone who wasn't born on our ground. The first law is that you only live in Sector A until you have children of your own. If you reach a certain age, realize that children will not be part of your future, and decide not to adopt, then you move away. That part is an unspoken rule; nobody will throw you over the gates, but if you don't add to the community, then you won't find work, and buying a house will be rather difficult as well. It's the social norm. Few leave, but most want to stay. As I said, life here is as close to perfect as it can get. When you do decide to have or raise a member of the next generation, you only get to do so until they have children of their own or decide to leave town.

As I said, the latter seldom occurs, partly because if they leave, they don't get to come back. And we see what the world outside looks like. It's dark and cruel. It's stuck in time in too many ways. Progress is seen as something to be feared, whereas here it is one of our core values.

When you reach that certain age and the time has come for you to see your first grandchild, you are asked to pack your bags and move to Sector B. If you happen to have multiple children, you wait for the last one to have a child of their own.

The second law is for Sectors A and B to never mix. When you leave the first chapter, you are bound to the second. Life in the other sector is just as lovely, only more relaxing. Resources from the young part are shared, and life is therefore made even easier for its residents. It sounds like punishment, but it is a reward. You work hard to deserve that peace, and even if you have to miss your kin for a while, they will come and join you when their time has come.

Some decide to have many children with large age gaps to ensure they will spend as much time with them as they can. Others have one when they are very young and hope the time will come soon so they can enjoy an early retirement.

I come from a traditional family, or at least I always thought so. Ever since I was a teenager, my parents preached to me how wonderful it is to have children of your own—to see a young soul look up to you and grow up to be its own person. Don't get me wrong, it does sound nice in many ways, but I never saw myself having children. I feel in many ways I can hardly take care of myself.

You should have seen the look on my parents' faces when they found out that I had a girlfriend. A real, serious relationship. I tried to hide it as long as I could because I knew exactly how they would react, and I was nowhere near ready for that kind of pressure. Keeping secrets in a town this small, however, is close to impossible, and when they finally heard the news about Fiona and me, they were thrilled—though possibly not entirely ecstatic, as her parents didn't have the best of reputations. They had six children and were planning to have more as long as they biologically could.

"You're not marrying the family, only the girl, after all. It's fine," my mother said with a fake smile.

I rolled my eyes.

"Marrying? Jeez, Mom, we're just dating. Who knows if it will even work out?" was my response back then. Fiona was great and all, but I was young and planned on not settling down anytime soon. Maybe things wouldn't work out; maybe I'd date many more people. Back then I was a little cautious when it came to love, but the longer we were together, the more I started realizing that Fiona was the one. She was critical of living here—well, not of where we were, but of where we would be going one day. She couldn't imagine living with all those old people; I mean, we weren't used to any. I told her that we would be old, too, then, but that didn't make the whole concept sound any better to her. She was similar to her parents in that way. Back then, I hadn't even told her that I wasn't planning on having children, although I believe we were in silent agreement on that. We often joked about all the places we would visit if we ever got exiled.

Unfortunately, life never goes as planned.

My feelings were never as muddled as on the day Fiona told me she was pregnant.

We were sitting in her parents' garden, watching her little brother play on the grass. We were alone, and he was too young to understand why his sister was smiling and crying at the same time.

---

A child changes everything. Everywhere, but even more so in Milton.

Fiona's parents were happy for us; they would have time to see their grandchild for years before their youngest child had one of their own. My mother and father were crying tears of joy at first. It was all they ever wanted.

They had been looking forward to the day they would be moved to Sector B all their lives. Until they laid eyes on their granddaughter and knew that they could never leave her voluntarily. If a child changes everything, so does a grandchild. The traditions were swiftly thrown overboard, and the tears of joy turned into tears of fear.

My parents were picked up on a Monday in a van driven by Thomas Miller, who went to the same school as I did. He was one of the few chosen to work for the town committee at a young age. Thomas had lost his parents as a young child; they died in an accident. When we were little, he was almost like a brother to me. My mom made two lunches for me to bring to school for years, one for each of us. As we grew older and Thomas was chosen to work for the committee, we lost touch.

Thomas stayed behind when the two officers got out of the car and made their way to our front door.

Ours, as in Fiona and I would now own the house.

My father's hand was trembling when he opened the door. His eyes were bloodshot. He hadn't slept a second last night. Mom didn't either; she held my daughter in her arms the whole night, holding my hand at the same time. I never believed that out of all people, my mom wouldn't be ready to say goodbye. She loved the life she had in Sector A of Milton and couldn't wait for the next chapter. Ever since they received the letter that told them they would be picked up soon, however, she'd spent every second fighting with my dad, who wasn't thrilled either but was too scared to break any rules.

"You wanted this," I overheard him say yesterday. "You wanted this life while you were young. You cannot change your mind now that you've grown out of it. Ben will come and live with us soon enough."

I shuddered at the thought. There was no way in hell I would ever leave my child and live in the next sector. I doubted very much that Fiona was into that idea either.

"In two decades? Three or possibly even four? What if our granddaughter decides to leave? Even if she doesn't, who knows if we will even be alive long enough to ever see her again?"

I didn't hear much more of their conversation, but Fiona and I had talked as well, and we knew we never wanted to be in the place my parents were now. But now that we had brought a child into the world in Milton, there was no way for us to get out of it.

I cried for the first time since I was a child when they guided my parents to the vehicle. They both tried to smile, but we all knew this was not a happy day. I tried to talk to the officers, to tell them that we needed them just a little longer to help with the child, but it was no use.

"They're gonna love the next chapter. Stay put, boy," one of them hissed at me.

The other pushed me back.

If this was such a happy day, why were they being violent? My gut was screaming, and I tried to shout at them. I shouted at my parents that they couldn't leave and at those bastards that they couldn't just take them. My body started trembling so much that I thought I would throw up at any second.

This was wrong. This was just wrong, and these people were smiling.

Smiling like shells with no emotion on the inside. Smiling gladly while taking my devastated parents away. Only Thomas looked serious; he was leaning against the side of the car, smoking a cigarette while avoiding eye contact entirely.

It was an odd sight, as I had never seen him smoke before.

At that moment, I was distracted by much more important things, of course, but as they finally drove away and the only sound we could hear was my little girl crying, I noticed that Thomas had left something behind.

A pack of cigarettes on the ground.

Now, seeing him smoke was a little unexpected, but throwing a pack of cigarettes on the ground was impossible.

Nobody ever littered in Milton. Especially not someone working for the committee. If I hadn't noticed, or if it hadn't been such a strange sight, maybe I would have continued my life in ignorance.

But I did, and I picked it up before anyone else saw it.

I don't know why—maybe it was just a gut feeling—but I went back into our house to open the package instead of throwing it away.

There were no cigarettes inside, but something else.

Polaroids.

There weren't many, and the quality was bad, but it was obvious what I was seeing on them.

Dead bodies. Lifeless bodies hanging in a row, with cuts so they would be emptied of their blood.

I even recognized a few faces. Neighbors who had welcomed grandchildren recently and were taken away to live in the other sector behind the forest.

Only now did I realize why our resources were so full, why we had so much, and why even the ones working for the committee were always young. I don't know how brainwashed they were, but this seemed to be all right with them. I understood why we had so much. We were not sharing with the elderly. There was no perfect place for their retirement. When they finished doing their work, they were disposed of.

Maybe they were moving on to a better place, but it was certainly not Sector B.

# SOMETHING IS WRONG WITH THE SNOW

I woke up in the most beautiful little place you could imagine. An old town with merchant houses and cobblestone streets overlooking multiple hills. And on top of one of those stood a small Baroque castle.

I had been ecstatic about coming here for a weekend trip with my boyfriend for our one-year anniversary. There's hardly ever any snow in the city where I live, so being here in December, with the smells and lights of the Christmas markets, felt like a dream.

When we arrived the day before, the air was crisp, and all the people in the hotel, the restaurants, and the shops were so welcoming. There wasn't any snow yet, but I could smell in the air that it would be coming soon.

When I woke up the next morning, the light coming from outside was almost blinding to my sleepy eyes, and I felt a headache settling in. I groggily got up from bed to close the blinds when I saw why it was so light out. A white sheet was gently resting on the homes and streets.

It should have been beautiful. If it weren't for all the red. Dark red stains on the white snow. Little drops here and there, but then there were whole puddles as well.

"Jacob?" I whispered, but my boyfriend didn't react. I repeated his name, louder this time, and he yawned loudly.

"What time is it?" he asked.

"Come here," I instructed. "It snowed."

"That's great, honey. I'll look at it later," he said and turned around.

"Please, come look at this."

He slowly got up from bed and walked toward me. When he looked outside, his expression changed from annoyed to wide awake.

"What the hell is this?"

We stared out of our window.

"It looks almost like blood."

"Wine, maybe?" he asked, still staring out the window.

I shook my head. "I don't think so. And how did it even get there? Everything around looks untouched."

Jacob took a deep breath and turned away from the window. "Ava, do you remember anything about last night?"

I swallowed. "I remember a lot of mulled wine."

"Yeah, same. No idea how we got back here, though." He laughed.

Jacob stumbled back to bed. "I'm sure there's a good explanation for it," he mumbled.

I kept staring out the window. A couple came into view; they walked down the street of our hotel, right past one of the bigger puddles, but they didn't even look at it.

After a while, I heard Jacob snoring, but I was fixated on the outside. More people came down the street, and some started shoveling the snow in front of their houses.

Nobody acknowledged the red snow.

---

After Jacob finally woke up again, we made our way down the creaky wooden stairs to get some breakfast in a cafe. The hotel was small and very old; the entire ground floor had this really ugly red-and-green carpet, and all the furniture looked like it was from the eighties, but that made it more charming. It almost felt like visiting your grandparents.

"Good morning. Did you have a good first night here?" the old gentleman behind the reception greeted us. He had a kind smile on his face and deep wrinkles under his eyes.

"Slept like a rock," Jacob said. "But weird question, do you know anything about the red marks on the snow outside? I told my girlfriend it's probably wine stains, but—"

"Oh, the red snow." The old man chuckled. "It's quite extraordinary, isn't it? Tourists especially seem to enjoy the mystery surrounding it."

"Mystery?" I asked.

"Well, you see, young lady, there is no definitive answer as to what causes the red snow. Some say it's drunk folks walking home through the snow while spilling the last bits of their mulled wine."

"But then there would be footsteps," I said.

He pointed his finger in the air. "Ah, yes. Very good! Well, the other theory has to do with the red bricks that you see around town. They say that when it snows, some of the flakes drop down the façades, take some of the color with them, and then drop to the ground."

His gaze started shifting from me to Jacob and back. "And others even say that the sky bleeds over our little town, to punish it."

"For what?" I asked.

"Who knows? Maybe the people who settled here upset the sky gods." The old man chuckled. "But don't you worry, it all gets cleaned up."

---

The old man was right. After we walked out of the cafe where we had breakfast in the town center, there was no sight of red snow anywhere, but I still couldn't get it out of my mind. Jacob and I discussed all the different theories but finally decided that it was probably a little trick the locals played on visitors.

A little mystery to add to the charm of the Christmas town.

We spent the rest of the day exploring the town some more. We jumped from shop to shop, simply to avoid the cold. It was also the reason we didn't hike up to the castle. I had underestimated how freezing it would be.

In the center of town was an old church that seemed really popular. I suggested checking it out, but Jacob was against it because he thought it would be boring.

Finally, it started getting dark, and we made our way to one of the Christmas markets.

This market had dozens of small wooden stalls selling little presents and a bunch of different food. There was a small ice-skating rink in the middle and a stage where music was played. The lights and smells of anise and cinnamon pulled you in and made you feel welcome and warm.

We had some hot beverages and waffles. We talked to some other people who were visiting town. Everything was close to perfect.

And then it started snowing.

As those little snowflakes fell from the sky, everything around us came to a halt. It felt as if the people around us stopped moving for just a second, and then there was one big, communal breath.

That was when everything got out of control. The jolly Christmas music from the stage turned into a distorted mess of sound. The fairy lights started flickering. And suddenly all the people around us started moving in all directions. Some were shouting, even screaming.

I was starting to get pushed around, so I grabbed Jacob's arm. "What the hell is going on?" I shouted, my voice trembling with fear, but the look on my boyfriend's face was the opposite.

He smiled as a snowflake fell on his face. He smudged it with his finger, leaving a trail of blood.

"It's the beginning of winter, Ava," he said with an eerie calmness. "Isn't it beautiful?"

I don't know what happened inside me next, but I pushed Jacob away and ran with the crowds. The town was still new to me, and at night I didn't recognize much, so I had no idea where I was going. All I knew was that something was wrong and that my gut shouted at me to run.

On my way through the alleys, I stumbled into a group of people.

Their faces were just as calm as Jacob's. A woman smiled and asked me who I was and where I came from.

"You're not from here," a man answered before I could say anything.

"Who brought you? Are you an offering?" the woman asked.

I stumbled back and kept running. I can't say how much time passed until I finally recognized the street where our hotel and Jacob's car were.

I didn't have the car key, so I had to get to the room. All I knew was that I wanted to get away from here as fast as possible.

The reception was empty, and I ran up the stairs to our room. When I opened the door, I realized that Jacob was already there and he was not alone; the old man from the reception was with him.

My heart was racing, and I contemplated leaving again, but then I thought I might be overreacting. Nothing had happened, and besides, I had nowhere to go. I would probably be safer here with Jacob.

"Ava, it's fine. You can come in," he interrupted my thoughts. I stayed frozen in the doorway.

"What's going on?" I muttered.

The old man gave me a sympathetic smile. "You are safe, girl. They have found someone else."

"Someone else?"

"Another offering."

"Grandpa," Jacob said in a stern voice.

"It didn't happen. She doesn't need to know," he whispered.

"Yes, I fucking need to know. What is going on? Why did you call him grandpa?" I shouted.

The fear was replaced with a rush of rage. I started moving toward the window.

"You don't want to see this, honey. Stay there," the old man said, but I didn't stop until I was almost at the window. And then I saw what they were looking at.

At the house across the street, a group of people were standing by a big open window that had a flagpole next to it. When I saw what they were doing, my blood froze.

They were hanging a body on the pole.

A million thoughts were running through my mind, but before I could act on any of them, Jacob had already grabbed my arm.

He pushed a syringe into my skin, and everything went dark.

---

When I finally opened my eyes, I was sitting in a moving car. It was day.

When the memories of the last night came back to me, I grabbed the door handle, but the door was locked.

"You wanna jump out of a moving car?" I heard Jacob say next to me. His eyes were fixed on the road.

My heart was beating so fast that I thought it might jump out of my chest.

"Are you all right, honey? You passed out last night after a few too many drinks—"

"Cut the crap," I interrupted him. "What the actual hell happened last night?"

He sighed. "So you didn't forget. What a shame."

Regret rushed through me. I should have faked it until we were out of the car.

"Don't worry, I'm not gonna hurt you. I actually really like you, Ava. You might not believe me, but that's a requirement."

"Requirement for what?" I whispered.

"For the offering, of course. Every December, on the first weekend, the blood snow arrives. And each of those two nights needs an offering. I'm really sorry, Ava, but if we don't do it, the snow won't stop. Until it buries us all." He was quiet for a second.

"I brought you to my old home, Ava, because you matter to me. And it wasn't certain that you would become a sacrifice, only a possibility. But you were lucky."

"Lucky?" I repeated.

"You weren't chosen. It would have been even better if you had blacked out, like on the first night. Everything would have been fine. But you made things really difficult for me."

I had been dating Jacob for a whole year. And I never realized what was wrong with him. I trusted him too much. I don't even know where this hell town is. Jacob surprised me with the trip, and I slept the whole way there. Now I understand he probably drugged me then, too.

I didn't say anything about that. I didn't confront him any further. All I needed was to get away from him.

"You said you weren't gonna hurt me."

Jacob smiled. "I won't. I'll take you back home, or I can drop you off on the way. Grandpa said it would be fine. He said nobody would believe you, even if you told them."

# OUR LOCAL GROCERY STORE STARTED SELLING PRODUCTS THAT DON'T EXIST

## Part 1

Nostalgia can be such a fine feeling. A smell linking back to an almost forgotten encounter, a movie that transports you right back to your childhood, a taste reminding you of a much simpler time. The town of Marville had a way of giving you this intense sensation every single day. I think it was mostly due to its seclusion. Marville is rather small—we only have the essential shops to fulfill our needs—but if we really wanted to escape to a bigger city, then we would have to endure hours in the car.

You might think we'd find it hard to breathe. Mom, Dad, and I hardly ever left town. If we did, then it was only for a bigger purchase of something we could not get here or for a vacation during summer. Nobody ever left Marville in autumn and winter, as that was when we'd make our money for the whole year. You see, this tiny place in the middle of nowhere is quite the tourist attraction. Maybe it's due to the beautiful nature surrounding us or the coziness of our unique little town, but as soon as the leaves start falling, the visitors stumble in. They take walks through our old, medieval town, have cake and coffee in our cafés, or go hiking through the woods surrounding us.

I always had a special place in my heart for the cold season. It brings some life into our town. Don't get me wrong, I do enjoy Marville, but the older I grow, the more I'm craving to see the big world, meet new people, see what is out there. The visitors give me a sensation of what that might be like.

This year I swore to myself to enjoy the cold months as much as I could, as I would be moving away for college next year. It would be the last year I'd help my parents in their coffee shop and the last year I'd get to spend with my two very best friends, who lived on the exact same street as my family. Little did I know that this year would be by far different than anything I'd ever witnessed here. It started with something as banal as can be.

Our supermarket.

I know we like nostalgia, but we still live in modern times and can buy the same things that are sold everywhere around the country. We only have one supermarket in town, but it is as big as they come. It sells everything from food to drinks, drugstore items, and handyman stuff. Our Coke was Coca-Cola or Pepsi. Our cereal Lucky Charms or Honey Puffs. Our Lay's were half-filled with air. You know, all the stuff you can get at most stores. The only difference would maybe be the fresh produce. Our milk, butter, and eggs come from local farms, which I always appreciated.

Well, now it seems they've taken the normality out of Marville for good.

---

It was a boring-ass Saturday, as it was every week in Marville, when we started noticing the changes. Damien, Tessa, and I were on our way to buy snacks for the evening and hopefully find someone to get us some beer.

"I feel like it's gonna rain tonight. We should do a movie marathon," Tessa exclaimed on our way to the store.

Autumn comes early in Marville. The hot weeks of summer were slowly coming to an end. We had spent almost every day by the lake, and the months passed like seconds. It felt like last winter was only yesterday. Damien's blond curls were growing out, Tessa's sun-kissed tan was slowly fading, and I was getting ready to go back to help my parents sell coffee and tea. Soon the first visitors would come in. Some come for a day, and some stay for days or even weeks at the local B&B.

"Ugh," Damien grunted. "What fucking movie have we not seen yet, Tess?"

"Do you have a better idea?" she hissed back.

Spending basically every single day together was starting to show its toll on us. These were the last carefree days we had, though, and I wanted to cherish them and do as little as we could as long as it was still time to relax. Soon we'd have to get back to studying and working.

The automatic doors to our local Marstore opened, and we were greeted by the cold breeze of the air conditioner. There was a distant melody playing from the store's speakers. Something old and cozy. I guess they were trying to get us into the holiday spirit already to frame a need for consumption.

Most grocery stores have a very specific setup. They start with greens and fruits because when you start shopping, your mind is focused and you might want to go for the healthy options. You start filling up your cart with them, and when you make your way to the end of the store, the focus is killed and you go for the sweets.

Well, my friends and I usually skip the healthy section altogether. Today, however, it caught our attention. We had only stepped in, and our awareness was sharp.

"What the fuck?" Tess whispered.

None of the fruits looked remotely like anything I'd ever seen before. There were bananas three times the size of the ones we know with a purple peel. The apples were tiny and came in plastic buckets. The cucumbers were shaped like pretzels. This had to be a joke or some kind of prank, but since when did grocery stores care to play with their customers?

"This is hilarious," Damien said and walked up to strawberries that all looked as if someone had taken a bite out of them already.

I had no idea what to say, and my initial reaction was laughter, though deep inside I knew this wasn't funny. I felt a knot tie in my stomach; something was awfully off. We continued walking through the aisles, looking for another customer or worker. Marville was a small place, after all, and we knew almost everyone who lived here.

We didn't see anyone inside, but our attention was focused on the colorful items on the shelves anyway. At first, I thought the crop had just been awfully weird this year, but the packaged products were even more astonishing. Every single item had been replaced by a new version.

Everything was similar to what we knew but just slightly off, just a tad different. The Coke was green, chip packages were vacuum-sealed, not leaving any air inside, and all the brand names had changed just enough to make us take a second look.

Rëësës, Mr. Plopper, or vanishED.

"Maybe the owners changed and they're only selling off-brand stuff. Because it's cheaper or something," I suggested.

"And they decided to exchange everything in one night? I was here yesterday, and I swear it was all normal," Damien responded while walking toward the shelf and touching anything he could get his hands on.

"Let's ask her!"

Tess started walking up to a woman dressed completely in black with a top hat completing her outfit. As she saw us approach, she turned around and smiled.

"Well, hello there, kids. How are you doing on this swell day?"

"Uhm, hello. Are you from around here?" I asked.

She shook her head, never breaking that smile. "I wasn't, but now I am."

Tess and I looked at each other, not sure how to respond to that.

"What do you think about the products in this shop?" Damien asked.

"They are terrific. Wonderful. Delicious!" she responded. "Oh, Logan, sweetheart, you should get some of these biscuits and broscuits for the coffee shop!" she said as she gently grazed her fingers down my face. They felt like sandpaper.

I had no idea how to respond. I'd never seen this woman before in my life. I thought she was a tourist.

Without saying another word, she turned around and continued shopping while humming a melody. It took me a little moment to realize that she was humming along to the music coming from the speakers. It was still the same song that was playing when we walked in. As if it was on a loop.

"This is so freaky," Damien whispered. "Are we dreaming?"

Tess chuckled, but I didn't feel like joking around. I was genuinely disturbed.

"Let's go to the register," I suggested.

The only cashier working that day was Matthew, a guy we knew from school. He was a bit of a bully and rude every time we came to buy anything, honestly, but today he looked different. He was smiling and humming just like the lady and waved wildly when he saw us.

"Matt, what the hell is going on? What happened to the store?" I almost shouted.

He shook his head while making intense eye contact.

"Absolutely nothing happened. What are you talking about?"

---

We didn't buy anything and just walked out. Damien suggested getting some of those weird snacks or at least the crazy fruit, but being in that store somehow made me feel nauseous. I felt like I was on the brink of passing out.

I was simply feeling wrong. That's the only way I can describe it, so I told my friends I would be going home for the night. The closer we got to our street, the more tired I became. I started wondering if I was hallucinating, but it seemed as if my friends were witnessing the same peculiar events as me.

We said goodbye, and we all went to our own homes to check with our parents.

As I opened the door to our home, a shiver went down my spine. I smelled something cooking in the kitchen, something both sweet and bitter, but the scent wasn't the weirdest part; it was the music. The same melody from the Marstore was coming from our radio.

"Mom? Dad?" I shouted.

"Oh honey, you're home! Come in, love. We were just about to have dinner!"

My mom was wearing a dress and white gloves, and my father was dressed in a brown suit.

"Is there a special occasion?" I asked.

"What could be more special than a loving dinner with your family, son?" my father responded in a dry tone.

I took a seat and swallowed. "Uhm, Mom, Dad, have you been to the store today?"

"Why, yes, I went just this morning to buy some flodders and branks," my mom casually answered.

"What?"

She pointed at the pan that was filled with some weird substance; it looked gooey and was formed into squares. Like a mixture of pudding and crackers. Both my parents looked at me as if I was the one losing my mind.

My stomach started rumbling again. Maybe I was getting sick. I wondered if I was having a fever. "I'm sorry, I'm not feeling very well. I'll take a little nap, okay?"

"You're not eating with us?" my mother asked with a strange twitch in her eye.

"I'll eat later," I mumbled and made my way up the stairs.

"You better!" I heard my father shouting from the kitchen.

Now, I don't have to tell you that something awfully off was taking place. I simply couldn't understand what it was, and I felt like I was losing my mind. And things didn't stop there.

---

When I woke up again, it was dark outside. A look at the alarm clock resting next to my bed showed me that I had slept for five hours straight.

I felt like I was starving and wondered if all the weirdness of today had just been a dream. I rubbed my eyes and stumbled out of bed, ready to go downstairs and grab a snack. Normally my parents would be asleep by now, but I still heard some commotion downstairs.

I grabbed my phone, and suddenly everything that happened earlier became far more real again.

**DO NOT EAT ANYTHING. WILL EXPLAIN LATER.**

Tess had sent me this text a couple of hours ago. I texted her back and tried calling but got no reply.

Slowly I opened my door to see what my parents were up to. At first, I thought the door was locked, but after pushing a little, I realized it was blocked by a pile of food lying in front of it. All things I didn't recognize.

I tiptoed toward the stairs. This was the first time in my life that I had ever been freaked out by my own home and family.

And then I heard them.

My parents were talking and laughing, but they weren't alone. There were a bunch of other voices I didn't recognize, but the one sound that stood out was the melody. They were still listening to it.

There was no way I was going down there to confront them. I got back to my room as fast as I could, locking the door behind me.

My heart started racing, a cold sweat was giving me shivers, and I felt completely out of my mind. I always knew Marville as the sole definition of the most wonderful place on Earth. It is safe and cozy and nice. It looks just like you would imagine Santa's village. The people are friendly, even the tourists. But now something else must have crept in here, something that doesn't belong, and it is somehow connected to that grocery store with the items that are all just slightly off.

I have no idea what to believe anymore, but I feel the deep need to get out of here.

Before more of them appear.

# Part 2

Overnight, everything around us had changed to the picture-perfect image of a town built inside a snow globe. It was only September, but the snowflakes were falling down like glittery, cotton-candy sprinkles. Neighbors were outside sipping something I assume was the new version of hot apple cider while they were decorating their homes. I didn't know what festivity they were preparing for, and I was scared to find out.

Marville was always a fine place, but the view I had this morning outshone anything I'd ever seen before. It was surreal. The street looked beautiful. Everything was radiating an atmosphere of coziness, and everyone who touched it was immediately won over.

And it all started with something as seemingly ordinary as a grocery store changing its products. Every little item looked as if it had been given a light touch to ensure it was just that little bit different than the original version.

*Why would anyone take that effort?* I wondered, while a part of me was sure that we had entered a new universe of sorts.

"Honey, what is going on with you?"

The voice of my own mother standing behind my door was sending shivers down my spine.

"You missed breakfast, boy. That is no way to be. You didn't even say hello to our visitors last night. If this behavior continues, we have no other option but to punish you," I heard my father's stern voice say. He was usually nothing like this. My dad is the kindest man I know, but whoever was knocking on my door was not my father. And that giddy woman was not my mother.

I could tell from the sound of their fingers scratching on my door. It sounded corrupt and malicious.

"Listen, Logan, baby, we need to open the café early this year but..." She took a long pause.

"But we don't want you to help," my father finished her sentence.

As if everything happening around me wasn't weird enough already. I couldn't for the life of me understand why my parents wouldn't want me to help. I mean, I never minded the work; I liked driving down to the shop with either Mom or Dad in the morning, being greeted by the smell of fresh coffee beans, and preparing muffins and brownies in the kitchen. I know it's not your typical teenage fun activity, but our coffee shop is nice, the people who visit are as well, and they always tip generously.

I took a deep breath. I couldn't hide from them forever. They were my parents, after all. Yeah, last night I was sure I wanted to get the hell out of here, but I couldn't really leave them here, could I?

I walked up to the door and opened it. My parents almost fell right into my room. They had been leaning on the door the entire time.

They were both wearing the same exact clothes as yesterday, but their faces looked messy, as if they hadn't slept at all. Mom's makeup was runny, and Dad's eye was twitching like crazy.

I decided to ignore their looks. I was afraid of what they might answer if I asked them about it.

"Why don't you want me to help?" I asked in the most normal voice I could force myself to speak in.

They exchanged a strange look.

"Just for now. You can help us when you feel better. I prepared breakfast. Go eat," my mother instructed with the biggest fake smile I had ever seen on her face. Then without waiting for a reaction, they turned around at the same time and walked down the stairs. Seconds later, I heard the front door shut.

When I heard the car engine start, I finally made my way downstairs. A part of me was scared shitless that last night's visitors would still be around, but the house seemed to be empty. However, as I got closer to the kitchen, I heard something.

The melody was still playing.

The tune I heard in the grocery store and that had followed me all the way home.

My heart was still racing like crazy when I jumped inside the kitchen. I had no idea why I did that; I thought it might scare away anyone that could be in there. I could have run out the front door, of course, but considering the entire town had just changed into a landscape from a picture book, I felt safer staying in here.

I was both relieved and shocked when I saw the kitchen.

There was no other person in here but instead piles and piles of food. It looked as if my parents had been cooking all night long. I didn't even understand when they bought all the supplies. The food here could have fed an entire football team.

There were fish, meat, and vegetables that all looked like jelly, and they smelled like nothing I had ever smelled before. There were bowls filled with mushy substances, all stacked on top of each other. Cakes that were made out of something that resembled concrete. As my eyes tried to process what they were looking at, my stomach started turning again. I was starving but simultaneously felt revolted. There was no way any of this stuff would ever touch my lips. If this was an art project, I would have been astonished, but my family thinking this was legit food that we had every day was a concept I couldn't comprehend. And it was all so much. I could hardly make my way to the kitchen counter to finally turn off that godforsaken radio. As the quiet settled in, I realized that the tune had been in the back of my mind all night long.

Well, now I was realizing that it wasn't in the back of my head but literally in my kitchen.

The silence was the nicest thing I heard since yesterday, but the quiet wouldn't stay for long. I heard our back door close shut. I didn't hear it open through the sound of the music, but whoever opened it was already inside. My eyes scanned the kitchen. Maybe I could climb through the window quickly, but what then?

"Hello?" I shouted. A part of me hoped it was one of my parents who forgot something, but another part of me really didn't want to see their faces, either. Mom's smile was still engraved into my brain.

"It's me. Are you alone?"

It was Damien.

I hadn't heard anything from him since coming home yesterday. I tried reaching him, but his phone went straight to voicemail every time. Tessa hadn't responded to any of my texts, either. I was positively freaked out since her text yesterday saying **DON'T EAT ANYTHING**. She clearly knew something, or she made that assumption because her parents had gone insane as well. And that left me with another fear. Damien was a little too keen on trying the snacks.

I didn't answer, but Damien was already standing in the doorframe of the kitchen. He looked miserable. He had bags under his bloodshot eyes, and his hair was going in all directions. We both looked at each other. It seemed like neither of us was sure what to say. Then his eyes wandered over the kitchen.

"Did you eat anything?" he asked.

I shook my head.

"Have you heard from Tess?" I asked.

He looked behind him and mouthed something I couldn't understand. Seconds later, Tess appeared behind him. She had scratches all over her face and arms and looked seriously disturbed.

"Logan, you need to come with us," she said. "We need to get out of this town as fast as we can."

---

We got inside Tessa's car. It was still snowing, and the ground was just slightly white. People were outside laughing and chatting, and for a second, it looked like a regular day in December. Except it was September, and half of the people out here didn't belong. They were all dressed in black, slightly old-fashioned outfits, and their faces were too perfect to be real. Their cheeks were all rosy, their teeth perfectly straight and white, their hair not a hair out of place. As we drove past them, their eyes and heads turned to watch us drive off.

They did not look happy.

"What happened to you?" I whispered to Tess.

"My mom. She went completely insane. She had made all these weird meals and tried shoving them down my throat. I kept resisting, so she became violent. The most fucked-up part was her face, however. It stayed perfectly still the entire time, as if something else inside her was controlling her."

"My parents were like that, too, but they didn't attack me. I'm so sorry, Tess," I responded.

She just shook her head in disbelief. "When that happened, I ran to my room and texted both of you. She followed me, though. It was so scary. Damien came over after he read my text, just in time. We fought off my mom and drove to the bookstore."

The bookstore was a small shop that Damien's parents owned. We used to spend hours there when we were younger, reading almost every book they had.

"What about your parents, Damien?" I asked, but then I remembered. His parents had left for a holiday. "Right. Never mind. Did you not eat anything?"

"Actually I did. I was starving when I got home, but we didn't have much in the fridge. I thought about going back to the store, but I don't know, something made me stay home. I still had eggs, so I fried them up. They looked normal, though."

"And you feel normal?" I asked.

He nodded. "As normal as you can feel in a situation like this."

"Maybe it's only things that get imported," I mumbled.

Until this moment, the entire absurd situation had felt insane and slightly threatening, but now we were sure that we had to get out. Tessa's mom was always loving and kind and certainly not violent. Whatever she ate had turned her insane, and soon it might do the same to everyone who lived here.

It felt so weird having this intense sensation of fear while looking at surroundings so beautiful and innocent. Kids were playing, the shops were all open, and everyone was getting ready for a season of glee.

The three of us had turned quiet. There was so much to discuss, to wonder about, but after the events of last night, I think we were all trying to make sense of it ourselves. At least my mind found it hard as hell to adjust. The contrast was insufferable. My brain was working overtime.

So much so that it took me a good minute to notice the music.

"Did you turn on the radio?" I asked Tess, who was sitting behind the wheel.

"No," she whispered, "it just started."

She was about to turn it off again, but Damien held her hand back. "Do you hear that? It's changing," he said.

He was right. At first, it sounded like the melody we heard in the store and that was playing in my kitchen, but the further away we got from the town center, the darker it became. We were really close to the town border, and the music sounded as if someone had thrown the sound of "La Vie en Rose" into a blender. The initial tune was strange but familiar. It gave me a warm feeling despite the fact that my head knew it was scary. But what it was changing to now was so much worse.

It was the sound of people crying.

And then the crying turned into screaming.

"Turn it off!" I commanded, but neither of my friends reacted. They were distracted by something far more horrifying.

We had escaped from the center of town, and our surroundings looked far different at first glance. There was no more snow and no strangers dressed in black. For a moment, it felt like we had gotten out of that nightmare.

But then we noticed them.

The bodies.

Tess slowed down. We didn't believe our eyes at first; it was simply too gruesome.

There were multiple people hanging from trees, their eyes opened wide in terror. At the end of the street, we noticed a car that had crashed right into a tree. Whatever was left of the people inside was now blood and goo.

"Stop the car!" Damien shouted, and we came to a swift halt. He slammed his door open and started running toward something at the end of the road.

*Shit*, I thought and hoped from the bottom of my heart that he hadn't spotted his parents in between the corpses.

I quickly unbuckled my seat belt and ran outside, following my friend. Tess stayed in the car, her expression frozen.

Damien turned around before I could reach him.

"Don't look," he whispered, but it was already too late.

There were people lying on the road. They weren't Damien's parents, but I did recognize a woman.

It was our high school teacher, Ms. Jones. The most intelligent and friendly person I'd ever met, lying in a puddle of blood with a pipe pierced through her insides.

"They killed them. Everyone who tried to escape," I whispered.

Tears shot to my eyes but were quickly followed by a feeling of nausea. I thought I'd pass out any second, and Damien looked just as pale as I was feeling.

He started saying something, but I couldn't hear a word. I tried to respond, but my words didn't make any sense. I suddenly started feeling this urge. I knew I would never leave. This was our end. We would stay here with Ms. Jones. "La Vie en Rose" played in my head, accompanied by cries and screams.

My thoughts were mush. No concrete thing came to my mind.

Then I noticed the car. Tess had come closer.

I don't know how we did it, but we somehow ended up back in the car, and Tess threw the car into reverse.

The further we got from the outskirts of the town, the clearer my thoughts became.

Those people hadn't been murdered. They had taken their lives at the border. I knew it because I felt it.

There was no way out of here.

We were stuck in our picture-perfect snow globe.

# Part 3

Marville was the most beautiful place on Earth. It looked like something taken right out of a book, and at times, I could swear it was. You could imagine sitting by the chimney, sipping hot chocolate in your pajamas, and looking at photos of Marville to complete the cozy atmosphere. All while listening to a tune that was almost forgotten. Something you can't quite place but that will make you feel warm and nostalgic all the way through. I believe that's how the other residents who were taken over by the new vibe were feeling. Though I can't say for sure whether they were feeling anything at all. They seemed like shells taken over by a higher entity. The ones who were quick enough to understand that the new living was just a façade didn't get far.

The border of suicide was keeping us inside the town that seemed nothing but perfect at first glance. As long as you obliged, ate the peculiar food, and listened to the otherworldly tunes. I still wasn't sure whether the screams of terror we heard as we reached the outskirts of town were warning us to stay inside or calling us to follow them. For now, and probably for longer than we'd wish, we would have to stay inside. It was still a better option than death. For just a moment, as we were driving back to town, still listening to the music, which now became softer and friendlier, I thought I might be able to get used to it.

I'd always wanted to change. Sure, Marville was nice and all, but we all crave something different after getting used to our mundane life too much. This certainly was more than just different. We had all the food that shouldn't exist. There was a whole new world to explore just in our grocery store alone. And it had been expanding over the course of the time that I had spent inside. Every store and every restaurant were now cooking and baking and preparing every item with the new products.

We had to drive very slowly as the snow had been falling nonstop. I couldn't quite say for how long we had been gone. We drove for maybe an hour in my definition of time, but as we entered the center of town, it felt like days had passed. The people, the real residents of Marville as well as the visitors, had been quite productive. They had started building little booths all over the streets. Tiny wooden huts selling tiny pancakes in the form of triangles colored all in black, there were multiple huts selling the wrong hot apple cider, and others were frying up red-and-white mushrooms that appeared to be taken out of a video game.

"Is this going to be their Christmas?" Damien broke the silence. We hadn't said a word after what we saw. It was too hard to process and even harder to say out loud. They wanted us to stay here. They didn't simply want to take over Marville; they wanted everyone who lived here to stay with them.

"I don't think it's their version. It feels like they are trying to copy what they imagine our life looks like. Just check out their faces. They are not simply different. They are mimicking us."

Tess was right. The visitors were observing us. At first, I thought they were angry in a way, as if they were trying to get rid of us. And while yes, they seemed dangerous, they also looked lost. On top of that, they were changing their outfits. At first, every single one of them was dressed in black, but now it appeared they were changing to different colors. However, just like the grocery store items, something about the clothes and looks was just slightly off.

"They are learning," I whispered as my gaze continued moving from visitor to visitor. They all stared back, but no one came closer or interacted with us in any way.

That was when I noticed that Tess had stopped the car. We were standing in the middle of the road, close to the town's marketplace. From here, I could see our coffee shop. The lights were on and the windows were fogged up. For a second, I wondered if I should walk over and try to talk some sense into my parents. I remembered sitting in there with my friends, drinking hot coffee, and chatting. We could still be doing that and have some delicious broscuits with it. My hand automatically moved to the door handle, but before I could open it, the car door locked.

It was Damien.

"Tess, why did you stop the car?" he asked.

"Oh, I just wanna jump out real quick and get some charcoal pralines from that booth over there!" she responded.

"Charcoal what?" I asked, and she pointed at a booth that was half in flames.

Tess started giggling. "They smell delicious," she said.

"They really do," I agreed.

I was starving. It felt like I hadn't eaten anything in a week.

Damien looked at both of us and then toward the radio. He started smashing his bare fist against it until it was bloody and the radio finally was broken. That didn't stop the music, however. It wasn't only coming from the car; it was all around us, playing from every corner of town. It had a way to play with our minds, and Tess and I were too hungry to fight it anymore. Honestly, I couldn't care less what would be on my plate at this point, I was just so damn hungry.

"Guys, remember what we just saw? All the dead bodies. They hung themselves on the tree because of whatever is out there. Don't listen to what is going through your mind right now. It's not your own voice you're hearing."

I tried listening to what he was saying, but it didn't make sense to me at that moment. I just wanted to enjoy the beautiful and peaceful surroundings. Tess cared even less. She unlocked the doors, quickly jumped out, and started stomping through the snow. Thinking about it now, I can't tell you what went through my head when all of that was taking place. I ignored Damien, who was shouting something after Tess, opened my own door, and made my way to the coffee shop that belonged to my family.

---

*Marvilllous* coffee.

The familiar sign stood up high, but it looked as if someone had given it a fresh coat of paint. The red color was dripping down, forming red droplets on the white snow. The door's bell rang as I pushed the thick glass open.

"Logan!"

My parents simultaneously shouted as they saw me. They were still dressed the same way with the addition of new aprons. I was still trying to make sense of the color of them. If I had to describe it, I would say they looked like the drops and blobs you see in front of your eyes when you rub them too hard.

There were about a dozen visitors inside. All heads turned and followed me as I stepped toward the counter where my mother was standing.

"Mom, I'm starving."

The words escaped my mouth before reaching my conscious mind.

My mother was still smiling. Her face was entirely frozen. Her big green eyes didn't blink once. Even when she started speaking.

"Of course you are, sweet boy. Everyone needs to eat."

"And who could say no to the delicious cuisine of Marville!" a woman's voice spoke. I felt her hot breath against my neck and turned to my left. She gently touched my face and started whispering. "A beautiful boy like this belongs in the most wonderful place."

For a fraction of a second, I felt content. She was radiating warmth and friendliness that perfectly matched with the cozy atmosphere of the café. But then her nails started digging inside my skin. I felt a swift rush of pain in my head. She removed her hand from my face and started sucking the blood off her fingers.

More people started getting up from their chairs, watching this peculiar interaction closely.

A man walked up to us and asked, "Is that correct?"

"What's correct?" I asked, but his question didn't seem to be directed to me. He was looking at the woman.

She didn't respond, however. Instead, she walked back to her seat as if none of this had just happened. The man came closer, and I was afraid he was going to have a taste of my blood as well. Behind him, another one got up from his seat.

"The muffins are ready!"

My father appeared behind me with a tray of something that resembled a muffin in no way. They looked like cubes of charcoal coated in a red, gooey substance.

He was standing right in front of me now. My father looked as if he had aged a decade in the last days. He looked tired, and the constant smiling had his face all rippled up.

"Can I have one?" I carefully asked. The muffins looked and smelled delicious. Like walking through a dark alley at night.

"You must!" my father almost shouted, his eyes twitching nervously. His hands were shaking.

"Eat!" my mother agreed, but when I saw her face, I noticed the same twitch in her eyes, and I could swear she was trying to shake her head. My parents were smiling, but their insides were shouting. They were trapped.

The look of suffering in their eyes seemed to be waking me up from a trance. I had felt so insufferably drawn to the insane food and the music. It had been playing with my head all day, and they almost took me over to their side. I was so close to giving in. I couldn't understand what was going on; I felt like I wasn't entirely in charge of my own head anymore. There was another voice in there with me.

I took all the strength I had left in me and ran outside as fast as I could. I didn't stop running. I ignored the voices and the music and the smells and just kept going.

I was completely out of breath and my pants were soaking wet and freezing from the snow when I realized that I'd run all the way home. During that short run, the sky had turned completely black. In a matter of seconds, the day had turned into night. Looking up at my house, I didn't feel welcome. This didn't feel like home anymore.

I felt trapped. Both my body and mind were stuck here. I had to eat eventually or I would starve. I couldn't get out, either, because the suicide border would not let me.

I was entirely sure I had lost my head, but something pulled me back to reality. There was a light glowing from Damien's house.

*My friends.*

During my strange moment in which I almost gave in to the new world, I'd entirely forgotten about them. A shiver went down my spine when I remembered that Tess had jumped out of the car as well. Had she already been turned?

As I ran up to his house, I saw his door opening. I hesitated for a second before I realized that it was Damien, who had seen me from inside.

"What the hell is wrong with you? And what happened to your cheek?" he shouted.

"I don't know. I went to my parents', and I almost ate something, but I didn't. And... where is Tess?"

Damien waved me inside, and I followed him to the living room, where Tess was sitting and shaking.

"She got really aggressive. It felt like she was possessed or something, but I caught her just before she could shove some of that weird Christmas drink down her throat."

"Are you okay now?" I asked Tess and sat down next to her.

She shook her head. "We don't exist anymore," she whispered and looked at Damien.

He sighed and sat down with us. "I tried calling my parents. They are out there. I thought maybe they can find a way to help us or make sense of this."

"And you couldn't reach them?" I asked.

They both looked at the ground.

"Yeah, I did. My mom picked up." He took a long breath. "She didn't know who I was."

"They had no idea what Marville was. They thought we were pranking them. Then we tried reaching anyone else we know that doesn't live here. They all thought we were crazy," Tess spoke.

"So then we went online. Everything works normally except when we look for our location. There is no Marville. GPS doesn't work. It's like we're in some sort of vacuum."

I was lost for words. Everything happening was entirely and completely insane, but this was the cherry on top. We were stuck here, and we could talk to the outside, but they were not aware of our existence.

---

We sat there for hours discussing our next steps, but there was nothing we could come up with that would help us get out. We couldn't hunt down every single person in town. We couldn't survive forever with no food, and that was when Tess suggested something.

"It all started with the grocery store. Maybe that's all we need to destroy."

It was the only idea that made the slightest bit of sense.

"How do we do it?" I asked.

"They should be closed now. We'll break in. Set a fire. Make an explosion. Whatever we have to."

We packed up anything we thought we might need. Weapons that would be useless considering we had no idea what they were capable of and as there were only three of us.

Finally, we collected all our courage and drove to the Marstore.

---

It wasn't closed. All lights were running, and there appeared to be people inside. From here, we couldn't recognize if they were residents of Marville or visitors.

"What now?" Damien asked.

"We go in anyway," Tess said confidently.

"All right. But you guys have to be careful. Last time the music almost got to you."

I nodded. I couldn't have them control me again. It was the most disgusting feeling I'd ever experienced.

The automatic door opened swiftly as the three of us stood in front of it, ready for whatever would happen next. At least that was what we thought at that moment. As we stepped in, however, we were not ready to be greeted by hundreds of eyes.

The store was completely full. There were people we recognized who looked nothing like they did before. Everyone was dressed old-fashioned like my parents were, and their skin appeared as if it would crack any second. Their faces were full of stress, and at first, I thought it was because of whatever was controlling them, but their fear seemed to be coming from something else.

The shelves were almost empty. They were fighting for the last items, stocking up on these unnecessary and nonexistent goods. They were screaming and fighting, scratching each other's faces, and pushing the weak ones to the ground.

"Let's get the hell out of here!" I shouted.

We jumped out of the store, shocked by what we had just witnessed while new customers were pushing us to the side, trying to get in.

"If they buy everything and nothing is left, maybe it will just be over. Maybe it will get back to normal?" Tess said hopefully.

"Or they'll kill each other," Damien added.

We stood in front of the Marstore, and I swore I was completely done with everything, so I did the least helpful thing. I sat down. I sat in front of the store that started all of this insanity, watching the catastrophe unfold in front of me. My friends fell down next to me, letting the numbness take over.

Hours passed, and the last people exited the store. Some were in tears, others drenched in blood. The lights of the store stayed on, but not a single soul was left inside. That was when I got up. I felt a tiny shimmer of hope when I realized that they must have taken everything.

I slowly walked inside, Tess and Damien right behind me.

The store was empty. Not a soul and not a product left. As we walked through the empty aisles, Damien finally said something.

"Do you hear that?"

At first, I had no idea what he was talking about. The only noise I could identify was the light buzz of the fridges, but then I realized what he meant.

It was quiet. The music was gone.

Tears shot to my eyes.

"Is it over?" I asked. I could already feel the relief rushing through my body. We finally felt peace.

Of course, it didn't last long, I realized when I heard Tess scream and not stop.

We followed her voice to witness the gory aftermath of the massacre. In front of the register were more dead bodies. Except these ones didn't look like they had killed themselves. They had been murdered as they tried to collect the last items.

The blood and intestines sticking out made my stomach turn and my eyes tear up. All hope was gone in a matter of seconds. We tried looking for anybody alive but quickly realized that we could not help anyone.

And that was when the next fear set in.

I ran out of the store without a word and again kept running and running until I was back in the town center.

*Mom, Dad.*

I prayed to a god I didn't believe in that they hadn't suffered as well.

I shoved the door of the Marvilllous café open, my heart beating so hard in my chest that I was sure it would explode. I fell to my knees when I heard my mom's soft whimper and the loud noises of my father throwing up.

The shop was a mess. Glass was shattered. Everything was emptied. My parents weren't able to say a word, but I was just glad they were alive.

People were roaming the streets, which were eerily quiet. The visitors were gone, together with their peculiar products. The snow had melted.

Nobody spoke. I don't think the victims were aware of what had happened. The few of us who hadn't eaten anything tried to talk to them, but it was no use.

Days passed. The town looked exactly the way I remembered it did before. The bodies disappeared. Our store was back to normal, selling Coca-Cola, toast, and straight cucumbers.

---

Tess and I both had scars on our faces reminding us of something so entirely unbelievable that you'd think it never happened.

And that's the thing.

Nobody remembers it happening.

Nobody remembers the parasite that infected us.

I wrote it all down, and even I don't believe it occurred. It feels like a story I made up. My face healed, and everyone around me had excuses for the scars and bruises they suddenly had.

We forgot what happened. All of us. And that's why we don't leave.

We never leave Marville in autumn and winter.

You see, this tiny place in the middle of nowhere is quite the tourist attraction. Maybe it's due to the beautiful nature surrounding us or the coziness of our unique little town, but as soon as the leaves start falling, the visitors stumble in. They take walks through our medieval old town, have cake and coffee in our cafés, or go hiking through the woods surrounding us.

That's how it always has been. Ever since the parasite affected us.

And I swear I would have forgotten again had I not found this little note in my pocket proving to me that the words I wrote down were not simply just a story.

It was a note written on a piece of paper that has a color I've never seen before. It looks like what you see when you rub your eyes a little too hard. I believe the woman in the coffee shop left it in my jacket when she took a bit of my blood.

**Thank you for sharing Marville with us. We are sorry our stay will be so short, but we can't wait to see your beautiful town with its wonderful residents again next year.**

With the note, she left a chocolate bar. I've never seen this wrapper before, but it looks just like something that shouldn't exist.

# MY DAD HAS A SECOND FACE

It only started a little while ago, but I fear it's getting much worse. My dad has started alternating between two faces that couldn't be more different. The first one has brown eyes just like mine, glasses that are much bigger than mine, and a beard that I won't be able to grow for at least five more years, as he says.

When Dad wears his bearded face, we look a lot alike, although he is convinced that I'm the spitting image of my mother. I'm not sure if that's true; Mum passed away when I was still in kindergarten, and I avoid looking at old photos.

In them, there are pictures of her, but none of Dad's second face, and they remind me of a time that I'm sure was much better than the one we have now.

The new face is harder to describe because a regular mind has difficulty interpreting it. It almost looks like a new layer of gray texture with dark veins was vacuum-sealed on a skull. It compares to skin in some ways; it can sweat, and it slightly trembles when he speaks. The sounds he makes are muffled and hard to understand because there is no hole cut for his mouth. There's none for his nose, either, but I can still hear him breathing underneath.

The only things exposed are two holes cut into the upper half, functioning as eyes.

Luckily, I don't see the second face very often; he can change back to the old one and does so most of the time, but an image like that is hard to forget.

I know this sounds entirely absurd and terrifying, but my dad is all I have, and he's not evil.

Bad people did this to him.

Dad used to gamble a lot and owed some people money. It's not something we talk about, but I picked it up through little clues. After Mum's death, he went through a hard time, but I swear that he always cared about me in the ways that he knew how to. We don't have any other family, just each other.

The gambling ended very abruptly. I wish I could have been happy about it, but what came after was much worse. That's when the seed for the new face was put into the soil.

One evening, my dad was pacing through our apartment, mumbling things to himself.

"Fuck. Shit. He'll kill me. Soran will *kill* me."

Then he looked at me, his brown eyes wide open.

"Do you have a friend you can stay with tonight, buddy?"

I would have loved to do that, but my friends and even their parents were probably all asleep.

"No, it's too late for that," he mumbled to himself again. "Go to your room, lock the door, and go to bed. I—I have to go out and take care of something. You're twelve now. You can do this, right?"

I nodded, but before I could even move, there was a knock on the door. From the look on Dad's face, I could tell these weren't visitors he was happy about.

After that knock, a number of things happened. Dad rushed me to my room, which I locked from the inside. He told me to climb in my closet, which I didn't; I sat down right next to the door. A few seconds later, our front door slammed open. I expected noise, shouting, maybe crying, but it was eerily silent. All I heard was an occasional whimper from my dad.

I felt so helpless.

A man spoke words in a language I didn't understand. After that, there was only silence, until finally the front door opened and closed again.

For hours, I was too afraid to leave my room, but when I finally did, it was morning. I tiptoed toward the kitchen, where Dad was having cereal. He smiled when he saw me, wearing his regular face.

Everything seemed normal. It wasn't visible at first, but after that night, my dad had changed.

At first, I only caught glimpses of it.

The first time, I saw it for a second in the window at night and was sure I imagined it. But then I saw it in the bathroom mirror, in his dark teacup, and sometimes in my dreams.

The shape that trembles and breathes with no mouth. It was fine as long as it was only in the mirror, but as time progressed, it started growing outside the mirror. Now his face changes at least one night a week, and it stays for hours.

I don't know what happened that night, only that I now spend a lot of time locked up in my room.

---

The description of the second face, I realize, resembles a mask in many ways, but it isn't. And the reason I know that for sure is that one night when Dad was sleeping or *appeared* to be sleeping, I tried to take it off. I was sick of it. I hated the other face. I wanted to see my regular dad again.

But it was impossible.

It wouldn't move, but when he felt my hands on his new skin, his eyes opened wide and he gave me the *sign*.

We never discussed the sign; he never speaks of it when he wears his other face. It's just something that I learned. When he pushes his fingernails into the palm of his hand, it means that I should run to my room and lock myself inside.

It's the only way he is able to communicate when the other thing takes over. He tries to protect me, even in that unimaginable state. It usually only happens when we have odd guests in our home or before he leaves to take care of something and doesn't come back before the sun. As it only comes out at night, I can avoid it most of the time.

The few times I have witnessed it, I'd rather try to forget.

He came into my room only once. His hands were all bloody, and he stained my white sheets. I kept my eyes closed and tried to ignore the muffled breath underneath his new layer of skin. I tried to hold my breath as long as I could so he wouldn't notice how scared I was. After a few minutes, I finally heard the door close again.

One night, I thought he wasn't even at home, so I got up to go to the bathroom. I had to go so badly, I thought I'd wet myself. When I opened my door, he stood there right in front of it.

No mouth, no nose, only two small cuts for eyes.

He made noises as if he was trying to speak, but no real words came out.

It was a terrifying sight, but he never tried to attack me, and I'd simply learned to lock my room every night and stopped drinking anything before going to bed.

---

In the morning, he'd always have his regular face back and be a pretty decent dad. He really was trying.

It took me a while to understand what happened and why the dangerous people even did this to him. I thought they were trying to hurt him, but now I know that they weren't punishing him. They were using him as a vessel. A body to carry the face and act on its behalf. To scare victims or do even worse things to them.

I know that now because he finally opened up to me.

We had dinner together, almost like a regular family sitting around our kitchen table. I can't begin to describe how out of character this is for us. We hardly ever eat together, and if we do, it's usually frozen pizza in front of the TV.

Last night, however, Dad cooked.

He'd made baked potatoes, green beans, steak, and even some really nice pepper sauce for the meat. He poured himself a glass of wine, and I had Coke in a fancy glass that I didn't even know we owned.

When I had difficulty cutting my steak properly, he helped me without a word. For a few minutes, we sat there silently; I even tried to chew as slowly as possible so I wouldn't be too loud. It felt as if I was having dinner with a stranger, and I had to be on my best behavior.

It wasn't really a stranger, though. Dad was wearing his regular face. He even smiled when he caught me staring at him.

"You like this better, don't you?" he asked. When I didn't respond, he added, "This face."

It felt odd because we never spoke about the obvious issue. I didn't talk to anyone about this; I kept it a secret because I was afraid that someone would take away the only parent I had left.

I nodded. Of course, I preferred his regular face.

Dad stuffed a big chunk of meat and potatoes in his mouth.

"So do I. This is quite the mess we found ourselves in, isn't it, son?"

Again, I only nodded.

"Do you even understand it? You're pretty young, right?"

"I'm not that young."

He looked me up and down. "Well, you are small."

He was in a mood. Normally, he was only like this after a night of losing. Agitated, slightly mean, but not violent.

"I'm old enough to know that you've turned into a monster," I hissed.

He dropped his fork and grinned. His teeth looked red from the bloody steak.

"I'm not a monster, son. I only work for one. Not voluntarily, but if I stop, he brings me incredible pain. He can rip my soul into pieces simply by stating my name. At least that's what it feels like." He sighed. "And imagine if he killed me, who'd take care of you?"

I shivered at the thought of my father being murdered and especially at hearing him talk about it. As if it were the most normal thing in the world.

"You and I, we get along well, don't we? I don't mind you being here, I really don't, but sometimes I think it'd be best if you simply left. Ran away. Disappeared."

I clenched my fists so that I wouldn't start crying. "Dad, what is going on?" I whispered.

He reached his left arm over the table and put his hand on top of mine.

"This thing inside me, it's fighting; it wants to take control. It really is a struggle, you see. Both of us want to be in charge, and switching back and forth feels numbing. If I could get rid of him, I could do so much more."

"Then why don't you? Kill it, kill the thing. We can run away. I don't care about this home. We can get help. We can go to the police!" I was practically shouting.

"I can't kill him. He has a mind of his own. And I'm not sure what would happen to me if I did."

His eyes appeared tired and sad for a moment, but then he smiled again.

"I—I don't get—" I started speaking but dropped my knife on the ground before I could form a sentence.

When I reached under the table to pick it up, I saw that blood was dripping from my father's hand.

I don't know how long he'd been digging his nails into his palm.

This was the first time this happened while he was wearing his regular face, which made me realize something. My dad has issues; I'm well aware of that, and I'm not trying to defend him. He has messed up often in the past, but when it comes to me, he always tries to be protective.

"You know if it weren't for you, I would have gotten rid of him long ago. He keeps fighting for you. It's really frustrating, you know, but I'm glad we finally got to talk. I've tried before, but it's not easy when I don't have a mouth."

He didn't simply grow a new face. He became a new person.

# THE PEOPLE IN MY HOMETOWN PRODUCE CURSED GOODS

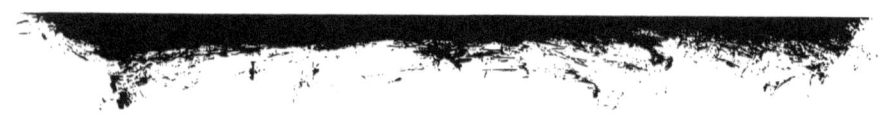

I was born in a town hidden behind the deepest and darkest forest. The golden fence posts surrounding our community stand tall and shine brighter than the sun. Behind the fence are people with the strongest spirit I have ever encountered, making the most bizarre and precious goods.

Tattletoe is the most beautiful town I've ever seen, but I wouldn't wish for anyone to visit it.

The people who run this town—we call them the committee—make sure that everything runs nicely and smoothly. We are told that the fence is here to protect us from the outside. If anyone ever did trespass, they wouldn't escape the town anyway; they'd be caught and brought right to the crematorium.

*The world outside is dark and cold.*
*You belong here with your friends and family.*
*This is the better alternative, trust us.*

That's what they usually say. And most people choose to believe them. The price they receive is a life fully taken care of, safely hidden behind the fence. They are happy with what they have.

There is no need to feel bad for our people, though. The fence isn't just there to keep us from the dark world outside. It protects the outside world from meeting the people of Tattletoe. And from the unexpected death hiding behind each corner, each cafe, and each shop.

In our town, everyone works. Not a single adult is unemployed. Some have better jobs than others, though; it's a gamble. I used to be a worker in our town's crematorium for years, and you can't imagine the things I've seen. That was until one lucky day when a new job opportunity opened up. It was unfortunate for the former worker who was burned to a crisp but incredibly lucky for me.

I was made an exporter of Tattletoe's finest goods.

---

Going from the crematorium to being an exporter has given me some insights into the workings of our town, which I'd rather have never known. Everything is a little hush-hush here, but there is a time when people are the most honest, and that is right before they die. The committee running our town does not appreciate one asking questions, but if you have to leave the gates and actually see the outside, there isn't much they can do to keep your eyes and ears closed, is there? All they can do is make sure you keep all your nasty knowledge to yourself. And they do a pretty darn good job at that.

"You might as well follow me in there, boy. Because what you are about to bring to the world will stain your soul for eternity."

Those were the last words the last exporter said to me. Mr. Deller was an old man by the time he stopped working. He was always a little stranger than the other people in town. He lost his wife when they were young. He only ever had one child—a son—who in turn only ever had one daughter. This is something quite unusual in our town. Having many children gives you a lot of prestige.

I didn't care what this would do to my soul, though. I was just happy to get away from the smell of burning corpses. No cinnamon in the world can overshadow the smell when you are right at the source.

Before leaving Tattletoe with my very first truck full of goods, I took a tour through town, simply to see what kind of things I would be sharing with the world and have a little chat with the ones who make them.

I started with the outer part of the town, the green and peaceful area where our gardeners take care of beautiful fruits and vegetables. The main things being grown here are citrus fruits. There are lemon and lime trees as far as the eye can see. I walked up to one of the trees, got on my tiptoes, and moved my nose as close to the fruit as I could to get a sniff of fresh lemon.

"What do you think you're doing, boy?"

The gardener was standing right next to me, staring me down with a gaze full of anger.

"I'm not touching!" I exclaimed.

He sighed. "Why try to smell something you can never have? Believe me, these lemons are no good. You are lucky not to try them. The limes are even worse."

"Why are they no good? They look amazing," I responded.

"That's because they will feast on your mind, take your free will." He looked me straight in the eye. "You're the new exporter, aren't you?"

I nodded.

"Listen, boy, they want me to send a dozen buckets full of lemons to some nearby town. And another dozen buckets of limes to a different town. When you get to those places, simply drop off the fruit. Don't talk to anyone."

And just like that, he disappeared again.

I dropped off the lemons in a town where they used them to make lemonade. They offered me a glass, but I politely declined. I brought the limes to a different town, where they wanted to make candy out of them. I don't know if I could have said no to those; they smelled so damn good. However, the gentleman didn't offer. When I saw the stains on his shirt, which looked a little too much like blood, I guessed it was for the better anyway.

I think that was the moment when I started realizing that the people who import the goods from Tattletoe were a little odd themselves. Although I was astonished at how insanely happy the people in both those towns looked. Not a single person was frowning. Their big smiles still haunt me.

I know what hostages look like, and they certainly were not living in those towns voluntarily. It was the Tattletoe curse that I had brought them in the form of citrus fruits.

All in all, my first day as an exporter went pretty well. An occurrence that happened shortly after that, however, made me almost want to quit altogether. I'd much rather have gone back to the crematorium.

It was the day I met the shoemaker.

The shoe store had always been one of the places that fascinated me the most in Tattletoe. From a young age, my parents had forbidden me to go inside, which of course only made me want it more. But I was a good kid and obliged my parents' wishes. I could only observe from the outside.

The shoemaker was a man named Theodore Tously. Tously's shoe shop must have been one of the oldest shops in town. From the outside, it looked like the most precious little place we had. Dark-blue tiles surrounded the big store window. The tiles were freshly painted every week because Tously didn't accept anything looking old and dusty. Inside the window, you could see some of the magnificent shoes he had made in the past, everything from crystal shoes to leathery boots. Every pair was unique, and you could see the hard work Tously put into them. I wished to own a pair of Tously's boots more than anything. Everyone in Tattletoe was damned to wear the same gray sneakers. Tously wouldn't allow the town to import any other shoes because he was afraid they could possibly outshine him.

He was a bit of a narcissist, as you might have guessed. And a cruel one, too, considering we're not allowed to purchase anything he makes.

My eyes were shining bright as I walked into the shop. It was the first time. Tously had classical music playing from a beautiful old-school record player, which added to the dark, atmospheric vibe in the shop. I couldn't stop staring at all the wonderful items I was suddenly so close to. Tously was working in the back of the shop and humming along to the music.

"Mr. Tously, I'm here to pick up an order?" I cautiously called into the shop.

He exhaled loudly, making sure I knew that I was interrupting him. "I'm almost finished," he grunted. "They asked me to make a couple dozen pairs of boots. Do I look like I mass-produce shit?" he shouted.

I shook my head.

"No, of course I don't. I'm a fucking artist." He got up from his chair and looked down at my feet. "You know, as you're leaving town, you might as well try on decent shoes. Nobody will see. I have just the perfect pair for you."

I swallowed. Those were the nicest boots he had ever made. "I'm not allowed to use any of the products, just exporting, sir."

"That's because you're weak, boy! Do you always do as you're told?"

I didn't know how to answer that question. We all did. That's how we survived.

He finally pointed me to the boxes with shoes, and I started loading them up.

---

This time I had to drive further. It took me almost a day to get to the place. They had a festival going and had invited many foreigners. As a gift to their visitors, they had ordered custom-made dancing shoes. It was really nice and kind of precious. They even invited me to stay, and for a second I was tempted to put on those boots that Tously had added to the order.

Almost.

I kept my gray sneakers on and stayed somewhat in the back. I didn't know if I was allowed to stay with the people who import our goods longer than necessary, but I wanted to see the festivities. While we have our own fun festivals in Tattletoe, we never dance much.

The music started, and the festival committee began handing out the shoes. Everyone was laughing, and the atmosphere was simply joyous. I didn't want to leave.

Until they started dancing.

It took a few minutes, but suddenly one person after the other fell onto the ground. Just like dominoes. A few were still shaking a little, but it stopped shortly after. Their eyes were wide open; I will never forget those empty stares.

---

I got back into my car and didn't look back. I wasn't delivering precious goods but cursed ones. You might be wondering why I would ever go back to Tattletoe after witnessing this. I knew they would make me export even more items like these, and there might even be more townspeople who would try to trick me as Tously almost had. But there were also people in Tattletoe that I needed to get back to. My family. My friends. People who needed me. I could never leave, and I could never give up the job.

The town committee was already awaiting me at the gates. I guess they had a hunch I wouldn't be too happy about my last delivery.

"We always try to tell you how terrible the world outside is, don't we?"

That was one argument. Of course, there was also the argument that they would kill my family if I ever disobeyed. They did offer me something that made my job slightly better, though: a privilege only granted to the most loyal workers.

When delivering the lemons to the town with no name, I was allowed to have a tiny sip of their lemonade. Not more than a shot, but I honestly have to say that it has helped me appreciate my job more. My mind just feels a little more free and easy.

# THE FIRST HOTEL IN OUR TOWN JUST OPENED, BUT ALL THE GUESTS ARE QUARANTINED

When they explained to me what my job would be, I was quite ecstatic. I had never in my life even visited a hotel, and now I was chosen as one of the few lucky ones who would help create a welcoming home for all the visitors who would soon be in our town.

The T was specifically designed to make you feel as if you were walking around in a dream. Slightly cloudy with soft lights and muffled sounds. Everything was a bit different; for example, the doorframes were all slightly different sizes and colors. The stairs that led to each floor appeared to never end until you suddenly found yourself at a different number. There was a glass elevator in the middle of the lobby, which very few were allowed to use.

I wasn't one of them.

Most walls were painted in a light lavender shade, but others were black. There were phone cords leading from each room that disappeared between walls, but all somehow ended up at the reception.

I'm not really sure how that worked, but it did look fascinating and odd at the same time. There were twenty-seven phone cords and twenty-seven room keys.

However, my favorite part of the interior was all the different lamps we got from one special shop out of town. Every single room had its own unique lamp.

I believed I was the luckiest girl in town for getting to work at the shiny new thing we had. Even more, I was thrilled to meet visitors. We didn't get those very often, or, to be more correct, mostly never. Our town was very secluded.

I already had a lingering feeling that I would regret my anticipation soon enough. Being happy in that town is a choice. One that you have to pay for with obedience. That was never one of my strong suits.

---

"You're here for everything and everyone but only after I ask. Or if it ever happens, the owner. But mostly you only listen to me, got it?"

Those were some of the first words Margery said to me.

Margery was basically my boss except not really. She ran the whole place, took care of everything, and knew everyone. If you saw her full cherry hair, her athletic body, and her tiny skirts, you'd never believe that she was already seventy-six.

"The young girl at the reception is Judy. She's seventeen or eighteen. Like you, she just finished school. During night shifts, we replace her with Jacob. Twins. Kinda *creepy*." She whispered the last word.

Judy waved hesitantly and smiled as we walked past her.

"You can chat later. But not too much."

We kept racing through the hotel as she explained the most basic things: how to make a bed, how to clean a bathroom, how to change a lightbulb.

"I am showing you these things so you can prepare today. When our guests arrive, however, you will not go to their rooms. They must stay quarantined. You will not open one door until I tell you to."

After hours of Margery telling me everything I wasn't allowed to do, I still had to prepare two dozen rooms.

At 8:00 a.m., I was sent home, exhausted but also sad. The guests were supposed to arrive at night, and I would miss it.

My second shift started the very next day at precisely 6:00 p.m.

The sun was slowly going down as I walked through the narrow, cobblestone alleys of the town, past all the shops, which were getting ready to close for the day. Most shop owners had made posters and signs to invite people inside. They'd been told there would be tourists, after all.

But nobody had left their rooms, and they weren't going to for a while.

The lobby was empty except for one person. Judy was standing at the reception, her chin resting on her hand as she doodled something on a piece of paper.

She looked up and smiled when she saw me. "Hey, Emma."

I looked at the wall behind her. Yesterday, it was full of keys. For some reason, my heart started beating faster.

"Are all the rooms booked?" I asked.

She nodded. "Every single one. And all for at least three weeks. Jacob checked them all in last night, apparently, which makes my job today pretty dull."

I leaned closer to her table and whispered, even though nobody else was around. "Did he say something? What were they like?"

She shrugged. "He said they were all polite and pleasant. A bit different from us but perfectly friendly," she said, raising her voice. Then she leaned in closer and whispered, "But I know he was lying."

"How?"

Judy looked around nervously. "I always know when he's lying. He raises his chin, and the tone of his voice changes. But that's not all."

She pulled out a piece of paper from underneath the one she was doodling on.

There were drawings of a bunch of different people. They all looked unique. Some were tall, some were wide, and some were dressed in a specific way. But they all had one thing in common.

They had no faces.

I remembered what Margery had said about the twins.

"Does he, um, draw things like this often?"

"Emma!"

Margery's loud voice surprised us. She was at the bottom of the staircase, but I hadn't even heard her walk down. Judy quickly hid the piece of paper.

The sound of Margery's heels echoed through the entire lobby as she walked up to us. My body stiffened, and I suddenly felt as if I was in trouble.

Margery looked at her watch. "You're five minutes early. You know you don't get paid for that, right?"

"I—"

"Never mind," she interrupted me. "I have a task for you. A very important one that I don't trust anyone else with. Follow me."

---

We walked into the kitchen where Hugo was cooking something with a tangy but unfamiliar smell.

Hugo, who was thirty years younger than Margery but actually looked her real age, was the chef. He looked the toughest but was probably the nicest guy in the hotel.

"One of our guests had a very specific wish. Normally, they all receive their meals at the same time, but this gentleman is special. When he has a wish, we're supposed to fulfill it."

Margery spoke in a strict tone.

"So I'm sending you to his room. You will knock on the door twice, and when he tells you to enter, you will. You will place the tray that Hugo prepared on his desk. You will *not* talk to the guest. Can you do that?"

I nodded.

"Good. The guest is in room eleven."

Margery left the kitchen, and I waited for Hugo to finish the tray.

"She's testing you. Wants to see if you can be trusted. You'd better do exactly what she says or she'll fire you," he whispered.

I swallowed. "Yeah, I know."

We both knew what that meant. Being fired is taken quite literally around here.

I took a deep breath before I knocked on the door of room eleven.

After my second knock, a deep voice whispered, "Enter."

With the tray resting on one arm, I slowly opened the door.

The sight of the man inside was so strange that I froze on the spot.

He was sitting by the window, looking at it but not out of it. The blinds were shut, and the only light came from the lamp on the nightstand next to his bed.

I couldn't tell you how old the man was, but his clothes made me assume that he wasn't young. He was dressed in an uncomfortable-looking checked brown suit and wearing a hat made of the same fabric.

Without turning around, he pointed toward the table in the middle of the room.

I tried not to shake too much as I quickly walked over to put down the silver tray. On the table, I saw a small box filled to the brim with keys.

Room keys?

I didn't want to stay in the room longer than I had to. It felt suffocating there.

I was ready to leave again, but then the man began to speak.

"I smell a lot of death in this town."

I stayed quiet.

"They are not educating the people enough. If they keep murdering all the residents, this hotel will have to grow exponentially."

Slowly, he turned his head, and I saw that he was wearing bandages all around his face. There was a slit cut in where his mouth would be.

I opened my mouth, but before I could speak, I felt a hand around my arm, pulling me outside. The door shut, and I realized it was Margery. "You did well, girl. He seems to like you."

My breath was fast and sharp.

I wanted to ask so many questions, but my fear took over. I've lived here my whole life; fear is the first thing they teach us. We know we can't leave this place and do everything we can to live a decent life. My parents have never asked a critical question, and they are the happiest people I know.

Margery walked me down the hall. When we reached the staircase, she smiled and hugged me. It was the first time she seemed human.

"The man you met wasn't a regular guest. He is the owner of this hotel. We do everything he says."

Many people I knew changed after they got their first job. They lost something inside of them: a glimpse of innocence. We do what we're told because we must. What other option is there?

"And the other guests?" I asked, making sure to stay as vague as possible.

"They are not guests. They are our new neighbors. Well, soon they will be. They are here to acclimate first. Until then, they must stay undisturbed."

I simply nodded, something I learned to do quite often. Mindlessly, I made my way back to the lobby. Luckily, Margery had no more tasks for the moment. She gave me a moment to calm down.

At the reception, Judy was replaced by Jacob. Night had come, and her shift was over. Jacob didn't greet me. He stayed silent, listening to something I wouldn't be able to get out of my ears or mind.

There were sounds coming from the telephone, carried through the cords from the rooms.

They were crying for help.

Jacob and I looked at each other, hopeless and empty.

Because we both knew that there was nothing we could do. They had to accept their fates just like everyone else here.

All I wanted was to get out and leave.

But unfortunately, in Tattletoe, quitting your job was not an option.

# AMY'S MISSING. HAVE YOU SEEN HER?

I didn't know Amy. I had never met her. Neither had any of my friends. Still, when I saw the poster of a missing girl in the town I used to call home, a suffocating feeling befell me. The feeling you have when something is entirely and utterly wrong. You can tell inside your soul that it's not how life is supposed to be. A girl so young, simply disappearing, leaving a family in pain. It's not something that should ever happen. And when it does, it can do strange things to the ones who witness it.

Parents were particularly careful with their children now.

"Only to school and back, and none of you will walk alone. Jonah, watch your brother!"

I heard a mother call out to her sons as I walked to the grocery store to get some eggs for breakfast.

Those words reminded me of something.

What do you call nostalgia that is only bitter and not sweet?

I faintly remember that we had a similar situation during my childhood. I was five or maybe six when a kid in town went missing. I'm not even sure whether I knew that child. I assume not very well. All I know is that the time was hard on all of us. Gately had a dark shadow cast over it. We lived in fear and dread. It was around then that many families left our town for good. Their homes felt stained. The memories of that time are blurry, but the emotions make up for it. When I think of that time in my life, a shiver goes down my spine. I don't think I will ever be able to shake it off.

I guess it felt even more wrong due to the contrast. Gately is absolutely lovely and vivid when the terrible isn't waiting around the corner. Most people are friendly and kind. The ones who never left were prone to assure that all the ones who stayed felt safe. I believe it worked. I, for one, had a pretty great childhood here. There was more than enough to explore, clubs to join, and events held regularly. Even when I went to college, I always looked forward to the times I would visit Gately.

Just like now.

I was looking forward to Dad's cooking and Grandma's baking. I was looking forward to seeing Maddie and Nicholas, my childhood friends, again. I was definitely looking forward to the carnival that would be coming to town after I saw all the posters advertising it. There was a big one next to the entrance of the grocery store. Although it hardly stood out, surrounded by the many faces of the same girl.

Posters of a missing girl. Just like all those years ago.

The picture was in black and white, but her shoulder-length hair must have been of the lightest blond. Her eyes resembled two black buttons staring toward the camera. She was neither smiling nor frowning. Her expression looked almost apathetic.

"Poor girl. She was so sweet. Gosh, and so young, too."

My head turned toward the voice. I wasn't used to people randomly chatting me up anymore. I guess that's a small-town thing.

"When did she go missing?" I asked the elderly woman next to me.

She didn't respond to my question. "Poor little Amy, I hope they find her soon," she mumbled before walking inside the grocery store.

The longer I looked at the poster, the worse I felt. It felt like it was hurting something inside me I didn't even know existed. Finally, I managed to look away and went inside to get the eggs.

---

As Dad, Grandma, and I sat around the kitchen table, having a late arrival breakfast for me, I was greeted by the face again. This time on a milk carton.

**Have you seen Amy?**

"I didn't realize they actually printed these on milk cartons," I mumbled.

"What do you mean?" my father asked.

"The missing kid. I thought these only existed in movies," I said as I held up the carton.

"Oh, that poor little Amy. What a horrible, horrible occurrence," my grandma chimed in.

"Absolutely. Such a tragedy," my father added.

"Did you know her?" I asked. "I don't believe I've ever seen her in town. Although most kids kinda look the same anyway, I guess."

Both Grandma and Dad were now looking at me, their eyes filled with disgust.

"Such a young soul. I hope she will be found soon," Grandma mumbled, ignoring my question.

"Who are her parents?" I asked.

"Yes, kids should be with their parents," Grandma said as she grabbed the milk carton. She started inspecting the picture with a look that I couldn't quite place. She was smiling, but her eyes looked scared.

"No, I mean, who is Amy—"

Grandma clawed her nails into the milk carton. With a strength I didn't know she had, she pushed so deep into the carton that it broke. Milk splashed everywhere, even on her face. But she didn't react. She simply put the carton back down and continued having breakfast.

"I sure hope they find the poor girl soon," she whispered.

"What the hell? Why—" I shrieked.

Dad cut me off before I could say anything else. His expression was stern. I knew that look. Grandma's mind wasn't as sharp as it used to be, and we weren't supposed to confuse her.

"Anyway, you should go visit your friends after breakfast," Dad said, changing the subject. He smiled, but the milk on his face and our table only added to the absurdity of the situation.

---

While my friends weren't acting as oddly as my family, the subject of the missing girl seemed to result in weird reactions from them as well.

I was hoping to find some answers with the friends I grew up with, but I only got more questions. Neither Maddie nor Nick knew the girl, and they weren't sure who her parents were, either.

"It's weird, right? I swear, it feels the same," I said.

"The same as what?" Maddie asked.

"Like twenty years ago, when the other child went missing. Was it a girl, too?"

Maddie and Nick seemed confused.

"There was another missing child?" Nick asked.

"Yeah, don't you remember? We weren't allowed to play for weeks, and a bunch of people moved away."

The two of them exchanged a look.

"That's strange. Are you sure you didn't make it up?" Nick asked.

"And did they ever find the child?" Maddie asked.

"Not sure," I mumbled. Suddenly, I felt even stranger than before.

Maddie smiled. "Of course you're not sure. Because it never happened."

"You shouldn't be spreading rumors. We should be focusing on finding poor little Amy, and that is all," Nick said.

I couldn't help but laugh. "What the fuck, guys?"

They didn't say anything, but Maddie started gently stroking my arm.

"It's okay, buddy. Horrible events like these can really screw with your mind. It will all be fine, though. We only need to find Amy."

---

I left Nick's home shortly after. In the past few years, I hadn't stayed in touch with my friends as much as I'd wanted to, but I still thought I knew them. Today they felt like absolute strangers. They were odd, just like my father and my grandma. Truly, just like everyone in Gately.

It's not that I had intended on speaking about the disappearance that much, but somehow I couldn't let go of it. I felt deeply involved even though I had no idea who Amy was. I didn't have any siblings who were the same age as her or even cousins, but it still stuck with me.

I presume all those pictures of her were part of the reason.

Her face was everywhere. I thought there were many posters when I went outside earlier, but now it seemed as if the entire town was plastered with them.

People kept saying how terrible it was. They kept repeating that we had to find the girl. Our town seemed supportive, for sure, but nobody seemed to actually do anything.

There were posters and pictures everywhere, but I didn't see anyone actually searching.

What had Amy's disappearance done to them? And who were the girl's parents? And why did nobody but me seem to remember the last kidnapping two decades ago? No matter who I asked, I simply wouldn't receive an answer.

To the point that I even started thinking of the unspeakable. I started wondering whether the people of Gately were somehow involved in the disappearance. Maybe it was somehow connected to the fact that this town was so prosperous and nice all the time.

Although, if they were doing child offerings, I suppose they wouldn't be actively hanging posters with her face everywhere.

Whatever was going on, it wasn't right. The people I felt so safe and close with suddenly seemed changed. They weren't warm and kind anymore, but empty and frightening. One wrong word and they turned manic.

The following days, I tried to avoid the subject of the missing girl altogether. I didn't even leave home much and stayed neutral with Dad and Grandma. I didn't see my friends much, either.

Until the first day of the carnival.

Nick, Maddie, and I had plans to go right after Nick finished work. I wasn't as excited about it anymore after the last few days, but it felt wrong to shut myself inside the whole time I was visiting.

This was my home, after all.

---

I'm not sure what I was expecting. The carnival didn't come to town often, so usually it would have been an exciting day, but as soon as we got close to the area, all of that was gone.

This carnival was nothing more than a shell.

The rides, the booths, the games. While all the lights and music were on, none of them were being operated. There were posters of the missing girl everywhere. People seemed to be walking around mindlessly. Townspeople I recognized, like the librarian or schoolteachers, were there, though none of them seemed like themselves.

They all had forced smiles on their faces, while their brows were furrowed. They were muttering words to themselves, the same ones they'd been repeating for days. Some of them had bloodstains on them, but none of them seemed to care.

When I looked over at my friends, I noticed the same stare.

"Did you hear about that little girl going missing? Bless her poor little soul," Maddie whispered in a voice that didn't sound like hers.

"Isn't it terrifying that one among us is capable of such horrors?" Nick asked.

I didn't say a word. I simply turned around to get home as quickly as I could. Whatever was going on at that carnival, I didn't want to witness it.

Everyone had lost their minds.

I ran all the way home. I had absolutely no idea what was happening to the town. The people didn't seem like themselves. And while I knew how absurd they were acting, this suffocating feeling inside of me wouldn't go away. I could only hope that somebody would find this girl soon.

I took a deep breath before going inside my childhood home. I was dreading seeing Dad and Grandma the way I saw my friends. I had no idea how to deal with that.

---

Grandma was alone. I wasn't sure whether that was a good or a bad thing. As I walked inside, I heard her rummaging through something in the living room.

"What's that?" I asked carefully.

Grandma didn't answer. She just kept sitting there, looking at pieces of paper. When I saw what she was looking at, I thought about turning around again.

They were posters of Amy.

But then I got closer, mostly because I was worried about Grandma, and I realized that those posters weren't entirely the same.

They had different dates on them.

*Last seen November 11th, 1990*
*Last seen November 11th, 1960*
*Last seen November 11th, 1930*

Nobody who stayed here remembered the last times.

Grandma had it right in front of her but didn't seem to understand it. I couldn't blame her. I couldn't quite understand why it was affecting us like this, either.

I just couldn't shake that image out of my head.

The picture of Amy with those black button eyes and ash-blond hair. That poor little girl must be afraid and cold, waiting for someone to rescue her. I guess that's why I'm writing to you.

We simply must find Amy.

Have you seen her?

# THERE ARE TWO VERSIONS OF MY CHILDHOOD TAPES

## Part 1

I was born right in the middle of the nineties, two years after my brother. All the memories of our childhood were kept on VHS tapes.

Tapes that we hadn't watched in almost two decades because, well, who still owns a VHS player?

My brother, Luke, would soon turn thirty, and I thought it would be a neat present to digitize all our old videos. My mom kept them in a box in our basement labeled *1993–1999 A Tapes*.

I had no idea what the A meant until I found the others. Our old basement was filled with all sorts of junk and memorabilia from past years. Dusty basketballs with no air, our old inflatable pool, sneakers I could still wear if I gave them a decent clean.

I got lost in there for hours, looking through all kinds of stuff until I stumbled upon a box that looked just like the first one. Except this one was hidden under a pile of old jackets.

*1993–1999 B Tapes*

At that point, I obviously had no idea what the difference between them was, and my parents weren't home, so I couldn't ask them. They'd gone on a cruise. I'd let myself in with the key I'd kept after moving out.

So I brought both boxes to my car. A week later, I picked up the boxes and a USB stick with all the videos from the shop.

I watched the first few, the ones in which I wasn't even born yet, just to check if everything worked fine. Then I put the stick in an envelope with a card so our family could watch them together after Luke's birthday and after my parents got back.

Two days after the party, my brother called me. He didn't tell me what was going on but commanded me to come over to his house as soon as possible. I'd never heard my brother sound more disturbed.

---

"What the actual fuck, Max?"

My brother looked even taller than he was; anger seemed to make him grow. I was a good bit shorter than him, paler, and weaker. My dark hair was curly and chaotic, and his was always styled right and the color of honey.

The only similarity we had were our greenish-brown eyes.

"I watched that shit with Ellie. You think that's appropriate for a two-year-old?"

"Can you at least let me inside before you start harassing me? I have no idea what you're talking about."

He moved to the side.

Their living room was a mess, with toys, clothes, and crumbs everywhere. It had been like that ever since they had Ellie. It made me like my niece even more, bringing a bit of chaos into my brother's sleek life.

"Are Ellie and Jacob not home?"

He shook his head. "They went to Jacob's parents'. He's pretty angry with you." He sighed. "Max, be honest. Why did you make those videos? How did you even—?"

"Huh?" I moved a stuffed elephant from the sofa and sat down. "I brought our old VHS tapes to a shop, and they—I told you when I gave you the stick. I thought you'd like to see them."

Luke frowned. "You look like you have no idea what I'm talking about."

He got his laptop and sat down next to me. He opened a folder with two video files labeled *Tapes A* and *Tapes B*.

"Did you watch them?"

"A few of the first ones."

"The A ones?"

I nodded.

Without saying anything else, he opened file B.

A video started playing.

The date at the bottom said NOVEMBER 1994 with the description PARK TIME.

At first, I thought it started with a dark screen. But as it turned out, it was just night. The quality wasn't great, but you could tell there were trees, and you could hear the occasional hoot of an owl.

"There is a similar video in the A ones. It's me, I just learned how to walk, and we're in the park, having a picnic. During the daytime."

"So what is this?" I asked.

"Wait."

Suddenly, there was light. Someone had lit a torch and shoved it into the ground. You couldn't tell who the person was because only their back was showing, and it was still too dark.

More torches followed, arranged in a circle.

When it was done, someone came with a child who looked a lot like Luke when he was little and placed the baby in the middle of the circle.

Even with the light, it still looked strange and blurry. There were voices, but I couldn't make out what they were saying.

"What the fuck?" I whispered.

I was speechless. And sick. Watching these hurt my insides, and I can't explain how or why. It felt as if it was too unnatural for us to comprehend, a sort of filter that lay over it, the sounds.

I wanted it to stop, but at the same time, I was too curious.

Luke looked at me with a concerned look on his face. "I'm going to fast-forward to one with you in it."

JUNE 1997 BIRTHDAY.

This one was during the daytime in our garden, but things looked slightly different again. Colors were much brighter, almost neon.

Two boys appeared in the frame, probably Luke and me. It must have been my third birthday, so Luke was five.

We were dressed in purple-striped shirts and pants but could only see our backs. We were running toward something that looked like a small bouncy castle, one I don't remember ever having.

We disappeared inside it, and the camera zoomed farther and farther out.

And then all you could hear were loud screams, but they didn't sound like they were coming from children.

When the two of us came outside again, the camera was still zoomed out, but you could still see that we were laughing and jumping. And there was something red staining our clothes and hands.

Blood?

I ran to the bathroom and threw up my lunch.

When I got back, Luke was waiting for me with a bottle of water. "Happened to Ellie, too. She kept throwing up and cried a lot."

I didn't like the idea that my little niece saw that, and I found it strange that she had such a strong reaction to it too, how she understood that something was wrong. Because, technically, nothing really bad happened in those tapes. They were just disturbing.

"Luke, I swear. I have no idea what that was. All I did was grab the boxes of tapes."

"Do you remember that birthday?" he asked.

"Are you joking?"

We went back to the living room. Luke had closed the laptop.

"I remember your third birthday. Some of your kindergarten friends were there, and Mom baked a cake. There was no bouncy castle and whatever the hell else that was."

My stomach was still turning. I've watched plenty of stuff far gorier in my life. I have no idea why this affected me so much.

"Mom and Dad come back tomorrow. We need to talk to them," I said in a determined tone. But Luke knew me well and probably heard the fear in my voice.

As far as I could remember, I'd never been scared of my parents before. But I also know that they'd been slightly particular when we were growing up. My parents had always been kind of eccentric; our house was always full of strange art, and they traveled all the time, even back then.

They never hurt us; if anything, they neglected us a little. But I didn't remember anything scary ever happening.

"I can go alone. Look, Mom and Dad are a bit weird. It's probably some very strange art project of theirs. But either way, I want to know what's up with that," Luke said.

"No, I'll come too. Maybe they'll be angry that we found them."

"Max, they kept them in the basement in an unlocked box. They wanted us to find them, or at least they didn't mind if we did."

I wasn't exactly afraid of my parents but of all the things I couldn't remember.

---

I stayed with Luke that night. Jacob and Ellie were still with Jacob's parents.

The next day, we drove to our old childhood home. Luke and I had both stayed in our hometown after moving out. His house was a twenty-minute drive from my parents', and I lived a bit farther away from both.

When we reached the driveway, I saw my parents' car and felt a cold shiver. I wasn't sure how we should do this, what we would say.

As it turns out, I didn't have to.

Mom opened the door before we even rang the bell. "Max, Lukey, how sweet of you to stop by."

She came closer to hug us, but Luke gently pushed her away.

"Where's Dad? The four of us need to talk."

Before my mom could answer, he marched to the living room where my dad was reading a book. "What the hell are the B tapes?"

My parents exchanged a glance. They didn't even try to act like they had no idea.

"Sit down, both of you. And calm down. It's nothing bad," my mom said.

My dad sighed and put his book away, then he got up. If anything, they looked annoyed that we'd disturbed their day.

Luke and I sat next to each other on the sofa, and my parents stood in front of us. For a moment, it felt like we were little boys again, getting in trouble for breaking something.

"Neither of you ever got hurt. We made them for a possibility, one that you didn't even get," my dad said.

"Can you please talk less cryptically?" I chimed in. It was the first thing I'd said.

"Those aren't real videos of your childhood. Just remakes. For your audition tapes. They were searching for child stars. Luke didn't make the cut, and then we tried with you, Max. But neither of you was chosen," my mom took over.

"They? Who are they? And chosen for what, a movie?" Luke asked.

My parents exchanged another glance. "Something like that," my mom said. "The filmmakers were looking for extraordinary children with specific instructions on how to show their personalities. The children who were chosen became part of this fantastic kids' show! But neither of you was."

Now Luke and I exchanged a look.

I had all those questions. Why would you do that to children that young? Why did you never tell us about it? And why did those tapes make us sick?

But the atmosphere shifted after my parents explained it to us. Mom went to the kitchen and started cooking. Dad was blabbering about their trip. They acted like what we had seen was totally normal.

That was the scariest part. How normal they thought those tapes were when they could even make a two-year-old sick. I felt like I didn't even know my own parents, and I felt strangely out of place.

Meanwhile, Luke looked like he would explode any second. Finally, he shot me a look and walked outside.

I followed, and we drove off without saying another word to my parents.

---

At first, neither of us was speaking. I suppose we both didn't know how to deal with the situation.

After a while, Luke parked next to a McDonald's. I thought he was just getting some food, but instead, he turned to me with a serious look.

"There's something you don't know. When you were sleeping last night, I watched a few more of the tapes. I mean, they made me feel terrible, but I had to know if anything, you know, really bad happened."

I swallowed, and Luke took a deep breath.

Then he shook his head.

"There was nothing like that. The tapes are messed up but in different ways. In ways that make you question reality."

"Okay."

Now he was looking straight at me.

"You know how Mom said neither of us made the cut? To be cast?"

I nodded.

"Well, after 1996, there was a third child in the tapes. And the more I think about it, the more I'm starting to remember things. I know it sounds insane, but I'm wondering if we had another sibling that we forgot."

# Part 2

"I'm your family, okay? That's all that matters."

I nodded, but the sinking feeling inside my stomach hadn't gone away.

I'd asked Luke to drop me off at home. Jacob and Ellie were coming back from Jacob's parents', and I needed some alone time.

I'd taken the USB stick with me. I had a feeling Luke would obsess about it, and that wouldn't be healthy for him or his family.

I, on the other hand, was single and lived alone. I had all the time and energy to go crazy.

Luke put his hand on my shoulder.

"I mean, I know all of this feels strange, but let's be honest, Mom and Dad have always been a little insane."

He tried to smile, but I saw a twitch in his eye. He knew he was losing control but tried his best to keep me calm. I was twenty-eight years old, and my brother still wanted to protect me. Even after moving out at just seventeen, he always stayed close and made sure we kept in touch.

It made me wonder how much of the bad things in our childhood he hid from me. Older siblings really don't have it easy sometimes.

"Luke, I'm fine," I said. "But I might take a little break from visiting Mom and Dad for a while. Just to wrap my head around things. As to the third child—"

"Look, no. Max. I think I let my imagination roll. That kid could've just been a neighbor or a friend's child."

"Oh, yeah, for sure. I still don't like that they used us for some weird audition like that. Never thought Mom and Dad were fame-seekers." I nervously laughed.

"Yeah, same, but try not to worry about it too much, okay?"

But of course, I did, just like him. We were stupid. My brother was trying to protect me, and I was trying to protect him, but in reality, both of us were already too deep into the mystery, and neither of us would let go of it.

---

As soon as I heard Luke's car drive off, I grabbed my laptop.

There were two things I needed to do.

First, I would start with the A tapes to see if there was another child in there with us.

Second, I would watch enough of the B tapes to understand a little bit better what they were about.

The first thing made me nervous; the second made me ill.

As I skipped through the A tapes file, I realized something. All the memories I had of my childhood came from what was filmed back then. I suppose it's not that odd; our brains aren't that evolved yet as kids. We mix the information we have with bits of memory and believe that we actually remember it all.

It was all fairly normal. A trip to the zoo, birthday parties, school plays.

I kept skipping until I reached 1996. A short fragment of Christmas. With me, Luke, my parents, some other adults, and a baby.

I didn't recognize those other adults. It might have been one of their kids, but my mom was holding it.

I paused the tape right there and switched to the B file to look for the same date. December 1996.

Even while I was just skipping through scenes, my stomach rumbled. I still didn't understand how it was possible. A few images and sounds couldn't possibly evoke such a physical reaction. Maybe it was just my nervous system warning me about something.

I tightened my fist and continued. No puking before I had some answers.

1996 LEIGH'S FIRST CHRISTMAS

It was set at a graveyard. It must have been evening, somewhere in between light and dark, but the contrast kept changing, making it difficult to focus on any specifics.

Then two gravestones came into the frame, but I couldn't decipher the names or dates.

Although one of them seemed to say Montroe.

Our last name.

I swallowed and kept watching.

An adult I couldn't identify brought the child into the frame. Leigh, I guessed. And the adult could've been my dad, although it was hard to say.

He laid the baby down on the ground in front of the gravestones.

All of a sudden, the light became crazy bright, almost burning my eyes. I looked away for a second, and the image had changed.

What I saw now was our family.

Mom, Dad, Luke, me.

And Leigh.

We were sitting on a blue sofa, and behind us stood a red Christmas tree. It seemed as if all the colors were reversed.

Luke and I kept moving and looking in all kinds of directions, but Mom, Dad, and Leigh were staring right into the camera. No movement.

Mom and Dad were both grinning. They almost looked proud. Then Dad's face turned serious, and the video stopped.

My heart was racing. There was no show or movie I could imagine that would want this as an audition tape, but I'd known that from the first few ones already.

Somehow I still tried to find a logical explanation, though. A reason why my parents were doing this.

Yes, they'd been weird sometimes, but they were still my parents. I didn't want to believe that there was something utterly wrong with them or imagine the kind of horrible people they were involved with.

At this point, I believed it to be some sort of Satanic cult.

My head joined my fast-racing heart. It felt like something would break out of my skull any second, so I closed the B file.

When the Christmas video of file A opened up, I watched a little more of it. It felt ironic but almost comforting to watch that regular-looking Christmas.

Luke and I were playing with presents, and the adults were drinking and laughing.

And then I saw a familiar face that didn't look as happy as the rest. My grandpa.

I don't know why I hadn't thought about that before. My grandparents moved away when we were really young, and not long after that, my parents broke off contact with them—or the other way around.

We didn't even go to my grandmother's funeral.

I took a picture and sent it to Luke.

---

He called me back an hour later, his first words being, "I found him."

"Who?"

"Who do you think? Grandpa. He lives in a nursing home in a place called Watton. I thought—"

"Luke, whoa, stop. You found Grandpa? How?"

I could hear him grinning through the phone. "He has Facebook."

I was quiet for a second. "Did you text him?"

"No. I thought we might pay him a visit. I looked up the town he lives in. It's a four-hour drive. I already took time off work. Maybe you could say you're sick or—"

I didn't even think about it.

"Yeah, okay. Let's do it."

---

"What does Jacob think of all this?" I asked the next day as we were sitting in the car.

Luke didn't answer for a while.

"I didn't tell him everything. Said the video was a strange art project of our parents' and that I'm in a fight with them about it."

"And about you leaving for two days?"

"Visiting our grandpa who we haven't seen in two decades."

I didn't question him further. It was his relationship, not mine. And it was probably for the best if fewer people got involved in this mess.

We arrived at the nursing home around noon.

A friendly nurse guided us to the garden where an old man was sitting on a bench.

I knew it had to be my grandfather, but it was strange to see how much he had aged. Especially after I'd seen him in the video only the day before, more than twenty-five years younger.

All of a sudden, I started getting nervous. The last time this man had seen us, we were children. He probably wouldn't even recognize us, and I didn't know how clear he still was in his head.

As we approached, he looked up and smiled. "Leigh!" he called as he looked at me.

"No, Mr. Montroe. This is your other grandson," the nurse said calmly.

"It's Luke and Max, Grandpa. Do you remember us?"

His expression changed immediately. At first, I thought it was anger, then disappointment, and finally sadness.

Luke and I were lost for words. We had planned all the things we would say and ask during our drive, but now my mind was blank, and from the look on his face, so was his.

Grandpa gave us a sad smile. "You boys have grown so much. Luke, you more than your brother, but still."

"Which brother?" Luke asked bluntly. "Max or Leigh?"

Grandpa shot him a confused look.

"He slips in and out. At times his mind is sharp, but often it's more foggy," the nurse explained.

"Great," Luke mumbled.

"I'm going to go inside and let you chat. I'm sure you missed your grandkids very much, Mr. Montroe," the nurse said in a friendly tone.

"No! Don't leave me alone with him," Grandpa said as he looked at Luke, who was just as confused as I was.

"Do you happen to have a phone number or any other contact information from his other grandson?" I asked the nurse.

She shook her head. "Unfortunately not. He brought him here a little while back, and he comes to visit at times. But it's hard to reach him."

"All because of that silly show," Grandpa whispered.

I got closer and sat down next to him. He didn't seem to mind me. "The show he was cast for?" I asked, gently placing my hand on his shoulder.

He looked me in the eyes and nodded. "I didn't know it would follow him like that, back then. I DIDN'T KNOW." He shouted that last part, and I instinctively removed my hand.

"Mr. Montroe, all is fine. Leigh is doing well," the nurse said calmly. "I'm sorry, boys, but I think now is not a good time for him." She helped Grandpa get up from the bench, but before he was standing, he looked at me.

"Not your brother. Your cousin. I raised that boy after—" He didn't finish the sentence but instead looked at the ground and sadly whispered, "Your parents should've died, not his."

---

"So what now?" I asked when we were back in the car.

Luke let out a big sigh. "We need to find Leigh, who I guess is our cousin and not our brother, so at least that's something. Maybe we can ask around and see if someone knows him. The town isn't that big, and he was some kind of child star, apparently."

I looked through the window at the gray buildings we were passing on our way to the town center.

"Did you see the look on his face when he said our parents should've died?" I asked.

Luke nodded. "They were probably the reason Leigh got cast. After they didn't want us, they tried with him instead. Maybe after his parents died?"

"You don't think Dad killed one of his siblings and their spouse to get their child for a TV show, do you?" I asked, half-jokingly.

Luke opened his mouth to speak but closed it again. After a while, he said, "Can you text Jacob and let him know we arrived? I forgot."

"Sure," I said, quickly followed by, "Shit." This shouldn't have made me feel so scared, but I knew something bad was about to happen. "He sent you a text an hour ago. 'Your parents just randomly stopped by. You know how much I hate when they do that.'"

Luke's eyes opened wide. "Call him, NOW!" he shouted.

I gulped. "It's going straight to voicemail."

# Part 3

"I'm going to kill them."

At the speed Luke was driving, we'd get back home in half the time we were supposed to, but I couldn't blame him. With the most recent news, I wouldn't be surprised if my parents were already working on Ellie's audition tape.

"We don't know that they—" I stopped to think over my words. "This happened decades ago. I doubt whatever production company that was still exists today. Maybe they just wanted to stop by."

"And that's why none of them are picking up their phones?" Luke hissed back. He was right. At this point, we couldn't know what my parents were capable of.

We both stayed silent for a while.

We were alive and healthy, and from what it sounded like, so was Leigh, but I'd still developed a fear of my parents and lost all respect for them.

"I remember them," Luke said all of a sudden.

"Who?"

"Leigh's parents. Our aunt—Dad's sister. And her husband."

I swallowed. Why was Luke only giving me truths in small portions? Before I could ask precisely that, he continued, "I'd forgotten. Repressed it, I guess, but I'm starting to remember their funeral now. It's strange. The only adults there were Mom, Dad, Dad's parents, and one woman I didn't know."

"You're trying to tell me you forgot an actual funeral until now?" I asked, fed up with being left in the dark by everyone in my family. If I had to go through this mess, I at least wanted to understand it.

"Yes, Max. Jeez, I'm not trying to mess with you. I don't get it, either. I was a child, too, when it happened. The memories are fuzzy, and I forgot until Grandpa talked about it. I told you I'd started remembering the third child, didn't I?"

"Yes," I mumbled. At the same time, I kept trying to reach someone. Mom, Dad, Jacob. "Maybe we should call the police?" I asked after a while. I didn't know why I didn't think about that before. It almost felt as if the outside world and authorities didn't exist.

Luke shook his head. "We don't know how unpredictable Mom and Dad are. I need to talk to them."

"Yeah, okay."

Luke started nervously tapping the steering wheel. "What's the first memory that you ever had?" he asked. "Like, the very first thing you ever remember."

I thought about it for a while. It's hard to say because, as I mentioned earlier, most of my memories were mixed with what I saw in the tapes. In the regular ones.

"I'm not sure," I said, although I did have one very early memory that I was sure was not from the tapes.

It's one of me and Luke. We were at home. It was night. Back then we still shared a room. There was a lot of shouting coming from outside. He came over to my bed and closed my ears with his hands.

But I couldn't say if it was real or if my mind had fabricated it, and Luke was already on edge with everything, so I didn't tell him.

Instead, I told him about something else I remembered, which I now think could have a meaning. "I remember a man visiting us once, a weird man. He was dressed in purple and yellow and had a very shrill voice."

Luke bit his lip, the same way he did as a kid when we were playing board games and he thought hard about his next move.

"We were wearing those same colors in that birthday video," he said.

I nodded.

"But it couldn't have been around the same time. You were too young in that tape."

"What's your first memory?" I asked him.

"Your birth. I think I was happy."

---

We didn't talk much for the next hour or so. We were both lost in thought. I was trying to remember as much as I could from my childhood, and I think Luke was doing the same. His expression darkened more and more the longer he was silent.

I had to ask him about more of his memories, but I decided to do it later. After he got his daughter back and knew that she was safe.

As we finally pulled into the driveway of our old childhood home, we discussed our game plan.

We'd start normal and calm. We'd let ourselves in with my key. We wouldn't shout or cause any trouble but act like nothing was up. Mom and Dad had no idea what we'd been up to or how much we knew.

Before we could do any of that, Mom got in the way, though. She'd already opened the door as we approached with a bright smile on her face.

"Boys, you're back! And just in time as well. We were just sitting down for dinner."

"How are you acting this normal?" I blurted out, forgetting that we'd planned to do the same thing and that Mom hadn't been with us these past hours. She had no idea about all the disaster scenarios that were going through our heads.

She answered me in the form of an eye roll. "You're so dramatic, Max. Sometimes I really wonder why you weren't picked. Maybe if you were better—" She stopped herself by clenching her fist. "Unimportant," she continued. "Come in."

Luke shoved her to the side and shot through the door. I quickly followed, leaving the door open behind me.

Our home has an open design with few doors, so you can quickly skim through the kitchen and living room. There was no one around.

"Where are they?" Luke shouted.

"Not up here." Mom shook her head and pointed her fingers down.

"Stay here," Luke said as he walked toward the basement.

Mom quickly followed him, making small jumps with each step.

Ignoring my brother's instructions, I went to the kitchen, grabbed a knife, and followed them to the basement. Of course, I had absolutely no idea what to expect down there, but at the end of the day, it was my family. And at the very least, I wouldn't leave my brother alone.

They had redecorated the basement. All the boxes with stuff were shoved in one corner. In the middle of the room was a table, our old garden table probably, with an orange plastic cloth that had balloons on it.

The table was set with plates, cups, and napkins, all in sets of six. In the middle there was a big plate with one of those huge silver covers that you sometimes see in hotels in movies, or maybe in real ones, too.

My dad was sitting on a small plastic chair. Mom stood next to him.

"Where are they?" Luke shouted.

Mom and Dad shot each other a look. "Who?"

"I'm not fucking playing. WHERE ARE THEY?"

"If you're talking about our son-in-law and our granddaughter, they went home around ten minutes ago after Jacob helped us set everything up," my dad explained calmly.

Our basement consists of two rooms: the big one that we were standing in at that moment, and a smaller one connected by a closed door.

I walked toward it, but Mom got in my way. My hands went to the knife that I had hidden in my back pocket.

"You're telling me Jacob helped you with… What the hell even is this?" Luke wasn't shouting anymore, but his voice had a low tremble. Even with parents like ours, family normally meant safety. The situation was absurd and quite frankly frightening. It didn't feel like reality anymore.

Everything seemed to happen ultra-fast and simultaneously in slow motion.

"It's a surprise party. Don't act like we can't talk to our son-in-law. Jacob loves us—"

"No, he doesn't," Luke hissed.

"And we love our little Ellie. She was playing the whole time. Luke, honey, call him if you don't believe us."

Now Luke was moving toward us, stopping dangerously close in front of Mom.

"We've been trying to call him for hours," I chimed in, but at the same time I remembered that there was never any service down in the basement.

"Luke, go upstairs and try to call him." I gave him a look that meant that I was fine down here. He hesitated for a second, then ran up.

As soon as he was gone, my parents' eyes were glued to me.

Both had massive grins on their faces and then shouted, "REVIVAL TIME!"

Dad got up and led me to the table, gesturing for me to take a seat.

"Stop this madness now. Why are you doing this to us?" My voice cracked, tears shooting to my eyes. I had finally reached the point where I just felt hurt.

Mom started stroking my hair the way she used to when I was little. "We? We didn't do anything. You did this, Max. When you couldn't perform well enough," she said.

"What—?"

They didn't answer but started rearranging things on the table until we heard Luke coming down the stairs. "They're both home and completely fine. First, he had no service, and then his battery was dead. Come on, Max. Let's go."

"No!" Mom shouted. "Not yet."

"You wanted answers, right? And we want to have dinner with you. If you stay, we will talk," Dad added.

Luke and I exchanged another look, and then, to my surprise, my brother proceeded to sit down.

This was our family, after all.

My mom sat down, took a deep breath, and started speaking. "Shortly after Luke was born, friends of ours told us about an upcoming project. A television show for children on the surface, but so much more below that. An opportunity to change everything in this world. But the project was only at the start. It would take more than a decade to evolve completely, which was perfect. We had all this time to prepare and become a part of it. The company behind it sent us instructions regularly, little clips we were supposed to film of Luke. And when Max was born of him, too. But..." My mom stopped speaking, disappointment written on her face.

"Neither of you made the cut," my dad continued. "You didn't seem to be right enough. But then little Leigh was born. We babysat him at times and took some footage. They loved him."

My mom took over again. "When his parents died," she said with no emotion in her voice, "we were sad, of course, but also thrilled because we thought we could adopt him. But your awful grandparents took him away from us."

Mom and Dad now looked at each other and smiled, and in unison, they spoke. "But it didn't matter."

"He was cast, and when the show was ready, they would find him and a way to get him on it. He was eleven when it started, and everything went perfectly. We even watched the show with you a few times! We wanted it to be you boys, but at least little Leigh was family."

Luke and I looked at each other, more confused than ever. Our parents had officially lost their minds.

"Can we talk now?" I asked. "Fuck it, I will because you're not giving us real answers. You're making the situation only weirder. What's up with this creepy-ass child's birthday dinner? Why are there six sets of dishes?"

They both grinned.

"Because we have fantastic news. There will be a reboot!" my dad almost screamed.

Luke's eyes shot open. "You're not doing any of this shit with Ellie, do you hear me? I'll get both of you arrested."

They both shook their heads.

"No, no, she's much too young. The new show will start very soon this time," my mom said. "The thing is, the show has an adult protagonist, and the last one recently died. Isn't that fantastic?"

Luke got up and called out, "I'm done. Both of you need psychiatric help. If you're ready for that, I might contemplate talking to you again."

I moved up as well, following him toward the door. But then he stopped all of a sudden.

"Wait a second. The show. It's that adventure time thing, isn't it?"

Both my parents smiled again and nodded.

"Didn't Max run away after watching that?"

"What?" I asked, but before I could get an answer, we were interrupted by the sound of a loud thump coming from the room next to this one. I heard a low voice whispering, "Help."

"Who's in there?" I shouted.

My dad answered, "Our star."

# Part 4

I woke up in a cold sweat after a dream that felt far too vivid to be a construct of my mind.

My surroundings were pitch black, but I smelled pine cones and trees all around me. It didn't matter that I couldn't see much; I knew I had to keep going. There was something waiting for me. Or someone. Nobody had seen me leave. I'd climbed out of the window.

I was afraid, but I didn't stop walking. It was as if I was being controlled by external forces.

Suddenly, two arms grabbed me from behind.

"Not you. They promised *you* would be safe," my mom whispered.

I had forgotten about this experience, possibly because I wasn't entirely myself when it happened. My mom brought me back home where a police car was already waiting. They'd been looking for me for hours.

She had saved me, but back then, I didn't know from what.

This must have been more than fifteen years ago.

Now I know that I was following my cousin's call.

"Do you have some water?"

The unfamiliar voice pulled me back to reality.

I still hadn't fully grasped the events of the last day. Luke and I had talked to my parents, who seemed to be going through some sort of manic episode.

Now, I was in a hotel, and my brother and his family were in the room next to me.

And I was here with my cousin.

"Uhm, no, but I can get you some from the sink in the bathroom."

He looked miserable. His eyes were bloodshot, and his dark hair, which resembled mine, was going in all directions. He was lying in the bed, while I was sitting on the sofa. I must have dozed off on it sometime early this morning.

He slowly nodded.

Luke had been hesitant about leaving me here with him, but I convinced him that after being drugged and tied up in our basement room, he was probably lacking the energy to hurt me. Besides, we were the ones who got him out.

And not without paying a high price.

I still have the look on my dad's face ingrained into my mind when he said that our star was next door.

His eyes opened wider than they humanly should be able to, and his grin was so bright that I thought the corners of his mouth might rip. The excitement quickly wore off, however, after I'd pulled the knife from behind my back.

It might have been a rash reaction, but for whatever goddamned reason, I chose *fight* at that moment instead of flight.

"Max, stay calm," Luke whispered, but I couldn't. My entire body was shaking. And then the most surprising thing happened.

My mom started laughing. Hysterically.

Then slowly she got up from the tiny plastic chair she was sitting on, all while still laughing. And then my dad chimed in and laughed even harder.

For a split second, I almost believed that my entire family was playing a prank on me, but then my mom started talking.

"Leave the show for the producer, dear. She'll be here soon. I even give you permission to slit my throat," she said with tears in her eyes. "Or your father's. But it should at least be taped, honey."

I was frozen and almost didn't realize that my dad had been walking up to me, his hands reaching for the knife.

Until Luke jumped in and punched my dad in the face, something I never believed I would witness. My dad, who had grown old over the years, fell back, and for a moment I felt pity. Even after all they'd revealed about themselves, I still felt bad for them. I still felt attached to them.

After the punch, things went really fast. Luke had taken the knife from my hand and was shouting at my mom to stay back. He walked up to my dad, but instead of helping him up, he grabbed the keys tied to his belt.

He threw them over to me, but of course, they fell to the ground. That was when I unfroze. I grabbed the keys and tried a few until one fit the other door in the basement.

Inside lay Leigh, falling in and out of unconsciousness. It was immediately clear to me that it was him because my grandpa was right: we looked very alike. Luke shouted some more things at my parents and helped me pick up our cousin. Together we carried him upstairs.

My parents didn't move, but as we walked up the stairs, I heard my dad say, "You're making a mistake. They will find you."

---

We were on our way to a hospital when Leigh started waking up more and more. He begged us not to go to the hospital but instead to drive to some hotel as far away as possible.

Luke didn't question him.

After picking up a clueless Jacob and Ellie, we were on the road.

On the drive there, Luke tried his best to explain everything to Jacob. He left out some parts, which I assume was because of Leigh.

"So I suppose they used us as bait. They said they wanted to plan something for your birthday. Recreate a party they had when you were kids or something. I shouldn't have gone along, I—" Jacob said after he had been silent for a long time, probably processing the insane story.

"I can't believe what you guys have been through," he continued with a hurt undertone. Either because Luke had kept this from him or because he genuinely felt bad for us.

When we reached the hotel, Leigh immediately passed out on the bed. I sat down on the sofa, making sure he kept breathing while listening to Luke and Jacob's muffled voices next door.

But now Leigh was awake. Finally, because we hadn't been able to ask him much and I was damn ready for some answers.

---

After texting Luke, the three of us sat on the bed, almost as if we were just boys, cousins, hanging out.

But I didn't even remember this cousin. To me he was a stranger.

"I swear everything is getting a shitty reboot. Even our murder show," Leigh casually said after a while.

"How can you be joking right now?" Luke asked.

He shrugged. "You get desensitized after a while."

"Can you tell us more about this show?" I asked.

"Do you want the short or the long version?"

"Maybe start with short," I said, getting nervous.

He shrugged. "I don't remember much about my parents' death or life before it. To be honest, I don't remember either of you, and I didn't even know you existed. I grew up with Grandma and Grandpa. When I was eleven or so, I saw an ad looking for actors for a new TV show. No idea why, but for some reason I thought that was exactly what I wanted to do." He sighed. "I thought there was no way I'd ever get cast. I was some kid from some boring-ass small town. Grandpa took me to auditions, he had no clue what this was about, and for some reason, I actually got the part. Everything else from that time is kind of foggy. There were a couple of other kids who I recently got back in touch with. And some motherfucker named Warly."

Luke and I stayed silent, listening to every word.

"The next part might seem a little absurd to you." He took a deep breath. "This show had an awful effect on kids. After watching it, they would run away from home. It was some kind of sick mind control from the production company. I know this sounds insane, but they took all those kids. I don't know how many of them died."

He looked at us, waiting for a reaction, probably thinking that we wouldn't believe a word. But we'd seen the tapes and had felt the effect they had.

"Did you ever go to the police?"

He shook his head. "No, and I suggest you don't, either. The risk is too high; they'll just send you to the producers. They have powers you can't possibly imagine."

"But our parents said that the adult in the show is dead. That's Warly, right?" Luke asked.

"Doesn't matter. He didn't matter. They can kill and replace any one of us. To be honest, I don't believe there is anything they cannot do, and running away from them is next to impossible. A while back, my friends and I had a terrible encounter with them. And then again. But we were able to fight them. Now for a while, I thought I was fine, but it never seems to end. And now they somehow got my uncle to lure me back in?"

I got up from the bed and started pacing around the room. "How the hell did my parents get you into our basement?" I asked.

He looked at the ground. "I don't have any family left besides Grandpa. When they reached out to me, I had no idea that they were connected to Warly, that they were insane—" He took another long breath. "Look, I can tell you everything else I know about this, but first, I need to know how you're all connected to this."

Luke and I exchanged a look, one that said, "Can we trust him?"

But then I thought about it. We could have been the ones in his place. We were lucky; they chose him instead.

Luke must have been thinking the same because, after some silence, my brother started speaking, telling Leigh everything that had happened since we watched the tapes.

When Luke was done, we both looked at Leigh. He had been quiet all throughout, but now he opened his mouth to speak.

"So this didn't start with the auditions. It was determined when I was a baby. And your parents knew everything?"

"I guess. Maybe yours did, too," Luke said.

"Did you tell your parents before looking for the tapes, the regular ones?" he asked, looking at me.

I nodded.

"And you'd never seen the other ones before? So they probably planted them there for you to find."

"But why?"

He was scratching the stubble on his face that didn't quite yet make a beard. "Did you feel anything when you watched them?"

"Yeah, they made me feel sick and overall a little strange," I said, my mind racing.

I looked over at Luke, but he seemed frozen. Cold sweat was forming on his forehead.

Leigh sighed. "If those tapes were made with some connection to the production company, they weren't normal. Watching them might do stuff to you and your mind. Maybe it already did. My guess is that your parents wanted you to see them, and we should find out why before it's too late."

# Part 5

It had taken power over me once before, and I realized that it could happen again. Maybe it already had. But what I couldn't get out of my mind was that Mom had saved me back then.

Why would she push us back in now?

"So what should we be prepared for?" Luke asked.

"Hard to say. I mean, if you can't trust your own mind, you just have to go with whatever you believe is real at the moment. There's no survival guide or anything like that. We just have to do our best and hope we survive," Leigh said.

"Fantastic."

Leigh gave him a half-smile. "It helps not to be alone. I wouldn't have made it without my friends back then. You have each other, and that matters a lot."

"Well, for what it's worth, you have us as well. Our parents might be dicks, but we're here for you, Leigh," my brother said. "Besides, someone who's already been in hell knows how to survive it."

"I'm still feeling normal, at least I think so," I said. "What about you, Luke?"

He started fumbling with the ring on his finger. "Mostly normal. Although I've never punched Dad before."

"And I never threatened our parents with a knife before."

"To be fair, they deserved that," Leigh said, and the three of us laughed.

For a moment, we really felt normal.

"Why do you think they chose you for the show? Why not Luke or me?" I asked after a while.

"I'm not sure. Maybe because I was Alex's age."

"Who's Alex?"

Leigh looked away. "He was the main character, next to Warly."

"The real star?" Luke asked.

Leigh nodded.

"So why don't we get that guy? Maybe if they have—"

"I don't know where he is," Leigh interrupted with no further explanation.

Luke started massaging his temples. "I have to go check on Jacob and Ellie." He gave me a look I didn't understand and walked outside.

---

"Do you know what happened to all those children that ran away from home?" I asked Leigh after a while.

He smiled, but there was still some sadness in his eyes. "They got to go home. Although most of them weren't children anymore at that point."

I bit my lip. The thought hadn't left my mind that I was almost one of them. And as hard as I tried to make my mind work, I couldn't remember more about that time.

"Is there a way we can see that show? I'd like to know—"

"No," Leigh interrupted again. "We left no traces of it, and trust me, you do not want to see it."

"But I already have. Well, when I was younger, I was one of the kids, but I don't remember it."

Leigh looked me up and down. "How old are you?" he asked.

"Twenty-eight."

"So you were eleven or twelve when Warly aired? Almost too old." He started rubbing his face again. "Did your parents ever tell you that I was in it?"

I shook my head. "You said that Warly is dead. Are you sure about that?" I asked.

He nodded and looked away again. I knew there was more to it; Leigh looked like he'd been through a lot, and I could tell that he wasn't quite ready to open up about all the trauma. But he tried.

"The producer slit his throat in front of my eyes. That's when I realized this wasn't really about Warly. He was a pawn just like the rest of us."

"Shit, that producer lady really is ruthless."

Leigh frowned. "Not a lady, a man. He was really charismatic, too, which makes him even scarier."

"Are you sure he was the producer? My parents were talking about a woman."

"Maybe it's a new one. Maybe that's why it's starting again. I have to make a phone call. Can I borrow your phone?" he asked.

I handed it over after checking if my parents had tried to contact us.

Nothing. No calls. No texts.

Leigh walked out to the hallway but came back seconds later. "The door to your brother's room is open."

I immediately jumped up and followed Leigh to the room next to ours.

It was empty, and on the white sheets, there was a red stain.

"Fuck!" I shouted. "Luke?" But of course, there was no answer.

"Maybe they went downstairs to get some food?" Leigh asked, but he didn't sound very convincing.

I shook my head. He would have told us.

"Maybe they left. Your brother seemed suspicious. Maybe he was scared for his daughter or—"

"No," I whispered.

Luke would never leave me alone.

---

The hotel was empty.

There was nobody behind the reception, no one in the lobby or the hallways. A massive building, simply wiped clean.

A nagging feeling spread through my body, the feeling that we had missed a lot during the short night that we'd spent inside the rooms.

"It's starting. They are here. They must be," Leigh whispered as he looked toward the front door.

"Give me my phone." I tried to reach Luke, but he didn't answer. I sent him a text, but of course, he didn't reply to that either. Something terrible was happening.

"We could leave. I don't see anybody outside. We could get weapons or reinforcements," Leigh said and looked me in the eyes. After I didn't answer, he added, "But you're not leaving, are you?"

I shook my head. "I'm going to look for my brother."

"All right, then I'm also staying. We're family, right?"

I wanted to trust Leigh. I felt bad for him. All of this mess was my parents' fault. They were possibly even the reason that Leigh was an orphan. Who else would have a better reason to mess with us?

I was starting to think that Leigh was doing just that. Because when I tried to reach Luke, I saw a text that Leigh had sent to a strange number. The message said, "It's not me," which I didn't understand.

And our current location.

But the message wasn't sent earlier when he borrowed my phone. It was sent around four a.m. Around the time I had dozed off.

Staying with Leigh might have been more dangerous than just going to look for Luke on my own, but right now I knew I needed him. He was the one they really wanted, after all; Luke and I were second choices.

All I had to do was not let him notice my distrust.

---

The hotel had eleven floors, a small lobby, a kitchen, an inside pool, and a conference hall.

The kitchen was locked, so we decided to check out the conference hall next. With a sinking feeling inside my stomach, I opened the big white door.

"What the—" Leigh whispered.

We were standing in front of a long table with chairs all around it. At the very top, across from us, sat Luke, tied to a chair.

He was wearing a purple blazer, and his head was tilted to the side as if something was wrong with his neck. There was blood on his face.

Leigh tried to grab my arm but missed it as I ran across the room to my brother.

"LUKE!"

His head slowly moved back to normal, and when he saw me, his eyes opened wide. Then his gaze went over to Leigh, and he shook his head. "Get out of here," he croaked.

"OH MAN!" I heard a different voice shout. At first, I couldn't tell who it was, so I looked at Leigh, who I thought was the only other person in the room.

But then I realized that there was someone else here who had been standing next to the door with a tape recorder in hand.

"Jacob?"

"Oh my god, Max! We're filming a scene right now. You fucked it up." He had a smile on his face, but his eyes seemed angrier than I'd ever seen them before.

"No," I whispered.

Then I noticed that he was holding something in his other hand. A hunting knife. "Did you hurt Luke with that?" I asked.

He nodded, like a proud boy.

Jacob was almost as tall as Luke and could seem crazy intimidating if you didn't know that he was actually super sweet.

Normally.

His eyes were opened wide as sweat poured down his forehead.

"Only a little bit. He's totally fine."

"Where's Ellie?" I asked, looking at Luke. For a split second, I saw the devastated look on his face and thought of the worst.

"She'll be right back," Jacob whispered, his eyes twitching for a split second. "Anyway, you and your cousin, especially your cousin, are more than welcome to join us?" he asked while moving the knife around.

I looked at Leigh, who was still standing at the door. He could've run away, but he didn't. Instead, he was making eye contact with me, and from what I interpreted, it looked like, "Together we can take him."

But before we could move, we started hearing the sound of heels walking on the wooden floor.

They stopped right behind Leigh. A woman started caressing his cheek with long, black nails, and Leigh lost all the color in his skin. She was wearing a checkered jacket, denim pants, and purple shoes. In her left arm, she was holding Ellie.

My eyes opened wide.

The woman smiled. "Hello there," she said in a playful tone.

"Give her to me, please," Luke begged.

The woman walked past Leigh and toward the table, where she took a seat on the right side next to Luke.

Ellie reached out her arms when she saw him, and my heart broke a little. But at least she seemed fine. She was smiling and didn't have a single scratch on her.

"Come on in, Leigh. We have a lot to discuss."

He walked toward me, and together we sat down on the left side of the table. It felt surreal, like we had just joined a regular work meeting.

Jacob followed and sat down next to the woman.

All of us were suddenly eerily calm—except for Jacob, who still had that insane look on his face.

"All right, let's get straight to the point. I was personally asked to take charge of the reboot of *Dr. Warly's Adventure Club*. And I have a proposition for you boys."

I swallowed.

"You're the new producer, huh?" Leigh asked casually. "What happened to the old one?"

"He is very busy, but he trusts me to do well with this task."

"Right. And what's stopping us from punching you in the face and running off?"

She shrugged. "Nothing. I wouldn't stop you. So no need to punch me. I am giving you an opportunity right now to start a conversation with us. As you know, we get what we want, and we will always find you again. What I'm doing now is giving you the opportunity to get the little girl out of here. We're not interested in her."

"How?" Luke asked, slowly coming back to his senses.

"I don't need all of you. And, believe it or not, I don't want you guys to hate us but join us, which I realize won't happen if we keep the babe. So I'm letting one of you leave with her. The other ones stay at the hotel with me and talk. That's it."

She gave us a big smile. "I will leave the room and let you discuss, though I expect an answer when I get back."

She got up from her chair, walked over to our side, and gave Ellie to me. Then she gestured something to Jacob, who got up and left the room with her.

I gave Ellie a kiss on her head and then gave her to Luke, who hugged her tight.

"There are no windows or other doors. We can't get out of this room," Leigh said.

I carefully touched Luke's face where the blood was starting to dry. "Jacob did this to you?"

He nodded. "You know we were wondering if watching the tapes did anything to us, but I didn't even think about the fact that Jacob had seen parts of it, too."

I swallowed. "Luke, are you normal?" I asked.

"I don't know, man. I'm not sure what normal feels like anymore. I think it's safest if you don't trust anyone."

"I agree," Leigh chimed in. "So what do we do?"

For the first time, I was sure of what needed to happen. "Luke, you go. You take Ellie and get yourself to a hospital. I will listen to what the producer has to say."

"Max, no way. No fucking way."

I put my hand on his shoulder and leaned in closer. "We've been cursed since the first moment Mom and Dad got involved in all this. But we're adults now. Ellie isn't. Get. Her. Out."

# Part 6

I started remembering Leigh.

And Alex.

And I now know what my mom did.

Before I ran away, before I watched the show, I was brought to the auditions. My parents had a big argument; my mom was shouting that I was too fragile, but my dad shouted back that Luke was too old.

"He won't be harmed! He will be a star!"

After the fight, Mom came to my room. She picked the clothes I would wear, combed my hair, and even put some makeup on my face. "We have to make a good impression." She smiled at me, but I knew she wasn't happy. Something was going on.

I'd forgotten all of that, but now it was coming back.

Parents weren't allowed inside for the auditions. They had given us all a sentence, put us in front of a camera, and filmed how we said it. I don't remember much more. Only that a number of children were filtered out.

Two girls were picked for the female roles.

For the male ones, there were three boys left.

I didn't know who they were back then, but now I realize it must have been Alex, Leigh, and me.

That was where things got really fucked up.

Two of us were supposed to be chosen for the show, and I thought I had a pretty good chance.

But then something happened.

My mother killed me.

---

The memories came back in little chunks, which I assume had something to do with how the following day went.

Because now, fifteen years later, Leigh and I were back at the auditions.

It wasn't easy, but Luke left. Leigh instructed him not to go to any authorities about this; he said it would make things even harder for us.

He promised we would be fine as he knew how to deal with them.

The producer sent us to separate hotel rooms to rest for the following day. We were on the eleventh floor, and our doors were locked from the outside, but we realized we could communicate by opening our windows. Our rooms were right next to each other.

"I don't know what will happen to us now, but can we be honest with each other?" I asked, sitting on the window ledge.

Leigh was silent for a moment. "Yeah," he finally replied.

"Why did you tell them where we are?"

"What?"

"The producer, you sent them our location."

Leigh huffed. "No, I didn't. I'm pretty sure it was Jacob, genius."

Right.

"But I saw the text!" I protested.

"Yeah... that wasn't to the producer. It was still dumb. And risky, though." He sighed. "Sorry, I should have told you. Remember how I said that I didn't know where Alex was? A while back he just disappeared, no contact, nothing. I sent that text to another friend that went through the Warly madness with us. This will sound weird, but I guess everything does at the moment. The Warly people have a way of creating new versions of us."

"Like on the tapes?"

"No. Worse. Those versions are real. They look like us, at least from a distance. They are more... fucked. Uncanny. And they can manipulate us. If you saw messed-up tapes from your childhood, it might possibly not have been the real you. Anyway, I warned my friend that it could happen again. I wanted to make sure that, whatever happened, she knew that it was me."

My head started hurting, but weirdly, it made sense to me. Maybe after all I'd witnessed in those days, things couldn't surprise me anymore.

"Do you think your friend can help us?"

"No, she's on the other side of the world right now. That's the only reason I texted her, wouldn't have involved her otherwise. But in case something happened, I wanted her to have our last location."

I swallowed. For a second, I had a bit of hope, but it was quickly taken again.

"Can you be honest with me as well?" Leigh asked.

I nodded, which I realized he couldn't see, but he continued anyway.

"Your parents killed mine, didn't they?"

"After everything I've learned about them, I think it might be possible."

After that, we both closed our windows.

---

I only slept for an hour or two that night. Though as I was lying in bed, it felt as if I was living somewhere in between the waking and the dream world. And that was where the memories came back more detailed.

The auditions. The three of us were sitting in a colorful room on small plastic chairs, surrounded by toys that we were too old for already.

Leigh was really chatty and seemed incredibly fun back then. Neither of us knew that we were cousins, but we got along well. Alex was quieter but had something very cool about him. I remember that now. Hanging out with them was fun; I don't think any of us were feeling competitive.

After a few hours inside that waiting room, they asked us back to the studio. Again, our parents were nowhere to be found.

Most of the lights inside the studio were turned off, but I could see that they had built a set. The ground felt like a sponge; every step we took was like a little jump. Alex was giggling until the voice of a man welcomed us. Next to him stood two other boys. I couldn't see a lot, but they had much resemblance with Leigh and Alex.

"Max," the producer said, "you did a wonderful job. However, at this time we can't consider you for the show. You will meet your mom in the parking lot."

That was it.

Leigh and Alex said goodbye to me, but their voices sounded different. Scared.

While I was sad that I wouldn't be joining them, I still felt relief, opening the door of the studio and getting out.

I remembered that my bag was still inside the dressing room where I was brought at the very beginning, so I walked there first.

And that was when I saw the corpses.

There were multiple bodies lying on the ground. They had been cut open, and a purple substance was leaking from them.

The substance made me believe that they were props, so with a beating heart I went to inspect them further. And that was when I realized that they all looked like me, in different years of my life. One of them, the biggest one, was wearing the same clothes I was wearing that day.

At first, I thought it was cool. I was thirteen and believed they had created them for the show.

But then I noticed that one of them was slowly moving his hand.

I stumbled back toward the door and started running.

I didn't stop until I found my mom's car.

The drive home felt like a fever dream.

"You will forget about this soon enough, my dear. It will be like a dream. Your father would have been proud if you made the cut, but I believe your cousin will do just fine. The producers will be happy."

She kept staring right ahead, hardly blinking at all.

I noticed the purple blood spatter on her skirt, but I didn't ask her about it.

At home, she played her part well, crying her eyes out because they chose Leigh instead of me, acting like she was disappointed because we couldn't be a bigger part of the production.

But now I believe that for a little while, she slipped out of the manipulation. And saved me, or at least won some time.

Those memories had been buried somewhere deep inside of me, but now they felt crystal clear. Especially after what Leigh had told me about the copies.

---

A knock on my hotel door brought me back to the present. I opened it, and a worker gave me a tray with breakfast. I asked them questions but received no answers.

An hour later, there was another knock. The same person brought me and Leigh downstairs to the room with the swimming pool.

When they opened the door, we heard the sound of a familiar-sounding jingle.

*Dun dun du du dun*

Leigh clenched his fist.

"There you are!" the producer welcomed us, but I didn't even look at her. I was overwhelmed by the strange surroundings.

I'd seen indoor pools before, but they had changed everything about it.

The room was lit with gray-and-blue lights. Inside the pool was a dark substance that appeared sticky. Around it, they had created fake bushes and trees. There were cameras running the entire time.

Besides the producer, there were a few workers, all dressed in the same overalls. One of them was Jacob.

"We are so excited to create a new audition tape with you! However, our new concept will be a one-man show. For this reason, we would like to estimate in advance who our new star will be. We only want the strongest one, the best."

The acoustics in the room made it sound like she was everywhere around us.

"I will be completely honest, neither of you was our first choice. We believed we had the best one secured, but he is... not currently in our possession."

"In your possession? What the fuck is wrong with you people?" Leigh shouted.

Even through the bad lighting, I could see that she was rolling her eyes.

"Anyway, whoever pushes the other one into the pool first wins. You will both be handed the same weapon to keep things fair."

Two of the assistants walked over and handed each of us a knife. My stomach started turning.

"You want us to fight? This is ridiculous. Neither of us wants to do this."

Leigh looked at me, but I couldn't make eye contact. My body was trembling.

"I will do it. I'll be your star or whatever. Just let Max go," he said, surprising both me and the producer.

She started laughing. "How very brave of you but this is not how it works. We *need* to see who is better."

I moved a step closer to the pool and looked at the substance. My sneaker touched the edge, and the fabric immediately started to melt.

"You want one of us to kill the other," I whispered.

"What if we don't do it?" Leigh asked.

"We will push both of you in and use one of our spares. We still have the option of a girl. And your brother, of course."

I swallowed.

There was no way I would kill Leigh, but having us both dead wasn't an option, either.

A timer started ringing.

"Go on!" she shouted.

Leigh and I looked at each other, both frozen. I was sure that if it came down to it, he would do it, but he stood still.

I took the knife and cut my palm.

Blood started trickling down. Real, red blood. Leigh saw what I did and copied me.

His blood was also red.

We exchanged another look and, as if reading each other's minds, started running toward the producer. Before I could do anything, Leigh had rammed his knife into her stomach.

Purple goo started dripping. She opened her mouth, but before she could say anything, I took my knife and slit her throat.

Workers started running toward us from all directions. This was our end. They would kill us both.

And that was when everything went black.

---

When I opened my eyes again, I was looking at an unfamiliar face.

Slowly, I came back to myself and took in my surroundings. Leigh was lying next to me, awake but just as confused. And Jacob was there, unconscious and tied up.

We were inside a moving van.

"Alex?" Leigh whispered as the stranger smiled and hugged him.

"How?"

Suddenly I felt wide awake and looked at the driver. Next to him was a baby seat.

Luke.

"You didn't think I would let you die in there, did you?"

I couldn't comprehend the situation. Tears started forming in my eyes. I didn't believe I would ever see them again.

Alex started speaking. "A lot has happened in the past year, something I will tell you all about. I was trapped for a long time but recently found a way out, but of course, I had to stay hidden. The only person who knew where I was was my mom. And yesterday, Helen called her. I didn't know what was going on, so I just drove to the location you had sent. That's where I met Luke. He was on his way to go in, with a gun."

"Great plan, Luke," Leigh mumbled.

"Yeah, I wasn't exactly thinking straight. Alex had a much better plan. We used gas to knock everyone inside out. I guess we were just in time."

"But you said getting out won't help us," I said to Leigh.

"It didn't. Not really. But we won some time. I have a place where we will be safe for a little while," Alex answered for him in a stern tone. "A friend will be waiting for us there."

"Where are Mom and Dad?" I asked Luke.

"I don't know. They just disappeared."

---

We got out of hell, but I believe I left a part of me in there.

So for now, we might be safe, but as I came to understand after getting to know Leigh better, there is no getting out of this anymore.

As we reached the town of Fereway, I realized that this was only the beginning for me.

Especially since we took Jacob with us.

# I WOKE UP INSIDE A REPLICA OF MY CHILDHOOD HOME

"Honey, breakfast is ready," my mother's friendly voice called from the other room. It awoke a warm and happy memory, one of our Sunday breakfasts where my mum would make the best waffles in the world, my parents would share the newspaper, and the smell of coffee would fill our whole house. While I was too young to have any of it then, I loved the smell of fresh coffee. My mum always used to mix in spices like nutmeg.

I wish I could have tried her special coffee, but she passed away before I was old enough for it.

My eyes shot open.

Whose voice had just woken me up?

I was lying on the couch in our living room. Well, my dad's living room. I moved out four years ago, just after I turned twenty.

Slowly, I got up and took more steps than necessary until I was standing in the doorframe between the kitchen and the living room.

"Dad?" I carefully asked, but nobody answered.

While it was always slightly emotionally painful, it wasn't unusual. I often heard Mum's voice in my dreams, but it was weird that I smelled waffles and coffee while the kitchen table was completely empty.

I shook my aching head. I had the most horrendous hangover that I needed to cure with more sleep. Upstairs, in my old bedroom, not on the uncomfortable couch.

*Dad must have made a toaster waffle before he went to work—*

Suddenly my thoughts were interrupted. Something was wrong. Terribly wrong.

I climbed up a few of the stairs and found myself in front of a thick, gray wall.

It sounds ridiculous, but the upstairs part of our house had either vanished or was sealed shut with a new wall. This sight felt so entirely absurd that my brain didn't even know what to make of it.

I instinctively took a step back, slipped, and fell down the few stairs, landing on my butt. I could swear I heard laughter. I slowly got up and walked toward the TV, but it was black.

"Dad?" I shouted.

"Where are you, Nick? Didn't you hear your mum calling you for breakfast?"

Every fiber of my body froze. That was Dad's voice, and it came right out of the kitchen.

I didn't understand what was happening, but I knew that something wasn't right, so instead of checking the kitchen, I decided to be smart and head straight toward the front door.

I pulled and pushed, but it wouldn't open. There was also no key in sight. I pushed aside the curtains on the small window next to the door, but all I saw behind it was black.

My heart started racing so fast I thought it would explode.

I swallowed when I remembered that I'd seen sunshine through the window in the empty kitchen earlier. Maybe I could get out through the window.

When I walked into the kitchen, I saw a little white booklet on the table that I swear wasn't there before. I picked it up and read the cover. All it said was NICK.

I was just opening the first page when I saw her right outside the window, scratching the glass with her nails.

My mother. My mother, who passed away when I was only seven. Or rather, something resembling her. I think the best way I could describe it is that she looked like someone had tried to recreate a human based on a picture that a child drew but with real flesh and skin. Her proportions were all wrong, her face was plastered with makeup, and her hair almost looked as if each strand had been glued on.

I felt too perplexed by the situation to even breathe. All I did was stare at it. And then a single tear rolled down my cheek.

When *he* appeared behind her, the copy of my father, I finally woke from my trance and stumbled backward into the living room. The copy of my father was far more realistic; only small components were incorrect. Like, he had a big mustache even though he'd shaved it off a week ago. And his nose appeared to lack nostrils. Small mistakes.

Holding that booklet that I found tightly in my hands, I crouched down next to the couch and hoped that this would all be over soon.

---

I can't say how long I sat on that cold living room floor. There wasn't anything I could do; the only way out seemed to be the kitchen, but at least it seemed they didn't try to come inside.

After what must have been at least an hour of sitting and contemplating my sanity, I decided to look into the booklet with my name on it and started reading the first page.

*The adventure of life*
*Pilot*
*Scene 1*
**We are inside a regular, suburban living room. The childhood home of Nick. We focus on the sofa in the middle of the room.**

**Nickis sleeping on the sofa, tucked underneath a light blanket, still wearing last night's clothes: Loose blue denim pants. Black T-shirt with a pocket. Converse shoes. His hair is frizzy.**

**A voice wakes him up.**
**"Honey, breakfast is ready!"**

"What the actual fuck?" I whispered to myself.

I skimmed through the pages, but hardly any of them made sense. A few scenes were normal, like the one describing me waking up. After that, it was a mixture of random words and nonsense. It was all bullshit, but I did not want to wait here until the *actors* of my parents came inside. I folded the booklet and shoved it inside my back pocket.

Holding my breath, I slowly tiptoed toward the kitchen window. It was the only way out for me. The glass was still foggy from the breath of my mother's copy. A shiver went through my body when I thought about it.

I collected all of my courage and peeked outside. There was no sight of anyone or anything. I held my breath just a moment longer, praying that this window wasn't a prop.

I probably could have broken it, but that might alarm the things and they'd come back.

But I didn't have to. The window opened like a regular one.

Finally, I could breathe again. I turned off my brain and climbed out the window.

---

I was staring at a blue wall, and above me was a warm, yellow spotlight. The fake house stood inside a massive storage hall. Cameras and other equipment were lying around, but there were no signs of any humans.

I walked around the hall until I found two doors. One of them had a sign glued to it.

**Audition for new Warly, this way!**

I decided to take the second door without a sign, which led me to a hallway. I ran through it and landed in a second hallway. I kept running until I finally found an exit. When I realized that I was feeling the real, cold air on my skin, tears started streaming down my face. The relief was replaced by fear when I noticed that the exit led me right into a forest. No roads, no sign of civilization. But I had to focus; I had to get away before they decided that I wasn't supposed to leave.

So I started running again.

I can't tell you how long I ran and how many times I got lost, if that even makes sense in those circumstances.

But finally, I found a diner where I could use a phone. I had escaped, and I was safe.

Ever since that moment, I've tried so hard to remember the location of the place. The police have not been able to find it with the bit of information I had. Of course, I left out the part about the creatures. Nobody would believe that shit, but I'm not able to let go of it. I need to find answers.

Before I end up back inside the studio.

Because when I fled, I took that script with me, and when I finally got home, I collected the courage to look at it and found another part that wasn't nonsense.

**Nick decides to trick the parents. He opens the window in the kitchen and climbs outside. He doesn't know where to go yet.**

**End of scene**.

They'd wanted me to leave—*no*, they even predicted it.

And now all I can do is keep wondering if there is a script for another scene. And whether I am in it.

# I'M PLAYING A GAME CALLED SMILE BUT NOBODY TAUGHT ME THE RULES

## Part 1

I wish I could tell you how my friends and I were sucked into the excruciating pain and darkness of this game. I wish I could tell you that we were tricked by a higher power and were now living through a curse, unable to free ourselves. But that wouldn't be entirely true. We wanted this. We wanted to join the sickness because it promised us a reward we couldn't say no to.

I made the conscious decision that I would be a damn part of this, and now I can't stop. And neither can my friends. Not until it's over.

When you start the game, when you are a part of it, there is no going back. And not knowing the rules could cost you your life. So if you ever get sucked into a game called Smile, maybe my advice could save you a limb or two. But be aware, I'm still figuring things out myself.

Let me tell you about Smile.

This all started when my friend Hailey got kicked out of med school. Becoming a doctor had been her dream ever since she was a kid, and having that taken away from her must have been heartbreaking. Ultimately, it also opened up her schedule for the upcoming madness. Hailey and Lucas were my best friends, and while we did have a past full of peculiar occurrences that led us to mistrust each other on one occasion or another, we had become closer than I'd ever been to anyone, including my family. And so of course the three of us were there together to help Hailey numb the pain of a future lost.

I had invited them to my apartment, a small but cozy place I scored on the ground floor of an apartment building. We were sitting in front of the TV watching silly cartoons when I read the email.

**SMILE**

It wasn't the first time I had gotten the weird email saying nothing but the word "smile." It had been happening for the last few days, but thinking this was nothing but spam, I ignored it. The email address was just a combination of numbers, the typical scam kind: 5252181131@smile.com

The emails were easy to ignore, but suddenly I was receiving the same word as a text message.

**Smile**

**Smile**

**Smile**

"Dude, your phone is blowing up," Lucas said. "When did you become so popular?"

"It's just spam." I held the phone in his face, showing him the last ten texts, all with the same message.

"Why don't you click it?" Hailey chimed in.

"Yes, Hailey, very smart idea. Why don't I open this obscure link that will surely not give me a virus?"

She rolled her eyes.

"Well, how about calling that number, then? It's not anonymous," Lucas said.

I thought about it for a moment, and I'd be lying if I said I wasn't curious. Besides, whoever was behind this had somehow gotten hold of both my number and my email address. I figured maybe I'd recognize their voice.

The phone rang five times, and I thought about hanging up, but then I finally heard them speak.

"Smile," an old voice whispered.

"Smile, Alex," they added in a louder tone.

I looked at my friends staring at me with big eyes. How did this person know my old name? I had changed it to Fynn a while ago.

"Who the fuck are you?" I shouted. I certainly didn't recognize this person, but the raspy voice sent shivers down my spine.

The response was a laugh followed by a short melody.

*Dun dun du du dun.*

"No way," I whispered.

"Welcome to the game, Alex, and don't forget to smile," they said before hanging up.

---

I tried calling again, but the number had been disconnected. For days, my friends and I tried to figure out more about this strange experience, but there was nothing we could find, having only the word "smile" as information.

But as it turned out, we didn't need to look for it. They were already on their way to us.

The three of us were sitting at a diner eating lunch when the strange man dressed in a purple jester suit walked inside. The second I heard him hum the melody, the hairs on my arms stood up. The man was wearing a mask over his face. A mask with a massive smile reaching from one ear to the other. There were a couple more people inside the diner, but nobody else seemed to pay attention to him. The jester made his way toward our table and dropped off a small purple package.

"Hey! Who are you?" Lucas quickly got up from his chair.

The jester shrugged, then took a bow before quickly disappearing outside.

The package had a card attached to it with the word *smile*, as well as a message on the back.

**The loveliest hello to you, our friends and game pieces,**

**We cordially invite you to join us on this wonderful adventure! There are many rewards to be won, much fun to be had, and many souls to be mushed. The three of you have been chosen as team W. How brilliant! In this package, you will find everything you need for the adventure. You will be looking for jesters, imposters, and even a princess! Thrilling, isn't it?**

**May the game begin, adventurers! :)**

We exchanged a quick look before tearing open the package.

Inside, we found a phone, a knife, and three masks that looked the same as the jester's.

"What the actual fuck?" Hailey muttered.

"Um, guys, check this out."

Lucas had opened the phone from the package. Inside, there was an app called *Contestants* that had personal descriptions as well as pictures of what we assumed were other teams. Some people were smiling toward the camera; others were wearing masks with the fake smile.

**Round 1: Take a photo of your team!**
**Reward: 100 dollars!**

The notification suddenly popped up, and just a second later we were looking at our own faces filmed by the front camera of the phone.

"Guys, smile," Hailey said, and while it felt extremely unsettling, I followed her command. Lucas, however, didn't change his serious expression one bit.

**Beautiful! Well, two out of three, but we'll get that fixed. :)**
**Round 1 starts in a few hours.**

We didn't believe it at first, but Hailey and I had both received the money. Of course, it was even stranger that they had our bank details. Everything about this game was deeply violating, but we had been sucked in. Not only did we need to find out more about what was going on, but parts of us were also excited about it. We hadn't been on an adventure for a long time, and at least this one paid well.

Hailey and Lucas decided to stay with me for the time being. We wanted to be together when we received the next assignment, and most of all we wanted to find out as much as we could about this game.

---

"Wasn't it strange that nobody paid attention to that weirdo in the diner?" Hailey asked back home. Lucas was in the bathroom taking a shower.

"Yeah, it's almost as if they knew what was going on. Like they purposely didn't look," I responded.

She nodded. "We should go through the photos. Maybe we'll recognize someone," she said and opened the app.

We swiped through dozens of photos. There was nobody in there I recognized in the slightest. Hailey kept looking through the phone while I researched some more on my laptop.

"Lucas has been gone pretty long. Do you think he fell asleep in there?" I laughed.

"Um, Fynn, they uploaded our photo."

Hailey's hand was shaking as she handed over the phone.

There were the two of us smiling awkwardly toward the camera, but that wasn't the horrifying part. Lucas was sitting next to us wearing the mask.

"Do you remember him putting on the mask for the photo?" she asked.

"No, he definitely didn't. Maybe they added it to the photo."

"Yeah, but do you see that?" She pointed toward the corner of the mask. It looked like there was blood dripping from it. The head was photoshopped onto the rest, but it was Lucas's face underneath. The lighting was much darker, though.

"Lucas?" I shouted toward the bathroom, but he didn't answer.

**Your friend broke a rule and had to pay!**

Finally, he opened the door. His eyes looked empty and red. In his hand, he held the knife from the package. On the corners of his mouth were deep cuts on each side.

"I had to do it," he whispered. "They know everything. My past, my family, my home."

"Shit, man, we need to get you to a doctor!"

Lucas shook his head. "I have a feeling we'd be breaking a rule. I can't break another one."

"How do you know you broke one?" Hailey asked as she got a towel for Lucas's bloody mouth.

"They sent me my punishment."

He wouldn't show us exactly what the text said and stayed quiet for most of the evening. But I knew my friend wouldn't mutilate himself like that for no reason. He had a reason, just like the rest of us. This game had sucked us in, and there was no going back now.

**Round 2: Find the jester!**
**Reward: 100 dollars for a photo! 1,000 dollars for an ear! 100,000 for his life!**

"An ear? His life? Do they want us to kill him?" Hailey shrieked.

"I mean, taking a photo should be enough, right? Sounds like we can choose."

"How are we even supposed to find him?" Lucas asked. He looked really messed up with those cuts in his mouth, but somehow he seemed even more sure that he wanted to continue. Not that we actually had a choice at that point.

"Um, guys, do you see that?"

Hailey pointed her finger toward my living room window. There was someone standing right outside it. I recognized the tips of his jester hat first. Then my eyes went to the creepy smile. He just stood there looking at us with his head slightly tilted, and then he started waving.

Before we could process what was going on, let alone take a photo, he grabbed something out of his pocket, threw it against the glass, and ran off.

As the initial shock settled, we got up and ran toward the window, but he had already disappeared into the darkness of the night. There was a stain on the glass from whatever he had thrown. Hailey opened the window and started climbing out. Living on the ground floor felt both handy and horrifying at that moment. This creep had gotten dangerously close, and worst of all, they knew where I lived. I sighed and followed Hailey outside.

"Fuck, fuck, why didn't we take a damn picture?" Lucas asked.

"Check this out, though. He left us a map!" I said. It was lying there on the ground behind the window, with a little ribbon around it.

"Um, that's not what he threw against the glass, though," Hailey said as she pointed the torch of her phone toward something slimy in the grass.

A bloody, cut-off ear.

That's where we stood. Sucked into the Smile game, not knowing at all what our next steps were supposed to be. Did the jester give us his ear so we wouldn't take his life? Or was this a trick to make us break a rule?

If you hear about a game called Smile, don't play it. Run as fast as you can. But I guess if you heard about it, it's already too late.

Just remember this one thing, for now: don't forget to smile. :)

# Part 2

The first round of the game left my friend with a nasty scar. The second round had given us an ear that was cut right off someone's head. And the worst part was that the round wasn't even over yet. *Smile* was not a game with no rules; the rules were strict, and the punishment was hard. We simply had to figure out how to play it.

The ear that we found lying on the ground next to my window was now safely placed inside a lunchbox that we put in the freezer. What else were we supposed to do with it?

We hadn't slept at all, but we weren't sure what to do next, so we were still sitting in my apartment planning our next steps. The map that was left for us was just a regular map of this town, and no matter how much we looked, we couldn't find any clues on it.

It was early morning by now, and the shimmer of sunlight coming in through the window gave me a feeling of hope. At least until I saw the bloodstain that the jester left on the glass last night.

"We have the damn ear. Let's just send them a picture and be done with it," Lucas mumbled.

"Maybe you shouldn't talk that much, Lucas. You'll get terrible scars."

He rolled his eyes and popped another painkiller. This was the third pill already.

"Hey, Hailey, why don't you tell us why you knew that we had to smile in the photo?" he responded.

Our eyes went to Hailey, who started fidgeting with her necklace.

"Why don't you show us the text they sent you, Lucas? We're a team, after all, aren't we?"

Hailey got up, her avoidant expression turning sinister.

Lucas stayed silent. Both of my friends seemed to have something to hide. It was bad enough that we couldn't trust the game we were so deep into; questioning each other was only making matters worse. Before they decided to put me on blast next, I brought the topic back to the challenge.

We still had a jester to catch.

"Okay, guys, calm down, yeah? Let's just figure out this damn game."

They both nodded, and Hailey got up to say something. "I looked through the other contestants on that app. I didn't recognize anyone, but what I noticed is how most are rather young. Teenagers, college students, though there are also a few people who look significantly older. Of course, there are also the ones wearing masks."

"So underneath the mask they probably look like me right now, nicely cut up," Lucas said as he moved his fingers to draw a smile in the air.

I tried thinking back to yesterday when we were sitting inside the diner. The other people must have been accomplices of the game. Maybe they were contestants like us, and sitting in the diner was a task they received, or possibly they were actors or game masters. Either way, it made no sense how they didn't respond at all to a man dressed in a purple jester costume singing and dancing through the diner. Not exactly something you witness every day. How far had this sick game spread already?

"Hey, check this out!" Hailey interrupted my thoughts. "There is a list ranking the teams."

I took the phone from her hands. We weren't quite at the bottom but not high up either with our one hundred points. There were even teams with points in negative numbers.

"One hundred points, so I guess that's our two hundred dollars minus the one hundred of Lucas. Did you check if they took any money off your bank account?"

He shook his head. "Nope, nothing gone. Guess they counted my cuts as payment. Don't even wanna know what they did to the bottom players."

"Yeah," I whispered. "Check this out, though. The team that is on number one has fifty thousand points."

"So that means they've probably been playing longer than us, right?" Lucas said.

"Yeah, or they've done worse things," Hailey chimed in.

"So you think the jester might be dead already?"

"One might be. We don't know how many there are," she said with a dark expression in her eyes.

---

Lucas kept scrolling through the game on his phone when suddenly something appeared to be changing.

"The numbers. They are getting lower."

I jumped up to take a look, and he was right. More and more teams were suddenly in the negatives; there was constant movement. Nobody seemed to be gaining points, however. I grabbed the phone out of Lucas's hand to take a further look. One team had just fallen from one thousand points to negative ninety-nine thousand.

"What? How the hell did they just lose one hundred thousand points?" I asked.

What happened next was even weirder. The group photo of the team changed to a new one. It had a gray filter on top, and the people had deep cuts in the corners of their mouths, but unlike Lucas's, theirs was turned upside down to a frown.

"Did they lose?" Hailey carefully asked.

"Hell knows what this means," I responded, "but whatever happens, we're not getting to that point."

A few minutes passed, and more teams lost points. None as many as team S, though.

*Dun dun du du dun*

The noise was loud and shrill. I almost dropped the phone out of surprise. Lucas grabbed it from my hands and started grinding his teeth. I could feel the anger inside of him.

**You have been patient! Congrats!**
**Round 2 will officially begin in 13:47 hours.**

"We weren't supposed to start yet! Fuck, that's why the others were lynched!" Lucas shouted and jumped up from his seat.

"Do you think so?" I asked.

"Why else would they only give us the info now? Shit, imagine what would have happened if we sent a photo of the ear."

"They probably would've ripped ours off, too. That damn jester tried to trick us," Hailey added.

We still weren't sure what exactly our next steps were supposed to be, but if this was really true, then maybe we had almost passed the next task. All we needed to do was wait for twelve hours and then send them the ear.

As we didn't have any information on what else we could be doing, we decided to rest for now. None of us had slept at all, and Lucas was still in pain.

---

It didn't take much for Lucas to fall asleep. Hailey and I tried researching some more until I couldn't keep my eyes open, either. I was passed out for what felt like forever. When I finally got up, the other two were in the kitchen making dinner and chatting. It was nice hearing them be normal with each other again.

We sat down to eat and try to distract ourselves, but in reality, all we thought about was that timer.

When it finally reached the last seconds, the three of us were curiously staring at the screen. The camera app opened. It was the back camera, but it had some strange filter on top.

"Are we supposed to take another photo?" Lucas asked.

I shrugged. They hadn't mentioned anything like that. All we had was an ear and a map. Had we finished the assignment without doing anything?

"Wait, I've got an idea," Hailey said as she opened the map we found yesterday. She held the phone above it, and on the screen, we started seeing signs. There were crosses that appeared on four different parts of the map.

Three of them were at random places around town, but one of them was far too familiar.

It was my street. The cross marked my home.

---

**Round 2 has officially begun! Go catch a jester! (Or parts of him)! :)**

"It's just showing my current location probably, right?" I nervously laughed.

"Must be. The other three places are all public places around town."

"I don't think so. I think they're all seeing it," Lucas interrupted her and pointed his finger to the window.

"Fuck me, not again."

The first thing I saw was the creepy smile of the mask. The person wearing it had pressed their face right on the window and was scratching the glass with their nail. Behind him stood two more masked strangers. The wrong smile burned its image into my eyes and brain.

The one in the front kept moving his head from left to right, and he was humming something in low tones.

"Fynn, did you lock the window when we got back inside yesterday?" Hailey whispered.

"I—I think so."

The strangers put their palms against the glass and started pushing.

I swear I thought I had locked the window last night, but it gave in to their pushes and opened wide.

Hailey quickly grabbed the knife from the table, but the masked people didn't seem to care. They didn't even move; they just stood there and kept looking at us.

They stayed right where they were, but we could clearly hear the tune they were humming.

*Dun dun du du dun*

Lucas ran to the freezer, grabbed the box, and before any of us could act, he threw it right over their heads. The smiling faces turned around, grabbed the ear, and ran off. I jumped toward the window and locked it.

The three of us were breathing heavily, and for a moment none of us said a word. I had brought us into some massive danger. Why the hell did I not lock that window?

Finally, Hailey broke the silence.

"We had the ear. We could have sent the photo. We were too slow," she whispered.

"At least we got rid of them. There might be others coming, though. We should go to those other locations now and find our own jester," I said, trying to sound as confident as I could.

---

"There are exactly three locations left. All in completely different parts of town. I think the best we can do now is split up to maximize our chances," Hailey said.

I thought about it for a moment. It seemed risky to split up, but all places were very public, and we had no idea if there was a time limit.

"Yeah, okay, guys, but stay safe. No risk-taking, yeah? Take a photo if you spot a jester, and that's it," I said.

Both agreed.

The marks were near the town hall, a mall, and a bowling center. Hailey took the car and drove to the bowling center, which was a forty-five-minute drive away.

Lucas and I both went to the subway, where we each grabbed a different line. Hailey had the game phone. We agreed that the two morbid alternatives were no option. All we'd do would be to take a photo and send it to Hailey right away so she could upload it in the game.

Sitting in the subway, I couldn't do much but wait and finally breathe. It would take me about thirty minutes to the town hall.

"Smile?" I heard a voice behind me.

It was a guy, about my age I guess, with short brown hair. I had noticed him looking at me from the other seat before, but I hadn't noticed that he had gotten up. Now he was standing right next to me.

"Sorry, didn't mean to freak you out. I saw your photo in the *game app*." He whispered the last part as he took a seat in front of me.

"So you're playing the game?" I whispered. He seemed normal, not crazy like the people in front of my window earlier.

"Yeah, long story. I figure you're on your way to the town hall, too?"

"Uh-huh, are you playing alone?"

He shook his head. "My friends went to different places. I have no idea if this is breaking any rules, but we're freaking the hell out. This game is so confusing and horrible and—" He sighed. "I don't know, maybe we can help each other."

I tried to smile. "Sure, dunno if I'll be of much help, though."

"Yeah, me neither." He laughed. "I'm Killian, by the way."

"Fynn."

Killian moved closer and started whispering. "Do you think there are more players in here?"

I looked around the car. There was an older lady, two men in the back, and some kids a few seats behind us. "Nobody I recognize."

When we arrived at the station for the town hall, we were the only ones leaving the subway.

The station was eerily empty and quiet.

"All right, let's go to the town hall, I guess? I doubt he'll be inside, but maybe on the place in front or—" Killian grabbed my arm and pointed to the platform on the other side. I didn't expect to see him at the station, but there was the jester. Possibly the same one I saw yesterday, but I couldn't be sure of that. He was at the very end, and in between us were the tracks. If we wanted to catch him, we had to run up all the stairs, get to the other side, and then run to the end of the platform. But we didn't need to. All we needed was a photo. I got my phone, but before I could take a picture, I noticed someone behind the jester.

It was Lucas.

Black hair, gray shirt, denim jacket.

It certainly looked like Lucas, but there was no way he could have made it here before me. He took the subway to the mall. I squinted my eyes to get a better look at his face, and I could swear I spotted the smile cuts at the corners of his mouth.

"LUCAS?" I shouted.

He looked at me, waved, and without hesitation grabbed the jester and pushed him right onto the tracks.

Killian turned around and started running up the stairs. I followed him as fast as I could. There was no sight of Lucas anywhere. We got to the other side and ran down to the platform where the jester was.

I thought Killian was about to take another photo, but instead, he kneeled down. "Grab my hand!" he shouted to the jester. I jumped down next to him and helped pull up the man. With all our strength, we got him back on the platform just before the subway train made it to the station. The jester got up, pushed both of us to the ground with unbelievable strength, and ran inside the subway.

I tried getting my phone, but neither I nor Killian was quick enough to shoot a photo before he disappeared.

That's when I heard my phone buzz.

**Hailey: We got it, we won the round.**

# Part 3

My friends could be more than mysterious at times. I knew that they had reasons for playing this game that they wouldn't tell me about. That there were things they knew and wouldn't share with me. None of this was a coincidence. The game hadn't found us; we had found it. And every single one of us was in it to win. No matter what it took.

Still, seeing the measures that my friend would have taken to win this game left a bitter taste in my mouth. I didn't like to admit it, but seeing my friend like that had woken up a deep fear inside of me. Not only because I started to see how far he was ready to go for this game but because I had never seen him happier than at the moment when he almost sent a man to his death.

The fear, however, was accompanied by a much stronger emotion. Anger. I was furious. Lucas could ruin everything for us with his impulsive behavior.

There were so many questions running through my mind, starting with how on earth we had won this round. There was a chance that Lucas thought he had cost the jester his life, but how would he have proved it? The man was alive and well because of Killian's quick decision-making. He had saved him. I was the one who simply followed, all while wondering if we were even making the right choice.

Killian, on the other hand, didn't even bat an eye before running to save the one who was torturing us. Could I trust this new player, or was he wearing a mask like everyone else playing the game?

---

Killian and I got inside the next subway that arrived and made our way back to the side of town we came from earlier. I needed to talk to Hailey about what had just happened, and Killian was nervous as his team hadn't completed the round yet.

"That was your friend, right?" Killian asked as we sat down in the empty subway. We had been quiet for the past few minutes, just collecting our breaths and thoughts.

I nodded.

"That's wild. Even from a distance, I recognized him right away. His face hasn't changed a bit," he continued.

"His face?" I asked.

He's wearing a mask in the photo. How would Killian even know what his face looked like?

Killian's face turned red, as if he had just said something he wasn't supposed to. "I mean it looks a bit distorted maybe. I don't know. Is he dangerous?"

Now I had no idea how to answer this question. *Was* my friend dangerous? "No, Lucas is a decent guy. I have no idea why he just did that," I responded.

"Lucas? I thought his name was—"

Killian was interrupted by the speaker announcing the next stop.

"Oh shit, I need to get off. Can I give you my number, though? I feel like we could help each other with this game."

"Sure," I said, and we exchanged numbers. Killian got up to leave, but before stepping out, he turned around once more.

"I'm sure we'll meet again soon. I'm rooting for you, Alex." He winked at me and left the subway.

---

I had no idea how Killian knew my real name. Or how he knew Lucas. I had no idea about anything that had just happened, but for now, my focus was on getting to my apartment and talking to Hailey. When I got inside, however, she wasn't there yet. But Lucas was, standing outside my front door.

"Yo, we did it!" he said and raised his fist in the air.

The sight of my friend filled me with an unspeakable rage. Before I knew it, I was pushing him against the wall.

"What the fuck, man? What is wrong with you?" I shouted.

Lucas stared at me with a confused look on his face.

"We agreed we would only take a photo. What kind of psychopath are you?" I continued.

Lucas pushed me away with unexpected strength. "What's wrong with you?"

"What's wrong with me? You're the one attempting murder for some shitty game! Was it worth the win, Lucas?" I hissed.

Suddenly, I felt an arm pulling me away.

"Whoa, what's going on?" Hailey asked.

"No idea, Fynn jumped me for no fucking reason."

"No reason? He pushed the jester on the train tracks. He tried to kill him without showing any remorse. And then he had the audacity to smile." I felt my chest moving up and down.

"What train tracks? Dude, I was at the mall. I didn't even see the jester," Lucas said.

"Then how did we win the round?" I asked.

"I saw him," Hailey chimed in, "at the bowling center."

She got the game phone out of her pocket and showed us the notification.

**Congrats, team W! You earned 100 points! Try to aim for more next time. :)**

"He was just jumping around, from one lane to the other in the center. The place was packed with other players wearing masks and some without. Everyone taking photos. They all seemed awfully normal, though," Hailey said.

"Good job, Hailey! The mall was packed with players, too, but I didn't spot any jesters," Lucas chimed in.

"You were not at the fucking mall, Lucas. What kind of shit are you trying to pull?" I almost shouted.

"Fynn, calm down," Hailey whispered. "Whatever happened at that station, we made it. Can we go inside now, please?"

I was still furious, but Hailey was right. We made the round. Our point score went up, and we each received a third of the money. They counted it as a team effort. For now, we were safe, but I would have to keep a close look at Lucas.

---

For the next few hours of the evening, I mostly kept to myself. I took a shower, got changed, and wrote down my thoughts. Lucas and Hailey excitedly talked about their experiences. The way they described both locations, it sounded like a normal game. Lots of young people gathering around to catch something, just like when Pokémon Go came out a few years ago. All while I almost saw a man die.

**Killian: We made it! My buddy caught a pic at the mall. He said it was crazy, people were trying to rip out the poor guy's ear... till security came. You guys all right?**

I walked up to Hailey and Lucas in the living room to show them the text.

"I met another guy at the station today playing the game. He was the only other one there, actually," I said. "Lucas, you said there was no jester at the mall, right?"

"This again? Seriously, Fynn? I left the mall after Hailey texted. Maybe that dude showed up afterward."

"Why do you have this guy's number, Fynn?" Hailey asked.

"Um, he asked for it. So we could help each other. Don't worry, I'm being careful."

Now Lucas seemed angered. "You don't trust me, but you trust some stranger? Ever thought that you just ran into some trap? Why were there no other people at the station? Hailey's location and mine were both packed."

Now that he mentioned that, it didn't really make much sense. I mean, sure, we weren't in the town hall but the station underneath. Still, most people would have taken the subway there; you can't get to the center in a car. And we saw absolutely no one but the jester.

"Do you know what team he was on?"

I shook my head. "No, but I could probably recognize him in the photo if he's not wearing a mask."

I scrolled through a bunch of pictures. More teams had gained points. There was also one more whose photo turned gray with bloody frowns.

"There, that's him." I handed the phone back to my friends. It was Killian and one other guy.

"Fynn, their team is the second-highest-ranking one!" Hailey exclaimed.

"Wait a sec, I think I know these guys. They went to Marden High," Lucas said as he grabbed the phone. "Yeah, I've definitely seen them. One of them worked at the coffee house in the center. You know which one I mean?"

Marden. That was the town right next to the one where Lucas and I were born. The place that had ruined both of our lives. The place that we had left behind us months ago to start over.

"We are basically on the opposite side of the country. This can't be a coincidence," Hailey quietly said.

"He knew my real name. And he said that he knew you, too," I said to Lucas.

*Dun dun du du dun*

"God, I hate this sound," Hailey said before she read out the notification we had just received from the game phone.

**Round 3: Figure out if you really know your friends! :)**

Lucas and I exchanged a look. This game knew exactly what was going on, and it was infuriating me. I was sick of being their game piece.

"I suggest we don't do anything before they send another notification. If they haven't changed the rules since round two..." Hailey said.

"Yeah, to be fair, there isn't much we can do with this info right now anyway."

---

We had no idea what to do with this information or with the fact that Killian knew who we were. Hailey suggested we text him, but Lucas and I agreed to stay put for now.

We decided to take turns staying awake so that one person would be awake when we received the next clue or assignment.

It was two a.m., and I was the only one awake.

Could I trust my friends?

I was wary of Lucas, but the more I thought about it, the weirder I felt around Hailey as well. She did know that we had to smile for the photo. She was the one who easily caught the jester, and I could still swear that I had locked the window last night, but Hailey stayed awake after Lucas and I went to bed.

My phone buzzed. At first, I thought it was the game phone, but that one only made the shrill sound.

I had just gotten a text from Smile. The number that had called me on the first day.

**Lovely Alex,**

**Do you know your friends? Come to [Redacted Location] alone and you might figure out who is fake and who is not. :)**
*Alone.*

They had sent this to me privately. It was clear what I had to do next. I made sure my friends were fast asleep before grabbing the knife and my mask and getting inside my car.

I didn't like going there on my own, but I had started to understand that this game took its punishment very literally. And I wouldn't like to find out what that looked like for this round. Besides, I didn't know what kind of messages Lucas and Hailey might be receiving from the game. I had to watch out for everything and everyone.

---

The address led me to the tallest bridge in town. The one that reached over the deep river with a steady stream. I didn't know what to expect at this place, but about twenty feet away, I saw two figures standing at the railing. As I moved closer, I received a new message.

**Fake friends need to be punished, Alex. Save your friend and push the other to their death.**

**Make the right choice and your team receives 100,000 dollars.**

I felt the knot in my stomach tighten. I had a terrible feeling that I would be looking into the eyes of Hailey and Lucas. A push from this height could cost someone their life.

I wouldn't be able to do this to either of my friends.

I thought I would try my luck to get some more information, so I texted back the number.

**What happens if I don't push either?** I texted back.

**We consider you a fake friend, too, Alex. You can spare your friend and choose to dive.**

For a moment, I thought about turning around and running. Forgetting all this ever happened and escaping somewhere they would never find me. But I knew that wouldn't be possible. They would just come for my family instead.

And so I took a deep breath and walked toward the two figures in the dark. As I got closer, I realized I had been half right.

It was Lucas, but Hailey wasn't here. The other person was Killian.

They were both standing on the other side of the railing with masks on so I could see neither of their faces. Killian's legs were shaking, but Lucas almost seemed calm.

"Lucas?" I quietly asked.

He didn't answer.

"Killian?" I said next, but he didn't answer, either. I could see his panicked eyes underneath the mask.

Of course, I didn't know this boy well, but could I really push him just to save myself and my friend? Even if I did kill him, I still wouldn't know for sure if that would win us the round.

I kept thinking and thinking while Killian was shaking even more. Soon he would slip, even without a push.

How could I know for sure that Killian was the fake friend? I had only just met him, and Lucas had been acting particularly shady and dangerous. He was the one who lied and almost killed the jester.

And suddenly something clicked in my head.

I collected all my strength and pushed Lucas over the edge.

# Part 4

**We cordially invite you to join us on this wonderful adventure! There are many rewards to be won, much fun to be had, and many souls to be mushed. In this package you will find everything you need for the adventure. You will be looking for jesters, imposters, and even a princess! Thrilling, isn't it?**

My first impression of this game was an image of completely random madness. With no clues or help, we were sent to hell. Though as the game progressed, I started understanding that this wasn't entirely true. While the game masters could be vague, especially when it came to the punishment, the assignments were often quite explicit and to be taken literally.

They had told us exactly what we would be doing in this game in the very first letter we received. We would look for jesters, imposters, and a princess.

That was what went through my head when I pushed him into the ice-cold river. I am quite aware that it was a risky and impulsive decision I took there.

In a matter of seconds, a waterfall of thoughts ran through my mind. The boy I called Lucas certainly wasn't who he said he was. Lucas wasn't his name; it was Leigh. My childhood friend who went through hell and back with me. But was that enough to consider him fake? I wasn't truthful about my identity, either, calling myself Fynn when I was still the same Alex. Even dyeing my hair and growing a beard didn't change that. In that sense, I would be just as fake as him.

But Lucas had lied. He kept secrets. He pushed a man on train tracks to die. That was what it all came down to. It seemed that he had betrayed us.

I thought I had to choose whether I would kill my friend who was appearing malicious or a stranger who appeared kind and compassionate toward an enemy. But that's the thing, right? Things are never as they appear.

And that was what clicked in my head when I looked into the eyes of the two men wearing masks.

I wasn't looking at Killian and Lucas.

I was looking at Killian and an imposter.

---

"Fuck, fuck, fuck!" Killian was still shaking all over. After I helped him get over the railing, he fell right to the ground.

At that moment, I couldn't really pay attention to him, though. I was standing at the edge, looking deep down into the river. I can't begin to describe how much dread and guilt I was feeling after what I had just done. I took such an impulsive action. What if it was wrong?

My heart skipped a beat as I felt my phone vibrate in my pocket. And I almost started crying when I saw Lucas's name on the screen.

"Where the hell are you guys?" he shouted through the phone.

"Leigh," I whispered, "are you okay?"

"What? No, I'm not. Both of you just disappeared. Where are you? And you're supposed to call me Lucas, idiot."

I wanted to laugh but only until I registered what he had just said.

"What do you mean both of us? Hailey is gone, too?"

"You mean she's not with you? Shit, I tried calling her, but she wouldn't pick up. Which one of you took the game phone?"

"Stay where you are. I'm coming home now," I answered and shoved my phone back inside my pocket.

The relief of Lucas being alive washed away with an awful new set of emotions. Where was Hailey, and if this really wasn't Lucas, who had I just pushed over the edge?

"What the actual fuck?" I heard Killian whisper. He was on his knees now, staring through the gaps of the railing. "How did he survive this?"

"This can't be possible. What is it?" he continued.

What I saw down there almost made me throw up.

From this distance, it really could be mistaken for my friend, but whatever this was, it somehow managed to survive a fall that should have been fatal and was swimming strongly in the river. We heard a shrill laugh before the creature lay on its back and got pulled down with the stream of the river with a big grin on its face.

I wish I could say that this was the worst thing I'd seen so far, but unfortunately, the fake Lucas was awfully familiar.

Except the last time I saw him he was much younger. I had to pull myself together and drive to the apartment. This night was not over yet.

---

"How did you know he wasn't real?" Killian asked inside the car.

After what had just happened and all the questions I had, I figured I would take him with me. Of course, I didn't trust this stranger, but his team had somehow made second place in the game. He certainly had to know things about it that I didn't. And he did kind of owe me after I had just saved his life.

"I remembered how you said something about Lucas's face being distorted. It reminded me of a show he and I starred in when we were younger. Well, it's a long story, but let's just say I have some experience with those copycats. But you know that, right? Because you know who we are?" I responded.

Killian stayed silent for a moment. "Your friend is Leigh, isn't he? He's the reason I started playing the game. He convinced everyone."

I knew I had to get home, but when he said that, I slammed on the brakes, locked the doors of the car, and turned to Killian. "What did you just say?"

I could tell that he tried to look calm, but his hands were shaking. "There was a video of him in which he told us about the Smile game. That's all I can tell you, okay? And now can you please get me home?"

Killian seemed so courageous when we had met in the subway, but now he reminded me of a scared child. It made me feel terrible; he had just looked death in the eye. And now I was basically kidnapping him because I projected my anger onto him. In reality, he had just been sucked into this horrible game, and it even appeared it was my friend's fault.

I took a deep breath to calm myself. "How old are you, Killian?"

"Twenty, why?"

"Did you see *Dr. Warly's Adventure Club* when you were little? You would have been around six or seven. It aired in Watton and the nearby towns. I assume it was on television in Marden, too."

"Um, yeah. That's how I knew you." He sniffed and then laughed. "I was your biggest fan. But that was years ago. In the video I saw recently, Lucas was all grown up."

I held the steering wheel tight.

"Yeah, it makes sense. They must have somehow lured him in. I know the people who are behind this sick game, and they are extremely dangerous."

"Yeah, I kinda got that when I almost just died. And I believe that they are specifically targeting you," he said.

"How so?"

"I hadn't actually received the location of the town hall yesterday. I saw Lucas and you at the subway station, and because he was heading in the direction of the mall, I thought I'd follow you. You were the only group who got that other location."

"They wanted me to see Lucas push the jester," I whispered.

"The jesters are just other players. They get the assignment to do things. My buddy Chris was actually the jester who brought you guys the package a few days ago."

I started driving again. There were so many things that were coming together but still so much that was unclear.

"I need to get home now. I think my friend might be in danger. You can go if you want, Killian, but I would really appreciate it if you came along and told us everything you know. And I mean *everything*."

He typed something on his phone and then looked at me and nodded.

"What is going on?" Lucas shouted first thing as I opened the door. I had only seen him a few hours ago, but so much had changed since then. I went from thinking that he was a murderer to being in charge of his fate to wondering if he was associated with the game masters of all this.

"I'll explain later. Has Hailey not come back?" I responded.

Lucas shook his head.

"I might know where she is," Killian chimed in from the back. "My buddy just texted me. He also had to push someone from a bridge. And he got to decide between two girls."

"What is he talking about?" Lucas shouted.

*Dun dun du du dun*

"I thought Hailey had the game phone?" I said.

"That was mine." Killian pulled out another phone from his pocket.

**Mix up! Congratulations team W., you won 10k as well as a new member.**

**Show your best behavior, kitty cat. You are among celebrities. :)**

Lucas walked over and grabbed the phone out of his hand.

"Kitty cat? What's that supposed to mean?"

"That's what they call me." Killian's face turned red.

My heart started racing.

"What does that mean? Did they just replace Hailey?" Lucas sounded as scared and panicked as I was feeling.

"Check the photos," I said.

They had been fast. Our team was now in the second position, and Hailey's face was replaced by Killian's. But Hailey hadn't left the game; she was now in the third spot next to Killian's former team member.

"Can you text your friend?" I asked.

"I tried. He's not responding anymore, but it looks like your friend survived?" he said.

"Or that's what they want us to think," Lucas mumbled.

---

*Dun dun du du dun*

**Congrats top 5! You all have been waiting for this moment, haven't you? The princess is close, but better watch out or she might steal your heart. :)**

Killian's hands started shaking when he read that message. His eyes were tearing up, and it almost felt as if he had become a whole new person.

"Finally," he whispered.

Lucas and I stared at him with questioning looks. There was so much happening at once. I had hardly gotten over the fact of choosing to kill Lucas, we had lost Hailey, and it felt like we all had our own agenda. Now we were supposed to be in the top five with a new team member.

"I don't think I want to murder some princess, even if it's another imposter. I still have a bitter taste in my mouth from pushing Lucas over the edge," I said.

"You did what?" Lucas asked.

"We won't murder her. We'll try to survive," Killian said in a dry tone.

---

We were sitting on the floor of the living room. In front of us lay the phone. There was nothing we could do but wait until we received another clue. We had tried reaching Hailey but couldn't get through to her or Killian's friend. Of course, we had thought about just going to the place Killian had seen his friend last, but we had a feeling the game masters were closely watching us and the round hadn't officially begun yet.

When Killian went to the bathroom and I finally had a moment alone with my friend, I decided I would try to get some information out of him.

"Lucas, did you tell the game masters about us? Are you the reason they found us?"

Lucas's eyes opened wide. "What the hell, no!" he said.

"You're telling me you didn't take a video of yourself forcing others to join the game?"

Lucas started laughing. "You're joking, right? Did you forget—"

He stopped talking as Killian stepped back into the room. We stayed silent after that. Even though we all had millions of questions in our heads, nobody asked anything. I don't know if the others didn't dare to ask or whether the game had just broken our spirit already.

It was dawn when the phone finally played that painful melody again.

**Round 4 will begin in 13.47 hours. Terribly sad news, your friend, I am afraid, is long gone! :( Your princess, however, will be awaiting you at the curious carnival in [Location Redacted] and isn't that all that counts? Don't forget your armor. :)**

# Part 5

Killian the kitty cat. This boy clearly had very specific intentions going into this game. He was connected to something in here, just as we were. The game had known my real identity from the start; they talked to me individually, made things personal. There had to be a reason that Killian had his own nickname. He kept saying how this game was targeting me and Lucas, but I had a feeling that he was playing an important role, too. Just the actual connection wasn't clear to me yet.

We still had many hours left before we could go looking for the carnival where we would search for the princess. Hours that should be used carefully to get more insights into the game or to get to know the intentions of our new teammate. It felt awfully difficult, however, to focus on the game when we didn't even know if Hailey was alive at this point.

"*Your friend is long gone.* They said it. That bastard teammate of his must have done something to her." Lucas was grinding his teeth. The scars on his mouth seemed to be healing, and instead of looking dangerous, he appeared sad and fatigued.

"We don't know if that's what they mean," I tried to convince both him and myself. I couldn't be thinking of this right now or I would just break down. I'd known Hailey ever since I was a teenager. We grew up next to each other, and worst of all, I was the one who sucked her into this whole mess in the first place when I shared my experience on the kids' show with her.

She became a target because of me.

I took a deep breath. It was time to let my friend in on what exactly I had experienced at the bridge. I was dreading telling him the whole truth because I was afraid he would take it wrong. I had saved Killian, after all, instead of the person that looked like my friend. His reaction was the complete opposite, however. He got up and hugged me.

"You're a freakin' genius, mate! Can't believe you figured out that it was an imposter. Though you really should've believed me when I told you I was at the mall."

"Well, you didn't make it easy. You've been so secretive."

"I've been secretive?" He laughed. "What about Hailey, then? If you weren't so keen on being quiet about everything, then maybe we could've gotten some info out of her. I mean, honestly, what will we do if she is still playing for the other team?"

I swallowed, not sure what to do with the information he just gave me. "Still?" I finally mumbled, but Lucas stayed silent.

"She was already in the game. You didn't join in the official first round. The game has been going on for a while now," Killian chimed in.

"Hailey played the game?"

Killian nodded. Lucas was still not speaking, but his expression told me everything I needed to know.

"She got us involved in this, didn't she?"

"Are you starting to understand that you can't trust your damn friends?"

---

It took us three hours to drive to the location of the carnival, which was hidden behind fields in the middle of nowhere. A shimmer of light sparked up the dark fields, and the familiar melody playing on repeat could be heard from miles away. The three of us had gotten dressed appropriately, and we were wearing our masks.

From a distance, it looked like a regular carnival. There was a Ferris wheel, carousels, halls of mirrors, food, and game booths. But instead of regular people, everyone except for us was dressed as jesters. Well, not everyone. The rest of the top five were spread around the place as well. Nobody approached us, though. Not before receiving instructions.

We kept an eye open, but so far there was no sign of Hailey.

*Dun dun du du dun*

**Shoot! All of you made it, how wonderful! The princess is awaiting you, but she is picky. Catch her first and don't get pierced! :)**

The timer ran out just as we received the message. The round had officially begun.

As if they had simply been waiting in the dark, observing us, the first group was walking closer to us. A group of young kids holding sharp weapons. Baseball bats with nails in them, knives, and daggers.

"God, they're just children. What is going on here?" I whispered.

"No fucking clue," Lucas responded, "but I'm certainly not gonna attack them."

The kids started getting closer, all humming the melody.

*Dun dun du du dun*

"Wait, I might have an idea," Lucas said. He stepped on the counter of an abandoned booth, standing high up, and then with all the volume in his voice, he started shouting.

"Welcome, welcome, welcome! It's time for another adventure!"

Then he took off his mask.

The kids were staring at him with big smiles on their faces, completely mesmerized.

"That's Leigh!" one of the kids whispered.

"Where are we going, Leigh? What will we do next?" another one said.

"We did everything you said! What's our next adventure?"

They were jumping up and down in glee. One after the other, they let all their weapons fall to the ground.

We were still trying to make sense of the situation when out of nowhere a jester who was sitting on the carousel next to us fell right off his horse. A puddle of blood was forming around them. This person had been hit by an arrow. Right in their heart.

Killian ran over and tried to help. I followed. The other players were still in a trance, staring at Lucas.

We removed the mask and saw the face of a man about my age. Blood was spilling out uncontrollably. We tried to stop it, to block the wound, but it was already too late.

"All right, kids, for the next adventure, everyone will go look for a hiding place," Lucas said in a shaky voice. As the other players dispersed, he put his mask back on, climbed down, and sat down with us next to the dead jester's body.

"Where did that arrow come from?" I asked, my blood-stained hands shaking. I looked around and didn't see anyone.

"Jen," Killian whispered.

"Who's Jen?" we shouted in unison.

Killian looked me right in the eyes and then said in the most distressed voice, "She's my little sister." Then he turned to Lucas and added, "She's the princess because you bastards made her."

Before we could react, another arrow was shot on top of the already dead man. We quickly took a step back. Killian and I ran to the closest booth to us, while Lucas hid behind the carousel's ticket shop.

"Why didn't you tell us?" I shouted after Killian and I had crouched down behind the booth.

"Because *he* was the one who told her to do it. She watched his videos every day. She already had a tendency to be brutal, but watching him brought out the worst in her. Damn, she's so young. She doesn't even know what she's doing." He was almost crying. "And then a few months ago, she just disappeared. I knew it had something to do with the game, so I joined to find her. It took me a while to figure out that she wasn't a player but a game piece. She's a fucking level."

"Okay, okay, Killian, slow down. Jen was brainwashed into becoming the princess of the game?"

He nodded. "There's something about her. Something that isn't quite right. She is very susceptible to messages of pain and torture. And Leigh somehow activated it again. It's like she feels no remorse... but I swear it's not her fault! If I could only get to her, I could—"

"Over there, the arrows are coming from the Ferris wheel," Lucas was shouting from the other side. "I think she only shoots when she's at the very top. We need to hurry."

Killian didn't even think before jumping up and running toward the wheel.

---

The space in front of the Ferris wheel was full of jesters, dancing around and laughing. More kept coming from different directions, all wearing the masks, but none of them did anything; they wouldn't even acknowledge us.

Killian was already in front of the Ferris wheel. He jumped inside one of the open wagons on the bottom. And then the wheel continued turning. Soon the princess would be on top again, shooting her arrows.

Lucas and I were just behind, fighting our way through all the jesters that kept appearing.

Before we could get to the Ferris wheel, however, the princess was back at the top, and sharp arrows were flying through the air. This time she was hitting random jesters around us. Not a single arrow was directed at us.

"Killian, you need to get to her, quick!" I shouted. These jesters were all innocent players, brainwashed into playing this game so far that they weren't even trying to hide from the shots. Bodies were falling all around us.

The situation was so surreal that for a moment I almost put my guard down. I was so distracted that I didn't notice that the jester standing next to me was not quite like the others. Not until I felt the cold knife against my throat.

"Hailey?" I asked.

The jester laughed and shook their head. Then they pointed toward another jester standing at the bottom of the Ferris wheel. This one was holding a gun and pointed it toward the Ferris wheel. At first, I thought they wanted to shoot the princess, but that wasn't their target.

While the princess was shooting arrows, Killian had climbed almost all the way up.

**BANG BANG BANG**

He was so close to getting to his sister, but just like that, he collapsed inside the wagon.

Blood dripped from the wagon as the Ferris wheel continued moving again and finally finished the turn.

As it stopped, the princess walked out with a big smile on her face. One of the jesters took her hand, and together they disappeared into the darkness.

I tried to look for Lucas to see what he was doing and why he wasn't helping, but I couldn't spot him anywhere. He was just gone.

And slowly everyone else was leaving as well until the carnival was empty except for the one other jester and me. The jester then took a step back, put the knife away, and removed their mask.

"Don't worry, Alex. I'm on your team."

# Part 6

I can't begin to describe what a rollercoaster of emotions I went through in these last couple of days. Days that felt like an eternity. Together with my friends, I got sucked into the loop of a game named Smile. The game of madness, randomness, and pain. I had lost Hailey. I had lost Killian. And Killian had lost his poor sister. Nothing went the way I had planned at all. As much as I tried to control the direction of the game, it was always a step ahead of me. I had officially lost control.

And now on top of it all, Lucas was gone as well. We had trusted each other with our lives on numerous occasions, and I never regretted it. I didn't regret it when I left the life I knew because it was clear to me that I had gained a new family. Lucas and I were like brothers. Brothers who went through the hell that was the TV show of Satan. A show we starred in as kids that made children who watched it do unspeakable things. Without our knowledge, our faces were involved in murder, kidnapping, and suicides. And while we didn't know what we had gotten ourselves into when we were that young and just wanted to act, we had been plagued by guilt ever since the memories of that time came back to us. And so we had sworn to do everything in our power to destroy anything that revolved around that show. But now I wasn't so sure anymore that Lucas was really on the same side as me. And Hailey, it seemed, had turned into a cold-blooded killer.

Suddenly, my family was gone, and I was standing there in an empty carnival, which had turned eerily silent. It was just me and this woman.

I didn't recognize her face at first. She had gotten older, just as I had. To be honest, I never expected to see her again.

"Janie," I whispered, but then my eyes shifted back to the Ferris wheel, and I couldn't focus on her anymore. I started running while typing on my phone.

"Alex, who the hell are you calling?" Janie shouted and jumped me from the back.

"A fucking ambulance. If it's not too late already." I pushed Janie away. "You did this. You killed an innocent boy for some shitty game. Why did you even come back? Did you side with them? Was this all planned out from the start?"

"Aw, Alex, I knew you liked me!" I heard someone laugh from the back.

As I turned around, I saw Killian's body drenched in blood, but he got up from the wagon as if nothing had even happened. And then I started realizing that he didn't have any wounds. I moved closer and touched his chest.

"This is paint."

I couldn't control myself. My mouth turned into a big smile followed by hysterical laughter. This situation was so insane, but the relief I felt was incredible.

The relief quickly turned to anger, however. I grabbed Killian by his shirt and started shaking him.

"You were never on our team, were you? You played with us."

"I'm sorry, Alex. We had to. This was the only way to free my sister."

Janie started typing something on her phone and walked over to us. "It's because of Lucas, Alex. Haven't you understood that yet? He is involved with Warly. He helped him to recruit the players. His video went all around. We believe that every kid who joined this game did so because they saw the video. That's how I even found out about it. He spoke to them on a level that not everyone can understand. But the ones that can lose all their free will. They didn't care if they would have died. They all followed Lucas."

"No," I whispered, "I was with him. All throughout the game. None of this is making sense. He cut up his own mouth, for fuck's sake."

"Ask your own friend. She got started because of him." Janie pointed to someone behind the Ferris wheel who was walking up to us. She was wearing a mask, but I knew this was going to be Hailey.

Instead of saying anything, she just walked to me and spread her arms around me. "I'm so sorry, Alex."

Killian and Hailey exchanged a look, and she said, "It's taken care of. They left and are already on their way back to Marden."

For a second he smiled, but then his expression turned dark again. "Why are they not saying anything? The round is over."

"Can anyone please just tell me what's going on?" I almost shouted.

Hailey sighed and sat down on the platform of the Ferris wheel. Then she told me the story.

"Weeks ago, this game found its way to some people I knew in college. They just called it Smile, and it didn't take long before they were entirely obsessed with it. They wouldn't tell me about any specifics, but from what I could tell, it sounded insanely morbid. One day I saw my roommate cutting up the edges of her mouth, and when I asked her what was going on and tried to call a doctor, she jumped me. She went insane and kept repeating that she has to play the game because Leigh the adventurer told her so. That combination of words already gave me goose bumps, but I thought it had to be a coincidence. I was in contact with Leigh all the time, and he never mentioned a game. When she finally showed me the video and I heard the oh-so-familiar tune, I knew that we were back in the Warly mess. But this time it seemed like Leigh was on their side. After we changed our names, cut so many ties, and everything, it was all back."

"Why didn't you tell me?"

"Because of the game. You know damn well that none of us could speak about it or they would harm anyone we care about. But the first time I played, I was assigned to a team."

"My team," Janie chimed in. "And just so you know, I never wanted to get back to any of this. I would have been happy never seeing anyone of *Warly's Adventure Club* again, but my little cousin played the game. I couldn't let anything happen to her, not after all the children that died back then. Well, and I couldn't let Killian do this all on his own."

"Wait, so Jen and Killian are your cousins?"

Killian grinned. "Yeah, also Killian isn't my real name, either. I stole that from a movie."

"And Hailey, well Helen, was helping you guys? All this time and you didn't care to tell me?"

All three of them turned serious.

"Look, Alex. It's not like we were completely in control. The rules of the game were being decided as things were already going. We had no idea what would happen. And frankly, after everything with Lucas, we couldn't know if you weren't involved as well."

Killian and Janie had a mission from the start, to save little Jen from the game of Smile. To wake her up and get her back home. They had to be careful because it was clear that the game masters would do anything in their power to scramble any plan they made. When Killian and Hailey had to switch teams, it could all have gone south. Everyone wanted to win the game, to get the princess. But if any other player found her, they would have brought her back to the game masters to collect their reward, so they came up with a plan with as many twists and turns that neither the game masters nor the other players would know what was going on. They created a distraction.

To Lucas and me, it looked like we were going to win. Killian would have gotten to Jen, meaning that our team would win the round and the entire game. But they couldn't have let that happen, not knowing that Lucas might be on the wrong side.

Killian had been playing for two teams this entire time. He knew everything but shared only breadcrumbs with me. With us. But now things were finally starting to make sense.

When Killian was as near as possible to the princess, almost sure of our win, the jesters came to play. The jesters were all extras. Here to confuse us and scare us. Game pieces that the masters found replaceable. Jen was shooting them down without a care in the world because that was what she'd been programmed to do.

Nobody would have expected a jester to start shooting a gun. To the masters and us, it seemed like a different team was going to win. In reality, however, Hailey had shot Killian with a paintball gun. While everyone was distracted, Killian's friend, who was disguised as a jester, brought Jen to a car and drove her off.

Now what wasn't clear to me yet was why they didn't go after Jen but instead came for Lucas. Or had Lucas escaped knowing the game was over for him?

"So what is happening now? We can't be so foolish to assume that they are not currently listening to everything we're saying," I said after they had told me about everything.

"It doesn't matter. Our team already won," Hailey responded. "When you started playing the game, they offered you something, didn't they, Alex? They let you choose your reward."

"They offered that all the children who were still under their spell, or brainwashed, would be freed from the game."

---

*Dun dun du du dun*

There it was. The abhorrent tune. Except this time we had been impatiently waiting for it. We were sure the game masters were listening to every word we were saying. It didn't really matter anymore at this point. But I knew that things weren't quite over for me yet. Especially with Lucas being away all of a sudden. Killian and Janie had given up on him and would have rather seen him dead, but I wasn't at that point yet. I knew there had to be more to the fact why my friend betrayed us. What I came to find out was just so much worse than what I could have imagined, however.

I lost the game. Big time.

**Congratulations on the win, team S! You must have the biggest smile on your face right now. You took your well-deserved reward. Though we can't promise that our princess will not rip out more hearts in the future. She's a first-class royal with a wonderful thirst for blood!**

The familiar voice was blasting from the speakers all throughout the carnival.

**Now, sweet Alex, our main adventurer... It is time to pay your debt as you lost, sweet child! Don't worry, though, the boys of** *Warly's Adventure Club* **are already awaiting you! We can't wait for you to join! Please follow our kind jesters. The rest of you may leave now. It has been a blast to play, and I'm sure we'll see each other again soon.**

It was finished off by the sound of a smile.

"There they are," Helen said and pointed to two jesters smiling at us. "Please be careful. You don't know what might expect you."

I took a deep breath and followed the jesters through the carnival. Everything around us was silent again. The lifeless bodies of players in jester costumes lay in puddles of their own blood. Poor souls who were sucked into this because they had listened to Leigh's video.

It should never have come this far. I should have known this would happen if we played with monsters.

The jesters stopped in front of a hall of mirrors. They opened the entrance and waved me inside.

---

Everywhere I saw myself. Distorted, small, tall. It didn't matter which mirror I looked into; I felt revolted by my own appearance.

And then a second face appeared from the darkness. And he looked worse than I'd ever seen him before.

Lucas.

"Alex," he cried out, "I fucked up. I really fucked up."

Before I could walk over to him, the mirrors changed. They had screens built in and were playing something. The same video of Leigh was reflected in each mirror. He was dressed in the green clothes that he always wore on the children's show. But this wasn't him as a child. It looked as if it had been taken a few weeks ago.

The melody played, and Leigh looked straight into the camera.

*Hello, hello, hello, adventurers! I want you to listen closely now.*

He smiled.

*I want to play a game with you. A game you will never want to finish. A game that will make each and every one of you smile from the bottom of your heart. Isn't that exciting?*

His face turned into a frown.

*I know you hate your life. I know deep down you would like to see the world paved in the color red, just as I! So why don't you join me and we can have lots and lots of*

The video broke off there and the mirror went back to normal.

"You fucking bastard," I said under my breath.

"We wanted to put an end to this. We wanted to save them!" I shouted.

"Alex, it's not like you think it is." We walked through the maze until we finally found each other. I didn't know if I wanted to punch him or apologize.

"It's true. I made the video for the producer. Well, no, that's not right. I made *a* video. He changed things, just like they did back then... The man behind *Warly's Adventure Club* reached out to me. I have no idea how he even found me, but he was extremely persistent, threatening everyone I know if I didn't listen to him or told anyone else about this." He sighed and looked to the ground.

"Then he made me a proposition. You know how all those children disappeared when we first aired our show? The children we wanted to save but couldn't find? He told me if he could take one video of me, then they would all be free to go."

"And you believed him?"

"He was very persuasive. That producer isn't a normal person, Alex. You should know that! He calls himself Mr. V and is this fucking eccentric cult leader or whatever, but—Look, Alex. He did let them all go. All those kids and teenagers playing the game, they were former hostages."

"Did you see the corpses outside? You didn't save them."

"But I tried!" He was shouting now. "And don't act so fucking innocent, Alex. You helped him, too. Why else did you make me cut open my own face?"

I swallowed and took a step back.

"What did he promise you, Alex?"

All throughout this mess, nobody had asked me what my intentions were to play the game. And I had no idea how to tell him.

"No need to be ashamed, Alex! You can tell him!"

A man with dark hair and shiny eyes had entered the room without me even realizing it. I had never seen him before, but I recognized his voice. He called me after we had already started playing the game, when it still seemed normal and all we did was take a photo of us. He called when I was alone. And he made a proposition if I played the game and won. And next to him stood Warly, with an expression of deep fear.

"He wanted to save good ol' Warly! Isn't that adorable?"

If you remember Warly, he was the adult in the show we acted in. He had once betrayed us and threatened many lives. We had abandoned him and sent him to prison, hoping to be rid of him. We couldn't risk having him around, but Warly was a victim. Just like us, he was sucked into the show without knowing what it did. He had tricked us, but I knew that he wasn't really a bad person.

We swore to forget about him, but when I heard his voice introducing us to the game, I knew they had somehow found him. The game master promised me I could save him if I played the game and did as asked.

The man took out a phone and started playing a message.

**I know this is insane, but look, you have to do it. Trust me. You have to or everyone else will suffer. We need to play the game. We need to Smile. You trust me, right?**

I had no idea that this was what they sent Leigh before he cut his mouth. He told me to take the message, and I did without knowing what exactly they would use it for.

"I wanted to step out at that point. When they told me to harm myself but I thought if you told me that I had to go through with it, there would be a good reason for it. I had no idea that reason was saving fucking Warly."

"I'm sorry," I whispered.

Leigh stayed quiet for a moment. Then he added, "Me too."

My friend and I had wanted to help, to make things better, but instead, we only brought about more suffering.

"I do have to admit, both of you are terrific actors. Not one of you ever spilled the guts... And don't worry, boys. I'm not a complete monster!" the man said as if he had just read my mind.

"I'm a man of honor, and I intend to keep my promise. Everyone who had been under our spell will be free after this game. However, Leigh, I'm afraid you did lose, so I will have to keep that video of you... for future purposes. I'm sure you understand."

"As to you, Alex. I bet your friends will forgive you eventually. Warly here, however, never will. I mean, losers don't deserve a reward."

Without batting an eye, he slit a razor-sharp knife right through Warly's throat. I had no other chance but to look at dozens of mirrors showing how the man I tried to save lost the life in his eyes as he collapsed to the ground.

As much as I prayed, this time it wasn't fake blood.

---

It took us a while to comprehend what had happened. I thought my friends and I would separate for good, but we didn't, and we never would. Not as long as we had this common enemy.

Mr. V did keep his promise, and the children were freed. Young adults were brought back to families who never thought they would see their children again.

It was a bittersweet end, though I have to admit that the bitter taste overrode.

It wasn't easy, but I think after much explaining we all understood that Leigh's intentions were coming from a good place, but he had been naïve and gullible. Just like me. It would still take a long time until we all trusted each other again. Especially as we gained two more members to our group: an old friend I never thought I would see again and someone I had grown really close to in those few days.

The horrific rollercoaster that was the Smile game was over. While the game ignited mistrust in all of us, we also understood that we were all sucked so deep into all of this, not being able to distinguish right from wrong anymore.

We had been victims and accomplices at once, but there was one thing we all agreed upon: Warly might be dead, but the adventure club will never be able to escape from this. Not as long as they know our faces.

So if you ever stumble upon a video inviting you on an adventure, don't listen to us.

# THE SOCIAL EXPERIMENT

## Part 1

Let me start by saying that I joined the experiment a while ago. I have tried before to talk to people about it, but nobody believes me, and I can't exactly blame them. I haven't been able to properly sleep, eat, or live since I made it back home, plagued by feelings of tremendous guilt. I hope sharing this will help my conscience.

**Day 1.**

The apartment looked pretty decent. It was small but had everything I needed: one room with a bed, although a pillow and blanket were missing. In the middle of the room was a table with two chairs. I wasn't sure why I would need two, as the main part of this experiment was me being alone in the room, isolated from the outside world. In the back was a small food elevator, like the ones you see in old movies. That was how I'd receive my meals. There were big abstract paintings. I had a chalkboard to write on, and of course, there was a laptop so I could communicate with... with whom exactly?

I opened the laptop. Everything was wiped. No internet access, no apps, no programs.

Only one little icon in the middle of the screen: **SOCIAL**.

I double-clicked it, thinking it might provide some more information.

**SOCIAL will start soon.**

**Make sure the laptop is charged at all times.**
All right, I guessed I had to wait.

I walked over to the chalkboard. Somebody must have been in this room before because "DAYS" was written on top with white chalk, with ten strokes underneath. I drew a circle around seven of the strokes instead of wiping them away. Next to it, I drew one stroke. For my first day.

They took away my phone. I had no calendar or even a clock, so I figured it could get difficult to keep track of the days. I realized I didn't remember if they had told me how long I would be staying.

My window view didn't offer much. All I could see were empty fields, and I could tell that I was pretty high up. I tried opening the window to let in some fresh air, but it was blocked. Probably so nobody would jump out after going crazy from the solitude. I was the kind of person who loved being alone, though. Add a pretty apartment, food being provided for me, and decent payment, and I was living my dream. I would have been dumb not to participate.

*DING DING*

The laptop was lighting up with neon green lights. I guess things were getting started! The Social app was running, and the screen had turned into something that looked like a chat.

**Social:** Welcome, John! We are very excited that you are participating in this real-life experiment. I am Social. Everything you need or that *we* need from you will be communicated through me. You will not directly talk to anyone else during your time here. Make sure that your laptop is charged at all times. Do you have any questions so far?

**Me:** Hello, Social. I am also excited! I haven't received any sheets, pillows, or blankets for my bed yet. Could those be sent over, please?

**Social:** That will be up to the other participants, as you will learn soon. Are you ready for the first round?

**Me:** Yes.

**Social:** As you know, you will be receiving all your food and drinks from us. What exactly that will be, however, will be chosen by another participant. For the first round, you can choose a meal combination for participant JULIA.

I was actually pretty excited about this. I was awful at making the right decisions—probably one of the reasons I changed my major three times. It might be interesting to put my fate into someone else's hands.

I scrolled down the list of food and drink items, wondering what Julia might enjoy. There were a number of breakfast items like pancakes, eggs, and bacon, but also a lot of random, disgusting-sounding stuff. Raw liver, bull testicles, sausage water. Pretty nasty. You'd really have to hate the other participants to send any of that. Unless you were into power moves.

Eventually, I picked toast with jam, scrambled eggs, and cheese with a cup of coffee and a glass of orange juice. Happy with my choice, I sent it in.

A minute later, the laptop started ringing again.

**Social: JULIA has chosen your breakfast. Walk to the food elevator now to pick it up.**

I wasn't too hungry just yet, but I was hoping for something nice to drink. I opened the small door of the elevator and got the tray out.

A piece of bread with something green on it. I picked it up, only to realize that the stuff on top was mold. I gagged and let it fall back onto the plate. I guess Julia was one of those people who liked power plays. I grabbed the glass next to it. At least she had sent me some water. My throat felt extremely dry, so I started chugging right away.

I really should have smelled it first.

What I was drinking wasn't water; it was vinegar. As the acidic taste filled my mouth, I couldn't keep it in anymore.

I ran to the bathroom and started puking into the toilet. The bitter taste of bile made me feel even worse, but I had no toothbrush or toothpaste, either. I wanted to rinse out my mouth, but there was no water. I couldn't even flush the fucking toilet.

This experiment was starting off pretty badly. I was just about to ask Social about this when I heard another ringing noise.

**Social: You just lost 50 social points.**

**Me: What the hell? What are social points?**

**Social: During your participation, you collect points. More points equal more power and more access. During this experiment, you have to make many decisions, one of them being who you want to be. Do you want to be nice or gain power?**

Me: I'm not sure I understand, but I'm really not feeling great. Is there any way I can get some water?

Social: That's not up to me, John.

Social: You have another decision to make! This time you will be sending an item to MANUEL.

Please select one item from this list:

Toothpaste

A shock collar

A knife

This list seemed even more random, but this time I really had to think it through. If I sent toothpaste, I would probably get more negative points, although at that point I wasn't sure what exactly that meant. The knife sounded like a terrible idea. I figured if I picked the shock collar, he could just decide not to wear it.

Social: Congratulations, you just received 30 social points! Walk over to the elevator now to see what MANUEL sent you.

It was a blanket. I felt like a real dick, but I kept telling myself that this was part of the experiment. Maybe those people didn't even exist.

My laptop let out another sound. There was a new icon on the screen: a green circle with a smiley face on it. I pressed it, but nothing happened.

Social: MANUEL has received and attached the shock collar around his neck. Press the green circle to send shocks.

Shit, had I just shocked him without even knowing? No, that couldn't be true. They can't purposely hurt participants.

I grabbed my blanket and took a nap. The experiment had only just begun, and I was already exhausted. The bitter taste of vinegar and puke in my mouth wasn't helping, either.

When I woke up again, it was already getting dark outside. Had I missed lunch? I walked over to the laptop, but there were no missed messages.

I was really getting fed up with this experiment when my laptop made another sound.

Social: Dinner time! Pick one meal for JACKIE.

I scrolled through the list again, but I had no idea what to do. Should I go with something decent and risk losing points? I went with a safe choice and sent a cup of vegetable broth, something I was really craving myself after throwing up. It wasn't a real meal, but it wouldn't make her sick, either.

After my choice was sent over, I went to the elevator to see what Jackie had sent me. It was a BLT and a bottle of Coke.

"THANK YOU, JACKIE!" I shouted out loud. I felt a little bad for only sending her broth, but at the same time, I was so happy to have something decent to eat and drink that would also kill off the terrible taste in my mouth.

**Day 2.**

The sound of a loud alarm blasting through the apartment pulled me out of sleep. I had no idea where it came from, but it wasn't from the laptop. The sound was followed by a robotic voice:

**SCORE TOO LOW.**
**WAKE UP IMMEDIATELY.**

It was still dark outside. It felt like it was the middle of the night. I got up from my bed, which felt like pure concrete. My head was aching from not having a pillow, but I was grateful that I had at least received a blanket. It was freezing cold. I realized that I didn't even have any spare clothes. Hadn't I brought any?

As I walked over to the laptop, the loud alarm finally stopped.

**Social: Good morning, John. Your social score has become dangerously low. Increase your score now by pressing the shock button.**

**Me: No.**

**Social: As a negative player, you will lose all perks, including nutrition. Remember, more social points equals more power.**

**Me: I don't care. I don't want more power.**

The music started blasting again. I felt like my eardrums would explode, and shielding them with my hands wasn't helping. As if this wasn't bad enough, a foul smell filled the room. I thought I would throw up again.

"Fuck this, it's not real," I said out loud and pressed the shock icon. I took a deep breath and pressed it two more times. Finally, the siren stopped.

**Social: Congratulations, John! You are now the highest-ranking participant.**

**Me: Yeah, because you fucking forced me to.**

**Social: It is now time to pick a meal for JACKIE.**

I felt bad for only sending her broth last night, so I chose pancakes and orange juice. After a few minutes, I went to pick up my meal from the elevator.

This time I almost threw up just by looking at it. On the plate, I found the head of a chicken. Raw and bloody. Next to it was a glass with what I could only imagine was blood as well.

I guessed I deserved that.

I was really fed up with this whole operation. I was hungry, tired, and sad. No money was worth this torture.

**Me: I want to get out of this experiment now. I am done.**

**Social: You can't leave. You will stay until the experiment is finished.**

**Me: What the fuck? You can't force me to stay. I never consented to any of this?**

**Social: Yes, you did. And you will stay until the experiment is finished.**

I started thinking about that. Did they give me a contract? As much as I tried to remember, I couldn't. I couldn't even remember what day it was today.

**Social: Do you remember how you came here, John?**

I didn't.

**Social: Do you remember what you did *before* you came here?**

I was so certain that I had joined an experiment, that they had offered me payment, but as much as I tried, I couldn't recall how or when that happened. I remembered things like who my family and friends were. I remembered what my home looked like but not what I had been doing lately. I had started studying psychology after giving up on coding. But when was that? My mind was blank.

**Me: WHAT THE FUCK DID YOU DO TO ME?**

**Social: We do not make any decisions for you. Play the game right and you will leave the experiment happy and healthy.**

**Me: Who are you? What is this?**

**Social: I am Social.**

**Social: Time for another decision! You can send something to a participant of your choice. Pick one of the following items:**
A gun
A bottle of water
A death threat

I decided to send a bottle of water to Manuel. It might cost me some points, but if I had really shocked him, he deserved this. After what must have been an hour, the laptop started ringing again.

**Social: You just received a video! Press play now.**

It was a video of a shirtless man, maybe in his mid-thirties. He stared right into the camera, and I could see the shock collar around his neck. Without a word, he picked up a knife and cut into his palm. With his other hand, he dipped his index finger into the blood and started writing something on his chest.

*Mary*

*No way*, I thought. *This must be a coincidence.*

I thought he was trying to write something else underneath. It would have been really hard to recognize what it was with the smudged blood, but I knew exactly what it said.

It was an address. One that I recognized very well. It was the address of Mary.

My mother.

# Part 2

**Day 3.**

I hardly slept through the night. I wasn't too afraid of what Manuel might do just yet, considering he was locked in here as well. What scared me, however, was that whoever these people were, they knew where my mother lived. And I had no way to warn her.

I needed to talk to Social, to figure out if they were a real person. Maybe I could somehow level with them.

I couldn't contact Social unless they initiated the conversation. I didn't know how long it would be until it messaged me about breakfast, so I impulsively walked over to the laptop and removed the charger.

**LAPTOP NEEDS TO BE CHARGED AT ALL TIMES**

The robotic voice filled the room again. I ignored it. I ignored the sirens and the smell and stared at the laptop. In hindsight, I was a pretty big idiot. Instead of thinking of a clever way to find a solution, I tried to force any reaction out of it.

The smell got stronger, and I started feeling weaker. I could hardly think anymore or move. Everything turned dark.

---

I woke up on the bed. My head was hurting like crazy. It took me a little while to get back to my senses, but then I noticed that the laptop was attached to the charger again.

Somebody had been in here.

Suddenly, an excruciating pain went through my entire body. I felt like somebody was choking me. Panting and shaking, I slowly reached over to my neck, where my fingers touched the metal.

Not only had someone been in here, they had given me a shock collar.

I slowly moved over to the laptop. Social had been messaging me.

**Social: I have received information that your laptop isn't attached to the charger.**

**Social: Somebody is on their way to fix the issue.**

**Social: Breakfast time! Please choose one of the items from the list for participant JOSH.**

Josh? Was there a new person?

**Social: JOSH has selected your items. Go to the elevator now to pick up your meal.**

**Social: Please choose one of the following items to send to participant JULIA.**

**A book**

**A gun**

**Five minutes of fresh air**

**Social: The item that JULIA selected for you will arrive soon and be attached by one of our workers.**

That bitch.

I didn't even get the chance to send anything because I had been passed out.

Another shock went through my body, even more painful this time. I picked myself up from the ground and got back to my laptop. I hadn't noticed before, but the shock icon was gone.

At least the chat was still open. This was my chance to contact Social.

**Me: Social, are you there?**

**Social: Hello, John! You have been very quiet today. Remember, less activity equals fewer social points!**

**Me: Were you inside my room?**

**Social: I never visit the participants.**

I thought about what to say. I had to be more careful.

**Me: Social, are you a real person?**

**Social: I am Social.**

I started to think that I was talking to a bot. If that was true, I could get some answers out of it as long as I asked the right questions.

**Me: What is my current social score?**

**Social: Your social score is +10. You are now the second-lowest-ranking participant.**

**Me: Who is on top?**

**Social: I am not allowed to share this information with you.**

I figured it must be either Julia or Manuel. Josh or Jackie would be the lowest-ranking.

**Me: Why is it beneficial to have many points?**

**Social: Higher points equal more power.**

**Me: Define power.**

**Social: In this experiment, we want to see how much it will take someone to get to the top. Being on top means more options for decisions. Decisions such as getting food, comfort, and freedom.**

**Me: Freedom, as in being able to leave?**

**Social: Dinner time! You may now choose a meal for participant JULIA.**

I was just about to pick bull testicles when another shock went through my body. My hands were shaking, and I could hardly breathe anymore. She was sending me a message. I had to be careful; she had total control over me at the moment. I picked steak, potatoes, beans, and a bottle of wine—the best options I could find. It felt awful sending someone who was torturing me these things, especially while I felt like I was starving, but I didn't want to risk getting another shock. I was still hurting from the last one.

After a moment, I went to pick up my dinner for the night. A chicken sandwich, coffee, and a bottle of water. The coffee was cold, but I didn't care. I hadn't eaten anything decent since that BLT, and I was even happier about that water. I took a few sips and decided to ration the rest. I honestly couldn't believe that Julia had sent me something decent. Had it not been for the shock collar around my neck, I would have thought that she was actually becoming nice. At least she didn't shock me for the rest of the evening.

I spent the rest of my day making up a game plan. I was done playing it safe. If I wanted any chance of getting out of here, I had to make it to the top. I still wasn't sure if Social was trustworthy. Okay, who am I kidding? It definitely wasn't trustworthy, but it felt too calculated in a sense. I don't think it wanted to torture me. It wanted to see how I would get through this.

The meal gave me some new energy. I went to the chalkboard and started writing down the info I had so far, along with things about myself—things I didn't want to forget, that would remind me that I had a life outside of this. I made sure to keep it vague, just in case they came back here.

**25** (my age)
**Kiwi** (the name of my cat)
**Psych** (my major)
**K & F** (the first letters of my two best friends)
**Julia: bitch**
**Manuel: has leverage & knife**
**Jackie: neutral so far**
**Josh: ?**

My thoughts were interrupted by the ringing of the laptop.

**Social: Time for another decision! Pick something from this list to be sent to a participant of your choice:**
**A towel**
**A death threat**
**A bracelet that keeps the participant from sleeping**

I wasn't sure what that last thing was supposed to be, but I guessed it was another form of torture. I picked the death threat.

If I got the same chance to take a video, then maybe this could be my way to communicate with Manuel. Either way, if he saw that I was wearing the shock collar now, he might go easier on me.

**Me: I want to send a death threat to Manuel.**

**Social: Great choice! Would you like to receive leverage information?**

**Me: Yes.**

**Social: The most important person in the life of MANUEL is: Sabrina, currently working as a nurse at Central Hospital. Always takes a bicycle to work.**

Oh fucking hell, Social.

A video recording app opened. The microphone was blocked. That was shit. I was planning on speaking. I had to get creative, fast. Social would probably check the video and make sure it was an actual threat. I grabbed the glass of blood that Jackie had sent me the day before. It smelled horrible, but I had kept it just in case. I started filling my mouth with the blood. I really had to fight not to vomit. I pressed play and got up in the middle of the room. Looking straight into the camera, I started spitting out the blood, trying to be as theatrical as possible—choking myself, coughing, with a freakish look on my face.

**Social: Recording complete. Video will now be sent to participant MANUEL.**

I could only hope that he understood what I had done.

**Social: You just received an item from participant Jackie. Walk up to the elevator now to pick it up.**

A pack of cigarettes.

**Day 4.**

The day started off with another lovely shock from Julia. I started cursing this person and her evil fucking mind. She was in here to win, showing no remorse. She had to be on top at this point. What reason could she have to shock me even more? I tried to get up from bed; I was feeling extremely weak at this point. My legs were shaking, I smelled horrible, and I was starving after only having one meal yesterday. Walking around the dry blood on the ground, I made my way to the table. I picked up the pack of cigarettes that I got yesterday. I don't usually smoke but thought it might distract me a little.

I opened the pack and noticed that it also contained a lighter. Obviously, you'd need one, but I didn't think about it until then. A lighter could get really fucking useful. I left the cigarettes where they were and put the lighter in my pocket.

Social opened the chat to inform me that I could choose breakfast for Manuel. I was already dreading what he would send me. At least this was my chance to talk to Social some more.

**Me: Social, is there a way to remove the shock collar?**

**Social: Only if another participant decides to send it to someone else.**

All right, that was some new info.

**Me: Is there only one of each item? Like the knife and the cigarettes?**

**Social: Correct.**

**Social: Choose a food combination for MANUEL now.**

**Me: Oatmeal and tea.**

**Me: Social, how long have the other participants been here?**

**Social: Manuel has chosen your breakfast. Walk to the food elevator now to pick it up.**

For fuck's sake. I had to be more precise with my questions. It only gave me a really short time frame.

I walked over to the elevator, expecting something smelly or rotten. I almost cried when I saw what was sitting on that tray.

Three kiwis.

While I was going crazy in the middle of the room last night, I had made sure my chalkboard would be in the picture—just enough for someone to notice if they really paid attention. And he did.

Why did he pick three, though? Did this mean he had been here for three days, just like me?

---

I spent most of the day thinking of other ways to send messages. Of course, all of this could still be part of the experiment. That thought was always in the back of my mind, but somehow I felt sure that Manuel and the other participants were just that: participants. Somehow tricked into this nightmare, like me.

Another alarm went off. My room turned red, and the sirens started blasting.

**SUICIDE ATTEMPT.**
**SUICIDE ATTEMPT.**
**SUICIDE ATTEMPT.**

What the hell? I definitely wasn't trying anything like that. I walked to the laptop, but there was no information, and just like that, the alarm stopped again.

**Social: You are now free to send another item to a player of your choice!**
**Bandage**
**Shock collar**
**Death threat**

This is where I made another foolish mistake, guided by pettiness, not logic. I should have tried to send another message or at least send someone the bandage. Maybe there really was a suicide attempt, but even if that was true, I wouldn't know who it was. In the end, hate and pain won out, and I sent Julia the shock collar.

As I logged in my choice, the collar around my neck snapped open. It must be automated.

**Social: Move the shock collar into the elevator now.**

At least a better option than being drugged again.

I didn't think everyone got the same options, because I was sent a book from Jackie. I was so happy that I would finally have some form of entertainment, but that was before I realized that the entire text was nonsense. I spent a long time going through every single page to see if, maybe, there was some secret message in there, but I couldn't find anything.

Eventually, I gave up.

---

**Social: Congratulations, John! You have received 200 social points. Tonight you may pick your own dinner.**

Under normal circumstances, I would have been ecstatic about this. Finally, I could get decent food. Some vitamins, some protein, and more water.

Under normal circumstances, I would have been proud. But how could I be proud if I got all these points by letting out my anger and frustration like this? A shiver went down my spine when I thought about how painful four shocks in a row must have felt for Julia.

That night I couldn't fall asleep, as much as I tried. I kept thinking about everything that had happened. I jumped up from bed as a thought struck me. "Please, please let this be true," I mumbled to myself.

Jackie had sent me two items today. That couldn't be a coincidence.

I opened the first page of the book and held the lighter underneath it. God, I remembered doing this when I was younger. She must have somehow gotten lemon juice.

"Help me I can't take it anymore."

I opened another page. This was extremely weird. The message said, "I'm John. Are you real?"

# Part 3

I know that many of the choices that either I or the others made during this experiment seem questionable, malicious, and occasionally pathetic. This is no excuse. I'm just asking you to keep in mind that we had spent days in solitude, hardly sleeping or eating, physically and mentally at the limit. At a certain point, all you care about is survival, no matter the cost.

---

**Day 5.**

**Social: Breakfast time! Please choose something from the list for participant JOSH.**

Breakfast. Apparently, the new day had already begun. It was still dark outside, and I hadn't been able to sleep at all. I kept thinking about everything. Why was there a message with my name in the book? Had I been here before, or was it a way to mindfuck me again?

After everything that had happened last night, I decided both Manuel and Jackie were trustworthy. I didn't trust Julia. She was my strongest competitor, and she was ruthless. I wanted all of us to get out of here safe and sound, but if I wanted to have any chance of getting control, I needed to play smart and gain points.

But first, I had to pick breakfast for Josh. This was good. I hadn't had any interaction with him so far. I needed to figure out if he was an ally or a competitor.

**Me: Social, before I pick Josh's meal, could you inform me about my ranking?**

**Social: You are currently the highest-ranking participant, John.**

**Me: Can you tell me how many other participants there are?**

**Social: You have had interaction with every object that is participating in this round.**

**Me: This round?**

**Social: Pick a meal for JOSH now.**

I went with a safe choice and sent him oatmeal and water. Nutritious but not luxurious.

I was really curious what he would get me or if I'd get any breakfast at all. Yesterday I wasn't able to send him anything because I was passed out.

A chicken sandwich, coffee, and a bottle of water. That was strange; this was exactly what I got yesterday, except this time the coffee was hot. So Julia must have skipped giving me dinner yesterday, and the food I'd found was the lunch Josh had sent me. I sent a steak dinner, and she decided to give me nothing.

I felt a deep urge to shock her again. Something inside of me was changing, and it scared me. As if I was just realizing that I had a dark, vengeful side. I was hateful. I had never talked to this person or even seen her, and yet I wanted to torture her, just because I could.

I stopped myself before actually pressing the button. These people were playing with my mind, and I let them. This was probably what they wanted: for me to stop caring, to abuse my power. I was at the top. That should be enough for now.

---

**Social: It is time for another decision! You can now choose to send one of the following items to a participant of your choice:**
    **Headphones**
    **Bandages**

**Razor blades**

I decided to send Manuel bandages. I had no strategy here; it just seemed like the safest move.

**SUICIDE ATTEMPT.**
**SUICIDE ATTEMPT.**
**SUICIDE ATTEMPT.**

The siren and robotic voice filled the room. Just the mention of suicide sent a shiver down my spine. My heart didn't stop racing until the siren stopped again.

**Social: You received a video from participant JULIA.**

It was a young woman. Her clothes were dirty and bloody. Manuel had made a rough impression as well, but Julia looked like she had been here for a long time. She looked tired, but her eyes were filled with rage. This didn't look like the decoy rage that I acted out in my video.

Her shock collar was gone, but I saw the bruises around her neck. That was when I noticed that she had a knife. She slowly moved it toward her throat. Her eyes never left the camera. I thought it was her way of threatening me until I saw the blood. She was actually cutting herself.

That was where the video paused. I hadn't noticed before, but I saw it in that moment. She was sitting in front of a chalkboard, and there was something written on it.

**DIE JOHN**

I felt frozen to the screen, even after the video had disappeared. Tears came to my face. This was all so much. Not knowing whether this was all just a trick, a mind game, or whether this girl had been pushed over the edge was ripping me apart. Had I given her the push? Was she really in danger? Was it too late?

---

After a few hours of internalized terror, I calmed myself again. This could all just be a trick. If it was, then it was working. I spent the entire day just jumping around in my room, no decent thoughts coming to mind. Eventually, the ringing of my laptop got me back to reality.

**Social: Hello, John. I want to personally congratulate you on how well you are doing in this experiment. I am impressed by your score and the choices you are making. You are constantly improving,**

and if you keep going strong, you will successfully complete the experiment soon. We are proud of you here at the Social Team. As a special treat, you will be having dinner together with the second-highest-ranking participant today. Enjoy! X

Me: Who is this? Social?

Social: Hi, John, this was a personal message sent to you by our head of research.

Me: Can I message them as well?

Social: I am afraid not.

Social: Today participant JOSH will be joining you for dinner. The meal will be picked by Social.

Me: Join me? As in face-to-face?

Social: Yes.

Me: I thought I wasn't allowed to know how other participants rank?

Social: *I* am not allowed to share information with you.

*All right, Social. Try to keep up the illusion that this is a legit experiment with all your fucking loopholes.* I almost typed this but decided to delete it. It might just cost me points again.

I really didn't trust any of this, but if it meant that I was actually meeting a real human being, I was all for it. I wished it was Julia, so I could set things straight, but maybe it would be good to meet Josh and figure out who this mysterious new person was.

**Social: Pick up dinner from the elevator now.**

**Me: Where is Josh?**

**Social: The other participant will be joining soon.**

I picked up my meal. Steak, jacket potato, greens, and champagne. This looked pretty great, although I only had one of each.

As I walked back to my laptop, I realized what Social had *really* meant by face-to-face. It was a video chat. On his side, it was still buffering. I made sure to turn my laptop in such a way that the chalkboard would be visible, and then I sat down.

Josh looked like he was about my age. You could see that he was mentally exhausted, but it was not as bad as with Manuel or Julia.

"So you are John?"

I was surprised to hear a voice. For some reason, I thought this would be muted. I had to be careful with what I said, though. First of all, I didn't know if I could trust him, and second, Social was probably recording all of this. I had to keep up the illusion that I was still trying, that I was a good participant.

"So you are my strongest competitor? Pretty good for someone who joined last," I said.

I had no idea if this was actually true, but maybe this would get me more answers.

"Hah." He forced out a smile. "Minus one," he said and nodded over. I think he was hinting at the strokes on my board. So I was right about that.

I was really nervous. I wish I had had time to prepare for this.

"I did something pretty... intense to get so high." He looked to the ground. "Some participant hasn't been sleeping for days because of me." I could really hear the remorse in his voice. But then he continued. "But you must have made even stronger decisions to be number one, I guess."

He was trying to get information out of me.

"I guess we both know how to play the game," I said and swallowed. I still felt the guilt deep inside of me. I took a big gulp from the champagne.

"I guess so. We're not at the losers' dinner," he whispered.

"Do you mean the others are talking as well?"

He nodded.

"How do you know?" I asked.

"Social."

"Which of them are the lowest?"

He shrugged. I guessed Social really kept the other rankings secret.

I was about to ask him, but the connection was already gone.

At least I had gotten some information, if Josh could be trusted. I knew that some of the other players probably talked as well today. I would have to ask Social about this, see if I could get more insight. And I knew that Josh probably gave someone that bracelet that kept you from sleeping.

I started feeling woozy. Had they put something in the drink? I somehow carried myself to the bed, and then everything went dark again.

**Day 6.**

The morning started off with the usual breakfast routine. I sent Manuel oatmeal and water. He sent me a glass of blood. Delicious, hadn't had that in days.

I didn't know how to feel about Josh after last night. He seemed somehow calculated, but he also made a genuine impression. So far, he'd always sent me decent food. The sleeping bracelet felt like something Social pressured him to do. He was playing the game to win, but he wasn't extremely evil. He was smart, though; he had figured out things pretty quickly, and he wanted to have control. Just like I did, as that was the only chance to get out, presumably. It also meant that he would probably be coming for me now.

---

I had been here for five full days already, and day six was starting off as awful as always. I tried to look for the book to figure out a way to send a message, but it was gone. So were the cigarettes. They must have taken them last night. Luckily, I had put the lighter in my pocket.

My hopes of getting out of here healthy were shrinking by the second, but I couldn't let this get me down. If I started losing hope now, I would probably die in here. I had to get into survival mode.

*Ding ding*

**Social: Hello, John! Today we have a very special assignment planned. You will be live-streaming the other participants and playing a game of choices. There are many points to be gained here, so do your best! Go sit down on your bed with the wall behind you.**

Four video screens opened up. I recognized Manuel and Josh. Julia was there as well. Alive. A feeling of relief washed over me. I didn't trust her, but I didn't want her dead, either. The last one must have been Jackie. She looked a little older than the rest of the group. The bags under her eyes led me to assume that she was probably the one who hadn't slept in days. That must really screw with your mind.

**Social: Welcome, participants! All of you have been doing well so far. Some did better than others, but don't worry. This game is a chance to change everything.**

**Social: Let's get started! Josh, choose a participant to fulfill the following task: Eat a raw deer heart.**

He didn't even seem to think about it. He responded right away.

**Josh: Manuel.**

**Social: Manuel, walk to the elevator and pick up the heart now. If you choose not to, you will not receive any food or beverages for the rest of the experiment.**

I could see him struggle. His eyes were filled with hatred. Eventually, he got up. Looking into the camera with tears in his eyes, he bit into the dark-red organ, finishing it off piece by piece. Josh didn't even flinch, and Julia looked more confused than revolted.

**Social: Next round! John AND Josh. You can both decide to either remove a tooth or a fingernail. The choice must be unanimous. What do you choose?**

**Me: Tooth.**

**Josh: Tooth.**

I sighed. If he had picked nails, we probably would have had to remove both. Josh wrapped his shirt around one of his teeth, closed his eyes, and abruptly pulled it out. Blood filled his mouth. He held the tooth up to the camera.

I followed. Normally, your mind tries to protect you; hurting yourself like this takes a lot of willpower. For me, it wasn't willpower, though. It was fear. Fear of whatever the alternative to this might be. It was painful as fuck but still felt harmless compared to what came next.

We all went through with the game. No questions asked. Nobody dared to disobey.

**Social: Julia can have a broken nose or all the hair burned off her scalp. Manuel, decide which option.**

Manuel was just shaking his head. His face was still red from the blood, and his eyes were full of tears. He was genuinely scared. Julia showed almost no reaction. Something had really broken her spirit.

**Social: Manuel, send your choice now or lose all your privileges.**

Finally, he typed.

**Manuel: Nose.**

Just like that, Julia turned toward the wall and repeatedly banged her face against it. As she turned around, blood ran all over her face; her nose was completely out of place. Still, she was calm. Not a single tear.

**Social: John, it is time for you to decide! Will Jackie cut off one of her fingers or be prohibited from sleeping for the rest of her time here?**

I could see the desperation in her eyes. How long can one survive without any sleep? A week? Two? I knew what she would choose if she could.

**John: Finger.**

**Social:** As Jackie is not in possession of a knife at the moment, one of our helpers will arrive soon to fulfill the task.

Jackie looked at her arm and smiled.

**Social:** You all did very well so far! Your wounds will be treated by one of our doctors shortly. Only one question left. One of the participants has to die. The majority wins. Who do you choose?

This couldn't be real. This was a whole new level of fucked up. I hesitated. How could I possibly answer this question? Manuel seemed to think the same because neither of us answered the question.

And we didn't have to, as the majority had already made its decision.

**Julia: John**
**Josh: John**
**Jackie: John**

# Part 4

*Participant files—Round 4*
**Participant JOHN**
Rounds: 4
Ranking: *not applicable*
Obedience level: Strong

Subject went through significant growth. At the beginning, decisions were purely altruistic in nature. As personal gain was made transparent, there was a change of tactics. At the end of the round, signs of resignation had become evident. A need for power and authority was established. After rising to the top on a score level, participant John had given up his own will entirely. Made deadly choices for a number of participants without signs of remorse.

**Participant JULIA**
Rounds: 3
Ranking: 2
Obedience level: Intermediate

The subject showed resilience and willpower all throughout rounds two and three. Inconsistent emotional state. Was almost removed due to a repeated suicide attempt. Strong determination to eliminate participant

John. At the end of round 4, the participant showed signs of apathy. Level of obedience is stable at this point.

**Participant JACKIE**
Rounds: 1
Ranking: 3
Obedience level: Strong

The subject showed occasional competent decision-making skills. Started off with a subjectively altruistic mindset; however, she would let other participants influence her choices. Of interest for future testing.

**Participant MANUEL**
Rounds: 1
Ranking: 4
Obedience level: Weak

The subject has poor decision-making skills. Lets his actions be guided by emotions. Has no explicit benefit for the experiment at this point and will therefore be eliminated.

**Participant JOSH**
Rounds: 1
Ranking: 1
Obedience level: Intermediate

The subject has surpassed expectations. He grew fast and showed a remarkable pattern in decision-making. However, his level of loyalty needs to be further examined.

---

**Day 7.**
I didn't even know how to put into words how I was feeling last night. I didn't sleep at all. For hours I was sitting on the bed, staring at the door, waiting for my end. Of course, I didn't know if I would actually die or not, but at that moment, the adrenaline was flowing through my entire body. Fear could be a real rush. My mind was not ready to die.

I thought about Kiwi, who had been left alone for days. I thought about my mother, hoping she would be safe. I thought about my friends, about my childhood. About the summers we went swimming in the lake, about the Sunday mornings watching cartoons with my dad.

I was not ready to die.

I felt hate. Pure, vengeful, bitter hate. For Social, for the experiment, for the other participants. This entire situation was so fucked up. I wondered if I would have done the same as Josh, if he had been the highest-ranking player. A part of me was scared to admit that I probably would have if it meant that I would be free. I thought about the other two and felt especially betrayed by Jackie. They couldn't have known that I was the highest-ranking player.

I kept staring at the door, waiting patiently, but nobody came. Maybe it had just been a mind game, after all. Maybe last night was just a farce.

---

*Ding ding*

**Social: Breakfast time! Today you will not have to choose. Go to the elevator now to pick up your meal.**

**Me: Prisoners on death row usually get to choose their last meal.**

No answer.

I walked over to see what would be on the tray. Maybe it was some sort of clue.

It was a finger.

Was this a sign from Jackie? Was the reason she picked me to die because of the choice I made for her?

I let it fall to the ground and broke down in tears. I lost all hope of ever getting out of this place.

The chat window was still open.

**Me: Social, am I still the highest-ranking player?**
**Social: Currently, the highest-ranking participant is Josh.**

Wait, had Social just given a name? They never answered questions on the rankings of other participants.

**Social: Hello, John, I want you to know that I am very impressed with your progress. I understand that it must feel surprising to see the other participants turn on you. Remember, the only reason they want you dead is because you are a threat. Wouldn't you murder someone if it meant getting your freedom back? We are sad that it had to come to this point, but we have provided something for you to make this a little easier. Make the right decisions. X**

**Me: Who is this?**

**Social: Hello, John, you just received another personal message from our head of research.**

**Social: You get to make another decision now. Do you want to continue and accept your destiny or put fate into your own hands? Go to the elevator now to pick up the items sent to you by the head of research.**

A bottle of vodka and a gun. One bullet.

**Social: Last night the majority decided for the death of participant JOHN.**

If this was making things easier, what was the alternative? What kind of gruesome death had they planned for me? I took a big gulp of the vodka.

I didn't even have to think about this.

**Me: Hey, Social, come and get me. Bring the head of research as well. I'd love to meet them.**

They could go fuck themselves if they thought I would make things this easy for them. I grabbed the bottle of vodka and poured it out in front of the door, making a trail toward the bed, where I sat down. I held the gun toward the door. If somebody came in, I had one chance to shoot them. My chances weren't great, especially as I doubted only one person would come in. So I kept the lighter close.

If I had to go, I wouldn't go on my own. I would take them with me.

I waited for what must have been hours, but nothing happened. Every time I thought I had figured them out, every time I thought things were ending, they just pulled another trick out of their hat. They must have cameras everywhere. How could I have believed that this was it?

The laptop started ringing again. The sound of pure misery.

**Social: Hello, John! We see that you did not decide to use the gun. You just gained 100 social points! We do not appreciate suicide attempts.**

**Me: What is this? Why are you doing this to me? Please just give me answers. If I have to die, at least let me know what the purpose of all this is.**

**Social: With a majority of 3 votes, the death of participant JOHN was decided. Do you agree with this choice?**

**Me: No, no, I do not.**

**Social: Adding your social score with the one of participant MANUEL, you could overrule the majority.**

**Me: What does this mean? What's going to happen now?**

**Social: You have two choices: Team up with participant MANUEL. If you can agree on another participant's death without discussion, it will be executed. Keep in mind, participant MANUEL could choose JOHN.**

This was no option. It was too much of a gamble.

**Me: What's the other choice?**

**Social: You can join another round of decisions. This time you will be making them on your own. If you gain 1,000 points in this game, the life of participant JOHN will be spared.**

This could only be another round of torture, but at this point, what did I have to lose?

**Social: First round: Give the gun to participant JULIA (200 points) or to participant JOSH (50 points).**

She had tried to kill herself before. If I sent the gun, this could be fatal. But then again, I would just send it, right? The decision was all hers.

**Me: Julia.**

Two hundred points. I moved the gun to the elevator. I hated giving it away, but I doubted it would have been of much use anyway.

**Social: Participant MANUEL is free to leave and go home (-200 points) or he will stay indefinitely (+200 points).**

Shit, I really, really wanted him to get out of here. To get back to Sabrina. But even more than that, I wanted to live.

**Me: Make him stay.**

Four hundred points. I felt like such a dick. I just kept the only person who had spared my life from freedom.

**Social: JACKIE will lose the rest of her hand (+200) or JOHN will lose a finger (+300).**

This was a really awful decision. A finger was nothing compared to a whole hand, and it would give me more points, but was I ready to sacrifice something for someone who had wanted my death?

**Me: Jackie.**

Six hundred points. If I hadn't realized it before, this game really showed me how weak the human mind is. You do anything some authority asks you to do, as long as it has perks for you. I felt like such a horrible human being. And it got even worse.

**Social: JOSH gets to speak to the head of research (-100) or MANUEL loses a toe (+200).**

I couldn't harm him even more.

**Me: Josh.**

Five hundred points. I hoped I wouldn't regret this decision.

**Social: You can end it all now! JULIA will be kept from all benefits, including sleep and nutrition, for one week (+500). Do you accept?**

Would she survive that? I didn't know. All I could hope was that she had something to drink saved in her room. Who cares? She wanted me dead. She didn't even flinch when she typed in my name. You have to do anything to survive.

**Me: Yes.**

**Social: Would you like to spare the life of JOHN (-1000 points)?**

**Me: Yes.**

Right after I typed it in, I ran to the bathroom to throw up. This had been the hardest moment of the experiment so far. I had never hated myself as much as I did at that moment. I hoped survival was worth this.

---

**Day 8.**

I woke up lying next to the toilet. The memories of yesterday came back to me, and I felt like throwing up again. Finally, I got up to see if there were any new messages from Social, any sign that this misery would end soon.

**Social: Dinner time! You may now choose a meal for participant JOHN.**

Why did this say my own name? Maybe they wanted me to pick my own dinner last night. I didn't care. I should have felt hungry, but the guilt kept me from even thinking about food. What time was it? I hadn't gotten a breakfast message yet.

As if Social could read my mind, the laptop started ringing again. The text was not from Social, though.

**X: Good morning.**

**Me: Social?**

**X: No. I would like to ask you a few questions if that is all right.**

**Me:** Does it matter what I say?

**X:** It always matters. Your decisions are what brought you this far.

**Me:** I don't remember ever accepting to come to this hell.

**X:** What do you remember?

**Me:** If I answer your questions, will you let me go?

**X:** Yes, Josh. After this conversation, you are free to go home. Do you remember your home?

Did they just mix up my name? I did vote for Josh to have a conversation with the head of research. I decided to just go with it.

**Me:** I do. I have a little apartment where I live with my cat, but you probably know all about that.

**X:** And you think the cat is called Kiwi? Yes, I can see that chalkboard.

How did they know that it was the name of my cat?

**Me:** Yes, Kiwi.

**X:** What does Kiwi look like?

I couldn't remember.

**X:** There are also two letters on there. K and F. Kristen and Fynn, right?

**Me:** How do you know that?

**X:** Do you remember what they look like? Or what Mary looks like? Do you remember your childhood home?

I tried to think of my mom. Blonde hair, brown eyes. She was about fifty. For some reason, I didn't remember more. What did she look like when I was younger? Why did my memory feel frozen? It was as if I was thinking of a photo, not a real person.

**X:** Keep thinking.

The image shifted. It was a woman with short hair. A kind smile. Her hair was black when I was little. Now it had turned gray. A name came to my mind: Margaret. Who was this woman?

**Me:** Do you know who Margaret is?

**X:** I believe that is your mother.

**Me:** Who is Mary?

**X:** That must be the mother of John.

**Me:** I AM John.

**X:** Are you sure about that? :)

More memories came up. Kiwi, my dad, my friends, the lake. Everything was wrong. They were simply images. They morphed into something else. College. A woman. Blood. A girl. She had a tattoo on her arm. A hospital.

I started remembering more. I had joined an experiment once. At college. I didn't remember much, except that the research was corrupt and evil. After I left that experiment, terrible things happened to me, to everyone around me. I decided to leave, and I traveled around Europe for a while, but wherever I went, things went bad for me. They must have found me. Or did I find them?

They wiped away everything and gave me false memories.

**X: Josh, you did really well here. I realize this experiment had its ups and downs, but eventually, you grew to the top. You showed no remorse. You are a true leader.**

Josh. Social kept calling me John, and I just accepted it. How did I forget about my own name?

**Me: No, I didn't. I only did what you made me do. I did what I had to.**

**X: Because of points? Numbers on a laptop? You decided to shock both Manuel and Julia. You sacrificed Jackie's hand. You gave Julia a gun even though you knew she was suicidal. Although you did spare John's life.**

**Me: Who is John?**

**X: You got to know him as JOSH. We swapped your identity with his and added him as an additional variable. He is on his way to become part of our team. Before this, he had been torturing Julia. And it worked.**

That was why she wanted me dead. And she probably convinced Jackie, too.

**Me: Why? Why did you do this?**

**X: All these people were normal human beings living their lives. Keep them in a room alone and give them the power to make decisions and they will lose all sense of humanity. And they are no exception. We have tested this in many settings already. Some humans, however, grow above. A very select few get to make rules, not follow them.**

**Me: And John is one of them?**

X: Hah. No. He had potential, but he is nothing like you. You are the only person who could remotely come close to me. This is why I need you. You were always one step behind me. I had to make sure you were strong enough to be part of this. To be part of the new life. And now I know. You have everything that it takes. I am extremely proud of you.

Me: You want me to start doing these sick experiments on innocent people?

X: This is happening. There is no way for you to change any of this. Our institution is far more powerful than you might believe. I am giving you the option to be on the side that *makes* the decisions.

X: I am not forcing you to do anything. Just think about it. You are free to go home now, but we will see each other again soon. Goodbye, Nine. :)

---

That was the last thing I remembered. I woke up in my apartment. My real apartment. Not the one from my memories, John's, or whatever they'd made me believe. My memories slowly came back. I wished they hadn't.

I thought about running away, starting over somewhere far away, but for some reason, I thought they would find me. For the same reason that the authorities wouldn't listen to me. They were powerful.

Yesterday I received an envelope with patient files, as well as this postcard:

**The next round of the Social Experiment will start soon. Do you want to be an object or a leader? :)**

---

I thought about this a lot. About joining them. Not as a test subject but as a researcher.

I thought about this a lot since I've been back home. I didn't know what would happen next, but this study did teach me a lot about human nature and my own mind. How arbitrary freedom and choice were. I followed them. Blindly followed some authority for made-up points and false promises.

I know I have to get back there. Not to become part of the research team but to save the ones I have left behind. I will not accept being this terrible person. I can do better. With the knowledge I have gained.

The envelope has no return address. So for now, all I can do is wait.

# EVERY NIGHT, A NEW WOMAN DANCES ON OUR STREET

She twirls around, her feet bare, the white nightgown soaked from the rain. Her hair is sticking to her forehead; normally, it's shiny and bright red, now almost black. So far, I've seen three women dancing before her. They were all dead by the end of the night.

And nobody ever went outside to help.

---

The first woman appeared a little over a week ago. It was a quiet night, and my parents were sitting in the living room, watching TV with my aunt. She'd arrived a few days earlier for my eighteenth birthday but decided to stay a little longer. She didn't visit very often, so I was really excited about that. I couldn't hear anything, but when I opened the door to my room, I saw the flickering of lights downstairs.

I'd gone to my room right after dinner because I wasn't feeling too well for some reason. My stomach was turning, and my body was heavy. I crawled into bed and was fast asleep before I could form another coherent thought.

Until the pain in my stomach woke me up just after midnight. After throwing up half of my dinner and brushing my teeth, all I wanted was to fall back into bed. But that was when I heard the sounds outside. It was a soft tapping accompanied by a quiet humming.

Hearing anything at all at night was completely out of the ordinary as we live on the quietest street in the country. So I walked up to my window and couldn't believe what I was seeing.

The sounds came from the feet of a young woman. She was dressed in a black leotard and tights, her hair was neatly put up in a shimmering bun, and her movements resembled those of a ballet dancer. Her body looked fragile, but her movements were soft.

I kept watching her, mesmerized by her dance while also wondering what was going on. Our neighbors are all very stuck-up. As I said, normally you don't hear a single sound at night.

I wanted to go downstairs to see if my parents or aunt were still awake so they'd see what I was looking at. I was sure they wouldn't believe me if I told them the next morning.

Something surprisingly non-ordinary happening on Jackington Street!

But then, before I moved away, the woman started doing something different.

First, her expression became more hollow. Her eyes opened almost as wide as her mouth, as if invisible strings were pulling them to the edges of her face. Despite the strange look, she didn't stop dancing, but it became far more rigid. She'd move one leg forward, then the other.

Finally, she fell to her knees, her head bowing as she hugged her shoulders, the bones sticking out underneath the skin.

My breathing became heavier as I realized that this wasn't simply a weird moment but that something was *really* wrong.

That was when she released her arms and looked up. My lights weren't on, but I could swear she was staring straight at me.

And then she screamed.

---

I stumbled back from the window and ran to my parents' bedroom. To my surprise, they were both awake with their lights on, standing behind their own window that had a similar view as mine. My mother whispered something to my dad.

"That was beautiful."

I stood in their doorframe for a moment, frozen in shock, until I walked up to my parents.

My father turned around and casually asked, "Oh, Andy, why are you awake?"

He came up to me and met me halfway, blocking most of the view to the street.

What I could see, however, was that a number of neighbors had turned on their lights when I walked from my room over to my parents'.

"Did somebody call an ambulance?" I asked.

My mother shook her head. "No, but somebody came to pick her up." Then she smiled at me. "Don't worry, nothing bad happened."

"But she seemed... sick or something. Definitely not right."

My mother gently stroked my arm. "It's okay, really, honey. Are you feeling all right? I thought I might have heard you throwing up?"

I'd already forgotten about that. "Yeah, I'm fine, just surprised. Nobody's supposed to make noise at night."

This time my father smiled. "You're right, but how about we talk about this in the morning? You should probably go back to sleep so you feel better tomorrow."

I didn't want to go to bed before understanding what was going on, but at the same time I felt drained, and I had difficulty even keeping my eyes open. I headed back to my room and looked down at the street again, except now it was empty.

---

The next morning, I was woken up by the smell of pancakes. Apple cinnamon pancakes.

I followed the scent to the kitchen, where my mother was standing behind the stove while my father and my aunt Aubrey were sitting by the lavishly decked kitchen table.

"Good morning, honey. Would you like some coffee?" my mother asked without a care in the world.

"Sure," I mumbled.

My dad was smiling. "Morning, buddy."

My aunt didn't look up from her plate.

"Did you see what happened last night?" I asked her.

"No, your parents just told me, though. Slept through it."

"What? How?" I asked. "You could probably hear that scream three streets away." I sat down next to Aubrey, and my mother poured me a cup of coffee.

Aubrey shrugged. "Maybe I'll see it tonight."

"Tonight?" I asked.

Aubrey finally looked up and stared right into my eyes.

"Aubrey," my father said in a stern voice.

"What? He's gonna see it again—or someone will tell him. Come on, John, there's no hiding it."

"Hiding what?"

My father loudly sighed. "Always such a pleasure when you visit, Aubrey."

Without asking, my mom started stacking pancakes on the plate in front of me.

"Mom, I can do this myself. Sit down and eat something, too. And can you please tell me what is going on? You're acting super strange."

"Oh, your aunt is making this bigger than it really is. You know how we and our neighbors cherish nightly rest? How we make sure not to make sounds that anyone outside our home can hear?" my father asked.

I nodded. After ten o'clock, nobody makes a sound on our streets. It's been like this ever since I can remember.

"Well, every ten years or so, the rules are bent a little. And when that happens, we see the occasional dancer at night. It only lasts a couple of days."

After finishing that confusing explanation, he shoved a forkful of pancakes in his mouth as if to say that the conversation was over. Like it didn't create more questions than answers.

"It's not the occasional dancer. It's one each night—and they are all women," my aunt added.

"But why? And how have I never heard of it?"

"Well, last time you were too young, buddy, and as it doesn't happen very often, people don't talk about it much."

My aunt rolled her eyes but didn't say anything else.

"It's a tradition. No more than that. And every ten years really isn't often," my mother added, and with that the conversation was over, and I was simply supposed to accept that this was normal.

But well, before all of this, I also accepted that it was completely normal that our streets had to be completely silent at night.

---

Aubrey disappeared right after breakfast to meet some old friends. Mom went to the market, and Dad went to work. Summer vacation had started a week before, so I had a bunch of free time on my hands, and I was determined to learn more about this dancing mystery.

I texted a couple of friends, but none of them had any idea what I was talking about. Not even Rudy who lived on the end of our street. But at least I had made sure that a couple of other kids would start asking their parents about this tradition we all had never heard of before. I wondered who else I could talk to about it; Aubrey would probably be the best option but not with my parents around. My dad, especially, was acting super strange.

When night came, I was determined to stay up.

A new woman appeared just after twelve. She was wearing a long, flowy dress and danced the foxtrot, alone.

On the other side of our street, a light was turned on, and I caught sight of a girl I hadn't seen before. She looked around my age, with dark red hair and an expression resembling mine. Shock.

The dancing woman turned around and suddenly fell to the ground, holding her ankle and twisting her face. I couldn't see well, but it seemed like she had hurt herself.

"I hope you're enjoying this!" she screamed as she got back up and continued dancing with a limp.

My heart started racing. I almost opened my window to ask her if she needed help when two arms pulled me away from my window.

"Dad?" I said, too loudly.

"Shh. Andy, you're only supposed to watch the dancing. Do. Not. Interfere." He closed my curtains.

"Dad, what the hell?" I whispered, and my father looked like he might punch me. Then he took a deep breath and walked me to my bed.

"I know this is all very exciting for you, but we have special ways of how we do things here. You don't want to get us into trouble, do you?"

"I don't understand."

I heard a muffled scream coming from outside.

"Do you?" he repeated in a stricter tone.

I nodded. Ever since I was born, my parents had indoctrinated my mind with strict rules, but this one seemed even more arbitrary than the nightly silence.

Dad sat there with me until it was over, not allowing me to take another peek. He said I wasn't allowed to watch if I couldn't follow his commands.

---

The following day, my parents and my aunt were gone before I woke up.

I made myself breakfast but couldn't stop thinking about last night. I really needed to talk to Aubrey. Someone who had gotten out of here and might tell me the truth.

I was pulled out of my thoughts when our doorbell rang.

In front of it stood the girl from last night. Not the dancer but the one I had seen through the window. Her eyes appeared bloodshot, and she seemed really nervous for some reason.

"Hi, I'm Eliza." She smiled politely. "Andy, right? Not sure if you remember me but I used to come visit a couple of times when I was younger."

"Oh yeah, are you visiting your grandparents?" I did remember Eliza. She was the Fleischmanns' granddaughter. I think her mom even went to high school with my parents. Her mom passed away a while back, and as far as I know, she didn't visit again after that.

She nodded. "Grandma asked me to come over to borrow some eggs. But, um," she carefully looked around, "I also came because I have some questions, and I'm pretty sure I saw you last night. Your parents aren't home, right?"

"Um, no, but how do you—?"

"Saw them leave. I've been watching. Sorry, this sounds weird, but I am completely freaking out." She walked right past me, toward our living room, not even waiting for an invitation.

"Are you all right?" I asked after closing the door and following her to the living room.

She shook her head. "Are *you*? I mean, that woman just died in front of our eyes."

I stood there frozen for a moment. "She what?"

"Died. At least I think so. She screamed, then fell to the ground. I'm not sure when she died exactly, but in a matter of minutes, two men came up and carried her away in a body bag."

I chuckled, not believing a word this strange girl was speaking. Eliza kept staring at me.

"I called the police, and they laughed. Can you believe that?"

"Look, um, Eliza. I'm not sure what you saw, but that woman didn't die. Apparently, this dancing thing happens once every ten years."

Her expression darkened. "I know. That's why my grandparents asked me to come. They said, as I'm part of the family, I have to be here for it. I thought it was some show or whatever, not this."

I sat down on the sofa. "Okay, why the hell would a woman die from dancing?"

She shrugged. "I don't know, but I do know that this is much bigger than just a dance. Because my grandma said that I couldn't leave. She said if I did, I would just die. Can you believe that?"

Now I was even more confused. "She says you'll die if you leave town? Is your grandma okay?"

"I thought she was. She never seemed that crazy before." Eliza started chewing her nails. "The thing is, I remember my mother telling me about something when I was little. She said leaving our hometown was the best thing she ever did, how she escaped a cult, basically. A few weeks later, she killed herself."

Eliza was now looking into the distance. The girl definitely needed some help, and I wasn't sure if I was the one who could provide it.

"I'm so sorry," was all I could say. "Maybe the woman last night was sick. I'm sure my parents would have said something if anything bad happened. They know everyone around here. And if you want to leave town, just do it? Your grandma will be fine."

She nodded. "Yeah. Sure," she whispered and walked back toward the door. "Could I still get those eggs, please?"

---

The dancer on the third night didn't even try. Her expression was empty, and she only stepped from side to side.

That night both my parents stood next to me.

"We should give him something again," I'd heard my mother whisper to my father earlier that evening.

"That didn't stop him the first night, either," my father replied. "It's time he learns how things work here. He might have a daughter one day."

I wanted to ask them more but was too scared. I started wondering if Eliza wasn't that crazy after all.

So we stood there together on the third night. The woman danced, sparsely. When she fell to the ground, she didn't even cry or scream.

"Pathetic," my father whispered. "She should feel honored."

My mother grabbed my arm tight and nodded. Her face was empty.

The woman lay there, her eyes opened wide, but she didn't move anymore.

"Is she dead?" I almost didn't dare to ask.

My father grabbed my shoulder for a second, then he left the room.

Just as Eliza had described it, two men wrapped her in a body bag and carried her away.

"Mom?" I said, not able to look into her eyes.

"Us women are born with a curse. We can try to run. I did. But it's no use. When our time comes, we can't fight it," I suddenly heard my aunt speak behind us.

"I don't understand."

My mother looked at me, tears forming in her eyes. "This is a tradition older than me, older than our parents. We don't understand it, but every ten years women have to dance, and they all die when they are finished. Something that has lived here longer than us takes them."

"Then why are you still here? *Why* would you come back?" I said to Aubrey.

"Because we can't fight it. If I don't come, I die either way. If I come, I at least have a chance not to be chosen."

"But why the hell would anyone from here even still have children? Why not let it die with them?"

"You heard your father. It's an honor to die for this town."

Aubrey took one more disgusted look at my mother and left the room.

When the final night came, I didn't want to watch. I'd talked to Eliza earlier that day about what my parents said.

Her grandparents told her the same story. She was even more disgusted than me. I still didn't understand if this was really some ancient entity or our own people who did this to the women. But Eliza was too scared to leave if that meant death.

Same as Aubrey. I knew I was born lucky, in a culture ruled by men like my father that will gladly sacrifice a woman if it means their lives are secured.

I had heard our door open and close earlier, but I was too scared to look.

---

She takes a final bow, and our eyes meet for a second.

I'm not the only one watching. The lights are on in every window. Some people wipe away tears, and when she is done, everyone claps, and they won't stop until she collapses.

I hope that at least now my mother will understand that this is wrong. Now that she lost her sister.

# I MOVED TO A NEIGHBORHOOD WHERE THE PEOPLE ARE TOO WELCOMING

It wasn't simply normal in the beginning; it was fantastic. I knew it as soon as the bus reached the neighborhood, as we passed roads with coffee shops and streets so narrow I thought we might get stuck.

The apartment I looked at was rather small, but it was enough for me and, most importantly, cheap. My workplace was only a twenty-minute bike ride away, but I would never go there. Everything seemed right, and I immediately signed the contract. I moved in a week later.

The best part was that it felt like home. I'd recently gone through a rough breakup and some other stuff. I needed a fresh start, and this was the perfect place for it.

This city had around a million residents, but the neighborhood made you feel like you were in a small town, or even a village. Very rustic and charming. And with all sorts of quaint traditions that my neighbor Linda would teach me.

---

The apartment came furnished, so I only had to carry in some boxes, which I decided to do on my own. I knew it was time for me to become independent.

Linda greeted me as I walked in and took the box I was holding from my hands.

"Oh, you don't need to do that! I got it." I smiled at the old lady.

"Nonsense! We are neighbors, and neighbors help each other. I'm not rotten yet, dear."

"Oh no, I didn't mean—" I paused and smiled instead. If she wanted to help, I'd let her help. Having a good relationship with your neighbors is always important, as they could make your life hell if they wanted to.

Besides, she stopped helping after the first box. She sat down at my kitchen table and watched me carry the rest in. After I brought in the kitchen boxes, I made us some tea. Moving my boxes to the second floor took me less than an hour, so I sat with her and chatted some more. That was when she told me about the first thing I had to do in the new neighborhood.

"All right, listen, dear. After you've settled in a bit, you get a long branch from a tree. You can buy it in one of our flower shops or get a fallen one from a real tree. After you remove all the leaves, you write your name on it and glue the branch to the door. The neighbors who wish to do so will write you little letters or glue small presents to the branch."

I'd never heard of anything like it, but it sounded sweet.

---

After walking through the streets for a day, finding a grocery store, a pharmacy, and of course the flower shop, I noticed a few things.

For example, many of the houses had at least one window with black glass. It made little sense to me; why not simply use a curtain? But I would ask Linda about it later.

Everyone was insanely friendly. People waved at me and smiled as soon as they saw me. A young woman with a little boy in her arm even came up to me and asked if I'd put up my branch yet, as she had a present for me.

"How do you know—" I started asking, and she immediately interrupted me.

"Oh, I'm a friend of Linda's and, well, word travels fast here."

I smiled. "Well, you don't need to get me anything. I already feel very welcome. Everyone is so nice. My name is Maira, by the way." I extended my hand.

"I know." She looked at my open hand for a moment but didn't reach for it. "You know, we have another new neighbor just on this street. A young gentleman named Julian." She pointed at an old, narrow house across from us with a branch taped to its door.

"I should get going. My other son is home alone. It was lovely to meet you, Maira. Welcome, again."

---

I decided to have a look at the new guy's branch, to get an idea of what I was to expect.

People had glued some notes on it. Some said "welcome" or "nice to have you here." Others were stranger.

"Count yourself lucky."

"Welcome to hell."

I reached for one of the presents when my hand touched something weird and slimy.

When I saw what it was, I instinctively jumped back.

An eye.

I can't say if it was human or from an animal, as I'd never seen one out of its socket, but it definitely looked real.

No matter how much I rubbed my hands against my pants, I couldn't get the feeling off.

That's when I noticed a guy watching me from a window next to the door.

He said something, which I couldn't hear through the window, but he looked angry. I got ready to leave when the door opened. "Wait!"

When he passed the branch, he looked at it with disgust on his face.

"Are you Julian?" I asked.

He nodded and came dangerously close. I couldn't help but notice that his eyes had the same brown color as the one I'd just touched. "You're new," he said.

"Yes."

I looked around and tried to think of a reason to leave. While he looked normal, nice even, he was giving me an off vibe.

He came even closer and started whispering in my ear. "It's too late for me, but you should try and leave."

I stepped back. "Yes, I was just about to. See you—"

"No, leave this neighborhood. Try and see if you can. Most of us get stuck here."

Now I was getting really nervous. "Listen, buddy, I really have to go and—"

"Do you remember your life before coming here?"

I laughed. "What kind of weird question is that? Of course I remember."

"That's good. I guess." He got a pack of cigarettes out of his back pocket and offered one to me.

I shook my head. From the things he was saying, it felt as if he was scared of something, but he spoke in such a calm way.

"Do you see the window above mine here? With the black paint? They have someone trapped in there. He cries all night long. The other day I went up to check on the people there. I really shouldn't have."

"Why?" Now I was really asking out of curiosity.

"It's hard to explain to normal people. They are broken humans, or something like that."

He was talking like a crazy person, but the weird thing was that he seemed really genuine. Maybe a little traumatized.

"Okay, listen." I was speaking in a really loud voice now, and people started looking out of their windows.

"No, you listen," Julian interrupted me again. "Is there an attic in your house? Or a basement? If there is, you might want to look at it. Or not. Might be better to stay delusional. Makes it easier."

---

I'd just moved here and had already met three eccentric neighbors. Still, nothing could have prepared me for what I was about to discover.

The following afternoon, I went down to the basement of my house.

The door was locked, but one of my keys fit the lock, which eased my mind a little. There couldn't be anything that bad waiting for me if I was allowed down there.

In reality, though, it was absolutely horrific. Linda simply didn't care if I saw it.

When I opened the door, I looked into the darkness but quickly found a light switch at the top of the stairs. Still, the light was quite dim, and it took my eyes a bit to get used to it.

The basement was one surprisingly big room. Twice the size of my apartment.

And filled with at least a dozen fridges. The big ones that you see at the supermarket with glass tops.

And inside them were organs.

I almost wished that this was about organ trafficking, but it got so much worse. I walked up to one of them and inspected it. There was a heart inside, which I swear was beating. And yes, I realize that's impossible.

But that's not even the worst part. The heart had all these flesh lumps, some small and some really big.

My stomach started turning and my brain was shouting to get the hell out when I heard someone coming down the stairs.

"Not everyone comes to live here. Some come to die," I heard Linda say.

She laughed when she saw my frightened face. "Oh, not you, dear. You belong here."

I was freezing and sweating at the same time. "What are... I don't understand. Why... are they *growing*?"

"Well, humans sometimes die, and when they are still fresh, we take whatever we can from them. We can make new ones out of the individual parts." She grinned like a proud child.

"New ones?"

"New humans."

My stomach kept turning. I wouldn't be able to keep it in for long, but I also didn't want to puke in the room of growing organs. I had to look away. "But how?"

She frowned. "There are many different ways to make a human. It's not all sex or science. We make sure all conditions are right, and then we pray. We do it our way, the way we were taught."

I swallowed. "Taught by whom?"

She rolled her eyes as if I just asked the stupidest question.

"The one who takes care of all of us. He is our leader and the leader of many more communities. Don't worry, you'll meet him soon enough."

That was the last thing I wanted. This was absolutely absurd, but she seemed so sure. This woman was insane; she probably killed people and experimented with their organs. Of course, no humans grew out of that. I knew I needed to get out of here, but I couldn't let her see how freaked out I was, so I kept asking questions.

"But how does it make sense? You kill one person and make a new one out of them? Why not use existing people and—"

"This way we can make more. A brain makes a new one. A heart makes a new one. And so on. The more substance we have, the more different creatures we can create. They all serve different purposes. You can see that by their looks. Some look just like you and me, and others are far more uncanny. Usually, the ones made out of hearts or livers—don't ask me why. But don't worry, we keep them hidden." She shrugged. "Anyway, you don't need to know every single detail. You know, I almost feel like you're using me. Pressing information out of me because you know I'm lonely and like to chat. It's very cheeky and manipulative. I don't like it one bit. Being used."

"No! I'm just curious, that's all. I believe you're a very important part of this community."

"Sure as hell I am." She looked away, but I could tell that she was slightly flattered. "You know you don't need to act all high and mighty just because you forgot."

"Forgot what?"

Linda smirked. "That you came to life here, grew out of a magnificent brain. One that our leader brought us himself. You are one of our most excellent copies, Maira. And we are so glad you found your way home."

I stayed silent.

"You can go now, girl. I can tell that you're too much of a princess to help with my work."

---

I didn't need to hear more. I ran up the stairs and through the door. As soon as I stepped out, I started running.

Out of the neighborhood, I thought, but I didn't even try. Instead, I ended up at Julian's doorstep.

He saw the look on my face and knew immediately. "You can't leave. Not as long as they don't want you to."

"Yeah, figured that one out." I bit my lip and looked around. I almost didn't dare say those next words.

"Is it odd that I don't feel bad about that? I mean, I kept trying to get out, but when I couldn't, I wasn't really disappointed. It's like I belong—"

"I know," he interrupted me. "I feel the same way."

# THIS IS NOT MY HOME

I woke up in the middle of the bed—the advantage of being single. I can use all the space I want. I woke up naturally, without an alarm, awakened only by the white light shining through the thin curtains. Mornings are usually dreadful for the simple fact that one has to wake up and become active, but it wasn't too bad that day. Believe it or not, I even smiled as I slowly moved my body to sit up.

And that's when I realized that nothing was right.

This was not my home.

This was not my bedroom, not my sheets, not my bed.

Slowly, memories started trickling back in. I went out last night. Decided to finally do the pub crawl we'd been planning for months. There was a lot of drinking, not enough eating, and I had the occasional blackout. Although I didn't remember meeting anyone I would have gone home with.

No, I did remember walking home with my friend Anne, who lives down the street. There was no way I met someone during the two minutes I walked home alone from Anne's place and decided to go home with them.

From what I could tell, I wasn't tied up or anything, and I didn't feel hurt or particularly odd. Except for my racing heart and my empty brain, I seemed okay. But it might have been due to the adrenaline suddenly rushing through my body.

I got up from the wooden bed with the incredibly comfortable mattress. The room I was in was clean and looked nice. Not the place you imagine ending up if you're kidnapped, and honestly, I didn't think I was.

There was a big forest-green chair in the corner of the room with a small table, a gray carpet on the floor in front of the bed, and a shelf filled with books.

It looked cozy and nice, almost the way I might decorate a new bedroom or guest room. For a second, I wondered if I did go and visit a friend after dropping off Anne.

But that was crazy.

I slowly made my way to the window.

Outside, I saw a regular suburban neighborhood. Nice little homes with pretty lawns and cars out front. Though it felt familiar, I didn't remember being here before. Looking down at my body, I realized I was wearing the same jeans and shirt I went out in last night. I went through my pockets, hoping I would find my phone in them, but all I found were my keys.

I shifted my gaze back to the street. In a way, it was calming to look out there. The sun was shining, the grass on the lawn was incredibly green, and all in all, it looked like a wonderful day in a pretty neighborhood. This did not look like the place a kidnapper would bring me to, but this also didn't look like a place close to my home. I live in a city.

I took a deep breath, calming myself down slightly when I saw the woman on the other side of the street. She looked like she was around the age of fifty, and coincidentally, she was also dressed as if she had just come out of the 1950s. Her red hair was blow-dried in that old-fashioned style, and she was wearing a sundress and a whimsical apron as she watered some plants on her porch. I suppose after a minute or two she must have felt me watching her, because she abruptly looked up right at me. Her expression was stern for a moment, but then she smiled and waved, and for a second, I felt slightly safe again.

When everything around you seems perfectly normal but inside your head nothing makes sense, it makes you wonder if you're the problem. This place wasn't scary; the gap in my memory was.

I took a deep breath and decided to go for the door. Ever since I woke up, I hadn't heard any sounds inside the house. Maybe I was alone. *Maybe I was an intruder, not a captive.*

I opened the door and saw a flight of stairs in front of me, wooden stairs that went around in a circle, leading me down to what I imagined was the living room. There was a big sofa, a TV, a table, all the regular stuff, but something was off. A bunch of picture frames sat on the shelves and hung on the walls, but none of them had any photos inside.

I decided not to check any other rooms but to look for the door leading outside as quickly as I could. Luckily, I didn't have to search long. The living room led to a hallway, which brought me to the front door. I hesitated for a second, worrying it might be locked, but I turned the knob, and sunlight greeted my face.

The woman I'd seen from the window was still standing on her porch and waved again as she saw me. This time I waved back as I crossed the street to go and talk to her.

"Wonderful morning!" she said as I approached her lawn.

"Um, good morning," I said and immediately added, "Sorry, this might sound weird, but do you know whose house I just came out of?"

She laughed. "That is a very weird question. You were just inside, weren't you?"

I scratched my head, wondering what to say next. "Yes, well, you see, I may have had a bit too much to drink last night, ma'am." I chuckled nervously.

"Oh dear, it appears you've lost your head, doesn't it?" she said. "But don't you worry. Everything's perfectly all right. I suppose you came to visit your friend. A young woman, just around your age. She left early this morning—where to, I'm not sure. And by the way, you can just call me Margie." She nodded her head like an old teacher.

A woman my age. That sounded a little more reassuring.

"Right, okay. Nice to meet you, um, Margie. I'm Tony. Can I ask you another weird question?" I paused for a second. "Where exactly am I?"

The woman smiled. "Would you like me to call you a cab, dear?"

"Yes, that would be very nice. Thank you."

---

The cab arrived only a few minutes later.

My mind was still quite scrambled, so I sat down inside the car and tried to make sense of what happened last night.

The cab driver was a middle-aged man with a marvelous mustache. His name was Maurie, and apparently, he got there so quickly because he lived in the neighborhood himself. Maurie had a warm smile and kind eyes, and

I finally felt far more at ease and only slightly confused. I got drunk, went home with some girl, and now I was acting a bit like an idiot.

"Did you have a nice time in our boring ol' suburbs?" Maurie tried to make some small talk.

"Yes," I lied. While that neighborhood and the people were all slightly odd, I realized that I was the weirdest of them all. And now I really just wanted to go home.

"Except, and I know this is going to make me sound really shitty—sorry, really stupid—I don't remember the name of the woman I visited."

"Margie? I was surprised to see her getting a visitor at such a random time of year," he answered.

"No, not Margie. The woman across the street from her. She's around my age?"

"Oh! Caroline. Sweet girl. Not many friends, though."

"Yes, Caroline, that must be her. You don't happen to have her number?"

"Eleven," he promptly answered.

"No, not her house number. I mean her phone number."

"No, sorry, but I can give yours to her if you'd like." He started rummaging through the compartment of the car and grabbed two cards as well as a pen. "Here ya go. My business card. One to keep in case you need another ride and one to write your number on so I can give it to sweet Caroline."

"Perfect, thank you!"

I didn't think I slept much last night because suddenly I felt incredibly tired, and before I knew it, my eyes closed and didn't open again until we reached my street, the one with my actual home.

"I'll need to run upstairs real quick and get some cash," I said, but before leaving I gave Maurie the card with my number on it. "I'll be right back!"

"All right, buddy, see you soon."

When I came back downstairs with my wallet, Maurie was gone. And I know this sounds very odd because throughout the car ride I'd felt safe and somehow at ease, but only now that I was back home did I realize something.

I'd never given Maurie my address.

That was the first time I visited Caroline's home, and even though I was incredibly confused back then as well, my mind became more and more scrambled.

As I write this now, in my regular home, in the regular town I live in, I can't seem to understand many of my actions. But when I'm there, around those people, things are different.

After that first visit, I waited for a call from Caroline, which never came. I tried to call the number on Maurie's card many times, but I think it was disconnected because the phone wouldn't even ring. And his card had nothing on it but his name and number. Googling them didn't bring up any results, either.

I asked Anne about that night, and she said I'd headed home after dropping her off, just as I remembered. For a while, I almost tried to make myself believe that it was all a big fever dream, except I still had that card from the cab driver.

Weeks would pass before I ended up in the far-too-normal neighborhood again. A part of me tried to forget about it altogether, and I think the more days passed, the hazier the memories became. I had to consciously sit down and make myself think about it, which was an odd experience. We normally remember weird occurrences much more vividly, except when our brain tries to make us forget traumatic experiences. Nothing particularly bad had happened during my visit, though. Not yet.

When I woke up in Caroline's home again, it felt just the same as the first time. It was morning, the sunlight woke me up, and I was dressed in the clothes I wore the night before, except this time it was sweatpants and a hoodie. I walked to the window and saw Margie again. This time she was cleaning her windows.

And this time I felt far more scared.

There was no logical explanation as to how I'd ended up back here. I hadn't been drinking the night before. I went to sleep in my own bed after watching some documentary, and I consciously remember checking if my door was locked (something I have to do every night now after once forgetting my key in the keyhole outside of my apartment door).

Somebody had brought me here.

I didn't waste time and went straight for the door.

"Hello?" I shouted, but nobody answered.

I saw a second door on the same floor as my room, but it was locked, so I went downstairs again. The living room looked almost the same except for one little thing: one of the frames now had a picture inside.

It was a selfie of a woman with blond hair, Caroline, I assume, and somebody else was sitting in the background with eyes closed. The photo didn't have the best quality, but I am certain that the other person was me.

I grabbed the picture and ran outside.

"Oh, hello there, Tony! How have you been, darlin'?" Margie asked.

I tried to collect myself, but my entire body was shaking. "What the hell is this place? Did I fucking die or something?"

Margie chuckled. "No, sweetie, we are all very much alive. I assume you simply came to visit your friend here. She's left again, hasn't she? Always so busy. Let me call Maurie for you."

"No. Call the police, please."

Margie gave me a sympathetic look. At least, that was what I assumed it was.

"No, honey, no police. Everything is perfectly all right here. But if you want to leave, I will call you a cab, or you could come inside and have some lemonade with me." She smiled.

I contemplated waiting for that Caroline girl to come back, but my gut told me to get the hell away as fast as I could, so I accepted Margie's offer for the cab, though not for the lemonade.

---

"Can you drive me to a police station?"

"Of course," Maurie answered, not even questioning my request.

"How do I keep ending up here?" I asked.

Maurie didn't answer.

While talking, I kept looking out the window, trying to memorize the surroundings, trying to figure out how I could come back here with the cops. However, I pretty much forgot about it in the moment.

"Who is Caroline, and why do I never see her?"

Again, no answer.

"You stole her picture?" Maurie finally asked.

This time I decided not to answer.

Despite my skepticism, he did actually drive me to a police station. I got out of the car and walked up to Maurie's window. "Can you come inside with me? Drive us back to the neighborhood?" I asked.

"I'm sorry—I can only drive you away, not back. You always come by yourself."

"What? I don't even know where that place is!" I shouted.

"I will see you again soon," he said, and before I could do anything, he was already driving off.

---

The police were no help at all. Even with the picture I had and Maurie's card, they simply laughed at me. I mean, my story did sound weird, but it was all true. They kept luring me to that place, and I didn't understand how.

So I figured I needed more evidence to show them that they were taking me, which was why I set up a camera.

This time, only two weeks passed before I woke up in the other home again.

But this time I wasn't woken up by sunlight. It was dark when I opened my eyes, and it took a moment for me to realize I wasn't in my own bed again.

I shot up, cold sweat running down my back, my hands shaking. And that was when I saw her for the first time.

A woman was sitting on the green chair, which in this light looked more black than green. I recognized her blond hair, but other than that, she didn't resemble the woman in the photo very much. Her skin was like porcelain, not the color but the texture. It was skin that looked as if it could break at any moment, and when she got up and walked toward me, I realized that parts of it were glued together. The hair was glued on as well. She moved and looked as if she were trying to mimic a human.

"Wh—" I tried to speak but swallowed my words.

"You are awake, my friend," the voice spoke, but her mouth hardly moved. "We were not meant to meet just yet. I am not ready," she giggled, "but at least it is dark."

My breathing quickened. If only I could bring myself to move, I could probably take her. I mean, I could probably even break her, but my body wouldn't move.

"Why am I here?" I finally said.

"Because every person needs a friend." She tilted her head and looked at me as if I was the one out of place. "Now go back to sleep. Everything is perfectly all right, my dear." She stood right next to me and caressed my face with her long nails.

The next day I woke up in the same bed, without Caroline but with scratch marks on my face.

I went to the window again. This time Margie was painting her walls. I almost went downstairs to talk to her again until I saw the other person. Inside her home, behind a window, stood a man. A little younger than her, probably, but not by much. Our eyes met, and his looked just like mine. Full of fear.

I ran downstairs and right toward the front door, ignoring the new photos in the frames. As always, Caroline was nowhere to be found, but I was thankful for that.

I crossed the street and shouted, "Who is that inside your house?"

"Tony! Dear, you've become quite rude. That is my brother. He is visiting for a year."

"Can I talk to him?"

She smiled, but it didn't look sincere. "Not yet, but *when* you come to live here for good, we'd love to have you over."

I turned around and went back to the house. I tried to look for clues, anything really, about what this place was and who those people were, but all I found were furniture and decorations that looked as if Caroline was creating a home for the two of us. In the kitchen, there were two of everything. Cups, plates, chairs for the dining table. Same in the bathroom: two toothbrushes, hair combs, towels.

She was preparing.

I almost ran outside again until I found a telephone. It was an old one, with a cord and everything.

I immediately tried to call the police, but it wouldn't ring. I couldn't call any friends because I didn't know their numbers by heart.

I did, however, memorize Maurie's number, just in case, and of course, he picked up.

"Can you bring me home?"

---

"Why do I keep ending up here? Please, just fucking tell me. Maurie, please," I begged.

He hesitated, as always, but to my surprise, he finally spoke. "I can't say why she chose you or how she found you. Only that she looked for a friend and that friend is now you."

"What about that man in Margie's house? Her brother?"

"Dear Margie has her very own way of finding visitors. Some family tradition. You see, everyone in the neighborhood has their own ways of doing things," he said, leaving me with even more questions.

"What do I do?" I asked, my voice full of desperation.

"From my experience, there is not much you can do. All I know is that I drive you home, but in time that home will not be the one you used to know."

---

My head was aching, my body felt empty, but I was back in my own bedroom again. I've already bought a plane ticket to go to my sister's, far away, hoping that will help.

Inside, however, I know that it won't. Especially after I looked at the camera footage. Nobody ever came here to take me. I got up and left on my own.

I don't know how, but they are slowly taking over my thoughts and actions.

And soon everything will be perfectly all right.

# MY BROTHER DIED BUT HE NEVER LEFT ME

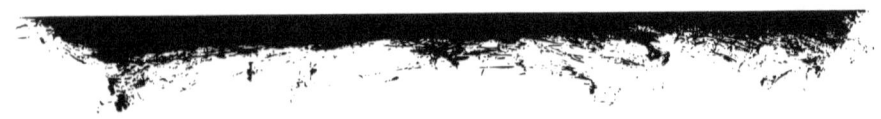

I was never a dumb child, but we only thrive in the context of the possibilities we are given. And I only had the context of a world so different that it shouldn't even exist. Of course, back then it all seemed normal to me.

We had the perfect life. The colorful, bright senses that you normally enjoy as a child before the world turns a few shades darker, or even entirely gray. Before the overstimulation of emotion turns into apathy. That was the biggest fear any of us ever had: losing the will to enjoy life. For anyone in Red Row, the world stayed just as it does to the eye of a child. Everything was bright and beautiful in our suburban town, and that's all you really need to be happy.

At least that's what they said.

As for all the suicides, they were another thing we grew accustomed to. Or something we accepted as perfectly normal from the start.

Red Row was a place bursting with emotion, and if you had none, I suppose you didn't belong.

It was the overall explanation I received after my brother took his life.

He jumped from Red Row Bridge, deep into the lake, and all we had left of him was a note, explaining that he didn't care and that he didn't belong. For everyone else, that was how the story of Miles Millstone ended. Some cried a little—sadness was fine in moderation—and after that, he was quickly forgotten. He was eighteen when it happened, and I was seventeen. When he died, we had a big celebration. That is probably what I remember most because it was so entirely the opposite of anything my brother ever was. But it was a tradition in Red Row.

Mum filled bright red balloons with helium, and each guest wrote a card about what they loved most about Miles. We filled our home with them. In the garden, people were drinking and chatting while Dad was burning hot dogs on the barbecue. Miles wasn't exactly popular, but still, our garden was completely packed with people whose faces had big smiles plastered on them.

Don't get me wrong, they weren't excited that he was gone. While Miles wasn't popular, he was also not despised but rather ignored. He was basically an extra on a film set. The smiles were forced, and so were some of the occasional tears. All the emotion was wrong and unfitting, but that was how the people of Red Row said goodbye when there was another suicide. And in their minds, Miles was just that: another reminder to stay happy.

When evening came, all the balloons were brought outside. Every person attached their card, and then they were let go, off into the air to say the last goodbye to another lost member of Red Row.

And just like that, Miles was gone and forgotten.

To everyone but me.

---

After the last goodbye, or the last hooray, my brother was gone and everything in Red Row went back to being just fantastic.

I don't think I even realized the loss of sensation, the lack of emotion, the depression I had slipped into. That was something nonexistent in Red Row. I had never learned about the possibility of feeling less or nothing at all. And the less I felt, the better I became at masking. When I couldn't find the energy to go to a party or hang out with friends, I would simply make up an excuse, telling them I was busy doing something even more brilliant than whatever they had in mind. My parents were often at work and didn't notice how much time I would spend being alone at home, doing absolutely nothing but staring at the wall, sleeping, or going from eating anything I could to nothing at all.

People described me as charismatic, fun, and outgoing. The complete opposite of my late brother. I don't even think I realized how close and similar I actually was to Miles until I started finding his notes.

Shortly after the funeral, my parents had filled boxes with all the things my brother had owned. Every sign of my brother's existence was neatly folded and stuffed in cardboard boxes. Everything he owned was bleak, and after all, that did not belong. I remember wondering how an entire life can fit into something as boring and irrelevant as cardboard.

"What are we gonna do with his stuff? Bring it to the attic?" I asked.

Mum laughed. "Why would we do that? It's just junk. We'll throw it out."

"Junk?" I asked, surprised at the carelessness in her voice.

"Rubbish, trash, unnecessary clutter," she responded with a half-smile and wide-open eyes.

"Shouldn't we go through it? Maybe he had a diary or something else that would give us a clue as to why he would do something so horrific." My voice was getting louder and shakier with each word. In theory, I knew that my parents were acting just in the typical Red Row way, not letting anything taint their bright lives, but I knew that this was simply not right.

My father got up from the ground next to a box, moving extremely slowly. My father wasn't an old man, but I remember how it looked as if each of his bones might break at any second. But then he stood over me, tall and scary with a smile on his face that simply looked wrong and unfitting.

"That boy was a waste. He never belonged, and now that he is gone, he will stay gone. Understood?" he shouted.

I'd never seen my father this angry.

"You better watch out, or you'll end up buried, too. Your flesh slowly eaten by the worms. Do you want that?" my mother added as if I wasn't feeling uneasy enough already.

"We can make that happen, no problem. Or are you gonna be good and happy and deserving of this wonderful life?" Dad asked.

"Screw both of you," I responded.

That was the first and only time my mother ever slapped me in the face. I was filled with rage at that moment. I remember it so vividly because while the entire moment was awful, I hadn't felt such strong emotions since my brother died.

It was the first time I went up to my room and cried. A part of me thought I would never stop until I was distracted by the bright light coming from outside. It was night already, but our garden was lit up in a warm, yellow light.

When I looked outside, I noticed what was going on. My parents were burning all the contents of the cardboard boxes.

The image of them standing behind that fire, smiling while they burned away their son's life, will forever be ingrained in my mind.

There was only one thing that survived the fire.

Miles's denim jacket that I had taken from his room the day we got the news about his death. I put it on and curled up in my bed.

---

They didn't notice that I'd kept the jacket. I suppose they had forgotten about him altogether or at least made themselves forget. Maybe I would have, too, slowly but surely. However, Miles made sure I wouldn't.

The first message from him was inside one of the jacket pockets. It was a handwritten note that said:

*Don't believe what they say, it wasn't a choice.*

My hands were shaking while I kept rereading that sentence. Did it mean what I thought it did?

---

Months passed, and I didn't find any more clues as to what happened to my brother. During that time, two more suicides occurred, and nobody was even thinking about Miles anymore. When I would wake up in the morning to my parents' laughter as they sat happily at the kitchen table, I wanted to puke.

The other two deaths happened only a few days apart. A man hung himself in his bedroom, and days later his wife did the same. To the people, it was a relief; they could hold two funerals at once, which saved them the hassle of buying more food for the party. The funeral was eerily similar to my brother's, and I felt dissociated the entire time. All the voices surrounding me just sounded like noise. At least four people came up to me to ask why I was acting so odd, and I couldn't even find the motivation to answer them or fake a smile.

On our way home, my parents kept picking fights with me, but I simply ignored them. All I wanted was to lock myself in my room and put on the denim jacket that was slowly losing his scent.

I'd left the note inside it, and every time I would put on the jacket, I would read it again.

That was what I was about to do that night, but to my surprise, the note had something else written on it now.

*Max. You need to be careful. They are watching. Act fine.*

My heart was beating so fast that I thought my chest might break open. I wore the jacket before we left, and my parents couldn't have been here as we had left together.

And on top of it all, it looked like his handwriting.

I had never been scared of my parents before; the only time that came close to that was the night of the fire, but now I couldn't believe I was wondering whether they had murdered their son.

But another part of me had a spark of hope that he might be alive. And hope was something I hadn't felt in a really long time.

---

More months passed, but this time I felt more active than ever before. I needed to be a part of the community if I wanted to understand it, so I started being social again. It took a while to force myself to do so, and it didn't always feel great, but the curiosity I felt had given me quite the push.

"Wonderful afternoon, neighbor. How's it going?" Mr. Anders called from next door when I walked out of the house that day.

"It's going great!" I called out as excitedly as I could. "How about yourself?"

"Oh, just fantastic!"

He was watering the plants on his lawn, or rather drowning them, but he didn't seem to care. He didn't care that his cousin had died just a week ago, either.

"My niece is giving birth soon, so what does it matter?" he joked back then.

The door to his house opened, and his son came outside. Benji was in the same year as Miles, but he was the complete opposite of my brother. He was president of at least four clubs, was friends with pretty much everyone, and never had anything negative to say about anyone. My parents adored him. When we were little, Benji, Miles, and I would sometimes play together, but that felt forever ago.

"Hey, Maxy, what are you up to?" He walked up to the tap and turned it off.

"Just going to the mall to get some guitar strings," I said and then with a smile added, "I'm just feeling like playing some music."

"Awesome, mind if I join?"

I couldn't think of anything I'd want less, but I nodded and lied about how wonderful that would be.

---

"Doesn't it kinda suck that people don't appreciate how good life can be?" he said out of nowhere. I'd never heard him say *suck* before, which was probably even more surprising than the question. The question seemed rude, too, considering I knew for a fact that he was speaking about my brother.

"You know, I don't even think I was ever sick before. Do you? Nobody is poor or hungry. We live in paradise. What more could there be to life?" he continued.

"Nothing, it's great," I mumbled.

Benji stopped walking, and I swear that his face turned serious for a second. "Well, then why are you like this? People can tell if you're not appreciative, you know."

I frowned for a second but smoothed it away quickly. "Why the sudden interest in my life, Benji?" I couldn't even hide the cynicism in my voice.

"Oh, I care about everyone! And I just don't want to see more people leaving us, you know?"

"Right."

"Besides. You'll turn eighteen soon. You'll basically be a real member of society then. That's huge."

I hadn't even thought about my upcoming birthday. "Yeah, that's pretty crazy."

Benji nodded. "Oh shoot, I just remembered I promised to pick up my cousin from the doctor's. You mind if I don't come all the way to the mall with you?"

I didn't care for him to come at all; walking next to each other was annoying enough. "Of course not, buddy, go ahead."

He came in for a hug. His face was so close that I could feel his breath, and then he started whispering, almost inaudibly. "We know you're faking it. You won't be safe for long." He took a step back, winked at me, and turned around to leave.

I couldn't shake off the goosebumps until I made it to the mall.

---

When I went back home, I was still thinking about Benji and wondered if he had something to do with the death of my brother. When I saw the light from his window and him standing right behind it, I quickly looked away and made my way inside our home.

My room had been locked, and the jacket was placed neatly right at the spot where I had left it, but sure enough, there was a new note.

*I know I didn't show it very well, but I have always cared about you.*

So far, I had tried to think of logical explanations. Dead people can't leave notes, after all. Something awfully strange had been happening since his death, and I was pretty sure my brother was trying to warn me.

---

On the day of my eighteenth birthday, I was tapped out. I had spent all the energy I had to act like the perfect Red Row resident, but it was all getting too much. I tried to think about Miles, I tried to be critical of everything happening without making anyone suspicious, but eventually, my mind couldn't do it anymore. I would wake up in the morning without a single thought going through my head, where there had been more than I could count before. It was as if I had used up everything I had.

When my parents came into my room with a big cake full of frosting and a letter on a tray, I couldn't even focus on them.

"I'm just as old as he was," I whispered.

"Who are you talking about?" my father asked, but I was too scared to answer. I swallowed.

"Thanks, Mum and Dad. This is great," I said, but the corners of my mouth wouldn't move up.

Mum looked at me with disgust in her eyes. "We knew you were a waste, too."

"You had so much potential," Dad added.

"What are you talking about?"

Mum sat down at the edge of my bed. Her long nails were digging into the wooden frame. "Look, sweetie. I know this might sound harsh. We love you with all our hearts, but we understand that not everyone can appreciate it when they're given everything."

"It's not your fault," my father continued. He tried to sit as well, but his bones were moving even stranger than the other day. "Being born in Red Row is a blessing. Now that you're an adult, you need to understand that you have a responsibility. For yourself and future generations. If you can't appreciate the best life, what else is there?"

They sounded so sincere that their words were somehow getting through to me. If this was the best there was, how could I ever feel better somewhere else?

"Have you ever considered that maybe you are the problem?"

---

I didn't even remember planning the party, but all my friends, all our neighbors, and even more people were there. Everyone had brought presents, and they were in such a cheerful mood.

Until I came down the stairs.

All heads immediately turned, and all eyes were glued to me. At first, I thought they might recognize that I was wearing the denim jacket.

Nobody said a word. It looked as if they weren't just looking at me but observing me.

"Are you enjoying the life we've given you?" a voice that didn't belong to either my mother or my father said.

I nodded, unsure how else to react.

"Do you want to leave Red Row?" another person asked while everyone else stayed still, watching me without blinking.

I shook my head.

"Splendid! Because you can't."

"None of us can!" someone else chimed in, and everyone started laughing at the same time. A laugh that sounded even more forced than usual.

"Well, there is one way to leave... but only if you truly do not belong," Mr. Anders said and mimed hanging himself with an invisible rope.

I ignored all their wrong faces and fake smiles and ran right through the front door.

---

It was cold that night, and I couldn't stop shivering. I had never felt that way before, but it didn't stop me from running. And I didn't even know where to go. The only thing I was wondering about was why Miles hadn't left me a note today of all days.

I stopped eventually. I can't say for sure why or what I was doing at that moment. Everything was happening filtered. I lost awareness. I lost the bit of free will I thought I had.

It was getting colder and colder until I suddenly felt a warm hand on my shoulder.

"Don't," a voice whispered.

In the state I was in, I was sure it could only be my brother.

"Miles—" I slowly turned around and immediately tried to back away, but he was now holding my wrist tightly, so tight that it was painful.

It wasn't Miles. Miles was dead.

"Let me go, Benji!" I shouted, but he didn't. Instead, he pulled me closer.

"Max, don't you know where you are?"

And I swear until that second, I had not been aware of my surroundings. I looked around and finally saw the water underneath me and heard the wind. I was standing at Red Row Bridge, at the place where Miles had jumped from.

"What is happening to me?" I cried.

"I'm sorry, Max. I tried to help, but they use *their* eyes to watch us, to make sure everything stays right. I tried to hide those letters because I thought you wouldn't listen to me, but if you thought it was Miles—"

It had been him all this time. I opened my mouth but couldn't bring out a word.

"Whoever or whatever created Red Row, it's not our people. Not really." He was quiet for a second. "It's the fact that we are born here. Things are great until you don't appreciate them, and when you don't, Red Row has a way to punish you. That's what happened to Miles."

I looked down again, at the railing, at the water.

"I know what you've been feeling lately, because I have felt it, too. And so did Miles."

"Are you joking? You are the complete opposite of who he was."

"We were a lot closer than you might think. We figured things out together. Your brother didn't give up. He never left voluntarily. We helped each other to stay aware... I know how crazy it sounds, but it only really happened when we got older. We had to focus so hard to make our brains work. We started planning how to get away, but Miles said he wouldn't go without you. But you weren't an adult yet, they were watching you too closely, and then—"

"And then he died," I finished his sentence.

"I thought about trying to leave anyway, but I owed it to him to take care of you."

Just then, I noticed the car behind him.

"Get in. We don't have much time. They'll be looking for your corpse soon."

---

I thought my skin would tear open. Every part of my body was hurting. I kept screaming, shouting at Benji to stop the car we were sitting in, the one he stole from his dad, but he kept pushing through. Leaving Red Row wasn't right; it didn't feel right; it was excruciating pain. I thought he had tricked me. I was sure he had. Maybe he had killed my brother, too. I couldn't breathe.

"You fucking bastard, stop!" I shouted, but Benji only pushed the gas even harder.

*We will die. We will die.*

The thoughts in my mind didn't sound like they belonged to me, but then finally there was a second of silence.

I have no idea how Benji was able to fight through it; he must have been in such pain, too, but he somehow did it. He got us out of Red Row, and I could finally, or maybe for the first time ever, think clearly. I woke up from a trance, from a constant state in which something in my mind was fighting until there was no energy left. But now it felt different.

I understood that we might have a chance at living.

And for Miles, I would make sure to take it.

# THERE MUST BE SOMETHING IN OUR WATER THAT TURNS ALL THE PEOPLE ODD

When the first corpse was pulled out of Velveton Lake, it was as if it had brought an infection that spread through town. People were surprised; they were scared and nervous. Nobody understood who this person was, who had died in the lake or been killed and disposed of in the water. Some were scared that a murderer might be among us, one of the unsuspecting residents of this town who possibly wasn't entirely innocent.

I couldn't tell you who that dead person was or where they came from. Nobody in our town could tell you, and if there were any who could, they never would.

We weren't told anything, either, when the other bodies followed. It became normal to us. A good thing, even. There was a lot of whispering about those people with unfamiliar faces. Though when the people of our town realized that none of the corpses came from this place, that not one of the dead bodies was identified as a former resident, they suddenly weren't that scared anymore. Especially when, for reasons that were unclear, life became more and more prosperous in our little town.

I was young when it all started, only six or seven, and I had no idea what any of it meant, nor did I have a grip on the concept of death. But of course, in a small town like ours, news traveled fast. Other kids had older siblings, and even if we didn't understand it, we knew about it. When all the adults acted as if the death of those strangers was no issue to us, we children started believing that, in fact, it couldn't be as terrible as our guts told us it was.

A few years passed, I grew from a child to a teenager, and the occurrences became far less frequent, though they never stopped. During that first year, around a dozen bodies were found. Now they found maybe one a year, and as always, it was the face of a person nobody in town could know.

I never understood why no measures were taken, why nobody from the outside was informed.

"That's because their faces don't belong to anyone we know," my mother would say.

My parents couldn't have cared less about who those people were, as our family was one of the many whose lives improved after the appearance of the dead strangers. My parents owned a restaurant that never got many visitors. Every now and then, strangers from the surrounding towns would pay us a visit, but not very often. I suppose people around here either didn't have much money or simply didn't enjoy themselves very much. We were on the brink of bankruptcy quite often, though I was too young back then to understand what it meant. All I could tell was that my parents were fighting more often than not and that almost nothing in our home was ever fixed.

Then the shift came with the water, and suddenly not only did our town change, but the entire region around us did too. Suddenly people were doing much better, acting far happier, and they were so much more active. The restaurant business boomed, just like the others. The darkness that came with the dead somehow awoke the motivation in the people here. My parents never fought anymore; they loved their work and our community.

So yes, as long as we didn't know whose faces belonged to the dead people, we were quite all right with them appearing, as it meant that our lives and our town were suddenly much more colorful, as if a paintbrush had gone over all the houses, streets, and faces.

I realize this sounds morbid and cynical, but it wasn't like our residents killed those people. At least as far as I knew. It was a mere coincidence that we had been chosen or that we lived at the very spring where the oddity arose.

As my friends and I grew older, so did our curiosity. When we turned sixteen, we were able to leave town more often and see what life looked like in the places surrounding us. My friend Mike was the first one to get a driver's license, and we would get out of town every now and then on the weekends. We'd go to the cinema in Marden or check out the mall in Watton, which meant that we weren't bound to the town we lived in all the time. It meant we got out, saw other people, and talked to those who didn't grow up in our town of corpses. It is only now, however, that I've grown old enough to understand that all those other places we visited from time to time were certainly not a great reference point. I only understand now that all the towns in this region I grew up in were peculiar, each in its own way.

I suppose it had something to do with our water. We all got it from the same spring, but it traveled; it changed and shifted. But we, here in my hometown called Velveton, were right at the source and therefore were getting the extra-special treatment.

We got to live happier, healthier, and luckier.

For me, though, my vision changed entirely on the night when my friends and I went camping by the lake.

We were just coming back from a trip to the cinema in Marden. It was me, my best friend Mike with his boyfriend Evan, and Evan's sister, Zoe. The four of us had been friends since elementary school, but Mike and Evan had only gotten closer a few months ago, so it was still all fresh and lovey-dovey. It also meant that Mike agreed to anything Evan suggested. It was the reason we even went to the cinema to watch some stupid kid's movie. And it was the reason the two of them convinced us all to go camping at Velveton Lake.

"Why the hell would we want to sleep next to corpses, Evan?" Zoe asked.

He shrugged. "Don't you guys wanna see, at least once, if these are really *strangers* or if the old people here are just lying to us?"

I didn't want to agree right away, but he was making a point. The thing was, people had left our town; we were not bound to it or anything. If someone had gotten murdered or had disappeared, we wouldn't even know. I still didn't like the idea of sleeping by the lake. I'd only ever gone there as a kid, and my parents stopped taking me there after the first body was found. Ever since then, and even though we had been living with this for a decade now, the lake creeped me out. I didn't want to be the next person pulled out.

But eventually, curiosity and boredom overrode our fear, and we decided to all go home, pack up some stuff, get food, and then head to Velveton Lake.

---

I had just gotten out of the house with my backpack and my sleeping bag when my neighbor, Mr. Jones, greeted me from his lawn. Marcus Jones had lived next to us for ages with his wife, Sandra, and their cocker spaniel, Buddy. Mr. Jones was quite all right; he even helped my dad build a treehouse for me when I was little.

"Going on a trip, Jo?" he asked while combing the grass with a hair comb and snipping off little bits by putting his fingers between the scissors and the grass.

Mr. Jones was a hairdresser, the best one in town, and he had the prettiest front yard in all of Velveton. After cutting the grass, he pulled out green nail polish and started painting some parts of the lawn. This would have been a peculiar sight if I weren't so used to my neighbors. Mr. Jones was actually one of the more normal ones. Like I said, the shift with the water turned our people a little odd. Some more than others. Everyone was extremely friendly, though, so I didn't mind if they acted weird.

"Yeah, we're sleeping over by the lake," I finally said. To be honest, I was hoping he'd talk me out of it, play the father figure since my parents were gone for the weekend.

"Let me guess, you kids wanna see a body?" He raised an eyebrow and grinned.

"Uhm, well," I started mumbling but was interrupted by Mike calling for me from the car. "I guess I gotta go," I said.

Mr. Jones smiled. "You know there hasn't been a new body in the lake this entire year. If you do get to see one, you should consider yourselves lucky. Have a good time with your friends!"

Nobody in their right mind would have gone camping by the death lake, and no parents should have allowed it, but well, most people here weren't in their right mind.

The weather was great—it almost always was in Velveton—and Mike even brought some beers that his brother got for us. If it weren't for the lake, this would have been a great summer evening.

Mike and Evan put up our tent while Zoe and I went looking for firewood before it got dark.

"Evan's been acting so weird lately," Zoe said while picking up some sticks from the ground after we'd walked far enough away from our little campsite.

"Lately?" I joked, but her face stayed serious.

"I don't understand his obsession with seeing a dead person. That's kind of creepy, right?" she asked, and I was glad to hear those words. When it came to death, our people were a bit too jaded and insensitive. They didn't see death as a bad thing because in some cases it brought them luck.

"Yeah, it's creepy, but it's not just him, right?"

She shrugged. "Doesn't make it better."

I agreed. "But why did you wanna come to the lake, then?" I asked.

"I don't think it's right, but I know my brother. He would have done this anyway. I'd rather be here if he goes crazy."

I chuckled, thinking she was joking, but again her face stayed dead serious.

And that was when we heard the screams. Screams of fear that sounded like they were coming from Mike.

Zoe and I immediately started running. The sky was getting darker, but luckily Zoe had brought a flashlight. As we got closer to the spot next to the lake where our tent was, all I could make out was one shape on the ground and another pushing him down.

When we got closer and they saw our light, the person pushing the other down started waving.

I grabbed Zoe by the arm.

I knew what was going through both our heads. Evan had lost it.

Before I could say anything else, Zoe had started running toward her brother, and I stood there in the darkness.

I swallowed my fear and followed.

"What the hell are you doing?" Zoe shouted while running.

"Don't worry, kids, all I gotta do is cut his face off. I bet that will work!"

That wasn't Evan speaking. Evan was the one lying on the ground.

We were finally close enough to really understand what was happening.

Mike was sitting on the ground next to the tent. We weren't able to see him earlier from our angle. His eyes were wide with shock, and he was shaking and screaming because of Mr. Jones.

My neighbor, Marcus Jones, was the one pushing Evan down while trying to carve into his face with a sharp knife. He didn't stop even when he saw us.

"It won't take long, don't you worry!" He laughed.

Zoe didn't even stop to think; she started running and tackled Marcus even though he had a knife in his hand. While my entire body was shaking and all the alarms in my head were going off, I followed my friend. Together we managed to keep him down until Mike finally got out of his shock and helped get the knife from his hand.

Evan had passed out, but aside from the cuts that would soon become scars, he seemed okay.

"What the actual fuck, Mr. Jones?" I shouted, still trembling with fear and anger. My own neighbor, whom I liked and trusted, had just tried to kill one of my best friends.

"Haven't you kids noticed how long it's been! I had to do something. For hell's sake, I have to start using polish on my lawn and flowers because they won't grow perfectly on their own anymore! My poor Buddy is sick and not getting better, and people are starting to get moody again."

"What?" Zoe whispered.

"It's been too long. No bodies have been in the lake for almost a year. Things are not right. It's going downhill, and you don't notice because you're still so young, but Velveton needs the dead to survive!"

"So you tried to kill my brother?" Zoe shouted and pushed her knee into his chest.

"I know it's not right. He isn't the right kind, but I thought if I cut off his face, well... Oh, I'm sorry, I knew it wasn't entirely right, but don't worry, his face will fix up real quick if he uses our water. But we still need to do something about the lake. We need a new corpse. It's important. Don't you understand?"

I got up from the ground. Mr. Jones didn't have a knife anymore, and there were three of us against him. Our highest priority now was to get Evan to a doctor. I went around him to lift Evan up by the shoulders when my shoes slowly started filling up with water. I hadn't even realized how close we were to the lake. I supposed Mr. Jones had planned to push Evan in as soon as he had cut off his face. I tried to ignore the water and grabbed Evan under his arms.

"Mike, get his legs," I commanded, when suddenly something touched my leg. I looked down, expecting some seaweed or sticks, but instead, my eyes met something I will never forget.

My heart started racing. "What the actual fuck is this?"

I was looking down at a body, a body that had washed up while we were trying to help Evan. When I saw that creature, I realized why Mr. Jones was trying to carve out Evan's face.

This corpse had no face.

The face wasn't cut off. It simply didn't exist. Where the eyes, nose, and mouth were supposed to be, this thing was blank. Empty. It had hair on its head, and its hands and legs looked exactly like a human's. That was all we could make out, since the rest of its body was dressed in a white gown. It also looked fresh. Not like someone who had been dead for a while.

"A new body," Mr. Jones whispered. "We are blessed after all," he cried.

I tried to speak, but no words came out. Even now I try to tell myself that it wasn't real, that it was just some extremely realistic doll, but deep down I know it's not true. That creature was certainly real, and I suppose we are lucky we only ever see the dead ones.

But to be honest, I didn't know who to be more scared of: the creature that had just touched my leg or my neighbor who was ready to kill my best friend.

---

Nobody in town cared what Marcus had tried to do. Not even Zoe and Evan's parents—can you believe that? They thought he did what he had to do and that maybe his heroic act had something to do with the new body finally showing up. The adults knew. They knew that the corpses didn't belong to humans like us, which was why they were never scared.

The people of this town had a very wicked understanding of the world.

I still don't know who the bodies belong to or why they have no faces. All I know is that ever since our town, and specifically our lake, was chosen for the faceless, life here became much better. Maybe it's some sort of payment.

Because it is not without consequences. There is something in our water, and it makes all the people here and in the towns around it peculiar. In Velveton, they appear blessed; in some towns, they enjoy killing; and in others, they are trapped.

I know all of this because I left. And I suppose because I have been gone for some years now, my mind is a bit clearer. I don't crave the perfect life of Velveton, not with the cost it brings. Though for some reason, I can't seem to get too far away. I moved to a nearby town, close to Velveton and also weird, but in a different way. I wish I could leave for good, but I can't. My body craves the water.

# SOMEBODY KEEPS SENDING ME THE SAME TEXT EVERY NIGHT

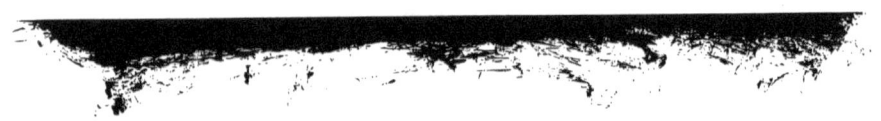

**D**id you lock the door?

    The first time those words appeared on my screen, my entire body immediately tensed up.

I was alone, in my studio apartment, lying in bed.

The worst part about living in a studio apartment on the seventh floor was that if somebody did come in, there'd be nowhere to run.

Without even thinking, I jumped out of bed and ran straight toward the door.

It was locked. Of course, it was locked.

Just a moment after I checked, I heard someone outside, softly humming a song. I held my breath, listening to see if they came closer to my door, but then I heard a key turn. Next door.

It was just the neighbor.

---

The next morning, all the paranoia and fear were gone as soon as I looked out my window at the lively town underneath.

The sun was shining, the roofs of the houses were colorful, and the lawns were nice and green. There were children walking to school and people driving down the roads on their bikes or going inside the bakeries and shops.

*This must be the safest place in the world.*

Even though I was looking down on them, I knew that I was at the bottom of the chain. New in town but ready to climb. At least that was what I had in mind when I moved here. Unfortunately, everyday life and a lack of discipline often got in the way.

I often imagined owning one of those beautiful homes. I was told that if I worked hard enough, I would be able to afford one of them soon enough. But I wasn't so sure anymore. Lately, I'd been thinking of moving away, maybe going back to my parents.

Right as that thought crossed my mind, my doorbell rang.

Joe was there to pick me up. He rang my doorbell every morning to pick me up for work. We both had jobs at the local newspaper, and after realizing that we lived on the same street, we started walking together every morning. Not because we were terribly close or anything like that. Joe was nice and all, but I think we only started walking together because we were both too polite to say that we'd rather be alone in the morning. We hardly ever got past the most basic small talk.

I knew exactly four things about Joe.

He was sixty-one, which was more than twice my age.

He had been married to a man named Marc for twenty years but wasn't anymore.

He loved cats but didn't want to get one because his apartment was too small.

The fourth was more of a guess. He moved here to start over. Like me.

It was Wednesday, so we'd already used up most of the regular small talk this week. The weather had been the same all week. There hadn't been anything particularly spectacular in the news. And I hadn't met many more people.

I think Joe pitied me because I was young enough to start over but seemed to be awful at making friends. This might be another assumption, though; our conversations never got that deep.

Maybe that was the reason I showed him the text.

He frowned for a split second but calmed his face just as fast. "Did you tell anyone about this?"

I shook my head. "No, maybe it was sent to me by accident."

He nodded. "Seems likely. Don't let it freak you out too much."

He smiled as a kind father does, but instead of calming me down, it felt like someone had punched my gut.

---

The workday went as always. I spent most of my day spell-checking articles, never writing any of my own.

Joe had to work longer that day, so I walked home alone. My dinner was already waiting on my doorstep for me. I ate, watched some television, and went to bed.

It was a quiet, usual evening until the clock turned to 11:20, and I received the same text as the night before.

**Did you lock the door?**

This time I decided to text back.

**Who is this?**

The response came after a few seconds.

**Phillip.**

My stomach turned, and the phone slipped from my hand.

Phillip was the name of my little brother. He had been dead for two years.

It felt too absurd while simultaneously too real. Of course, this wasn't my dead brother texting me, but just reading his name was enough to shatter me entirely from the inside. I'd never gotten over what happened to him.

My little brother was fifteen years younger than me. When he died, he was only seven. I was twenty-three then and had moved back home temporarily after college.

Tears formed in the corners of my eyes. I shoved my nails deep inside the palms of my hands, a nervous habit I'd formed.

Maybe someone was pranking me. Maybe a different Phillip was texting me. Or maybe I was hallucinating.

But Joe had seen the other text, so it had to be real.

I went back to the door and rattled it like crazy. I knew it was locked, that the door wouldn't open, but I couldn't stop trying for some reason.

Finally, exhausted, I left the door alone and went to bed. Plagued by nightmares of my little brother, it simultaneously felt like the longest and shortest night.

---

The next morning when I walked up to Joe, I noticed he wasn't alone. A young man was standing with him, chatting with him animatedly. I even caught a smile on Joe's face.

"Good morning, May. You look terrible," Joe said.

"Didn't sleep well," I responded. I looked at the other guy, but he didn't look back. He was quite handsome, but his eyes looked just as bloodshot as mine that day. And it looked like he had some bruises on his arm.

"Got another text?"

I nodded. "I'm not sure it's by accident anymore."

"What kind of text?" the new guy suddenly asked and quickly added, "Sorry, don't mean to be nosy."

"This is Louie. I met him yesterday. He just started working at the printer," Joe explained.

"I'm also your next-door neighbor, I think. At least I was told the girl next door worked at the paper, too. Did you make all that noise yesterday?" He laughed nervously.

"I thought my new neighbor was a woman. I heard her humming in the hallway."

Louie's face turned as red as Joe's hair. "Yeah, no, that was just a visitor."

Joe and I exchanged a quick look, but then the three of us started walking to work.

After a few minutes of silence, Louie asked, "So what is this whole text thing about?"

I started chewing my lip, wondering if I should tell him.

"Somebody keeps texting May if she locked her door," Joe answered for me. When did this guy get talkative?

"That's odd." Louie scratched his head. "It's always locked, right?"

"Of course. Every night."

I planned on walking home alone after work, but then I heard someone call my name.

It was Louie.

"Wanna walk home together? Joe told me to catch up with you. He has to work longer."

"You two seem to get along quite well," I said. I didn't even mean to, but I think I sounded slightly sarcastic.

"Afraid I'm gonna steal your best friend?" Louie joked, and I actually had to laugh.

"Kinda."

Louie smiled. "He told me I remind him of his son. He was around my age."

"Was?" I asked.

Louie nodded. "Car crash. Joe made it. His husband and son didn't."

I felt a sting inside my chest. Poor Joe. "Was he the one driving?" I asked.

He nodded again.

"Was it his fault?"

Louie shrugged. "We all have a past, right?"

I didn't say anything until he suddenly grabbed my arm. The entire atmosphere shifted in a second.

"What's yours, May?"

I looked into his eyes, and all of the former friendliness was gone. I wasn't sure if what I was seeing was anger or fear.

I tried to free my arm, but he wouldn't let go. We were only a few houses away from home, and I suddenly did not like the idea of us walking in there together.

He probably caught the look of fear on my face because he suddenly let go. "I'm sorry," he whispered and looked around the street. There were no other people outside. "I just... I know I'm not supposed to ask, but that text you get about the door is so weird. Why would they ask you if the door is locked if they're the ones locking it? And why are they locking it only at night? What is it we and the other people really do here in town? She comes to me almost every—"

Now I was the one grabbing his arm. "Stop talking."

---

We walked up to the seventh floor. Dinner was waiting at both of our doorsteps. I wouldn't have gone up with him, but I knew he wouldn't do anything.

None of us would.

That night I slept through the text but woke up when I heard someone scratching at my door from the outside.

"You didn't lock the door," I heard a familiar voice speak.

My body tensed up, and my breathing stopped.

The doorknob rattled.

*"You can call for help, but it will be too late. Somebody must die."*

I shivered.

"That's what the intruder said before opening the door and walking up to the little Phillip—"

"Stop!" I screamed and walked up to the door. "Why are you doing this to me?" I shouted and punched the door.

"WHY?"

Then I heard a loud bang from the wall behind me. It sounded like my neighbor was hitting his fists against it.

"Don't." I heard Louie's muffled voice from behind that wall, but I ignored him.

"I want to leave!" I shouted, and then I heard the lock turn from outside. The door opened, and in front of me stood a woman.

I didn't know her real name. She'd introduced herself as Ms. M. I'd met her many times before, and every time she looked calm and friendly. She was supposed to appear like a therapist, one you could trust.

But I knew it was just her shell.

She tilted her head.

"Oh, May, you'll never make progress like this. Where do you want to go?"

"Home. To my family," I cried.

"Oh, to your brother's grave and your parents who will forever rightfully blame you?"

She was right. There was no other place for me to go. This town was something out of a dream. A place that accepted anyone with nowhere to go. They provided you with an apartment and a job, and if you worked hard and fit in with the community, they gave you chances to grow and become even better.

"Do you remember what we told you when you moved here?"

I nodded. "I will never leave, and I will never disobey." I clenched my fist. "But why were you sending me those texts?"

"To remind you. We had a feeling you weren't happy. You weren't grateful. We wanted to remind you of your past."

My past.

I'd just been back from college for a short time. I wasn't ready to get serious about life yet. My parents were gone for the night and asked me to watch my brother.

I didn't think it would be a problem if I went over to my friend's house for just an hour. Phillip was fast asleep in bed.

I hadn't realized that I didn't lock the door before leaving.

"Did you make Louie ask me about that?"

Ms. M smiled. "I thought the two of you could connect. He's blaming himself for dead children as well." She chuckled.

I didn't respond to that. Whatever happened couldn't have really been Louie's fault because he would be in prison and not here. They wanted us to believe it was our fault. So we would stay.

"But he found us. And we are here to give all of you a second chance at life."

I took a deep breath. "I know. And I appreciate that."

When the citizens stayed long enough, they really got turned. When they moved into their houses, their brains were washed so thoroughly that Ms. M and the others in charge could do whatever they wanted with them. I realize how terrible it sounds. But when I came here, I really thought I didn't deserve a decent life. It was surreal enough to feel better than death.

"No, you don't. You know you can think about leaving. But you never really will leave. You will just make things a bit harder for us."

I swallowed. There was someone else in the hallway. Backup. She usually brought someone with her.

"Step one is easy. Me coming here, to talk to you. Sending you some silly texts. Step two is more physical. And step three is something you never want to witness. You can't use your second chance when you're buried underneath the town. Do you want to continue to step two?"

I shook my head. She was right. If I just did what I was supposed to, things went smoothly for me. I didn't have to worry about the regular things in life. I didn't have to buy my own food, make sure I had a job, or try hard to earn forgiveness. Everyone here had done something.

Everyone had a past.

As if she was reading my mind, she smiled once more and got ready to leave, but there was one thing I couldn't shake off.

"Ms. M, how do you know what the intruder said to my brother? Did you make that up?"

She turned around one more time. "May, I never lie, and I do not like questions."

# SOMETHING IS NOT RIGHT WITH THE NEW FAMILY

## Part 1

When you've lived somewhere long enough, you don't realize how strange it actually is. You believe what they tell you is normal.

And if you don't dig too deep, this town we live in appears heavenly. When you come to live in Agsbury, you sure are taken care of for the rest of your life. All the houses on all our streets are beautifully crafted in their own individual ways to make a family feel welcome and happy.

We are told this exact fact when we are assigned to help with a new house. It started out small many years ago. A tiny village with just the basic necessities, like a small grocery store, a school, and a doctor's office. But it has grown exponentially to a town with more than a thousand people.

I can't say exactly what it looked like in the beginning because that was way before I was even born. All I can say is that during the sixteen years of my life, I've enjoyed living here.

Every week we have a big market in the center of town where we can buy everything that our hearts desire. When the market isn't there, we have a number of shops and boutiques run by the people who live here. There's a cinema and a theater and different clubs you can join.

It rarely happens that a person or a family moves away from here, but when they do, their house is renovated or a new one is built.

During the last few months, I helped with the finishing touches of the newest house in our town. It is especially exciting to me as it filled the empty spot right next to ours, meaning we would get new neighbors soon.

I kept waiting and waiting to see who the new people would be. Every day when I came home from school, I checked if they were there yet. When the holidays started, I began spending significantly more time sitting by the window in my room, looking for a moving truck.

When the new family finally moved in, I completely missed it. My friend Jules had stayed over, and we had fallen asleep watching *The Grinch*.

We both woke up early in the morning from loud sounds and commotion coming from next door.

We both jumped up to look out the window, where we saw a few neighbors standing in front of the new house.

With Jules right behind me, I ran downstairs to the kitchen where my parents and my little brother were having breakfast.

Mom smiled when she saw me. "Good morning, you two! Our neighbors arrived, and I heard they have a son just your age!"

My dad, who was cooking some eggs and scraping the pan like crazy, didn't turn around or wish us good morning. He looked like a wreck.

Mom laughed when she caught me looking at him. "Your dad didn't get a minute of sleep."

Finally, Dad turned toward us. "What an inconvenience, moving into a new house in the middle of the night."

"Did you see them yet?" Jules asked.

"Not yet, but I was going to go over soon with a basket of muffins. You girls can join me if you like," Mom asked.

My dad shook his head. "Mary, maybe you should give them some time to settle in first?"

Jules looked disappointed, and for some reason, I felt the same way. I know it might sound weird what a big deal this is to all of us, but as I said before, Agsbury was a bit different. And new people in such a small town can change a lot.

Dad went to work, and we all ignored what he had said.

Mom had spent the morning baking muffins and filling a pretty wooden basket. She said we still had dozens of them in the basement from back when we moved here.

"So everyone is just gifting each other baskets back and forth?" Jules asked. "I saw a bunch of them at our place, too."

Jules had been my best friend ever since I could remember. She lived down the street and was almost like a sister to me.

My mom chuckled. "Well, it's not about the basket, it's about what's in it! And, well, about the gesture. We want to make the new family feel welcome."

---

The door was already open, but we still knocked. The house that I'd only seen empty was now filled with furniture, decorations, and at least six different baskets filled with muffins. Jules and I exchanged a look and tried not to laugh. I guess it wasn't about what's inside, either.

"Oh, hello!"

A woman my mother's age approached the door. She was wearing a yellow dress, and her black hair framed her face, which had at least three layers of makeup on it.

"Hi there! My name is Mary Lawrence. This is my daughter Charlie. We live right next door." My mom squeezed my shoulder. "And this is our dear friend Julia."

"How nice to meet you," the woman said with a bright smile. "My name is Helen Lester. Please, please come inside. My husband Anthony is just in the living room."

We followed her through the house, and I couldn't help but wonder how quickly they had furnished everything inside. When I was here, the whole house was still bare. How did they do all that in just one night?

Mr. Lester was sitting on the sofa staring at a blank television, motionless, but when he heard us approach, he quickly turned toward us, although he didn't stand up.

"Anthony, honey, these are our new neighbors. Mary, Julia, and," she took a short pause as if she had to remember my name, "and Charlie."

His serious face swiftly turned into a smile even bigger than his wife's, though I could swear I saw a twitch in there. "Good day!" he called out.

"Poor Anthony hurt his leg working in the house." Helen's smile turned into a dramatic frown.

"How unfortunate," my mom responded in a tone that sounded slightly judgmental, though I couldn't say why.

Jules and I stood behind her awkwardly that entire time until we heard a new voice calling hello into the house.

Another neighbor with a basket full of muffins.

---

"What a lovely couple, weren't they? Though it was slightly odd that they never introduced that son I heard about. He must have been in there somewhere, right?" my mom asked me as we walked back home. We left shortly after the other neighbors came in, and Jules went back to hers.

I shrugged. "We didn't introduce Dad or Benny, either."

"Yes, yes. All in good time, I guess."

---

For the rest of the day, I couldn't shake the feeling that something about those people and the entire interaction was off. I didn't mention anything to Mom because whenever I tried, she responded in a very strict manner.

And I probably would've just ignored my thoughts as I normally would. There was a new family every year; the only thing different about this one was that they lived so incredibly close. I told myself that I felt an attachment as I personally helped with the house.

But when I saw *Ethan*, I realized there was something much bigger going on.

Most people in Agsbury go to bed awfully early. My parents turn off all the lights before ten, and all the noise just disappears. When I'm not ready to sleep, I often sit in the nook by my window and draw something.

It's quiet and relaxing most of the time, but that night I looked outside and saw a pale face staring at me with wide, empty eyes from the window next door.

My body froze in a moment of shock. When my breath came back, it was short and rapid.

I'd recently gotten used to looking at the empty house, and I suppose for a moment I forgot that it wasn't empty anymore.

But whoever was staring at me did not look all right. Through the darkness, it was hard to say, but this person kept scratching at the window. When our gazes met, he pushed his head against the window again and again and again. I couldn't say for sure, but it seemed like he was screaming.

Until all of a sudden, he was pulled away from the window, and it all stopped.

I'm ashamed to admit how long it took me to finally get into action. As my thoughts became clearer, I finally walked to my parents' bedroom, trying to somehow explain what I'd just witnessed.

"Charlie, this is more than absurd. Do you hear yourself?" my mother said in the aforementioned strict tone.

"I—I know, but I swear something happened. We need to check on them."

"We've met the Lesters, and they seemed like perfectly fine people. Now calm down," my mother said.

"We didn't meet the son!" I shouted, to which my mother responded with a stern look.

Now my dad, who was sleepy and groggy, chimed in. "You met them? I thought we said we would wait."

My mother just shrugged, and then Dad got up from bed and left the room.

Mom and I exchanged a quick look and then followed. "Howard, what are you doing?" Now, Mom sounded more scared than strict.

I thought Dad would go next door, but he walked to my room and straight to my window.

And then he waved.

Slowly, we walked up to the window, Mom making sure she was a step ahead of me. When I reached the window, I couldn't believe my eyes.

Mr. and Mrs. Lester were standing by the window where I witnessed the horrors earlier, looking at us with the exact same smile while waving.

"See? All is fine. It is dark. You must have hallucinated," Dad said.

"Yes," my mom added. "Now let us let the neighbors sleep. I will make you some warm milk to calm you down, Char—"

"No," my dad chimed in. "It is late, Charlie. Just go to bed."

---

To be honest, I thought the subject would just be dropped. My parents didn't say a word the next day.

I think we were all a bit surprised when the Lesters rang our doorbell around noon.

And this time they had their son with them.

During daylight, he didn't look scary at all. His brown eyes appeared bloodshot but not empty, and his face wasn't that pale but had a nice touch of color. His hair, which yesterday had gone in all directions, was neatly styled back.

My parents invited them inside, and we all sat down in the living room.

"Dear Charlie, we want to sincerely apologize for Ethan scaring you like that!" Helen said without blinking even once.

"A dumb, boyish prank." The father awkwardly chuckled while gently nudging Ethan, whose face distorted for just a fraction of a second. But then he really looked as if he felt bad.

"I'm sorry. That was really stupid of me," he said. "I didn't mean to scare you."

He sounded sincere.

I looked at all the concerned faces around me and let out a short laugh. "It's really okay. I was just surprised, not scared," I lied. The lie seemed to help, though, because suddenly all the adults seemed far more relaxed.

"Well, now that the issue is resolved, how would you like to join us for a barbecue?" Dad enthusiastically suggested.

---

They stayed the whole afternoon. The Lesters were really nice, saying all the right things, and even Mom was warming up. Ethan was rather quiet but friendly and polite. He talked about how he liked to play soccer and that he'd already seen all the sports fields we had in Agsbury.

Dad liked that.

Benny asked if Ethan would play video games with him, which he politely agreed to. So the three of us went inside while the parents stayed in the garden.

Ethan and I were alone in the living room for just a minute, sitting next to each other on the sofa, while Benny went to get his games.

"So have you met many people here yet?" I asked, trying to make small talk.

Ethan looked around the room really quickly and then came really close to my face. "I have no idea what happened last night," he whispered. "I don't think I've ever met you but—" He pulled his shirt up a bit and pulled his pants down just enough to show something written on his lower stomach.

No, not written. Carved. With a knife or something similar from the looks of it, though the wound didn't appear fresh.

"It's upside down," he whispered. "But can you read it?"

He pulled back quickly as we heard footsteps approaching, but I did see what it said.

# Part 2

The books in the library, the movies in the cinema, the games we could play. All of them were limited to a specific collection. A way to mimic what was on the outside to give us a sense of having entertainment and choices when in reality we only learned and saw what we were supposed to.

Of course, I didn't know it then.

And I never should have known. I never would have figured it out if it weren't for that slight coincidence that got the suspicion rolling.

Ethan says it might have been fate.

I believe it was my dad.

---

My name written on the stomach of a boy I'd never seen before had to mean something. Of course, after what I'd seen in the night, I wasn't yet sure whether I could trust this Ethan.

I had been living a happy and fulfilled life in Agsbury. There was never anything that I missed, nothing I desperately longed for.

He was the only factor that led to the disruption of my belief system, and what kind of person would I be if I let some random guy do that? I had a mind of my own, after all.

So I tried to ignore the issue. I told myself that I'd ask Ethan to leave me alone if he tried to bother me again. He should play his weird games on his own.

I was set on that, but then Ethan surprised me.

For the next few days, we saw each other occasionally. We'd get the mail from outside at the same time, we'd be at the grocery store picking something up for our parents, or we'd be at the sports center at the same time.

And every time he acted awfully normal.

During each of those occasions, Ethan acted just like everyone else. He waved, said hello, or he'd ask me something simple like, "Do you know where the green beans are?" but it never went further than that.

He treated me just like a regular neighbor. He had entirely adapted to our way of living.

And that was what got my blood boiling. He ignored the issue, which resulted in me not being able to ignore it any longer.

This boy had brought some kind of change to town. I just didn't know what exactly was going on.

Of course, I couldn't talk to my parents about any of this. Not after the way they reacted on the night I saw Ethan's strange act through his window.

I didn't even tell Jules, my closest and oldest friend. For reasons I couldn't explain, I felt I had to keep it all to myself. In Agsbury, we don't voice criticism or speak of bad emotions. Most of the time we don't need to, and when you do feel negative, it feels silly to bother others with it.

You don't want to be the odd one out.

So I thought the best thing I could do would be to befriend Ethan to try and figure out more about him.

---

"So this is where you usually hang out?"

Ethan's gaze switched between Jules and me.

We were sitting at the coffee house overlooking the marketplace. Getting him to join us for coffee was easy; I just acted like it was a spontaneous idea when I saw him helping his mom out in their yard. She was thrilled by the idea of him socializing as well.

"Not exclusively, but often. We usually come after school, but it's the holidays now," Jules said.

Ethan nodded. "It's nice. Good coffee," he said and added three cubes of sugar to his cup.

"Yes, it's the absolute best. Well, to be honest, it is the same roast you can get at the market, but it does taste nicer when someone else brews it, I think." Jules kept talking.

Ethan nodded and kept adding sugar cubes to his coffee.

"That's a lot of sugar," I said when his cup was starting to overflow. Jules hadn't even noticed.

"Oh." Ethan looked down. "Sorry, I think I zoned out for a moment. Last night I—"

He was interrupted by the waitress, who came over with a pot full of fresh coffee. Without even asking, she started pouring coffee into Ethan's cup, which was already filled to the brim.

"Oh, look at you, your drink is all sugared up! We should add a bit more caffeine or the sweetness will go to your head!" she cheerfully said as she removed his cup and filled a new one with coffee so hot that it looked like it was boiling inside the cup.

---

Ethan was really fun once he warmed up. He seemed witty and fit well into our little group. I was starting to think that he could hang out with me and Jules more often.

We sat in the coffeehouse for another hour that practically flew by, talking about all sorts of things. As it turned out, we had a lot of the same favorite movies, books, and artists, which made me wonder how he'd grown up.

"What was the place like where you lived before?" I asked.

Ethan didn't even think before answering. "Typical, not spectacular. A place to live, not to love. We had neighbors but no real community. And our house wasn't as nice as the one we live in now."

I thought his reply sounded a bit strange, but Jules nodded in agreement.

"Makes sense, your old one wasn't built by Charlie, after all."

"I didn't build anything." I rolled my eyes.

"What about you guys? Did you always live in Agsbury?"

I thought about it for a second. "Well, ever since I can remember, so I suppose always."

Jules nodded in agreement.

"So you were born here?"

Jules answered before I could. "No, nobody is born here. You come to Agsbury when you become a family. My mom said you have to apply and they mostly consider people who already have children. It does make sense because the houses are all too big for just a couple or a single person."

"Sounds logical, so you were probably just too young to remember moving here."

Jules nodded. "All I know is that our families must have come here only a year apart from each other because Charlie and I have known each other since kindergarten."

For some peculiar reason, she said that in a threatening tone. Was Jules afraid that Ethan, as my new neighbor, would replace her as a friend? It felt flattering, though unnecessary.

Ethan ignored her and looked at me. "What about your brother? How old is he, like ten? Do you remember him being born?"

I opened my mouth to answer but couldn't when I felt a pulsating pain going through my left hand that was holding my coffee cup. I immediately dropped the cup, which spilled all over the table.

"What the—?"

"Oh dear, I am sorry. I must be losing my mind missing your cup like that. Let me make that up to you with a free piece of pie?" It was the waitress who, without me noticing, was back at the table.

I hadn't even asked for a refill.

On our bike ride home, all I could think about was Benny. He'd always been my brother, but I had never thought about his birth until Ethan asked about it. It must have been here in Agsbury, but why couldn't I remember anything about it?

Jules and Ethan were talking about all kinds of things on our way home, but I stayed silent. I was too occupied with my own thoughts.

I hadn't even realized that we were already back on our street.

"Do you guys wanna go to the cinema or something tomorrow?" she said once we were in front of my house.

"Yeah, that sounds good!" Ethan said, and I nodded.

We said our goodbyes, and Jules cycled on.

Ethan was just about to head home as well, but I grabbed his arm before he could. "Why are you acting like nothing happened?" I surprised myself with my sudden courage.

Ethan's face shifted for a second. He frowned, but then he forced it back to a smile. "I'm trying to be normal. Well, for my parents." He looked around the street. "They like it here. It makes them happy. I want to be happy, too. I shouldn't have jumped on you like that. I just found it so weird that your name was on my skin when I'd never even met you before. And I'm pretty sure that it had been on my stomach before we even moved here. Like someone tried to make sure I wouldn't forget, you know?"

He shook his head before I could answer. "Sorry, I think it's best if we just don't think about it any longer. I actually get an awful migraine when I try to. I'll see you tomorrow?"

Maybe Ethan was able to shove his suspicions down, but I couldn't any longer. I contemplated talking to my parents about Benny's birth during dinner, but for some reason, I couldn't. It seemed like a bad idea, though I couldn't explain why.

I acted normal, just like Ethan, but that night I couldn't sleep again.

I'd never had trouble with sleep before, but something about me had changed ever since the Lesters moved in next door. And it wasn't just me who acted differently.

That night I realized that there was something wrong with my family as well.

I was lying in bed, my eyes open and focused on the ceiling, my thoughts flowing in all sorts of directions.

And then I heard it.

A sound through the usually suffocating silence. I got up to look at Ethan's window, but this time it wasn't coming from him.

It was coming from downstairs. That was strange.

My parents were *never* up at night.

My heart was racing inside my chest as I slowly made my way down the stairs, following a voice to the kitchen.

It's hard to say where my nervousness was coming from. That was my home, after all, the place that should make me feel safe. And the thing is, I wasn't scared of an intruder. We didn't have any crime in Agsbury; it was the safest place you could imagine.

I was so scared because the person whose voice I was hearing was my father.

He was speaking so quietly that I wasn't sure what he was muttering at first. But then I realized it was a name.

"Lucia."

His whisper slowly became louder.

"Lucia."

"Lucia. You are dead."

"We are all dead."

The unusual sight of my father at night like this, talking that way, sent a shiver down my spine. For a moment, I just stood in the doorway, not sure what to do.

Finally, I whispered, "Dad?"

With a sudden movement, he turned around, and our eyes met. I can't say which of us looked more distressed.

"They are growing corpses. You die the second you set foot here," he said.

"Wha—?"

My breathing stopped when I suddenly felt a touch on my shoulder.

"What is going on here?"
It was my mom. And I'd never been happier to see her.

---

Mom walked Dad back upstairs to their room. Then she came back and heated up a cup of milk for me.

"Your father did something horrible," she said after a long silence. "But he never meant to. He's a good man, a truly good man. Sometimes his head becomes a bit broken." She looked at me, wiping away a single tear from her cheek.

"But please don't worry, my child. I will call the doctor tomorrow, and he will be fine. Go back to bed now, and I will bring you the milk, okay?"

She smiled at me, and we hugged. For a moment, I really felt better and safe again. I walked toward the stairs but turned around one more time to ask my mother something that had been bugging me since the afternoon.

"Mom, what was the place like where we lived before here?"

My mother smiled and answered without thinking about it for even a second. "Typical, not spectacular. A place to live, not to love. We had neighbors but no real community. And our house wasn't as nice as the one we live in now."

# Part 3

Getting rid of Jules wasn't easy, but it had to be done.

I vividly remember meeting my best friend. It's one of the few memories I have that appear somewhat clear in my mind, a happy moment without alteration. Of course, it was easier then because I was younger.

Although I can't say how old for sure. I'd been trying to remember whether Benny was already born. I'd been trying that for different memories, but he only appeared in more recent ones.

But the image of Jules was as clear as day. She was like a ray of sunshine, dressed in a white skirt with lots of bright lemons, almost the color of her hair. Her mom had the same lemons on her apron. We went over to their house after they'd invited us to a barbecue.

The parents were chatting loudly. Our moms connected right away, and so did Jules and I. After we ate, we went inside and played games.

Thinking about it now, it was a lot like the day Ethan's family came over.

We like to repeat stuff.

After that day, we were inseparable. She introduced me to everything I know and love. I used to look at her and feel like I belonged.

The last time I looked at her, I wished that she would drop dead.

---

Mom and Dad were both gone. Mom had work to do, which was odd for a Sunday, but sometimes that was what it was like, and we never questioned her work. Dad had gone on some kind of play date with Benny. None of us mentioned last night during breakfast.

Jules and I were in my room, getting ready for the cinema. I knew right away that there was a reason why she came to my place before: she wanted to talk about Ethan.

I meant to keep things to myself, at least for now, but after the night I was feeling awfully nervous. Instead of drinking the milk last night, I'd poured it out because I didn't want to sleep; I wanted to think. Now, with only two hours of sleep and a mind going in all directions, I started regretting my decision.

It made me more emotional and less careful. When she asked about Ethan, Jules probably wanted to know if I had a crush on him or something.

You can imagine the look she gave me when I told her about everything else. The words came out of my mouth like vomit.

The engraved name, the view from my window on his first night, the things my father said.

I was pushing my fingernails into the palm of my hand to keep myself from starting to cry.

"He looked so scary. Nothing like my dad," I whispered after I'd poured out everything that had happened without a pause. Jules had been watching me carefully and quietly the entire time. "But, Jules, I don't think he's going crazy. I think he tried to warn me." I whispered the last part even though we were all alone in the house.

My friend got up and sat down right next to me on the bed, with no distance to move. She put her hands on top of mine, which were still formed into fists, and gently pried open my fingers.

Then she moved her hands to my wrists and grabbed them tightly. "God, you are so stupid."

Her tone was mellow, cold.

"What?"

She sighed. "Insufferable, really. If it weren't for your mother, you'd probably be long dead. I don't even want to know how often your parents drug you, although I can assume."

I stared at her face that showed not a single sign of emotion.

Her grip became even tighter. "I am sorry, Charlie. I hoped we could earn our place in Agsbury alongside each other. Of course, I would have gotten married first and worked to be accepted as a member with my own house. And then you could have tried the same. We would have been like our moms. With our upbringing, we would have had many years to live. Now only one of us does."

I tried to pull away, but now her nails were digging into my flesh.

"What on Earth are you talking about, Jules?"

"Only worthy ones are chosen to live in heaven, Charlie. Our families worked so hard to come to Agsbury. They spend all their time becoming important members of the community. One day, they will be chosen to become the soil that nourishes our earth. The earth that gives up happiness, fortune, and health in return."

Finally, she was showing emotion but in a way that made my blood freeze. Her eyes were wide open the entire time as if she'd forgotten how to blink, and her teeth were grinding loudly against each other as she tried to force the biggest smile I'd ever seen.

"Where did you learn all this? What soil? You mean when we die and are buried?"

"When we are offered, and buried, silly. But only when it is our time to leave Agsbury. And I have no intention of leaving the community anytime soon. But you..." She sighed. "You don't understand it, Charlie. Even with all the years your parents have tried to prepare you, you've stayed clueless. Do you know how hard it is to be friends with someone so dumb? If it weren't for your lovely mom, I would have abandoned you much sooner."

She loosened her grip slightly and tilted her head.

"Oh, poor Charlie, you look so scared. Don't worry, it will all be fine. You won't be turned into soil before you turn eighteen. I will talk to your mother, and she will wipe your little memory as gently as she can. And then we can have a bit more time together."

While all her words were like daggers in my brain, I had to focus. It was possible that my friend had lost her mind, but after everything I'd witnessed these past days, I think the truth was much more complicated.

And whatever happened, I couldn't let her talk to my parents. I had to keep my memory clear.

So as Jules kept blabbering about her fruitful future, I slammed my head against hers in a moment of surprise. I didn't even think about it; my body simply started to act, and my brain tried hard to keep up. She instinctively let go of my arms, and I got up as quickly as I could, ignoring the pain in my face.

She followed fast and grabbed my shirt to pull me down to my knees.

"HELP!" she shouted, but I shut her up by pushing my elbow into her stomach. She dropped to the ground, and I quickly jumped on top of her, pushing my knee into her chest.

As the adrenaline rushed through my body, I tried to think of my next step. I wasn't used to fighting anyone. And then we were interrupted.

"What the hell?" a new voice spoke.

It was Ethan who had come inside without our knowledge.

Nobody in bloody Agsbury ever locks their door.

"Get her off me." Jules started crying.

Ethan didn't move. He looked at our bloody faces.

When Jules said, "Charlie has gone mad," it looked as if something inside of him clicked.

"Do you have tape? A rope maybe?"

Jules and I both stared at him.

I took a deep breath. "Jules said my mother drugs me. Can you hold her down while I look for something?"

---

It was in the honey. There was no scent to it, but it made the most sense. She kept it hidden at the back of the highest cupboard. And we never had honey with breakfast or any other meal.

But it was always in my milk.

Getting Jules to swallow the honey mixture I made wasn't easy, but we managed. My heart was racing the entire time. My mind was so focused on hoping that nobody would come home that I didn't even have time to process what had just happened. Together with Ethan, I had drugged my best friend, tied her up, and hid the sleeping girl in my closet.

The pain only got to me as Ethan and I biked all the way to Agsbury Lake, and I'd told him everything I'd learned from my father and Jules. Agsbury Lake was my favorite place because I could always go there to be alone.

Of course, back then I didn't know that the people of Agsbury regularly fed it with corpses because they believed that it nourished our water.

Ethan looked surprised after everything I told him, though not as much as me. Maybe because his old life was more recent than mine.

"I don't know why I never questioned anything before. Agsbury really does feel like heaven, but lately, everyone seems to be breaking a little. Jules said something about them turning people into soil. When they find me—" I stopped talking.

"We need to get away," Ethan said firmly.

"There is no place in Agsbury where we can hide, and we can never get far enough on our bikes. And what about our families?"

I wrapped my arms around my legs.

"So what now?" he asked.

I shrugged. "I'm sorry I pulled you into this." I took a deep breath. "Why did you even help me and not Jules?"

Ethan started tapping his fingers on the ground nervously. "When I saw you there, something in my mind shattered. For a moment, I remembered the night we came here. Your dad was there. And other adults. They—" He paused for a moment. "They hurt me. Tried to make me comply or whatever. Jules was there as well, with all the adults. I think it was some kind of initiation, and she seemed weirdly into it. She had that look your mom always has. The one my parents now have as well."

I swallowed. "Was it that night you carved my name into your skin?"

"Yes. I don't remember everything but... I know it was bad. And it's our families that did this to us. We need to get help or—"

"Charlie!"

Both of us turned around in the same second to see where the voice was coming from.

It was my dad, walking down the path that leads from the street to the lake.

I jumped up. "Shit, shit, shit. What now?"

Ethan looked just as clueless as me. And even more afraid when his eyes met my dad's.

At the top of the path, I saw a car. We didn't have a car. Nobody in Agsbury did.

There was no need for the residents of Agsbury to have cars. We had bikes for short trips inside the town, and if we wanted we could buy skateboards or roller skates. But nothing with a motor.

If you are someone with important privileges, you do drive a car at times. For example, if you pick up a new family, and Dad was a trusted resident. But I had no idea why he had it now. Was he trying to get rid of us?

"Get in the car! Now!"

Ethan and I both turned to the water for a split second. Should we try to swim? I didn't even know where the lake ended.

"We don't have much time. Get in the car now. Benny's already inside, hurry!"

---

"How did you know that we were at the lake?"

"After I found Jules in your closet and saw that your bike was gone, I just assumed. You used to run away to the lake often after we'd moved to Agsbury. I think you were too young to understand the full extent, but your gut already knew this place was wrong. I wish mine had as well."

Only as we reached roads that I'd never seen before did my heartbeat start slowing down. Lately, I'd been too afraid of my own family. If my dad hadn't mentioned Benny, I probably would have jumped in the water.

Now I was glad that I hadn't. After my father finally, for the first time in my life, really told the truth.

"Agsbury was a paradise. A place that you didn't choose but had to be chosen for. If you showed enough determination and love to grow this community. We met one of their spokesmen on a holiday once. He told us about this wonderful place where families live together in happiness, where there is no crime, no hate. Of course, we didn't believe much of what he was saying at first, but they get to you eventually.

"You were only ten back then. We didn't have much money and little support from our respective families.

"Agsbury was going to fill all those voids for us. So we wrote our application and had many interviews and trials. It took almost a year until we finally received the acceptance letter. Your mother couldn't believe her eyes. I'd never seen her happier than that day."

Ethan and I stayed silent, absorbing all the words my dad was speaking. I was sitting at the front next to my dad while Ethan was in the back with a fast-asleep Benny.

"There were so many rules. We weren't allowed to conceive more children, weren't allowed to leave, even for vacation, weren't allowed to own a car. When I think about it now, I believe we were insane for wanting it, but they had a way to be persuasive."

I didn't like where things were going.

"And we were happy. We'd convinced ourselves to be. Your mother especially. Even when she learned about the ritual. Once a year, a family is chosen. Often it happens when their youngest child turns eighteen. I want to spare you the horrifying details, but these families never truly leave Agsbury. They believe, and I used to as well, that dying and becoming a part of Agsbury's grounds was the greatest honor. The town feeds on the dead and pays its residents with good fortune."

My stomach started turning. "But wait. We moved here before Benny was born. This isn't adding up," I said.

My dad nervously looked through the mirror at Benny. "They don't always wait until the child turns eighteen. He needed a new family."

I looked at the sweet face of the boy I had only known as my brother and couldn't help but imagine what they'd done to his parents. This couldn't be real. "Dad, where are we going?"

He took a deep breath. "We're getting away before they notice that the car is gone. Where to, I'm not sure yet." He looked at Ethan. "I know this is a lot for you, too. I'm sure you don't want to leave your parents but—" He stopped talking.

"Why now?" Ethan suddenly asked. "Why should we even believe you? I know you were there on my first night. Why didn't you help us?" He was almost shouting now.

"Because I needed time to become myself again. Normally, when a new family comes, their children are still pretty young. They can be persuaded easily. For you, it was hard. Your parents tried to talk you into it, but you couldn't be convinced. But they wanted this so much and showed all this determination. They would have done anything. And I saw it on the night you moved in."

We were taking paths I'd never seen before, luckily with no people in sight. I couldn't believe other residents hadn't tried to flee. I wondered how people could be persuaded so easily but remembered that I'd been the same until now.

"But the moment something in my mind really shattered was when I heard them call you by your real name. Charlie," my dad continued.

Ethan and I exchanged a confused look.

"It reminded me how they wipe everything from our old lives. You having the current name of my daughter." He looked at Ethan through the mirror. "It reminded me of her real one."

"Lucia," I whispered.

A tear was forming in the corner of my dad's eye. "I am so sorry for everything we've done to you, children. I pulled you aside that night." He was talking to Ethan again. "Pressured you to not forget your name. I thought I could do *something* at least. But it took me some time to collect the courage and formulate my plan. I wanted to get more children out of there, but they have very smart ways to trick the outside world as well. If I went to the authorities, they'd only put me in jail for kidnapping."

I felt like I would throw up any second. "Dad, what about Mom?"

"Your mother would happily die to become soil for the grounds of Agsbury. And she'd take us with her. For now, we need to save ourselves."

# I WENT BACK TO KICKY-KIDS' FUN LAND. IT'S NOT SO FUN ANYMORE.

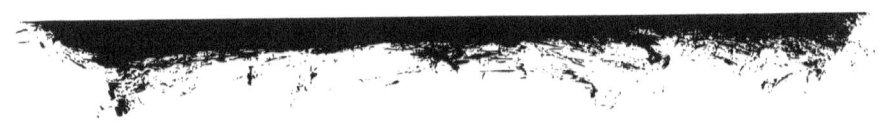

They were always there, not actively present but sitting somewhere in the back of my mind. The memories. Memories of long slides and big trampolines, as well as colorful tables where we had snacks and juice boxes. Memories of a climbing tower with leaves and tree branches where you could climb like a monkey. The monkey tree is the most vivid one for some reason. The rest are mainly colors and a few noises. Noises of children's laughter and faint, repetitive music somewhere in the background. As a child, you don't notice music as much.

The colors I see when I try to think of the Fun Land are mostly green. Probably the monkey jungle I'm thinking about, but there are hints of bright pink and yellow, too. Most distant memories of activities I did as a little kid are like that. I'm twenty-three now. It was pretty long ago, so I suppose it makes sense. It also makes sense that I remember blurps of color instead of real events and faces. I must have been six or seven then. I can't say for sure because of the gaps in my head. Well, my mind.

The children's fun land with the monkey-climbing trees, snacks, and music. It would be one of those memories you simply have of your childhood. You don't remember it all, but it is still a fine piece of nostalgia buried somewhere inside of you.

I'd done loads of stuff as a kid, and nobody actively thinks about it on a regular basis. The only reason I'm starting this trip down memory lane is because, for some unspeakable reason, my memories of Kicky-Kids Fun

Land suddenly became completely sharp and vivid. That's not how brains are supposed to work.

It sounds bonkers, I know. It's odd because I know what the blurry memories look like, and it's strange because now I can distinguish between those and the new, vivid ones I suddenly have. Sounds strange? Yeah, it is, but that's not all. The memories didn't just come back to me; they also came back to Maxy Miller, my childhood best friend, who I probably hadn't talked to in more than a decade.

---

I woke up from a long sleep after a drunken night at the bar. I hadn't been drinking in forever, and my tolerance was crazy low. After basically falling into a coma back at home, I had the most vivid dream. The following morning, my eyes opened wide as the beams of light shining through the drapes kissed—or rather, hit—my face. First, there was pain. I'd forgotten how horrible hangovers can be, but then I repressed the pain to focus on the dream I'd had that night. The dream that awakened all those memories of Kicky-Kids Fun Land. Suddenly, it felt as if it had all happened only yesterday, and I even wondered if I'd somehow gone there while being completely hammered.

No, that couldn't be, because in those memories I was a kid, and so were all the other kids there. You know how you always see yourself in a third-person perspective when you think of something that happened? Well, I saw child Jamie running around the plastic—or trampoline-like—soft floor. It was all green. Forest-green tiles mixed with poison-green. They bounced a little when you ran fast enough, and we always did. That was when I remembered Maxy. Well, I never forgot about his existence, of course; we simply weren't as close after going to different high schools.

Tiny pink plastic tables with rainbow-colored chairs around them, which seemed much bigger then. The same irritating tune repeated over and over again, accompanied by children screaming, laughing, and crying. Our poor parents must have left with a migraine each time.

I was surprised by how vivid those memories suddenly were, and for the first time in years, I missed my old friend and wondered how he'd been doing. The headache was suddenly very much present again. I groaned and tried to suppress the pain just a little longer as I reached for my phone on my bedside table. As if he'd somehow read my mind, I saw a Facebook message from Maxy.

**M: Hey man, how's it going?**

Typical Max. We hadn't spoken in years, and he texted as if we never stopped being friends.

"What the fuck," I mumbled to myself. This was too much of a coincidence. Had he somehow read my mind? Well, it turned out that I had no idea how much further this would go.

After a little chit-chat, I got to the point and told him about my dream, about my memories of Kicky-Kids, and that I'd seen him in it. That last part sounded really weird, and I almost regretted saying it until he texted back.

**M: ... no fucking way, Jamie. That's exactly why I texted you. I had a dream like that.**

I broke into a cold sweat, not knowing whether it was due to my hangover or the absurdity of the situation. It was all too crazy, but luckily my old friend agreed. I wasn't alone in losing my mind.

**M: Do you remember where it was? Can't find it on Google.**

After jumping, or rather crawling, out of bed, I chugged down some water with a few painkillers and called my mum. Her memories were even more blurry than mine. She said we went to a couple of different places for kids back then, and she was right. Kicky-Kids didn't ring a bell, but then again, she didn't remember any of the names.

Finally, my friend Max did find something. On a forum for our town. After talking about it some more, we decided to meet again to catch up with some coffee and take a walk toward the industrial area where the Kicky-Kids building was supposed to be.

What could be the harm in checking it out, after all?

---

"I mean, they probably shut it down, right?"

We spent more than two hours at a café Max suggested, near the district he'd moved to. He'd only moved back recently to help out after his dad broke his hip. He had been in a relationship during most of college, but they broke up more than six months ago. That was most of the catching up we did. For the rest of the two hours, we talked about our childhood—the only common topic we had. Finally, we addressed the elephant in the room.

"How the actual fuck did we have the same dream last night?"

I stayed silent for a second. I'd been thinking about it all day. I'm not exactly a superstitious person; I studied psychology. I'm aware of the abilities of our minds.

"Maybe we saw some commercial? Subconsciously woke up that memory?"

"Maaaybe. Still weird, though. I swear I remember every second. Even how you fell and messed up your knee."

I swallowed.

That was exactly what I had seen in my dream before I woke up this morning. For some reason, that particular moment hadn't felt cheerful. Or maybe I'm only thinking that because I woke up with a racing heartbeat.

Now Max was grinning. "Wanna go check it out?"

I nodded. That was the main reason we met up, after all.

---

Neither of us expected it to still be around. Many old places were shut down, especially in the industrial area. And if it was still there, we would've found it more easily online.

That was why we stood with our mouths wide open as we looked up at the enormous green neon sign that read **Kicky-Kids Land—Fun for Young and Old**.

I gulped.

"Looks exactly the same," Max said as if reading my mind.

I expected the building to appear old or run down, but it was clean and the sign...

"The sign is lit up, which means there's electricity," I said. "They're still open."

"Should we go in?"

"Hell yeah. It says young and old, right?" I grinned.

I swore in that moment it didn't matter that we had lost touch for years. It felt as if I was back with my best friend, and we were up for a crazy adventure.

The door was open, and as we entered the foyer, I could already hear the familiar music in the distance. There was a big desk in front of us where you would pay, but the hall was empty.

"What now?" I asked.

Max shrugged and then pointed toward a big, half-circle doorway with a thin curtain hanging from it. That was how you got to the main hall of the fun land. We could hear laughter and music coming from behind it.

That was the first moment I got a little nervous. We had been acting pretty impulsively.

"Should we go?" I asked.

"Inside?" Max misinterpreted. I'd meant we should leave, but now I was curious. We could take one tiny peek and leave after.

Max led the way, and I followed. Before we knew it, we stood in the fun hall of Kicky-Kids Fun Land. It looked exactly the way I remembered it. The plastic tables, the gummy floor, and the rainbow chairs. There were colorful slides and even indoor swing sets. The walls were painted with teddy bears, lollipops, and fire trucks.

Everything looked exactly the way it did back then, but it was incredibly eerie.

"There's no one here," Max whispered.

I swallowed. I could have sworn I'd heard children laughing and screaming. Now, all we heard was the music.

Max and I looked at each other.

"Maybe they're getting ready to close down? It's pretty late."

He nodded.

A knot was tightening in my stomach.

"We should get going," I said as I took one more look around the big hall, but then I noticed something.

"Wait, where's the jungle where you could climb?"

Max took another step inside, and I reluctantly followed. He'd always been a little braver. Or dumber.

"That wasn't here," he answered after a bit. "That was a different fun land or whatever."

"Are you sure? How many of these are there?"

Max didn't answer. He was now confidently walking toward the other side of the hall.

"There's someone there!" he exclaimed. "Hello?" he shouted.

"What the fuck, man?" I hissed. "We're not even supposed to be here."

As I caught up to him, I saw the person he was talking about. But they didn't look quite right.

"Is that a clown?" I asked but didn't expect an answer. The tall man had white makeup on his face, a red wig, a big red nose, and a black-and-white clown costume. He started moving toward us, but not in a normal way; he was somehow jumping as he walked, moving extremely slowly. I grabbed Max's arm and got ready to get the hell out of there, but then the man smiled and waved.

"I fucking hate clowns," Max whispered. Only then did I notice how tense he was. I supposed his confidence was slowly fading.

"Hello!" the clown called back in the same tone as Max. I'm not sure if my friend noticed as well, but somehow his voice even sounded like Max's.

"Hey, sorry, we just came in here. We wanted to see if this place still looked the same as it did when we were kids." I nervously laughed.

The man came closer, and I noticed that it wasn't makeup on his face but a mask.

"Hey... this place is sorry. I hate kids," the man said. Now his voice was even stranger. It sounded partly like Max but also somehow like me.

"Is he screwing with us?" Max tried to joke, but I could clearly hear the nervous undertone in his voice.

"Let's get the hell out of here." But as I turned around to where the exit should be, I realized it wasn't there. The door was gone. All I saw in front of me were giant-sized colorful toys, climbing racks, and slides.

Something had changed while we were inside, and I cursed myself for not listening to my gut and following a guy I hadn't talked to in years. Suddenly, I even wondered if I really ever came to Kicky-Kids before. Everything seemed utterly and horribly wrong. I felt as if I was waking up from a trance. Why was I here? Why were there music and lights but no people except for one clown? And why was there no proof of this place even existing?

I hadn't thought about it until this day, and apparently, it had melded with other memories of mine. Had it been planted inside my mind? I looked at my old friend, who suddenly didn't seem so familiar anymore.

I blacked out pretty badly last night. Had he done something to me? Was this even the Maxy Miller I remembered?

I looked back, but the clown was gone, and the sound of children playing and laughing was back. But now the two of us seemed to be alone in this massive hall.

I didn't even look at Max again. I simply started running. If I couldn't find the door, at least I needed to get away from him. I ran toward something that seemed to be a ball pit. The music and laughter got louder, and my mind was too overwhelmed to even think clearly.

This couldn't be a prank; the door had disappeared. It was there a few minutes ago.

I kept running without a safe goal, and as I tried to quickly turn around to see if he was following me, I tripped. I fucking tripped and fell, my knee hitting the ground so hard that my arms quickly followed. As I tried to get back up, I saw him.

The clown standing right in front of me.

"... not supposed to be here. Hell is fun," he said in that voice that was both mine and Max's. I wanted to get up, but my body was frozen. I could hardly even breathe. Just when I thought it couldn't get any worse, he took off his mask. Underneath, it revealed something so utterly wrong and uncanny that I will never be able to wipe it from my mind. His face had been sewn from different parts of human faces.

I was sure this moment would be my last until someone grabbed my arm and pulled.

"Move!" Max shouted, and not knowing what else to do, I followed. We ran to the other side of the hall, where the door had suddenly reappeared out of nowhere. I was certain it had been in a completely different corner when we came in, but it didn't matter.

We ran and ran until we pushed open the glass door and were back on the street.

I fell again, and so did Max, but we were outside. Completely out of breath, I turned my head slightly to see if we were being followed.

The clown wasn't behind us. Not only was he gone, but Kicky-Kids Fun Land was gone, too. All we saw was an old, gray brick building. No sign and no music. It was the middle of the day, and while there weren't that many people out on this street, it seemed completely normal. As if we hadn't just escaped a nightmare.

I looked at Max, who was just as out of breath and shocked as I was. I felt guilty for believing he'd tried to lure me in there. For believing he wasn't himself. He was the one who saved me.

"How did you find that exit?" I finally muttered as we were getting away from that street as fast as we possibly could. I was leaning on Max because I could hardly walk. He grabbed for his phone with sweaty hands to call for help, though I had no idea what we would even say.

"The walls move," he finally said after taking a deep breath. "I remembered from my dream."

---

I remembered the fun land vaguely. The one with the monkey climbing park. That one was real. Max and I really did go there as kids. Maybe it shut down or became a different place.

The place we visited that day was not real. Kicky-Kids Fun Land did not exist. And neither did the memories we had of it.

Of course, they couldn't have been. The memories were far too sharp to be real.

I have no idea who or what planted them in our heads to lure us to that place, but we were lucky we got out alive.

# I USED TO LOVE WATERMELONS. NOW THEY SMELL LIKE DEATH TO ME.

Home doesn't feel right anymore, it doesn't feel safe, and I'm afraid for my family. Something has invaded our apartment. It probably shoved itself inside the elevator, crawled over our welcome mat, and now that it's inside, I'm not sure how to get rid of it.

I don't know who invited it in or, worse, who sent it. I don't know if it randomly found us, but I believe it's here to stay. I felt the shift, the rising tension. Our comfortable and cozy little home turned cold and tense.

It started when I woke up one morning, with a bitter taste of blood in my mouth and a rusty stain on my pillow. When I went to the bathroom to rinse my mouth, the water turned a light shade of red.

I didn't love what I saw in the mirror. Bags under my eyes, my long brown hair frizzy and even darker than usual, pupils huge despite the bright white light of our bathroom.

I looked like a mess, but who doesn't this early in the morning? The trails of fresh wounds inside my mouth were new, though. When I touched my tongue, I felt deep, rough cuts all over it.

*It had opened my mouth and cut me in my sleep.*

For a second, I thought I saw something in the mirror, but when I blinked, everything was fine.

That was the first sign that something was wrong, accompanied by a headache that felt like a million worms pushing their way out of my skull.

Fucking painful, let me tell you, but I swallowed some ibuprofen and tried to ignore it.

Of course, I didn't think of an intruder right away. An intruder who made cuts in my mouth and brought me headaches, an intruder who wasn't human—who would suspect that?

The taste of blood was there again the next day, but by then I had convinced myself that I was biting myself in my sleep. I went to school as always but couldn't tell you about a single conversation I had there. I remember walking to the bus stop with my best friend Mina as always, but for the rest of the time, the autopilot inside of me was in charge. Apparently, we even had a test, which I only remembered when we got the results back and I'd passed for whatever reason. I couldn't explain why I was feeling so weird, but people usually can't. Understanding our own weird emotions is next to impossible sometimes.

The following night, however, I understood what I was feeling. It was fear.

There was something in here with us. I heard it scraping its claws into our walls. Sometimes I'd hear a whisper or quiet laughter in an unfamiliar voice. It went away as soon as I opened my eyes, but I still felt a presence. The first night I heard it, I collected my courage and went to my parents' bedroom. My dad carefully walked through every room, trying to figure out if someone was inside, but there wasn't anyone here but the four of us.

"Lona, habibti, are you all right? You've been acting weird these past days," my Mom said with a slight accent. It comes out stronger whenever she's worried.

I live with my Mom, my dad, and my fifteen-year-old brother in a small apartment. He's one year younger and three centimeters shorter but still acts like he is the king of the family. To me, he is just an arrogant little shithead.

"Isn't it obvious? She's just crazy for attention," my brother chimed in.

"Leave your sister alone," was all my father said. And after that, we didn't talk about the noises anymore.

My family seemed fine. Our home seemed fine. And I tried acting the same.

The melon was my breaking point.

You see, my favorite food in the entire world has always been watermelons. Watermelon salad with feta and olives, watermelon as a snack with lime juice and cinnamon, or even frozen watermelons blended into a slushie. It might be hereditary—my grandparents used to grow watermelons. The taste and smell of watermelons are one of the very few memories I have of Syria.

This was a great way to start my Saturday. The house was quiet. Mom went to the market, Dad was probably asleep, and my brother was at soccer practice. Additionally, there was no scratching or other signs of weirdness that day.

I got that big knife that my dad likes to use out of the drawer, balanced the melon on our kitchen table, and started cutting into the thick rind.

As soon as I cut into it, though, a foul smell filled the entire kitchen. I dropped the knife, my eyes watering, and went to open the window. The smell was spreading faster than hellfire.

That fucking melon was rotten. I didn't even know they could get this foul, especially as this one looked so good and fresh from the outside.

I was already getting a plastic bag to throw that whole mess away, but as I opened the drawer with the bags in it, I heard a sound behind me.

A cracking sound.

Slowly, I turned around only to see that the watermelon was breaking open without a hand touching it. As it opened wider, some rich, black substance dripped down.

Thick, black worms slowly crawled out of the black goo while the melon opened in half.

Worms. Just like the ones in my brain.

I ran out of the kitchen to my parents' bedroom, but to my surprise, my dad wasn't there.

I grabbed my shoes and ran outside, slammed our front door shut, and headed for the elevator.

I needed to get out of that place.

We live on the sixteenth floor, and whenever I'm in the elevator, I feel a little dizzy from how fast it goes. After that melon, I felt extra nauseous.

Three floors down, the elevator came to a sudden stop. The doors slowly opened, and I looked at the last person I wanted to see at that moment.

It was Noah, sports bag in hand. Fuck, of all the times. Whenever we'd see each other, it would be really awkward, and I avoided those moments as best as I could. Even though we lived in the same building, I'd been surprisingly successful.

Noah used to be my best friend. Well, one of my best friends. There were three of us: Noah, my still-best-friend Mina, and me. We grew up together in the same apartment complex in Berlin Neukölln, played in the sand of the communal playground, and went on little adventures that seemed big to us then. We were not only neighbors but also went to the same school near Berlin's Teufelberg. Needless to say, we were inseparable. Until we turned fourteen and Noah suddenly didn't give a shit about us anymore. It was just after my birthday, and I still wonder if something happened that day or if he just found new friends and new interests.

He cut us off, and after that, he'd barely say hi to Mina or me if he saw us. And we became a two-friend group.

So yeah, meeting Noah now of all times, while putting my shoes on inside an elevator, probably wasn't great.

"You all right?" he asked as he stepped inside.

I nodded.

He opened his mouth like he was going to say something else but stayed quiet. It was weird. We used to talk so much.

Finally, we arrived at the ground floor, and I basically jumped out of that elevator. But I heard no steps beside me.

Noah didn't follow.

I turned around for a second, and our eyes met. There was an odd look on his face, one that I couldn't quite place, but I ignored it and headed for the door.

---

As the crisp March air hit my face, I realized I had nowhere to go. I didn't even bring a jacket. Mina's home wasn't an option because she'd ask questions, and I didn't feel like explaining what was going on.

So I just started walking, ignoring the cold. Ignoring what I had just left at home. Ignoring the way Noah looked at me. Like everyone has been looking at me lately. Like I'm losing my mind.

God, losing your mind is lonely.

I was shaking, not just from the cold. I felt sick and gory. Violated. I knew there was something in there. Something haunting us.

I kept walking and walking. At least it was early enough in the morning that there were hardly any people around. Finally, I ended up at the playground and sat down on one of the swings.

And my mind just turned blank.

I ignored those voices shouting that something was wrong. I needed a moment to not think about anything. Until I realized that my mind would just keep going on its own.

I unfocused my eyes, unfocused my mind, and suddenly I wasn't looking at the familiar playground but at a gloomy place. A place that felt like the inside of that rotten watermelon. Around me, I heard voices in languages I didn't understand shouting and screaming in agony.

Something was coming closer, trying to touch me. When it was close enough, it whispered something in my ear. A question in an unfamiliar language.

Suddenly, someone tapped my shoulder, and I was pulled out. I blinked and was back at the playground.

"Lona?" the voice in front of me asked.

I swallowed, tried to collect myself. None of this was actually happening, and I needed to calm down.

"What the hell, Noah? Did you fucking follow me?" I asked, surprised at the mean undertone in my voice.

He just stood there, his face looking as if it had lost all its blood. "Yeah. I thought I saw something in that elevator. Well, I thought I was imagining things, but I still felt like I had to come after you. And when I saw you sitting here, I knew it was real. Fuck, Lona. What is this?"

"What is what?" I asked, my heart still pounding in my chest.

"When you just sat there, totally spaced out, your entire eyes were black. How is that possible? And in the elevator..." He paused for a second. "When the doors closed, your reflection... It wasn't y-you," he stuttered. "Your skin had all those cracks, your teeth were crazy sharp..." His eyes were wide open while that waterfall of words poured out of his mouth. Words that shouldn't make sense but somehow did.

His curly black hair, which used to be all over his head, was now more wavy than curly and styled well with a middle part. I always loved the contrast between his dark hair and the light blue eyes—and I couldn't believe I was thinking about his eyes while my mind should be focused on what was happening to me.

"I—I don't know," I lied.

I knew it, but I tried to ignore it. Tried to convince myself that it was something else.

Nobody heard the noises because they didn't come from the outside. I heard them inside of me. And the reflection I saw of myself in the morning, even if only for a second, wasn't a hallucination.

I saw the thing that was inside of me.

The intruder wasn't in our home. It had nested in my head and in my chest while slowly changing me.

And Noah saw it.

"I don't know," I repeated. "I don't know what's going on with me. I didn't do anything. It just started." I had to fight back tears at that point. "It's—God, and the melon. How did that even happen? Did I do it?" I kept blabbering and blabbering on.

"Melon?" He raised an eyebrow.

"Watermelon, actually. Rotten and filled with thick worms. God, how am I supposed to go back home?" I replied.

We stayed silent for a while.

"Want me to go with you?" he finally asked, and despite my skepticism, I nodded.

---

I didn't feel like going back home, and it felt even weirder taking Noah with me. But I couldn't stay outside forever. And while it was weird, it also felt somewhat familiar. Like old times. Although it was a little odd how quickly Noah accepted this whole mess and was now even trying to help me.

I walked into the apartment first, with Noah right behind me.

The melon was still on the kitchen table, although it looked nothing like what I'd seen earlier.

The frightful image wasn't the melon this time—it was my father, who sat there staring at the sweet pink mess. And the look he had on his face.

He looked at me, his eyes piercing through mine.

"Wh—where were you this morning?" I asked. "I thought you worked all night. You usually sleep—"

"Who are you?" he said in a tone that I'd never heard from him before. Anger and fear all mixed up. It was weird; my dad knew Noah well, even if we weren't friends anymore.

And that was when I realized that he wasn't talking to him. He was looking at me.

"Who are you and what happened to my daughter?"

I took a step back, almost bumping into Noah, who was right behind me. I looked at my dad, my sweet dad, whose eyes were bloodshot and full of fear. He'd never looked at me this way. Then I looked at Noah, whose face was a mixture of pity and fright.

I took another step back, away from Noah and into our dim hallway with the big mirror.

Now that my eyes were open, I saw it clearly.

The creature inside my shell.

# NOBODY WARNED US ABOUT THE SCARECROW BEFORE WE MOVED HERE

My parents decided to move to this town on a whim. There is no better explanation. They were fed up with the high prices of rent in the city; in Sutton, they could afford a whole house with three bedrooms. I had my own room, they had theirs, and we even had an extra room for guests that would never come.

My parents didn't know that then, though.

The town was cute enough, at first. A small town center with shops and a marketplace. We also quickly realized that the people here loved all sorts of community activities: fruit and vegetable contests, a celebration for each season, and regular town meetings.

Everything they could think of to distract themselves from what was wrong with the town.

I wasn't happy with the decision to move at first but budged when I saw how happy it made my parents. Besides, I only had one year of school left and was already planning to move away for college. We couldn't have known that I never would.

We moved here on the first of October, one year ago, and were quickly welcomed by most of our neighbors. The first ones were the Millers, who lived right next door to us. Mr. and Mrs. Miller came over with a huge wooden basket filled with all kinds of baked goods and massive smiles on their faces that never seemed to disappear.

We were busy unpacking the boxes in our living room when they knocked on our door. Mom went to open it while Dad and I listened to the voices.

"Oh, what a wonderful decision you made by buying this house," we heard the woman say.

"And at the most perfect time as well. We saw that you have a daughter. She looks about the age of our Ethan. Oh, maybe he can tell her about all the fun a young person can have in Sutton!" The father spoke faster than a normal person should.

Mom didn't get a single word in.

"Yes, wouldn't that be wonderful! The three of you should come to dinner sometime. We would love to introduce you to our town," the mother continued. "Have you met Harry yet?"

Slowly, Dad got up and walked toward the door.

"Oh, you must be the husband. Hello!"

My parents were city people, and I could tell they were already overwhelmed by the warmth of the people and couldn't help but grin.

When the Millers left, we started snacking on all the goods they brought but were interrupted every couple of minutes by new neighbors bringing more stuff.

After the last ones, my dad closed the door and sighed. The three of us looked at each other for a moment and then started laughing.

"This will take a lot of adjustment," my Mom giggled. "But it could be worse, right?"

"Well, at least we didn't have to worry about lunch or dinner today," I added. We had a bunch of casseroles, pies, and salads. Everyone brought us something.

"They are a little peculiar but nice, I guess," Dad said. "I'm sure we'll get used to it. And a bunch of parents are already planning friendships between you and their kids, Avery. You're already so popular," he joked.

"Yeah, maybe I can become Harry's friend."

"Oh yes, what was that about?" my Mom asked. "They all talked about this Harry person, but nobody ever told us who he actually is."

"Maybe the mayor?"

Due to the fall holidays, I had to wait to start school. I also wasn't planning on making friends here. I had my friends at home, after all. So I spent those days with my parents, and the next day I went to the grocery store with my Mom so we could stock up on everything we didn't have yet.

We walked to the town center, and it only took us ten minutes to get to the store one of our neighbors recommended. I expected a real grocery store, but it was more like a tiny kiosk with only the bare essentials. They had no name brands and were mostly stocked with vegetables and dairy items.

The woman behind the register gave us a big smile. "Wonderful choice of items you made here. You know, everything we sell is produced locally."

"Oh, that's nice," my mother said.

"Yes, it is, isn't it?"

"Even stuff like toilet paper?" I asked.

"Well, no, not everything. But almost everything. We do not rely on the outside much, and we don't need to. Harry wouldn't like that," she whispered that last sentence.

Mom and I exchanged a curious look.

"Yes, well, who exactly is this Harry? We keep hearing that name and—"

Mom stopped speaking when she saw the woman's face change completely. She'd lost all her color.

"You will learn soon enough. But hopefully not too soon. Just remember, we all stick together here."

This confused us even more, but the woman wouldn't answer any more of our questions. Instead, she tried to distract us with all sorts of information about the upcoming fall festival.

I wish she had been right and that we'd had more time. But as it happened, I saw Harry that night.

---

My parents had already gone to bed, and the street was so quiet that you could have heard a pin drop outside. I was in my room, watching a show, when I heard footsteps. If you can call them that. It sounded more like someone dragging themselves over the floor.

I walked over to the window but couldn't see much at first. The street was dark, and all the lights in the houses were out. I'd noticed people pulling down their shades earlier in the evening, but as my eyes adjusted, I saw where the sound was coming from.

I saw a man in ripped clothes with something that looked like straw hanging out from his arms and legs. His movements seemed awkward and slow, and his body was all crooked and bent, almost as if he were hurt. But every now and then, he would slightly change directions, going in a zig-zag line. I couldn't really see his face until he stopped right in front of our house and started looking up at my window.

Suddenly, I was painfully aware that my room was the only one around with a light on.

My breathing got heavier, but the rest of my body was frozen.

And that's when my door opened and the light went out. I tried to scream, but no sound came out, and a hand suddenly pulled me out of my room and into the hallway.

It was Dad.

"Did you see that?" he whispered. I saw Mom standing in front of their bedroom door.

I nodded, not really able to speak.

"What a freak," my mother said.

"Joanna."

"I'm just saying, it's the middle of the night. He looks like he's on drugs."

"Why did you pull me out here?" I asked, my voice finally back. I didn't want to admit that my parents might be as scared as I was.

"We saw him looking up. And when we came to the hallway, your light was on."

"He was looking at you," my Mom whispered.

Dad walked back to my room, and after a while, he said, "He's gone."

---

When morning came, the three of us had calmed down. In the daylight, our fear from the previous night seemed ridiculous.

"It was probably just a drunk guy coming home from an early Halloween party," Dad said during breakfast.

"Yeah," I agreed. "I still didn't like the way he stared at me, though."

Mom kept rearranging the scrambled eggs on her plate, not really eating anything. "Do you think that man was Harry?" she asked after a while. I'd been thinking the same thing. We were able to laugh about it, but it didn't change the fact that something about this place really didn't feel right.

---

That evening we were invited to dinner at the Millers'. At first, I didn't want to go with my parents, but I felt like it might be a good way to find out more about Harry and Sutton, so I went along.

Mom brought a bottle of her favorite wine. She'd gotten a box full from the city before we moved, and the Millers were ecstatic about it. We sat down at their dinner table, which was already filled with lots of appetizers and decorations. The people here were great hosts; you had to give them that.

Mr. Miller opened the wine and poured everyone, including me, a glass.

"This is fantastic! I don't remember the last time I had wine this good," Mrs. Miller exclaimed.

"I'm glad you like it," my mother said. "I still have a few bottles, if you'd like one for another time."

"No, no. I wouldn't want to take the last memories you have from home."

"Oh, don't worry. I can order more once we're out."

The Millers exchanged a strange glance but didn't comment any further.

"Ethan!" the father suddenly shouted. "We are starting dinner!" He looked at us apologetically. "Our son is sometimes just so lost in his own world."

We'd already started eating when he finally came into the living room. He resembled his dad with his black hair and tall stature. His mom was the opposite: short with red curls. He was also dressed very casually in a T-shirt and ripped jeans while his parents looked like they were at a dinner party in the '50s.

"Ethan, meet our new neighbors, Eli and Joanna Russell. And their daughter Avery."

"Hi," he mumbled as he sat down in the free chair opposite me.

Ethan was the first person in Sutton that we met who didn't smile when he saw us.

He was quiet the rest of the dinner while his parents, as usual, kept speaking without a pause.

Toward the end of dinner, my Mom decided to finally interrupt the strange couple by telling them about what we saw last night.

For a moment, there was silence. The Millers looked very uncomfortable but didn't stop smiling.

"That was Harry," Ethan finally said.

"That's what I thought, but we really don't understand this. Does this happen more often? Does Harry have some kind of psychological problem?" my mother bluntly asked.

Mrs. Miller shushed her. "Sorry, Joanna. That was rude of me!" She looked around the room. "It's just—we don't talk badly about Harry."

"Oh, I wasn't trying to. The man was staring at our daughter at night. We were just a bit concerned, that's all."

"We don't want you to feel uncomfortable. Everyone here is so happy that you moved to Sutton," Mr. Miller chimed in. "It's just not simple to explain who Harry is."

"Has he ever harmed anyone here?" Dad asked.

Again, silence.

The dinner ended quickly and awkwardly after that. We left with more questions than answers.

The following day, my Mom suggested we take a little day trip so we could explore nearby towns and maybe find a place with a decent grocery store.

None of us admitted it, but I think that all of us were kind of creeped out and just wanted to get away for a bit. The neighbors here were open and friendly at first glance, but something was really wrong with them. I could see the regret in my parents' faces. We didn't belong here.

We packed a few essentials and got in the car.

We drove for five hours until we finally gave up. That was when we realized that there was no way of leaving Sutton. The GPS was all wrong; the streets came to dead ends. We tried to drive away the same way we came, but it almost seemed like those roads were gone.

The three of us felt as if we had lost our minds.

Finally, we came to a long road and figured it would lead us out.

The road was empty. We hadn't seen any houses for at least half an hour. There was nothing but fields.

Dad pushed the gas harder, and we were finally able to breathe properly again. Until we saw something on the road. From this distance, we couldn't recognize what it was, but as we got closer, we realized it was a person, and they were slowly walking in our direction.

We came to a sudden halt right in front of him.

I immediately recognized the shredded clothes and the straw. Everything about him looked fake, except for his face. A human face with thick eyebrows and thin lips.

We stood there for a moment as he dragged his body toward our car. Mom locked the doors.

He opened his mouth, but no words came out. Then he reached his arm toward my mother's door. That's when Dad threw the car into reverse. When we were far enough away, he turned the car around.

We were almost out of gas but still somehow made it back to our new house.

---

When we got back, I saw Ethan sitting on his front porch with a book. My parents didn't want me to go over, but I convinced them that it was fine. They decided they would knock on some neighbors' doors to find out how to get out of town.

"Tried to leave, huh?" he said as I approached.

I nodded.

He gave me a half-smile that felt genuine.

"What is going on here?" I tried to hide the panic in my voice.

"You fell into the trap. Once you move to Sutton, you stay here for good. The only escape is death."

I swallowed. "That's ridiculous."

He shrugged. "Doesn't make it any less true."
"We came here before, to look at the house. We left after that."
"That was before you actually lived here. Now it's too late."
A million thoughts raced through my mind, but I realized there was no use denying what he was saying. We had just driven for hours through a tiny town. I knew that he was right, even if it felt wrong. So instead, I turned to anger.
"Then why the fuck did no one warn us?"
He got up from the porch and came closer. "Because they are all insane. After the man who lived in your house died, they were just so happy to get new residents. New neighbors. They can't leave, so they try everything to get at least a little change, a little glimpse into the outside. It will probably happen to you and your parents soon enough."

---

My mother cried the entire evening. My father went from reasoning to anger to silence to apologizing.
We tried calling and texting people from the outside, but every time *we are trapped* would turn into *we are so happy*. *This is hell* would change into *you should move here as well*.
The next few days were much the same. We tried to leave a few more times. By car, by foot, with bikes. While we didn't meet Harry again, we also didn't find our way out. The town felt like a maze.
Slowly, weeks passed and insanity turned into everyday life. My parents started dressing and acting like the neighbors. They joined town events and made friends that were just as lost as they were.
Harry wanted us to stay. The townspeople wanted us to stay.
And Sutton became our new reality.

# WHEN THE LIGHTS ON THE STREET START TO FLICKER AT NIGHT, IT'S A WARNING TO STAY INSIDE

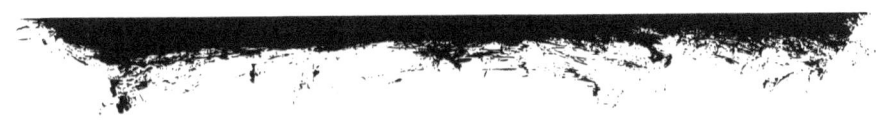

I grew up in the heart of Harvey Lane. In the big house with the perfectly painted window frames and the grass in front that is always cut in the most symmetrical manner. The people who live in our town are the most helpful you could ever imagine. If a brick on your house is hanging only slightly loose, they will come by and help to fix it right away. If your dog runs away, the entire neighborhood will be on the lookout. If you're down with a cold, your neighbor is quick to ring your doorbell with a steaming pot of chicken soup. It's a community filled with kindness and *heartred*.

That's what my mother always says. It's her version of hatred because the latter clearly does not exist anywhere near Harville.

Despite the apparent perfection, I don't enjoy living here at all. I hate the appearance when, deep inside, I know that not everyone can be this happy and friendly all the time. I know I'm not. I haven't been ever since my father left my mother and me just the day before my fourteenth birthday. Without saying goodbye or giving a reason. The last thing I heard of him was the big fight he had with Mum. I don't know what they talked about—only that the smashing of the door would be the last I'd hear of my dad. I imagined my mother would be sad, but she smiled nonetheless and told me how it was his own fault for voluntarily leaving the most wonderful place on Earth.

It didn't take her long to find a replacement and get married again. Doug is even more enthusiastic than her, and it makes the bile in my stomach rise every time I talk to him. Two years had passed, but I still couldn't warm up to Doug. Not because he treated me badly in any way. He was always grinning and making dumb jokes. He'd cook dinner and help with my homework. On the outside, he acted great, but every time he was around, my gut would scream that something was awfully off about him.

Admittedly, I enjoyed my time in Harvey Lane when I was a child. Mum and Dad would take me to the playground, and I would play until my eyes could hardly stay open anymore and my feet were sore. That's where I met my best friend, Elias, too. He has the kind of eyebrows that always made him look a little mad, and I think as he grew up we both started to take on the anger we were missing here. Back then, though, we'd happily play all day while my parents sat on the grass with the other families to have picnics and talk about the wonderful life of Harville. If you looked at the people here, you might understand why they enjoy being here so much. There are no problems in our small town. We don't have poverty, violence, or anger. Everything is regulated so you never have to worry, even if you're alone. Maybe the reason we never leave is that everyone who lives here is afraid of the reality of the world out there.

Of course, that's only what it looks like on the outside. They don't speak about the disappearing children in public, after all. At first, I was too young to understand. Every year or so, there would be whispers about another girl or boy being lost without a trace. I would hear Dad speak to Mum about the dangers of Harvey Lane and feel the anxiety build up.

"These things happen everywhere, Marcus. You are simply more aware of it due to the contrast. It's easy to be upset by something when all you know is peace and harmony," my mother said in a melodic voice.

"It's easy to be upset when our child could be next," my father responded in a stern tone.

That's about the time Mum noticed that I was eavesdropping. Her smile disappeared from her face for a split second. It was the last time they discussed the matter of the children at home. I, on the other hand, had lots of questions, but at night when I was in bed, Dad came up to me to assure me that I would never be in trouble.

"As long as you're back inside before the streetlights turn on, you will always be safe in here with your mother and me. All right, buddy?"

He patted my head, and moments later, I forgot all about the only dark side of Harville.

---

That was a long time ago. I was far beyond the age of being home by dark, and I knew for a fact that my dad would not be there when I got back.

Honestly, I had been trying to spend as much time away from home as I could.

I wasn't exactly afraid that whoever or whatever was making children disappear would take me next. I was almost an adult by now. Besides, Elias always said that those kids weren't taken. They ran away because they couldn't bear this utopia that was more shine than substance. He wasn't wrong. If it weren't for my only friend, the only other cynical person I knew here, I would have been long gone as well. But with him, I had somehow gotten used to the simple life we lived here. I didn't know anything beyond it, after all.

Things were going pretty all right, all things considered. The last disappearance had been months ago and was not framed as one.

Dylan Dullens. The thirteen-year-old son of one of the most well-known families around. The Dullens are always around whenever anything in town took place. Mrs. Dullens always organizes the annual Christmas festivities. She gets the big tree for the town center, takes care of decorations, and leads the carol singers through the streets. Mr. Dullens is the head of the homeowners' association. He's the one you need to talk to if you want the slightest change in town. And he'll always forbid it with the friendliest smile. They have four other children, who are all extremely popular and pretentious. When Dylan suddenly stopped coming to school, everyone was told that he was sent to a prestigious boarding school across the ocean.

We knew it was a lie, but nobody said a word. I think most parents were just glad their children were still around.

After Dylan, we hit a quiet phase for children but an exciting season for Harville. There were even more festivities, and the few streets with broken pavement were repaired. The town looked better than ever before, and its residents were so cheerful that it could hurt your eyes and ears. I gave up trying to talk to Mum and Doug about any of the issues. They always had different reasoning and would simply try to convince me to join a club, a neighborhood party, or the Scouts. I had stopped joining any events in town a while ago and had tried to distance myself from my stepfather and mother as much as I could.

---

Ignorance can be bliss until the problem comes close enough for you to worry.

It started with a flickering streetlight, the way they do when a bulb is close to dying. The bulb was tattered but not yet broken. A first warning sign that it needed to be changed.

As I walked down the empty street toward home, I passed the flickering lamp and looked up. Little insects were attracted to the slowly vanishing light before it suddenly went dark. It didn't feel too strange, except the same thing happened a few feet farther at the second streetlight on Harvey Lane. I glanced back, and the first light was shining brightly.

I kept walking, and the flickering followed me past every lamp until I finally started running. Right toward the pastel green door of my childhood home. I slammed the door shut, locked it three times, and crept toward the window, my breath slow and my heart racing.

All the lights were off.

I sighed, telling myself it must be a power outage. Those happen quite frequently here, but when I reached for the light switch next to the door, our home wasn't dark anymore.

"What are you doing here?"

My heart skipped a beat when I heard the deep voice behind me.

"Doug, what the fuck?" I shrieked.

"Julian, my boy, you know we don't swear in this house," he said, his mouth forming into a half-smile.

"Why were you standing in the dark?" I asked, my voice still slightly shaky.

"You shouldn't be here, Julian. You know that, right?" he said, moving a step closer. His face and voice both sounded friendly, but he was acting even stranger than normal. "Not now and not then."

"Um, where's Mum?" I asked nervously.
"Tonight's the town meeting. Things aren't going too well lately. Haven't you noticed more people being sick? And the fields are too dry this year. It's—pardon my directness—suboptimal."

He was right. I'd had to bring soup to three different neighbors in the last couple of days, even though people hardly ever got sick in Harville.

"Why didn't you go with her? You never miss a meeting."

"I had another obligation."

Doug stared at me the entire time he was speaking. I could swear he didn't even blink once. I felt incredibly uneasy being home alone with him, but luckily, the doorbell saved me. It was Elias, who had come over to watch a movie after getting stood up for a date. I'd never been happier to see him.

When we turned around, Doug was gone.

We heard the news in the morning. Jeanie, the girl who lived three doors down, was gone. This time, no bullshit explanation would spread through the town. We knew because of the big bloodstain right in front of her house. There was an investigation that, of course, led nowhere. People were mourning, but they were doing it in the Harville way. Her parents didn't show a single tear, and nobody wore black. And everything in town went on, nice and swell. Even more so than usual. There was no need for bringing soup. The streets were clean, the grass was green, and the weather was warm. Life moved on quickly. Everyone seemed to forget, but Elias and I didn't. All this time we thought we were safe now that we were older, but Jeanie was already seventeen.

And I felt even more messed up knowing that I had been out there, right on that exact street the same night it happened. Was it somehow connected to the streetlights?

The following week, Elias and I decided to do something we had never done before. We went to a town meeting. It started at eight p.m. I knew both Mum and Doug would be there, and after the previous week, I had been avoiding them as much as possible. Especially when I saw the big bright smile on Mum's face when she prepared scrambled eggs while nonchalantly speaking about the girl who we lived next to disappearing. I could have sworn I saw her eye twitch a little when she spoke about how hard it would be to clean off the blood, but that was all. We cycled to the town hall but left our bikes a street over to make sure nobody would see us. Nobody under the age of eighteen was allowed at the meetings. When we were sure that everyone was inside, we quietly made our way to the front hall.

It was empty. They were all in the big meeting room.

"Maybe this was a bad idea," I whispered.

"Shh."

Elias quietly walked up to the door, which was open just a crack. He waved me over, and I reluctantly moved closer.

"They're all clapping," Elias whispered as we hunched down next to the door.

"A big Harville congratulations to the Murries!"

The clapping became louder, and cheering followed.

The Murries were Jeanie's parents.

"We are all so happy to have you as a part of our community! We know best how wonderful the honor of sacrifice is," Mr. Dullens spoke. "All our families have given, and we all receive. Just the way it should be."

My heart was racing, and I wanted—no, I needed—to hear about what kind of Satanic ideas they were preaching, but after that bit of cheering, they went on with the regular program as if nothing had happened.

---

"Sacrifice? What the actual fuck?" Elias almost shouted after we made our way back outside.

I stayed quiet for a while. I had known for a long time that something was off about the picture-perfect appearance of Harville. Just not how bad it was. The parents here give up their own children to have what? A nice neighborhood? My entire body was shaking.

"That night," I mumbled, "I think I was supposed to disappear."

I thought about the streetlights. If I hadn't been freaked out by them so much, I wouldn't have run home. It was almost like something was trying to warn me. Or someone.

And maybe my dad didn't leave voluntarily, either.

# MY MOTHER IS PERFORMING A PUPPET SHOW FOR US. WHEN IT ENDS, WE DIE.

"And the wolf was so hungry that he slit open the princess."

She moved around the puppets she'd made for us when I was six. The ones that were all dusty and ripped. Nobody had touched them in years.

"But the princess was strong and wouldn't die, so the wolf tried to run—"

My little sister Abby was enjoying all of it. She had no clue that Mum was going through something that seemed like an intense manic episode.

"Make the wolf come back!" Abby shouted, and Mum smiled.

"Mum—" I started, but my voice broke off.

She kept moving the dolls, and I stopped listening to what she was saying. We'd been inside the basement for hours watching the puppets and listening to my mother changing her voice. Somehow I couldn't move. And I didn't dare. Behind the self-made puppet theater, my mother had a large kitchen knife. I thought of ways to trick her or overpower her, but it simultaneously pained me too much to see her this way.

So I sat there frozen, watching her slowly lose her mind.

Mum and I had built the stage for the puppet show when I was little with the help of my grandpa. We used wood that Grandpa cut into pieces that fit, and then Mum and I painted them. We even added a curtain from pieces of an old red dress my mum owned.

The puppet show became my biggest obsession. We'd spend every weekend creating new puppets and decorations. It was all self-made; we didn't buy a single one. For their hair, we used strands from old dolls or cut strips of cloth. Mum made all their dresses herself with her sewing machine.

When I look back at my childhood, those are some of my sweetest memories.

But as I got older, we stopped using the puppet show. When my sister Abby was born many years later, puppets weren't really in fashion anymore, so the whole ensemble moved to our basement.

I'd moved out of my childhood home years ago but still regularly visited my family. Today was one of those random visits. I still had my key, so I let myself in. After shutting the door and shouting hello, I waited for a response, but the house was eerily quiet. My mum had said she'd be home all day.

"Hello? I'm home," I shouted again, this time louder, and then I heard my sister calling me from the basement.

I took off my coat and then walked down the narrow steps to the basement. Our basement was just one room, filled with boxes and some old furniture. When I saw that my mother was presenting a show with our old puppet set for my sister, I couldn't help but grin. This was the last thing I was expecting to see.

Abby was wearing a cute little dress and a crown and kept giggling.

"What's going on here?" I said in my best older-brother voice. Abby was sixteen years younger than me, so we always had a very playful relationship.

"A puppet show!" Abby answered excitedly.

"I always thought she didn't like this thing," I said to my mum, who was crouching behind the wooden box that was our puppet theater.

I took a seat on the carpet next to Abby and saw that my mother was holding a jester puppet in her hand, one of the first ones we had made back then.

"The princess demanded a show. Who am I to resist?" she said in a deep voice, and Abby looked at me and nodded.

The nostalgia immediately hit me, and I stayed there, watching the little show my mother put up for us. It took me a little while, however, to realize some of the stories were specifically directed at me.

She switched the jester for a witch and changed her voice again to make it sound more rusty and creaky. "The prince is here, and he thinks he can simply join us after he left this home. He doesn't belong here anymore!"

The prince was the puppet my mother had specially made for me back then.

The wooden theater was big enough that my mother could crouch behind it and disappear completely, but suddenly I saw her peeking at us from the side. Our eyes met, and I felt a knot in my stomach. Something about her seemed off.

I looked at Abby, who didn't seem to notice a thing.

Suddenly, my mother dropped the puppet of the prince and continued with a whole different story as if nothing had happened.

"This is the story of the frog and the witch who could not make a wish. The frog was purple; the witch was orange. Colors are fun, and numbers are two."

I looked at my sister and whispered, "Is she running out of ideas?"

Abby giggled. "I like it."

Abby was five. I think she didn't care what the fairy tales were. She just liked looking at the puppets.

I had no idea how long those two had already been in the basement before I arrived, so at that point I thought my mother might simply be a little fatigued.

She continued the nonsense story for a while, and I sat there and watched. Not because I cared about the tales but because it felt wrong to go upstairs. In a way, I felt glued to that strange show.

This went on for what felt like hours. At times the story and her voice were clear and coherent, but then it became odd and dreamlike again. There were moments when I actually thought I wasn't awake.

When the strange story was done, my mother peeked at us from the side again. She disappeared a second later but left a mark on the side of the box. A bloody handprint.

Then she held up the puppet of the jester with one hand, and with the other she held a large kitchen knife, making it look like the jester was slashing at the air.

"Mum?" I nervously asked, but she didn't respond. "Mum, are you okay? What's with the knife?"

"We collected lots of props because we thought we might need them!" she said in a high-pitched voice I'd never heard before.

She kept ignoring me and put on a new puppet to continue with a different story.

---

I can't say how much more time passed. I felt sick to my stomach while the rest of my body was in shock. I had never seen my mother like that before, and I simply couldn't move.

"The wolf took the clothes of the little girl and went to the forest to—"

After three or four more stories, I decided it was time to end this.

"Hey, Abby. Should we go upstairs and get a snack?" I asked her, trying to find a way to remove her from whatever was going on with our mother.

"No!" my mother shouted. She put both her hands on the stage and lifted herself, showing us her face. Her eyes were twitching, and her mouth was twisted into a big smile. "The show is not over yet. The princess wants to see the show."

I turned to my sister, who started looking a little afraid. She was only five and probably couldn't grasp the odd situation, but she was starting to notice that something was off.

"Okay, why don't we take the show upstairs? I can carry the puppet theater upstairs and we can sit on the sofa?" I suggested.

My mother stayed silent for a while. I slowly got ready to get up until Mum started speaking again.

"I have one more tale to tell. This time it is about a prince." She looked up from the box for a few seconds, staring at us with an intensity I'd never felt before. "When the prince was only a kid, he lost his father, the king. The king had been very sick, and when he could live no longer, the prince was very sad. So the queen found many ways to distract him and make him happy. And one day he felt better. So did the queen, and she found many things to do, though she never found another king. She didn't need one. The two of them had each other."

She stopped for a moment, and little Abby started squeezing the fabric on my leg. She turned her face toward me, and I noticed something I hadn't seen before. Abby had a cut on her left arm. Had my mother done that to her with that knife?

My breathing became heavier. I thought about jumping up as quickly as possible, grabbing Abby, and running upstairs. My mother wasn't the youngest anymore, I could have overpowered her, but she did have a knife. And I didn't want Abby to get hurt. But if I could outrun her...

"But then, one day, there was a princess, and she was the sweetest thing she'd ever seen," she continued the story, her voice getting louder.

She let the queen fall and grabbed the jester puppet again.

"The jester said to the prince, 'Be aware. The princess might look sweet and nice. It might feel as if you've known her your whole life.'"

Finally, something clicked inside of me.

"Can I join the show?" I asked as I very slowly got up and moved toward my mother.

She didn't stop me.

I grabbed the puppet of the wolf, but I had no idea what to say. Behind the box, I finally saw my mother in full. Her skin had lost all its color, and while Abby had one cut on her arm, my mother's body was covered in them. Her clothes were ripped, and everything was stained with blood.

I looked down at my own lap. Blood was staining my pants, but the pain wasn't registering in my brain.

She kept going on with the show, her voice getting weaker.

"The jester danced around and kept performing. She hoped the prince would not come home because she knew: if the show stopped, the creature would slaughter them both."

I saw her eyes that were filled with fear and regret. She tried her hardest to continue but couldn't go on.

"I'm sorry," she whispered. "She tricked us both." Then she collapsed from exhaustion.

"It's okay, Mum." I held back my tears. "You tried your best."

I grabbed the jester puppet.

And continued the show.

# WELCOME TO HEAVEN

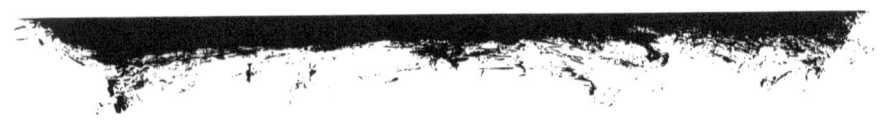

Would you choose to live in a town where everything was always right and everyone was always nice in exchange for simply never questioning how it came to be?

I never thought I would be the kind of person to give up my free will in a subtle way like this, but in this specific case, the perks simply outweighed the costs.

It all began after my aunt passed away. We weren't very close; she and my mother had lost touch in recent years, so I was more than surprised to hear that I had inherited her house, a house I'd never even visited before. I hadn't even attended her funeral, as she'd requested in her will that it be held in the town where she and my mother were born.

Despite her generosity, I never intended to move there. I believed I was too young to be living in my own house in a tiny, incredibly secluded town. Instead, I asked my boyfriend to join me on the five-hour drive to check the place out and put it up for sale.

As we drove past the sign that read *Welcome to Heaven* in big, cursive letters, it was as if we'd stepped onto the set of a movie.

The side of the road was lined with big apple trees that all looked exactly the same; they were bright green, flecked with huge red apples. The road we drove down became significantly smoother, birds were chirping, and we saw a small river glowing in the sun.

And that was only the beginning.

The closer we got to the center of town, the more beautiful it became. We passed little farm stands that were made to look like strawberries, blueberries, and figs. There was a bakery inside a brick house emitting scents of vanilla and warm butter, and cafes with people sitting out front. I slowed down to look into different shops selling clothes and jewelry. For a town so small, it had anything you could wish for.

"I thought this would be some boring little village," Ian mumbled from the passenger seat.

"Me too," I agreed. "But it's so nice."

We pulled into the street of my aunt's old home. There were houses in all kinds of colors with small chimneys and cute little front yards where people were tanning in the sun or watering their plants.

Some waved at us as we passed, and to our surprise, most of them didn't seem much older than us.

"This should be it," I said as we reached house number seven.

We walked up the gravel path to the front door, and I rummaged through my purse for the key, but, surprisingly, the door was unlocked. As I stepped over the threshold, I smelled cinnamon, as if someone had been baking in the kitchen very recently.

Ian followed close behind, the two bags with our clothes and other things hanging over his shoulders. "Wow," he mumbled, and I shared the sentiment. It wasn't anything major, not a huge hall or anything like that, but the interior just felt so homey and nice. There was a small fireplace in the living room; everything was still furnished. There was no television but a massive shelf filled with hundreds of books. We continued to the kitchen, and I opened a few cupboards, which were all fully stocked.

Ian opened the fridge and turned to me with a confused look on his face.

"Did your aunt live on her own?" he asked.

"Yeah, I think so. Why?"

He pulled out a carton of milk, opened the lid, and smelled it.

"The stuff in here looks fresh."

I joined him and saw the fridge full of produce, cheeses, and meats—not a single thing rotten.

Aunt Maggie had died a month ago.

"That's really odd," I whispered.

I moved away from the kitchen and found the staircase leading upstairs to the bedroom and bathroom. On top of the bed, I found a letter addressed to me.

My dearest Eleanor,

You might have been surprised to receive this present. When I got ill, I wondered whose life I could make infinitely better, and I ultimately landed on you. You are in the prime of your life and deserve happiness. So now, I am giving this home to you, and as you will soon learn, it will be the best thing that ever happened to you.

Enjoy it with all your heart.

You will learn that you never have to endure stress again, and you won't feel anger or sadness, only luck. And there's only one thing you need to do in exchange.

Never question *why*.

---

I called my mom to tell her that we'd arrived safely. She'd been a little suspicious of the whole thing at first, and when I told her about the letter, it didn't exactly ease her mind.

My aunt had moved away when she was in her late twenties. She was a good bit younger than my mother. After she moved to this town, they lost more and more touch, and I believe my mother was afraid the same thing would happen to me. She hadn't even known that her own sister was sick until it was too late.

I convinced her that we would only be staying for a little while and that I had every intention to simply sell the house and get back home.

That was the only time I called my mother the entire time we were in Heaven. After that call, I left my phone on the desk in the bedroom and didn't pick it up again. I simply didn't feel the need.

---

The following morning, our doorbell woke me from the best dreamless sleep I'd had in years. Ian wasn't next to me, but I smelled fresh coffee downstairs.

When I got down, Ian was already on his way to the door. I walked up next to him, and we were greeted by five friendly strangers, one of them holding a big basket.

"Welcome!" they all said in unison. Two of them were women, three were men, and they all looked very different but somehow similar. They had the same posture, the same cheery grin, and similar sets of workout clothes that I immediately envied.

The tallest of them stretched out his arms, gesturing for us to take the basket.

"Wow, is this for us?" I asked.

The basket was filled with chocolates, bath oils, lotion, fruits, and a bunch of other fancy-looking items.

"Well, yes, of course," one of the women said as she linked arms with the tall guy. She had golden hair that shimmered in the warm sun and freckles all over her cheeks. "We saw you arriving yesterday but didn't want to bother you on your first day. You're Eleanor, right?"

Ian and I exchanged a look.

"Yeah, but you can call me El," I laughed. "And this is my boyfriend, Ian."

"Lovely. I'm Lea, and this is my husband, Marc."

The others introduced themselves as well, but I immediately forgot their names.

"Did you settle in well?" Marc asked.

"Yeah, I mean it almost feels like a hotel," Ian answered. "The whole house is fully stocked. It's kind of crazy."

The five neighbors exchanged a look I couldn't quite place. It almost appeared like confusion.

"But I didn't find any personal things from my aunt. This used to be her home. I thought we'd have to pack her things or something—"

"Stop right there, honey," Lea interrupted me. She grabbed my wrist and squeezed it so hard I thought it might bruise. "Don't question it, just enjoy." She winked at me and added, "I hope we become marvelous friends."

"Oh, well, we're actually not planning to stay very long," Ian said.

They all started laughing hysterically.

One of the guys from the back wiped away a tear and said, "You'll change your mind."

With that, they turned around and left.

The ease I'd felt that morning suddenly turned sour.

"Where the actual hell are we, El? This feels like *The Truman Show*," Ian laughed after we'd closed the door again.

But we had yet to learn how right they were. Because as the day came to an end, we'd both agreed to throw our plans of selling the house aside and stay forever.

---

I can't say how long we'd been in Heaven—days or possibly weeks. You know the old expression, time flies when you're having fun.

Ian was gone for the afternoon to play tennis with Marc. It was the very first time since our arrival that I felt the smallest sense of boredom. It wasn't a bad feeling, simply one that prompted me to find something to do.

And so I decided to do something I hadn't done in a while: read a book.

I picked up the first one that looked interesting from the shelf and flicked through it, but for some reason, I couldn't read it.

"Must be a different language," I mumbled to myself.

I picked up the next one, but it was the same, and the one after that and the one after that. All these books were simply decorations, I realized, and I laughed. What a fun way to fill a shelf! I almost turned away to find another thing to do when one specific book caught my attention. It was tiny, smaller even than my palm, and didn't fit in with all the rest; it almost disappeared between them.

I pulled it out with my fingernails, and when I opened it up, a piece of paper, folded multiple times, fell out.

I picked it up from the ground and opened it only to realize that there was writing on it. Writing I could understand.

*I have to write this down because I always forget. I don't remember when I came here. I don't remember why.*

*Everyone is always so nice. Why are they so nice? My neighbor Trisha started talking about her family. It made me wonder if I have one, too.*

*I found Trisha in her hallway. All the blood was drained from her body. Where did all her blood go?*

*Two men appeared next door; they went into Trisha's house and came back out with a big black plastic bag.*

*Nobody here gets to grow old.*

*I remembered someone. Lucy. And her little girl. What was her name again?*

My breathing stopped at the mention of the name. Lucy was my mother.

The paper held only one more sentence.

*I will be in the black bag soon. I know it.*

Aunt Maggie had written these, probably shortly before her death, and as if the content weren't strange enough, I noticed that the handwriting looked very different from the one on the letter I found on the first day.

---

I sat in the living room for so long that I didn't even notice when it got dark or when Ian came home. There was so much fog around my mind that I didn't even react when he turned on the lights, or when he kissed my forehead, or when he started a fire in our fireplace.

"El? What's that in your lap?" he suddenly asked.

I looked down at the piece of paper with the last words I'd ever read from my aunt and swallowed past a hard knot.

"I—I found this."

He grabbed the paper, and his eyes scanned the page. Then he crumpled it without another word and threw it into the fire.

"Let's forget this ever happened." He smiled brightly, showing all his teeth, and then proceeded to go to the kitchen to start dinner.

---

The following day, I did just what Ian said and tried to forget all about the strange letter. My aunt had been sick, after all. It was no use to think about anything, really. We were happy, and I wouldn't have wanted that to change for anything in the world.

And I would have continued living on like that, happy and oblivious, if it hadn't been for the intruders in our home.

Ian and I had spent the day at the local community pool, tanning in the sun, going for a swim, and having drinks with our new friends.

When we came home, we were so happy and content that we didn't even worry about the strange car out front. Or that all the lights in the living room were on. We never locked our doors; no one in Heaven did.

But as soon as I saw the two people in our living room, something snapped inside of me.

"Mom? Dad? What are you doing here?"

"Eleanor!" My mother got up from the sofa and hugged me so tight that all the air left my lungs. "Why do you think we're here? You sent me all those strange texts, and you wouldn't answer any of my calls. We got worried about you!"

"What texts?" Ian asked, and I shrugged. I had no idea what she was talking about.

She pulled out her phone and showed me dozens of texts from my number.

*Ian and I decided to stay in Heaven.*
*We are so happy here.*
*We need time to ourselves, to settle in.*
And a bunch more like that.

"Well, I haven't written any of those, but I agree with them." I looked at Ian, and he nodded.

"No, you don't understand, honey. I received the same messages from your aunt when she moved here. Exactly the same ones, word for word. I should have questioned it more then, but—"

"So what? It *is* great here. Why don't you stay for a while? I'm sure you'll understand then."

"Eleanor, have you lost your mind? This isn't like you. You wouldn't answer any of our calls or—" My father started to rage, but then Mom turned around to look at him. I couldn't see her expression, but my dad suddenly fell silent.

"Actually, I think that sounds like a terrific idea," she said.

---

The four of us had a nice dinner and went to bed soon after.

When I woke up, I was in the backseat of a car, with Ian passed out next to me. My father was behind the wheel, with my mother in the passenger seat.

"Mom?" I mumbled, slowly coming to my senses. "Where are you taking us? We have to go back." Suddenly, my heartbeat started racing.

My mother kept shaking her head, and when she turned around, I noticed tears in her eyes and a big scratch going down her cheek.

I blinked a few times. Sleep was claiming me, and I could hardly keep my eyes open. The last thing I heard was my mother saying something strange.

"I don't care that you're an adult. I don't care that that house belongs to you. That place is not right. And I'm not losing you like I lost her."

---

I've been back home for a few days. Not in Heaven but in my real home, with the family I'd almost forgotten about.

I talked to my parents for a long time. Dad doesn't understand anything and thinks Ian and I lost our minds. But Mom seems to get it, especially after I told her about the note I found. She's trying everything to keep my mind sharp, hardly ever leaving my side.

I've been strong so far with her support, but I can't say the same for Ian. He seemed cooperative at first and listened to my parents. I thought we might be able to get through this.

But yesterday, he disappeared without even a goodbye, and I have a damn good hunch where he went.

# THEY WERE OUT OF LEMONS

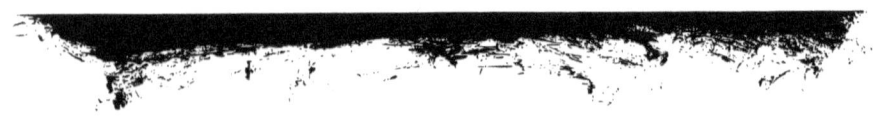

I was never too fond of sweet stuff. Marzipan made me sick, chocolate never made me feel joyous, and the worst flavor I could imagine was that of sugary pears. Lemons, on the other hand, were to me like a gift sent from heaven. A sour lemon with just a bit of sweetness was all I needed to be happy. There was nothing better than the addition of lemon juice to improve some dish or pastry. Fish with a dash of lemon juice, lemon zest sprinkled on top of a roast chicken, a cup of hot lemon water with a bit of ginger and honey when you had a cold. Since I was a little child, I would eat only lemon-flavored ice cream and popsicles. Cakes, muffins, and pies always taste better with a layer of lemon curd. Or have you ever tried lemon meringue? It's breathtaking.

Of course, I'm not talking about the synthetic lemon flavor that you get in some types of candy. They taste like soap and are a massive insult to the fruit. I am talking about the real deal. A fresh and juicy lemon wrapped in its bright yellow natural package as if it were kissed by the sun herself.

We were spoiled in more ways than one. We can only miss all these things because we had the privilege of knowing them. Going to the store at nine p.m. to buy some fresh fruit isn't a given for everyone. I had never imagined how accustomed we had all gotten to the convenience.

"They were out of lemons."

"Well, that's a bummer," my boyfriend Nicholas said with a sympathetic undertone to his voice. "What did you get instead?"

"A can of tuna."

His eyes opened wide with excitement. "That's terrific!" he exclaimed.

I raised an eyebrow.

"Oh, don't give me that look. You know tuna is amazing."

I shrugged. "I guess, but what dish are you gonna make with a can of tuna? There were no peppers, no tomatoes, or even bread."

I used to be optimistic, an enthusiastic person that saw challenges instead of issues, but that was a long time ago.

He grabbed the can of tuna from my hand and placed it in our pantry, next to some kidney beans and half-rotten potatoes. The last few we had.

"You know, I think it's great that we have a little more to eat, but please don't sneak out on your own anymore. You know I don't like that. If anyone had seen you with this—"

"I know. I'm sorry."

Nicholas was much better at adjusting. He used to be a chef, and no matter what type of food we were stuck with, he would make the best of it. But even someone as creative as him wasn't able to make this life actually bearable.

I had lost my energy. My motivation. I hated everyone and everything.

My hate began when they started bunkering any substance that some dumb news channel told them was important. I laughed at them with their dozen packages of toilet paper, wondering what on earth they were planning to do with all that. Of course, we hoarded a little as well. Enough flour and yeast to bake bread. Some frozen vegetables. A few canned goods. Non-perishable stuff. Soap. Vitamins and medicine.

Not to prepare for some apocalypse but to make sure that we would be able to live decently during a two-week lockdown. Two weeks. That's what it was supposed to be.

Two weeks in which you don't have contact with anyone. To minimize the spread so that the hospitals could have some leniency. We all knew the disease couldn't be stopped easily. That was never the goal. The goal was to spread it over time so that there would always be enough people around to help the ones in need. But humans don't think logically in a time like this.

People bunkered more food than they could ever consume in a year. Especially the ones who didn't need it. A grandmother who lives on her own cannot easily go to the market to buy twenty packs of beans and bottled water, but someone with a big car and time can. They started fighting for a pack of flour or hand sanitizer. They filled up their basements to the brink, which meant that the ones who didn't do the same found themselves staring at empty shelves every day. No matter how early they woke up or how many stores they visited. All the goods were already placed in the basements of a few people who simply couldn't get enough.

But I don't need to tell you that. You were there to witness it.

My anger and dread grew even bigger when I realized that buying all those resources didn't even stop them from going outside. Had they stayed home with all the goods they had bought so they would be prepared for a lockdown, then maybe things would have worked out. But unfortunately, everyone got bored of the initial thrill quickly.

When the clubs started closing, people started throwing private parties. When the restaurants started closing, they would meet and chat at the bakeries. When the schools closed, childcare institutions had to be opened for the children of police officers, doctors, and nurses.

The perfect breeding places for infections.

The regulations coming from the governments came too late and were too vague. There weren't enough places to get tested, so people were told that they probably just had a common cold.

It spread, faster than it ever should have, and eventually we were overwhelmed. There was no way to help everyone, and the few who were still healthy and able to work had to try hard not to get infected. Especially when the disinfectants started running low. Had the regulations been clear from the beginning, then maybe things wouldn't have gone this far, but eventually we reached the point where both economic and social systems collapsed.

There were hardly any professionals left to help. The hospitals had become one of the most dangerous places to be, and we should be forever grateful for the few volunteers who still tried to see a shimmer of hope and help. Among them were the ones who worked in the empty stores. There was no way to import any new foods, so you were limited to buying one product, which usually was a canned good.

Nicholas was right. Tuna was terrific.

I was just being fussy. We were incredibly lucky, after all. It's just that for some reason I never gave up the hope that I might find a fresh piece of fruit, maybe even a lemon. I kept dreaming of seeing the yellow piece of happiness, holding it in my hands and inhaling its smell. I had almost forgotten what it was like. What I would have done for just a tiny bit of fresh fruit or some fresh vegetables. Even the taste of some bitter Brussels sprouts would have made me feel ecstatic.

"You know things will get better, right?" Nicholas pulled me out of my train of thought. I noticed I had been more absent lately. And tired.

"Sure." It made me feel horrible that I had become so pessimistic. He tried as hard as he could to make things slightly better, and the fact that we hadn't killed each other yet after all those weeks in quarantine was basically a wonder.

He grinned.

"Promise not to go outside alone again, and I will give you a surprise."

"A surprise?" I asked skeptically.

"Yeah. It's nothing too big. I found it in a trash can, and it doesn't look too great, but maybe if we believe in it, it could grow and turn out fine. You know, like our own little project to prove to us that everything will turn out okay in the end. That things will get better." He scratched his head nervously and then pulled something out of his back pocket.

He opened his hand, and in his palm, he held a small lemon seed.

# MORE CHILLS FROM VELOX BOOKS

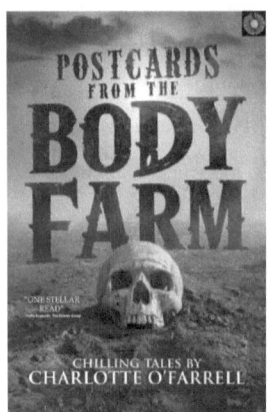

# MORE CHILLS FROM VELOX BOOKS

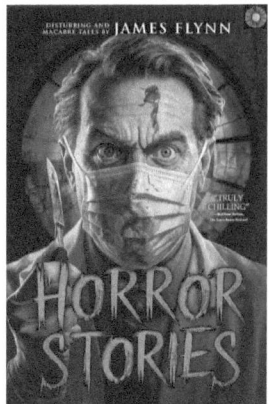

# MORE CHILLS FROM VELOX BOOKS

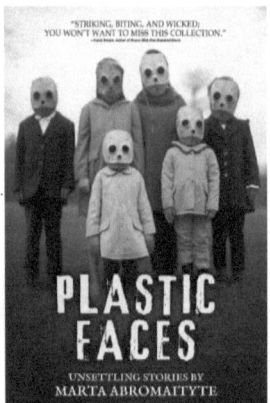

www.ingramcontent.com/pod-product-compliance
Lightning Source LLC
LaVergne TN
LVHW040041080526
838202LV00045B/3431